THE
MOUNTAINS
BETWEEN

by

Julie McGowan

THE MOUNTAINS BETWEEN

ISBN 978-1-909278-85-1

THIRD EDITION

Sunpenny Publishing - www.supenny.com

MORE BOOKS FROM JULIE McGOWAN:
Don't Pass Me By
Just One More Summer

MORE BOOKS FROM SUNPENNY LIMITED:
Some Day, Maybe, by Jenny Piper
Sudoku for Christmas
Blackbirds Baked In A Pie, by Eugene Barter
Dance of Eagles, by JS Holloway
Going Astray, by Christine Moore
My Sea is Wide, by Rowland Evans
If Horses Were Wishes, by Elizabeth Sellers
Far Out: Sailing Into a Disappearing World, by Corinna Weyreter

Best Wishes

Julie Melymere

For my parents, whose story inspired this one.

*

I would like to give special thanks to the following people:

My husband Peter, and children Daniel, Catherine,
Robert and Elizabeth, for encouraging me every step
of the way and always believing in me.

Barbara Daniels, for her professional eye.

Ann and Allan, Vi, Rosemary, Debbie and Linda,
for their unfailing support.

My amazing publisher and editor, Jo Holloway, and proof reader
Andrew Holloway, for their expertise, and for making this whole
process so much fun.

Part One

1929 ~

1

Jennie

Jennie heard Tom's voice calling her, but she ignored him and scrambled over the gate into the ten-acre field. She ran head down, forcing her legs to go faster and faster, her breath coming in great racking sobs, until she reached the corner of the field where the land sloped down towards the railway line, and she would be hidden from the house. As she flung herself face down onto the grass and the sobs became bitter, painful tears, Mother's words echoed in her head, refusing to be quelled.

You were never wanted! You were a mistake!... A mistake... a mistake!... Never wanted...!

The day had started so well. The Girls were coming home and Jennie had been helping Mother in the house – as she always did, but more willingly this time, excitement tightening her chest because her sisters would soon be here and the summer holidays would then have begun in earnest. Mother, too, seemed happy; less forbidding, and the crease between her brows that gave her such a disapproving air had been less pronounced.

Never wanted!... A mistake... Your Father's doing!

Eventually there were no more tears left to cry, but the sobs remained; long drawn out arpeggios every time she inhaled. And the more she tried to stop them the more it felt as if they were taking over her body.

She sat up and wrapped her arms around her knees in an effort to steady herself. A small girl dressed in a starched white pinafore over a blue print summer frock, with two mud-brown plaits framing a face whose eyes looked too large for it. She stared at the mountains – her mountains, her friends, keepers of her secrets. But today she wasn't seeing them, could draw no comfort from the gentle slopes of the Sugar Loaf which stretched out like arms to encompass the valley. Today the mountains were majestic and aloof, wanting no share of her misery. In her head the scene in Mother's bedroom replayed itself endlessly before her.

She'd been returning a reel of thread to Mother's workbox – a sturdy wooden casket kept in a corner of the bedroom. Inside were neat trays containing all Mother's sewing things, and one tray full of embroidery silks, the colours rich and flamboyant as they nestled together. Jennie had lifted the silks up and let them run through her fingers, enjoying their smooth feel and the rainbows they made.

Then, for the first time, she'd noticed that what she thought was the bottom of the workbox was, in fact, too high up.

She lifted the rest of the trays out and pulled at the wooden base, which moved easily to reveal another section underneath. There was only one item in it; a rectangular tin box with a hinged lid on which was a slightly raised embossed pattern in shiny red and gold. She traced the pattern with her fingers. It was an intriguing box. A box that begged to be opened.

Jennie had lifted the tin clear of the workbox when suddenly Mother appeared in the doorway, her face bulging with anger.

"What do you think you're doing? Put that down at once!"

Taken unawares by her mother's arrival and the harshness of her tone – excessive even for her – Jennie turned suddenly and the box had fallen out of her hands, the hinged lid flying open and the contents scattering over the floor. Had she not been so frightened by Mother's anger, Jennie would have registered disappointment, for the box, after all, held only a few old papers.

To Mother, though, they seemed as valuable as the Crown Jewels. With an anguished cry she'd pushed Jennie aside and scrabbled on the floor to retrieve the documents.

"I'm s-s-sorry," Jennie stammered, "I didn't mean ..."

But Mother wasn't listening. She was too busy shouting.

"Why don't you ever leave things alone? This is mine! You had no business! You're always where you're not meant to be – always causing me more work! Either under my feet or doing something you shouldn't!"

Her voice had grown more shrill as she spoke, with a dangerous quiver in it, so that Jennie didn't dare offer to help – or to point out that the things her mother was accusing her of were grossly unfair. She'd given up doing that a long time ago. "... It's not right – I didn't want... Three babies were enough!"

Mother had been looking down, thrusting the papers back in the box, continuing to exclaim about the unfairness of her lot as she did so, almost as if she were no longer addressing Jennie. But then she'd snapped the box shut and swung round to face her daughter.

"You were never wanted, you know! It was all a mistake! All your Father's doing!" She turned back to the workbox, her shoulders heaving with emotion.

There was a moment's silence.

"What did Father do?" a crushed Jennie had whispered.

Mother's hand had swung round and slapped Jennie across the ankles. "Don't be so disgusting!" she'd hissed. "Get out of here!"

Jennie knew, as she sat on the grass, that Mother had meant it. She was used to her mother's tempers, her insistence that the house, the family, and at times the farm, were run exactly as she wished, but this was different. The expression on her face as she'd spoken the dreadful words was one that Jennie had never seen before. It had been full of a strange passion – and something else which Jennie, with her limited experience, couldn't identify. But it had frightened her.

Never wanted! A mistake!

It changed everything. Nothing in her world would ever be the same again. Her eight years thus far had been secure ones; lonely at times, being the youngest by so many years, and hard when Mother's standards were so exacting. But happy, too. Happy in the knowledge that she was well-fed, clothed and housed; well-cared for (didn't that mean loved and wanted? It appeared not). Happy on the farm, surrounded by her mountains, and in the company of her beloved father.

Father! Jennie's heart beat faster in alarm. Did this mean that he didn't want her either? That he too saw her as some sort of mistake? Her relationship with her mother always held uncertainty, but Father's affection never seemed to waver.

A kaleidoscope of images of herself with her father rushed through her mind. Making her a wheelbarrow all of her own, so that she could 'help' him on the farm, when she was only four. Holding her in his arms when she cried because a fox had got in and wreaked havoc in the hen-house; comforting her because she'd been the one to discover the terrible decapitated remains. Letting her help to make new chicken sheds, safely off the ground – not minding when she'd splashed creosote on the grass. Urging the cows to milking, his voice kind and gentle, calling each cow by name and helping her to do the same until she could recognise each one.

Surely he loved her! He had to love her!

Panic was rising inside her and she wanted to run to her father and beg him to tell her that it wasn't true; that she wasn't simply a mistake. But fear stayed her. There was the awful possibility that he might tell her even more dreadful things that she didn't want to hear. It would be the same if she asked The Girls, and as for Tom, well! – he had never disguised the fact that a sister six years younger than himself was fit only for endless teasing.

The words were still playing in her head when suddenly the panic eased. What else had Mother said? … *All your Father's doing!* She didn't know what her father had done, but surely if he'd done it then he must have wanted her?

She lay back on the grass and closed her eyes. Perhaps if she went to sleep she would wake up and everything would be just as it was. She could go back to the house and carry on as usual and the lead weight in her chest that was making breathing so difficult would be gone.

The hot July sun soothed her. Mother would be cross if her skin burned, but Mother being cross about such a thing didn't seem quite so important at the moment. Convincing herself that her Father loved her and wanted her was, she instinctively knew, the only thing that would help her to push her mother's awful words to the back of her mind.

Katharine Davies sat on the edge of her bed, her shoulders sagging uncharacteristically, her breathing rapid and shallow. The papers were safely stowed away again but the episode had unnerved her too much for her to return downstairs just yet. Jennie was too young to have understood the implications of what the papers contained, but what if she told the older children of their whereabouts? A hot flush spread over her anew as she considered what they would think of her. She tried hopelessly to calm herself, but memories of nearly seventeen years ago refused to go away.

"Edward! Oh Edward!"

The voice was her own, urgent, pleading as his hands caressed her, explored her; and she wasn't urging him to stop. Oh no! To her everlasting shame she wanted him to go on, to satisfy the craving that had taken over her whole body. And he had: gone on and on until she felt she was drowning; until she had screamed her ecstasy.

I love you Katie. I'll always love you! Edward had held her afterwards, murmuring into her hair, promising to take care of her. And he had. But it hadn't been enough.

The memories sent prickles of shame up her spine until her neck was on fire. Yet, unbidden, the feeling was there again; that same burning physical wanting that had gnawed away at her in those early years, trapping her with its demands, its insatiability.

She stood up abruptly, angry that her body should be betraying her after all these years when she'd thought she had it firmly under control. She clenched her hands tightly in front of her. She must, she would, maintain that control.

She forced herself to think of what must still be done, which chores in the dairy or in the garden would best exercise her treacherously unreliable body.

She thought fleetingly of Jennie as she moved swiftly out of the bedroom. She shouldn't have spoken to her as she did, but doubtless the child would get over it – would probably look at her with those sheep's eyes for a day or two and then it would pass.

But you meant it, nagged the mean voice of Conscience.

She clutched the crucifix hanging round her neck, as if gathering strength to push the voice away. *I'll pray about it tonight,* she vowed, making for the stairs.

"Bessie! You'd better see about scalding the milk or it will turn in this heat! Then come and help me clean the dairy."

The girl, plump and homely, turned from the large stone sink where she was peeling potatoes, ready to make a cheery remark until she saw the expression on her employer's face. Best not look in the churn, madam, she thought, or the milk will turn never mind the heat.

Jennie **saw** her mother in the dairy as she entered the back of the house and tiptoed up the back stairs. She didn't want Mother to see the grass stains on her apron.

She'd thought long and hard once she'd finally stopped crying, and had decided that if she tried, really tried, not to let Mother see her doing anything wrong, and not to argue with her ever again, then perhaps Mother would forget that she was 'a mistake' and decide that she was the best-loved and most wanted of all her children.

She sighed as she reached her room. It would be hard work. There seemed to be so many things that Mother had definite and immovable views on. Take her apron, for example. Aprons weren't meant to get dirty. Mother's aprons always stayed spotless – except for the apron she wore over her apron to do 'the rough'.

Not that Mother ever did the really dirty jobs. They were done by Bessie, the latest in a long line of girls who stayed until they could take Mother's demands for perfection and her sharp tongue no longer.

She put on a clean apron and went to the recently-installed bathroom to wash her hands and face, careful to wipe the basin clean afterwards and replace the towel just so. The bathroom was a sufficiently new addition to be treated with exceptional respect. Then she returned to the kitchen by the front stairs so that Mother would think she had been in the house all along.

"May I go now, please – to meet The Girls?"

Jennie didn't want to look Mother in the face; instead she fastened her gaze on the shiny gold crucifix.

The crease between Mother's brows deepened as she surveyed her daughter. She opened her mouth as if to speak, but closed it again. Then her shoulders dropped a little as she appeared to relent from whatever it was she had been going to say.

"Very well. But wear your sunbonnet – and keep your apron clean!"

Jennie went meekly to the little room behind the kitchen and fetched her sun hat before letting herself out through the back door, forcing herself to walk sedately in case Mother was watching her as she crossed the farmyard – immaculate as ever because the cows weren't allowed to cross it lest they make it dirty.

Once round the corner of the barn she ran again to the gate of the ten-acre field. But she didn't climb over it this time. Instead she divested herself of her apron and sunhat and hung them on the gatepost before turning to a smaller, iron gate which led to the lane running parallel to the field.

She began to skip along the lane, sending up little clouds of dust as she went. It was impossible, somehow, to walk once you were out-of-doors and alone, even when you were feeling pretty miserable. Had she been feeling happier she would have tucked her skirts up into the legs of her knickers and tried a few cartwheels. But as she thought this, the awful words bounced up at her in time to her skipping... *Not wan-ted... not wan-ted... not wan-ted...*

The engine hooted as it pulled out of Nantyderry Halt, diverting Jennie. No need to think about anything else now The Girls were home! She broke into a run as they appeared at the end of the lane. They were each wearing their school uniform and carrying a small case; Tom would take the van down later for their trunks. Their uniforms bore the badge of the convent school at Monmouth, which they attended not because they were Catholic but because it was the best school in the area, and they boarded, not because it was far away but because that was what the best families did.

Jennie threw herself into the arms of her eldest sister, sure of a rapturous response.

"Steady on!" laughed Emily, swinging her round. "You nearly knocked me over! Let me look at you! You've grown again while we've been away! Laura! Don't you think she's grown?"

Laura, a year younger than sixteen-year-old Emily, but inches shorter and already more buxom, hugged Jennie more steadily.

"At least an inch taller," she agreed.

"Does that mean I can use your tennis racket this summer?" Jennie asked excitedly, turning back to Emily. "I've been practising like mad against the barn wall with the old one, and you promised me yours when I was big enough."

"We'll see," came the reply. "You'll have to show me how good you are."

But Emily's eyes held a merry promise and suddenly she caught hold of Jennie and danced round with her again.

"Isn't it wonderful? I've finished school for good! My very last day! I can hardly believe it!"

"It won't be so wonderful if we're late for dinner," Laura reminded her, picking up her bag and beginning to walk up the lane. "Jennie, your dress is terribly dusty – Mother will have a fit!"

"It's alright," said Jennie, "I can cover it up with my apron – I've left it on the gate."

But as they reached the gate, there was Tom, Jennie's sunhat perched ridiculously on his head, and the apron held aloft.

"Give it back, I mustn't get it dirty!" Jennie cried, hers arms flailing wildly as Tom held her easily at bay with one gangly arm.

"Please, Tom!" Laura sounded as urgent as Jennie, as the gong for lunch sounded from the house. "You know she'll get into trouble."

Emily sauntered through the gate behind her sisters. "Give her the apron and the hat, Tom, and carry these bags in for us." Her voice sounded almost lazy, but Tom was aware of the authority behind it. He was taller than both his sisters, but Emily always managed to make him feel small.

He relinquished the garments to a relieved Jennie, tweaked each of the long brown plaits hanging over her shoulders, and then grinned. "Better not spoil the homecoming, I suppose."

But he didn't move to embrace his sisters. Instead they all hurried in for dinner.

Come along! Come along!" said Mother as Father stopped to kiss and hug his two elder children. "This dinner will be getting cold."

Jennie contrived to sit between Father and Emily and at once felt happier, although tears threatened again when Father asked her in his gentle voice what she'd been doing all morning. Fortunately Mother began speaking to Emily, and as it was unwise to talk at the same time as Mother she didn't have to answer.

Edward Davies surveyed his family with a degree of pride as they sat round the large, scrubbed kitchen table. All four children well-grown and healthy – no mean achievement when you compared them to the malnourished rickety children over in the valleys, many of whom would be lucky to survive infancy. He would have liked another boy, for the farm, but he loved his daughters nevertheless.

Not that Katharine would have been happy with another boy – there'd been enough fuss as it was when Jennie came along, so he'd thanked God that He had seen fit to bless them with another girl. For some reason Katharine saw girls as a blessing and boys as a kind of blight. *Poor thing,* she would say whenever she heard of a mother being delivered of a son, no matter how longed-for. She treated Tom well enough for all that, Edward allowed, although he never saw the look of pride in her eyes that he had seen other mothers bestowing on their sons. But then, he reflected, Katharine was not like other mothers in a good many ways.

He watched her now, talking to Emily. She was still a handsome woman, despite her nearly forty years, with no hint of grey in the coils of rich brown hair which she wore piled high like Queen Mary. She'd kept her figure too, which was petite, with delicate wrists and ankles, but her body had always curved in and out in the right places.

Beautiful she'd been, when he first met her; beautiful with no idea of her beauty, which was what he'd found so appealing. Large grey-green eyes, more green when stirred to anger or passion, had beguiled him, and a relentless determination to set the world to rights according to her own view of things had been particularly attractive in one who looked as if she should languish and be pampered all day.

They first met when she was only eighteen, and had returned home from being a children's nanny to care for her younger brothers and sisters following the death of both their parents – her father having discreetly drunk himself to death after losing his wife from septicaemia.

Edward had watched her over the next few years as she struggled valiantly to prepare her siblings for adult life, while he himself was struggling to make a go of his first smallholding. But it had been some time before he'd plucked up courage to court her formally; there had always been an elusive quality about her that held him back, whilst at the same time tantalising him. She was twenty-three before the demands of her family had ceased and she had begun to take Edward seriously and allow him any degree of familiarity – and then, to his joy, what sensuality had been unleashed! And he had loved her! Oh, how he had loved her!

And I still love her now, he mused sadly. But it had been many years since the passion which had simultaneously driven and mortified her had been given rein. The determination which had enabled her to take over successfully from her parents had been channelled into 'getting on' in the world – or at least in the important bits of the society in which they moved, while the passion had been supplanted by a strange mixture of worldliness and godliness.

And, he thought with a sigh, *if cleanliness really is next to godliness, then she'll have a special place reserved for her when she gets to the other side.*

"The Talbots are expecting you from the beginning of September," she was telling Emily now, "so you will be able to have the school holiday here as usual."

Emily nodded, her mouth full. She was to be employed by the family who lived at The Manse in Llanfihangel Crucorney, to care for their two young children while Mrs. Talbot recovered from the imminent birth of their third child. Emily had mixed feelings about staying at home until September. She seriously doubted whether she could survive six weeks of Mother without sparks flying. The most confident and headstrong of the four children, and with a finely-honed sense of humour, she was aware every time she came home of the growing urge to kick against the restrictive rules of 'proper' behaviour by which their lives were governed.

The others all seem to have found ways of coping with it, she thought. Laura, stolid and naturally more placid, was the most easily convinced by Mother's edicts and could be quite shocked if it was suggested that they should be disobeyed, or even mildly distorted. Tom, mischievous and loud, had already escaped by allying himself with Father and spending all his time out on the farm, the only place where Father's word was law.

And what of little Jennie? Emily looked down affectionately at the small girl sitting docilely beside her. She, more than any of them, bore the brunt of Mother's abrasive tongue. How would she cope during the next few years as she became increasingly the only one under Mother's domination? She seemed happy enough out on the farm, playing and running free. But indoors she was a completely different child; withdrawn and somehow more solitary than when playing for hours on her own outside. Judging by her pale face and heavy eyes she'd probably been in some sort of trouble already this morning.

A wave of protective love for her baby sister swept through Emily. *I'll give her a good time this holiday,* she vowed, *and come home as often as I can to see she's alright.*

Emily's own future was already mapped out for the next few years. She was to spend the time until she was eighteen with the Talbots – approved by Mother because, although they lived in a thoroughly Welsh village, they were of English stock and very well-connected – and then she was to fulfil her long-held ambition and begin her nurse training. This had also met with approval, as she was to go over the border to Ross-on-Wye, and nursing as a career for genteel young ladies had gained a lot of ground since the war. Emily felt excited and impatient for the next two years to pass every time she thought about it, and no dire warnings of how hard a life it could be would deter her. The rules and regulations governing every aspect of a probationary nurse's life could be no more confining than those she'd lived under for the past sixteen years.

"I'll help you unpack," Jennie told The Girls after dinner, hoping that Mother had heard her being helpful, "and then there might be time for some cricket. I want to show you how I can bowl over-arm – Tom taught me!"

Ever since she'd discovered the range of sport to be played there, Jennie had longed for the day when she too would be attending the convent. She'd wondered at first how the nuns managed to run in their long habits, and had imagined them tucking their skirts up into their knickers like she did for cartwheels. Emily and Laura had shrieked with laughter when she'd mentioned this and explained between chuckles that special mistresses were brought in for games. But Jennie preferred the image of the nuns running to and fro, their black wimples flying out behind them, and refused to replace it with the more prosaic picture of a sturdy-thighed young woman in an Aertex shirt.

D id Mother get cross with you this morning?" Emily asked casually. The three of them were sitting on the hay bales in the shady Dutch barn after half an hour's cricket in the hot sun.

"N-no," faltered Jennie, aware of Laura's concerned mother-hen gaze upon her. "Well, not really ... She was a bit worked up about getting things ready for you both coming home." She sought to change the subject. She didn't want to tell them what had really happened because everything they did together after that would be done out of pity for her – she knew they already felt sorry for her being so much on her own – and more than anything she wanted them to love her for herself. "Mother says we can all go to the market on Tuesday," she said with desperate inspiration. "Will you both come?"

Laura reached over and hugged her. She'd seen the pain in the large grey eyes that were so much like Mother's. "Of course we will. Come on – I need a drink of water. Then we'll try you out with Emily's tennis racket."

S unday was as hot as the day before, but airless and humid. It was a relief to go to Holy Communion and sit in the cool, dark church at Nantyderry. Unless it was pouring with rain Mother preferred to walk down the narrow winding road from the farm, she in front with Father, her back ramrod straight, and the children in miniature procession behind.

They left the house sufficiently early to enable them to pass the time of day with their neighbours, done in strict accordance with the neighbour's prominence in the community. Thus, Ced Griffiths, from the next farm along, who sat on the parish council, would be greeted with considerable warmth, and Mrs. Protheroe, widow of Major Protheroe of Nantyderry House, with conspiratorial respect meant to convey equal standing. The vicar's wife, always referred to at home as 'poor Mrs. Simmons', received a smile of pitying condescension, due to her inability to make her unruly children behave in a manner fitting for a Reverend's family, while the farm labourers' families received not a glance, unless it was winter and the children were sniffing with colds, when Mother would glare at them and 'Tuttut' very loudly. At such times Mother's own children would stare steadfastly ahead so they could pretend not to see the rude gestures directed at Mother once her back was turned.

For once Jennie was eager to go to church, desperate to engage the Almighty's help in the seemingly impossible task of keeping Mother happy and becoming a favoured child.

"Come *on!*" she urged her eldest sister, dragging her away from the bedroom mirror. "Mother will start shouting at us in a minute."

Emily, too, had been looking forward to the morning, because she'd put her hair up for the first time and wanted Ernest Gronow, whom she knew was sweet on her, to see how elegant she'd become. Not that she had any intention of returning his interest: had no intention of becoming involved with anyone for at least ten years – and who would want to be called 'Mrs. Gronow' anyway? But it was amusing to turn her head from time to time during the interminably long service and see his round face glow like a beacon because she'd caught him watching her.

"Emily! Sit round!" her mother hissed the fourth time. Tom craned his neck to see what had interested his sister and caught the tail end of Ernest's blush. He smiled. He could have some sport with Ernest next time they met.

Tom himself had no desire to be in church. He felt uncomfortable in his starched white collar and flannel suit, already getting too small for him so that his bony wrists protruded too far from his sleeves and his turn-ups were too high up his boots to look right. He and Father had been up since four-thirty, milking the cows, feeding the animals, and delivering the milk, more hurried than usual so that they could get back and rush around even more to be washed and changed and ready for church and the remainder of their so-called day of rest.

Laura sat next to Mother, holding herself taut in an effort to prevent her stomach from making indelicate gurgling sounds which she couldn't help but would get blamed for nonetheless. Only Father and Tom were allowed a light breakfast on Sundays because of rising so early, but the girls and Mother only had a weak cup of tea so that there was nothing in their stomachs when they took Holy Communion. And by the time they returned home it was too late, as food would then 'spoil their dinner'.

Mother stood, sat and knelt at the appropriate times, her face pious and rapt throughout. *She still notices everything, though,* thought Jennie, receiving a frown and a "Keep still!" for fidgeting. She must have eyes in the back of her head!

The prospect of Mother with another pair of eyes intrigued her, and she spent several minutes imagining where they would be and how Mother would manage to brush her hair without hurting them. Lost in contemplation, she was surprised to receive a sharp poke in the arm from Tom as the congregation rose for the final hymn.

Oh, damn! She hadn't spent enough time beseeching God to help her, and now it was too late! *And now I've sworn as well!* she thought in rising panic. *And in church, too! ...* Perhaps it didn't count if you only thought it, but then God was even worse than Mother for knowing everything you did, including what you thought.

She tried to pray as well as sing, but it was impossible and she got another nudge from Tom because she kept missing the note. *I'll say extra prayers tonight,* she vowed, trying surreptitiously to rub her arm – *and next week I'll remember not to sit next to Tom.*

"An excellent sermon, Reverend Simmons," exclaimed Mother as they shook hands in the porch.

"Yes, excellent," echoed Father cheerfully. Glad of the opportunity to sit down, he hadn't listened to a word of it. Leaving Mother to exchange social niceties with the ladies of the parish he strode over to Ced Griffiths to indulge in fifteen minutes of farming talk, while The Girls stood shyly but provocatively eyeing the young men from under the wide brims of their straw summer hats.

Jennie saw Tom amble over to Ernest Gronow, nudge him – Tom was a great one for using his knobbly elbows – and nod towards Emily. She watched in fascination as a deep red flush spread above the white of Ernest's shirt collar, until his whole face looked on fire.

"He's taken a real shine to you," Tom told Emily with a grin as they walked home. "Breaking his poor heart, you are."

But Emily tossed her head, pleased with the feel of her hair tucked up under her hat, and looked haughty. "He can mind his own business," she said, "and so can you, Tom Davies."

"I'm sweating!" announced Jennie, remembering Ernest's red face and feeling hot for him.

"Animals sweat, men perspire, but ladies *glow!*" Mother immediately reproved, but she didn't sound too harsh. She'd enjoyed the outing to church and was feeling particularly satisfied because Emily's prettiness and ladylike appearance had been commented on by several people. Not that it would do to let Emily know that, and risk her becoming vain, but it reflected well on herself to have such a personable daughter. She didn't think that Laura would impress with the same qualities, but she was undoubtedly going to become striking in her own way and could make an excellent marriage.

She glanced at Jennie, walking hand-in-hand with her father, and could feel no emotion at all, except perhaps a faint irritation. She'll have to improve greatly if she's going to match up to her sisters, she decided, taking in Jennie's rather sallow complexion and deep-set eyes that permanently had dark shadows under them. But then, it wouldn't matter too much, as she'd already marked Jennie down as the daughter who would stay at home and help care for her parents as they aged. Mother was a great fan of Queen Victoria, and she'd kept her youngest daughter at home.

"Ced Griffiths is thinking of giving up Pontypool market for a while," said Father over dinner in the pleasant well-proportioned dining room. "There's so little money about that people will only buy vegetables when they're nearly going off, so you're practically giving them away."

"And that certainly wouldn't suit Ced Griffiths," observed Tom with a chuckle.

Mother gave a disdainful shudder. "I don't know why anyone would want to go to that dreadful hole anyway."

"Now, Katie," reproved Father in his gentle tones, "It's not their fault if there's no work to be had."

He realised his mistake as soon as he'd finished speaking. Mother hated to be called by what he considered the pretty diminutive of her name.

"They may not be to blame for their idleness, but they don't all have to be so dirty!" she snapped. She rose and began to clear the dishes, indicating to the girls to help, effectively curtailing further discussion.

Pontypool was about nine miles away from the farm, in the opposite direction from Abergavenny, the nearest of a string of mining and industrial towns in the Welsh valleys for whom this second decade of the twentieth century had been disastrous. Repeated strikes for better pay and conditions had only resulted in demoralised men crawling back to jobs for less instead of more, and now shrinking world markets and steel production being moved to more favourable coastal sites made their prospects even bleaker.

Mother, however, could only see sloth in their enforced idleness, and had a deep mistrust of their chapels and public houses which seemed to spawn each other on opposite corners of every mean little street. She much preferred Abergavenny, with its air of bustle and purposefulness as a little market town, proud of its place as the gateway to the beauty of the Black Mountains and Brecon Beacons. Here, life might be tough if you were a struggling hill farmer, but at least more people were Church, and the Blorenge mountain separated you from the awfulness of the mining communities.

And that's the best part of the day over, thought Jennie as she put away the clean cutlery while The Girls washed and dried the dishes. Mother took herself off for her afternoon nap, claiming that she would never rest properly in this sticky heat, but nevertheless everyone would be expected to be as quiet as possible until she arose.

"You can play with your dolls in the parlour," she told Jennie before mounting the stairs, "and then later on we can look at the Big Bible."

"Thank you, Mother," Jennie responded dutifully but dully, and went to fetch her dolls.

She sat on a tapestry stool in the parlour with the dolls on her lap and wondered, as she did each Sunday, what she was supposed to do with them. She'd been told repeatedly that they were very expensive and she was lucky to have such beautiful dolls, and she was sure if she was a doll-type little girl she would be thrilled with them. But there was something sinister about their bright staring eyes, while their rosebud mouths, which Mother claimed to be the epitome of beauty in ladies as well as dolls, seemed petulant and cruel.

Not that Jennie had ever analysed their features to this extent; all she knew was that she couldn't cuddle them and croon to them the way she could to Mopsy, the old rag doll she'd pushed around the farm in her wheelbarrow when she was younger and which was now tucked safely away in the back of a cupboard in her bedroom, lest Mother should find her and deem her too old and tattered to keep any longer.

Jennie thought of Mopsy now and wished she could fetch her to cuddle. She felt in need of the comfort that the familiar feel and smell of her old friend – a mixture of mustiness from the cupboard and old dirt from outside – would give her. But to go upstairs now would be to make the floorboards creak and incur Mother's wrath.

Jennie gazed around the room, hoping for diversion, but everyone was occupied. Laura was busy with her embroidery, which she did exquisitely, and, to Jennie's amazement, with great enjoyment; Emily was writing a letter, while Father and Tom were reading the local papers. They were both back in their working clothes – and thus seated on hard chairs – attendance at church being Father's only real concession to the Sabbath.

Jennie thought about undressing her dolls and then dressing them again but it seemed a rather pointless exercise and their frilled and flounced clothes had so many tiny buttons. The oppressive stillness and heat began to overwhelm her and her head began to ache faintly, but she wouldn't admit to it because that would mean a dose of Syrup of Figs, which she detested and which always left her with a gripey stomach-ache.

"Can I go outside, Father?" she asked, her voice high and loud in the quiet room.

"'Mmm?" he replied absently, his mind still on the news–paper.

"May I go for a walk around the garden? It's very hot in here."

He put the paper down and looked across at his daughter. He noticed her pinched, solemn countenance and smiled kindly. She looked a bit off colour and the room was very warm. "Of course you may," he said.

Jennie laid the dolls on the stool and left the room hurriedly, before Father could remind her about taking a hat. As long as he didn't tell her, it wasn't so bad to pretend to forget.

She was only allowed to walk around the paths edging the formal gardens when wearing her best clothes, and besides, running and shouting would be totally inappropriate on a Sunday. She ventured along the drive until it became too dusty, and then turned and followed a path that led to the side of the house and the part of the garden which the parlour overlooked. She could see her mountains now, except for the very tops of them which were hidden by a shimmery heat haze.

At the bottom of the garden was a large rhododendron bush where she'd discovered a blackbird's nest in the spring. The baby birds had flown, but the mother bird was hopping agitatedly about nearby, hoping to distract her away from the nest.

"It's alright," she said, "I won't hurt you or your babies," and then she laughed as the bird stood still, its head on one side, as if considering what she'd said.

The thought of the mother blackbird's concern for her family brought back all the feelings of yesterday. Jennie probed at them like she did with her tongue at the gap made by a tooth falling out. They felt much the same; raw and faintly bloody, and much too big ever to be filled properly again.

She made her way back the way she'd come, keeping a look-out for one of the farm cats to distract her away from her thoughts and pausing to lean on the garden gate and gaze at the front of the house, feeling a rush of love for its solid beauty. She liked the way the windows each side of the front door seemed to wink at you in the sunlight, and the large cream stones making a pattern up its gable ends. The woodwork was picked out in Father's favourite apple green and cream, except for the front door, which was heavily varnished, with a gleaming brass knocker and letter box.

I never want to leave here, Jennie thought fervently, not even sure in this mood whether she wanted to board at the convent. *Even if Mother doesn't love me, I can't stop loving the farm and everything about it.*

There was something so comforting in the rhythm of its day-to-day activities. Very soon Father and Tom would be back outside for afternoon milking, the pigs and chickens would be fed and preparations made for the beginning of a new working week, each day with its clearly prescribed tasks, varying only slightly according to the seasons.

The best day this week would be Tuesday, Jennie decided, because they were all going to the market. But first, the worst day of the week had to be endured; Monday Washday. Mother would be in a foul temper all day, exclaiming constantly that she didn't know how a family could get its clothes so dirty – although as it was the same every week you'd think she'd be used to it by now.

The large boiler in the washroom between the kitchen and the dairy, from which Father and Tom would only extract a small amount of water for washing and shaving since they never used the bathroom, would be lit at first light. The Girls would strip and change the beds before breakfast, after which everybody tried to keep out of the way as much as possible until they all sat down to dinner – always cold meat from yesterday and re-heated vegetables, because Mother wouldn't have time to cook as well and The Girls, when home, would not be allowed to do it as Mother wouldn't be able to oversee their activities in her kitchen.

"Come along! Come along! I'll never get done at this rate!" was Mother's constant cry to anyone who happened to be in the same room as her and dared stop to take a breath.

By this time Bessie would be red-faced and breathless from her exertions with the dolly, and her arms reddened and sore-looking from hot water and soda, and even Mother, who scrubbed the collars and dealt with the underwear, would, true to her edict, be 'glowing'.

I'll get up early tomorrow and see to the chickens and collect the eggs, Jennie decided, as the first step of her plan to become indispensable to Mother. She conjured up a picture of Mother smiling benignly and crooning words of praise and love – which, in truth, Jennie had never heard in her life – as her youngest child became the mainstay of her existence. *And I'll strip and change my bed myself, and then…*

Her plans were interrupted by large drops of rain plopping purposefully on her head as, in the distance, the first rumblings of thunder could be heard. Jennie hurried up the front path and entered the house just as Mother was bustling down the stairs, issuing orders.

"Turn the mirrors round! Laura! See that all the cutlery has been put away! Leave that front door open, Jennie, and go and open the back door!"

Jennie scuttled off to do as she was told, relieved that her mother was too preoccupied to question why she had been outside. A flash of lightning illuminated the now dark kitchen, followed closely by a burst of thunder that seemed to be right above the roof, making Jennie jump as she opened the back door but filling her with excitement rather than fear.

Mother, though, was frightened by thunderstorms and insisted the doors had to be left open so that a thunderbolt coming down the chimney could find its way out again, and all precautions had to be taken so that lightning shouldn't hit metal or glass.

"Why don't you put your crucifix inside your dress until the storm is over?" Tom had once suggested, and had had his ears soundly boxed, as apparently he should have realised that the wearing of the crucifix automatically protected Mother from the risk of electrocution and it was blasphemous to suppose otherwise.

The storm was heavy but brief. Afterwards Jennie stood at the front door breathing in the scent that the rain had unleashed from the rose bushes lining the path, and watching the early evening sun – released now from the oppressive clouds – making the raindrops sparkle on spiders' webs. The evening was still but fresh, the air sweet, with that indefinable quality of Sunday restfulness and peace, and for a while her mother's recent malevolence was forgotten.

2

Harry

The walk up the steep road to the top of the Blorenge had warmed them, but now, standing at the top with the ever-present stiff breeze whipping round his body, Harry was glad he'd brought his thick scarf with him. Wrapping it round his neck and tucking the ends into his jacket, he looked down over the land laid out before them, wondering as always at the beauty of this bit of creation. To their left was a deep ravine, the 'Tumble', covered in bracken and mountain streams and falling away to the village of Govilon, criss-crossed by little pathways trodden for centuries by meandering sheep and explored by countless children on Sunday School outings. Further down was the glint of canal and river in the pale sunlight, more visible now that the trees were starting to change colour and drop their leaves. And opposite, the majesty of the Sugar Loaf dominating the skyline, its lower slopes a patchwork of field and pasture flecked with copses and isolated farmhouses, with Abergavenny nestling beneath its embrace.

After a few minutes of contemplation Ivor said, "We'd better be getting back. Mam'll be fretting if I'm late for tea."

The two boys turned back towards the way they'd come. A different world below them now: a world of pit head wheels and slag heaps, of ironworks and blast furnaces, of narrow terraced streets punctuated by chapels and public houses. The town where they'd lived out their lives so far; which filled their very being, like the coal dust which permeated every brick and stone, doorstep and window-sill, and the lungs of every miner in Blaenavon.

They passed the edge of the Keeper's Pond, the landmark at the top of the Blorenge, and began their descent down the twisting road. It was only mid-September, but the air already held a hint of rawness, and below them lights were already beginning to twinkle.

"Have you asked again?" Harry questioned his brother as he

strode to keep up with the other's longer gait.

"'Course I have. There's no-one being taken on at the moment. Still beats me why you want to work down the pit, though, when you've got a cushy little number where you are."

For the past year Harry had been working as a delivery boy for the large Co-op store at the foot of the steep hill on which Blaenavon was built. It was known as 'Bottom Cworp' (so pronounced by all the locals, in the way the Welsh have of slurring their vowel sounds) to distinguish it from 'Top Cworp', which was half way up Llanover road, leading out onto the mountain.

But Harry didn't want to be a delivery boy – he wanted to do a man's job, like his older brother Ivor. He was determined to follow Ivor down the mine just as soon as they were taking people on again. His Dad had been laid off after the long strike, like a lot of the older men, but just occasionally they took new ones on and when they did it was fit young lads they wanted, from whom they'd get more work for the same day's pay.

"You just make sure you keep asking," Harry told his brother now.

"And after a week you'll hate it as much as the rest of us," Ivor said. "You'd be better off following our Dai up to London." He quickened his pace. "Anyway, forget about it for now – I've got to go back down the place in a few hours."

He suddenly grabbed Harry's cap and threw it up in the air. "And you'll have to get a few more muscles on you, anyway, boy, if you want to do a man's job!"

And he was off down the road with Harry's cap, his youngest brother chasing after him, both of them laughing.

For these couple of hours they were just two carefree lads again, one a head taller than the other and broader-chested, but there was no mistaking the likeness between them. Straight dark hair, blue eyes, and a directness of gaze that ran through the whole Jenkins family.

Ivor had long been Harry's role model. The youngest in the family, Harry had always tagged along behind the other three, treated with indifference by his other brother Dai and mothered by his sister Lizzie. But it was always Ivor he wanted to emulate. Ivor had joined that close-knit world of those who burrowed underground, the miners who greeted each other as they made their way to the pit-head at the start of each shift, creating a camaraderie it was impossible to infiltrate. And Ivor could join them in the pub of an evening when he was on 'early turn' and raise a pint glass with arms made muscular from hours of hard physical graft. Ivor was already the man Harry longed to be.

The two brothers parted at the corner of High Street with a brief:

"See you – tarrah!" from Ivor and a "Tarrah! Tell Mam I'll see her tomorrow," from Harry. Not for a moment would he tell Ivor how much he'd enjoyed his company, even though to meet like this on Harry's afternoon off from the Cworp meant so much to him. You just didn't say so if you wanted to sound like a man.

Harry made his way to his Nan's house in the middle of a higgledy-piggledy row which faced onto High Street. The shop Nan kept at the front sold a mixture of things: sweets and chocolate that kept the children coming in when they had a halfpenny or penny to spend; fruit and vegetables which were delivered from Abergavenny, and some grocery provisions, mainly tinned and jarred goods. The shop made an income of sorts, and Nan eked out a further living by renting out some of the rooms on the two floors above.

Of her seven children, only two were girls – Mary, Harry's Mam, and Maisie, her youngest daughter who still lived with her. All her other children were married, but all still lived in Blaenavon, so Harry had spent a comfortable childhood secure in the knowledge that wherever he went in the town there was someone nearby who was related to him either by blood or marriage, and who could therefore be relied upon to help him if he was in trouble, or provide a bit of diversion or the odd halfpenny if they were feeling flush.

Nan's lodgers came and went, except for Bill, who helped her in the shop and stayed because he was in love with Maisie – a spirited girl who so far had shown him little encouragement; but he lived in hope because she hadn't encouraged anyone else either.

Harry had been living at his Nan's ever since his Dad was laid off. It had been Nan's idea. "One less mouth for our Mary to feed, and one less pay packet for the Welfare to know about." And her eyes had twinkled at Harry, her favourite grandson who reminded her so much of her husband, promising a stay as cosy as she could make it.

She was in the kitchen as Harry burst in, his cheeks gleaming from his walk and hunger already gnawing at him from the smell of whatever Nan was lifting from the fireside.

"Barley stew?" he sniffed appreciatively.

"When our Maisie gets in," Nan said.

He crept up behind her as she gave the contents of the pot a stir, and put his arms around her, squeezing her squashy girth. "With dumplings?"

Nan smacked his arms from around her middle. "Get on with you, you daft beggar! Yes, there's dumplings. Would I ever make you a stew without?"

They'd have to hunt around a bit for the meat in the stew, but there would be plenty of vegetables that were past their best for selling in the shop, slices of potato and glistening pearl barley for thickening, and delicious gravy, so who needed meat? Like all the more efficient housewives in Blaenavon, Nan was an expert at making a lot out of very little to fill empty stomachs.

She was a comfortable body, almost as wide as she was tall, her stout figure enveloped in a wrap-around print apron that puckered and strained across her cushiony bosom. Wisps of white hair were already escaping from the coiled bun at the nape of her neck, framing a face that was undoubtedly wrinkled, but plump enough that it didn't matter. Nut brown eyes stared straight out at a world that had been full of hardships since her husband had died before Harry was born, succumbing to the same invidious disease that was now creeping unchecked through the lungs of so many men in the town.

Maisie was soon in through the door, looking as immaculate as when she'd left that morning. She worked as a clerk in the colliery office, one of the few women in the place – which she enjoyed immensely, but which kept Bill in secret anguish that she might eventually fall for someone else's charms. Bill joined them when he heard Maisie's voice, sitting opposite her as Nan bustled about serving up their meal.

"I've been out with Ivor today," Harry told her between mouthfuls. "Asked him to keep looking out for a place for me at the pit."

"You'll be lucky," Maisie said, "There's talk now of them closing Milfraen before very long – the Federation's pressing for steel props to be put in, but of course that will cost the Company money, so it's easier for them to close the whole damn place and throw a few hundred more out of work."

"Don't swear, Maisie!" Nan said quickly. "No need to bring pit language to this table!"

Maisie winked at Harry, because they both knew the sort of much stronger language some of the miners favoured. "Better to hang on to what you've got and be grateful," she told him. "There'll be any number wishing they could swap places with you before long."

The evening passed like many another – idle chit-chat around the fireside, where Nan eventually joined them after 'finishing up for the night'. Her chair was to the left of the fireplace, with mahogany arms and faded chintz cushions. The chair on the other side of the fireplace had different cushions, and neither matched the horsehair sofa, just as the chairs round the table where they ate were all different. But any surface that could be polished shone smartly, and now glowed in the light from the fire.

Sometimes Harry skimmed through a newspaper or read the latest thriller he'd fetched from the library, but often it was difficult because the gas lights would start pop-popping as the gas started to run out, and it wasn't economical to feed more pennies into the meter just to read a book.

On Tuesday evenings Nan would don her double-breasted tweed coat, which strained across her front, wrap a scarf around her head and set off down the hill to Horeb Chapel and 'Ladies Bible Study'. She'd been attending for as many years as Harry could remember, and possibly in the same coat, which led him to question one day whether the ladies didn't know as much as they ever needed to know by now.

Bill had laughed. "It's not the study they go for – it's the tea and biscuits and good bit of a chin-wag afterwards!"

Other evenings would see various members of the family calling in, usually the men on their way to whichever pub for a pint or two.

Later, from the street, there could occasionally be heard familiar sounds – men coming off the afternoon shift, having been replaced by those on nights. Later still, the clattering of boots and the odd raised voice as the pubs emptied. Then quiet, as those with work prepared for another heavy day, and those without spent long hours wishing.

This particular night changed abruptly at three in the morning when the town was awakened by the sound of the colliery hooters signalling an emergency. Within minutes fire engines and ambulances were being manned and people were heading for the pit head, the families of those on the night shift at the forefront.

Harry bumped into Nan at the top of the stairs. His eyes met hers in mute enquiry. Two of her married sons worked down the pit.

"It's alright," she said at once. "They're both on afternoons this week."

"It's not alright," Harry said hoarsely. "Our Ivor's on nights. I'll go up and see what's going on." He turned back to the bedroom to fling some clothes on.

Bill's voice came from across the landing: "I'll be with you now, boy."

They soon joined the clatter of boots running down High Street.

"Where is it?" Bill called across to one of the men.

"Milfraen!" he shouted back, in time to his trotting feet. "Rock fall, I believe. Whole tunnel blocked off."

The pit head was full of running feet and voices calling to one another, issuing terse directions, anxious faces suddenly looming eerily out of the dark into the puddles of light cast by the offices where Company officials talked hurriedly to one another. Harry and Bill pushed their way through the hubbub to find the two uncles who they knew would be preparing to go down with the rescue crew.

"Ivor!" Harry shouted at them. "Our Ivor's down there!"

The two men glanced at each other. Both knew which seam Ivor was working on.

"Don't worry. He's probably helping to get the others out already. And if he's not – well, we'll find him," one of them said to Harry, while the other made a face at Bill and jerked his head to tell him to get Harry away.

Bill grabbed Harry's arm. "Look! There's someone else needs our help."

Harry turned in the direction Bill had indicated and saw his father walking towards them, his face dark and grim. Harry looked into his eyes and saw his own anxiety reflected there, so that there was no need to say anything. Bill urged them further away from where the rescue operation was moving smoothly into the well-known routine, and passed Harry's Dad a cigarette.

"Where's Mam?" Harry asked.

"At Nan's with Lizzie. She wanted to come up here with me, but I told her Nan and Maisie would need her. No place for a woman up here."

The growing band of people watched as the rescue party headed for the cage to take them down below, knowing that the next time the big wheel turned it would be bringing up either survivors or bodies. There wasn't much they could do except stand and stamp their feet and speculate on how many were trapped and what their chances were. Those who had lived through this sort of thing before murmured about the additional hazards gas and rising water levels could cause with every passing hour that the mine stood crippled.

Women, unable to sit at home and wait any longer, began to arrive. With scarves and shawls pulled over their heads to ward off the cold night air, tangy with the taste of coal dust, they stood in huddles separate from the men so that it didn't matter if a tear or two was shed even before the worst was known.

They look like the women at the bloody crucifixion! But how many healthy innocent men are being sacrificed this time? Harry thought bitterly.

Milfraen was the oldest of the three colliery workings and rumours of its neglect were rife. Captain Jackson, the Company manager, could be seen in the yellow light of the engine room, apparently overseeing proceedings – a hard, flinty-eyed man who rode about town on a tall chestnut gelding, thinking nothing of using his riding crop to swat at small boys should they get in his way. The Company owner kept well away from the source of his wealth, so it was towards Jackson that most vitriol was directed; it was he who had remained implacable to the miners' demands and scorned the

Federation; he who had watched with a satisfied gleam in his steel grey eyes as the men crawled back to work after each strike, for less than they'd earned before; and it was he who had made the final decisions about how many should be laid off as the slump continued, so the ranks of unemployed rose ever higher.

"Huh!" said one old hand grimly, "the only thing that bugger will be bothered about is if any of the trucks are damaged. They cost more to replace than the men."

As the hours passed the mutterings became more muted, the atmosphere more expectant, broken only occasionally by ripples of anxious whisperings every time an official moved from one office to another. Even the air became still.

It was daylight before the cage wheel began to turn and the first of the casualties was brought up. It finished turning when there were nine bodies laid out on stretchers, to be taken to the shed designated as a mortuary for formal identification.

The first one was Ivor.

3

Jennie

Waking early on Tuesday morning, Jennie rushed to the window to check on the weather. If there was so much as one little cloud over the Skirrid, Mother would insist on taking mackintoshes and umbrellas. But the sun was shining and the sky was clear. Relieved, Jennie smiled at the mountains, splashed her face and hands with cold water from the jug which stood on the dresser and quickly dressed.

Entering the kitchen, she realised it was even earlier than she'd thought and The Girls were not yet about. Father and Tom were still out on the milk round and Bessie, who had to walk nearly two miles from the far end of Nantyderry, had only just arrived and was in the dairy with Mother, washing down the utensils. Any other morning Jennie would have gone through and offered to help, but today she stood uncertainly by the kitchen table. Monday had been a very bad day, incurring Mother's anger very early on, and Jennie wasn't sure of her reception this morning – especially without The Girls there for moral support.

She hadn't meant to make Mother so cross. Following her resolve of the previous day she'd crept out early in the morning, before even Mother was downstairs, opened the coops and let the hens into the orchard, shooing out the birds that were still roosting and finding their eggs fresh and warm in the hay. Then she'd taken the eggs into the washhouse and carefully cleaned and dried them before replacing them in the basket, which she took into the kitchen and placed proudly in the centre of the table so Mother would see them as soon as she came into the room.

As the house was still very quiet, Jennie had gone back to her bedroom and begun to change her bed, already feeling a heady glow from anticipating Mother's pleasure. She'd heard Mother go downstairs, and Bessie arrive, and later the sound of the milk van returning. She was struggling to make a bundle of her dirty bedclothes to carry them downstairs when she heard the back door slam, Tom's voice talking rapidly, and then a loud cry from Mother.

Her heart began to thud. Something had gone wrong! Perhaps Tom had bumped into the table and broken the eggs; or perhaps it had been Bessie as she laid the table for breakfast.

But it was worse than that. The latch of the high gate going into the orchard hadn't been closed firmly enough; all the hens had escaped and were now scattered over the flower garden, the vegetable plot, the yard, and some had ventured into the barn.

Mother had pounced on Jennie as she re-entered the kitchen.

"It was you, wasn't it! *You've* done this, you stupid girl! Why can't you leave things alone? Now we've got to get all the hens back, and there's all the washing to do – I'll never get done!"

She began to shake Jennie as she spoke, until Jennie thought her teeth were beginning to loosen.

"I was trying to help!" she spluttered disjointedly. "I didn't m-mean to let them out! I was t-t-trying to give you a nice surprise!"

She burst into tears as Mother released her, and ran into the arms of Emily, who had just come down to see what all the commotion was about. Emily automatically put her arms around the distraught child, but Mother stayed her.

"Leave her alone – it's too late for her to be crying now! Come outside with the rest of us and help round up the hens!" She turned to the sobbing Jennie: "There'll be no market for you tomorrow, my girl! Go to your room!"

I think you're being a bit hard on the child," Father remonstrated when he came in for breakfast, while The Girls held their breath at his temerity. "She was only trying to save you some work, and the catch on that gate is very stiff. She wouldn't have let them out on purpose – not like Tom here would have done at her age!"

Mother said nothing until breakfast was nearly over.

"I suppose she'd better come to market with us," she grudgingly relented. "She'll only be under Bessie's feet otherwise. But she can stay in her room this morning and not get under mine, now she's put me so far behind!"

Everyone breathed a silent sigh of relief, and Bessie found a moment to sneak some bread and jam up to Jennie and tell her that she would be getting her treat after all.

"Thank you Bessie," was all Jennie had said, in a woebegone little voice, her face a picture of misery.

It wasn't right, Bessie thought. Always picking on that young one, her mistress was – she'd have trouble with her nerves later on, she'd bet on it. She'd seen her jump before now when her mother spoke sharply to her – and she'd cleaned those eggs something lovely, bless her.

Bessie went heavily downstairs and took out her feelings on the washing dolly.

Jennie had been allowed downstairs again late in the afternoon, when the kitchen was hot and steamy and smelling of ironing, with Mother pressing the shirts and blouses that Bessie couldn't be trusted to do properly, and the sheets already folded over the rack suspended from the ceiling, to air. Mother's only comment had been a warning to 'keep out of things'.

She'd gone quietly out of the house in search of Father, needing the comfort that his reassuring presence always gave her. She found him walking the cows in for afternoon milking, and fell into step beside him. Luckily Tom was elsewhere.

"I'm thinking of increasing the herd," Father told her. "Just a couple at a time – and it's your turn to decide on names for the next ones I buy. So would you start to think about it?"

She nodded and gave him the ghost of a smile. She knew it was his way of making her feel better. "I like Mildred," she said, remembering a character from a book she'd just read.

"Mildred's a fine name for a cow. If I see one at the market tomorrow, then Mildred it will be."

Tom was waiting for them at the cow shed. Jennie didn't feel up to dealing with his teasing, so didn't go in. At the door Father leaned down towards her. "Those old hens enjoyed their little trip out of the orchard, you know. They'll be cackling about it in the hen-house for days."

She felt the familiar conspiratorial warmth that she always felt when she was out and about on the farm with Father. There was a twinkle in his eye as he spoke, so she reached up and put her arms around him and for a moment hugged him hard – something she hadn't done since she was much smaller. Surely Father couldn't be so kind all the time if he didn't love her at least as much as he loved the others.

And now it was market day, made all the more exciting because she would be allowed to spend the time with Emily and Laura instead of following Mother sedately about as she shopped. They were all ready straight after breakfast, Mother so impeccably dressed that no-one would imagine she was a farmer's wife. She and The Girls were to take the train in, avoiding the cattle market altogether, and would meet up with Father and Tom at the Angel Hotel later in the morning for the journey home.

Tom and Father had already gone on ahead with the milk van, which Jennie would have liked to have done too, because she knew that they would have taken the road into Abergavenny which went past the old workhouse – and Tudor Street.

Since very small, the phrase 'like someone from Tudor Street' had been used whenever she had muddy boots, or a dirty face, or tangled hair, so that its inhabitants now held a great curiosity for her. Tom had told her that the children played in the street, often without shoes, and the smaller ones even without any underwear, but perhaps that was just Tom teasing her again. Mother, when asked, dismissed it as a 'slum' that lowered the tone of Abergavenny, and where you would catch diphtheria (which was much worse than pneumonia) if you so much as set foot near the place. Jennie gathered from this that Mother must be unaware that Father and Tom drove through there every day, ladling pathetic amounts of milk into jam-jars, Father often refusing their pennies and halfpennies when he knew there was a sick child in the family.

Good morning, Mrs. Davies!" The treacly voice of Dr. Moxom stayed them as they were walking down the hill from the station towards the town. Dr. Moxom attended all of them except Father, although he came from the far side of Abergavenny and there was a doctor in Goytre whom they could have used. But Mother maintained that Dr. Moxom was far better trained than any doctor she'd come across, and was so understanding of *women's problems.* Jennie sensed from the slight undertones in which this was said that it would be wrong to ask what those problems might be. But Mother was probably right, because Dr. Moxom was apparently a great favourite with other ladies in the area too. Father, equally steadfast for once, refused to be impressed, and stuck with Dr. Pritchard who was just as interested in animal ailments as human ones.

Dr. Moxom seemed quite old to Jennie, but she knew he was considered to be rather handsome, and he certainly oozed charm in an oily sort of way. He raised his hat and bent so low over Mother's hand that Jennie thought for a moment he was going to kiss it, which she imagined would feel quite tickly as he had a large, walrus-like moustache (which he seemed rather proud of, as he often stroked it as he talked).

"Just the lady I wanted to see!" he exclaimed, holding Mother's hand for a few moments more than was necessary and patting it with his other hand. "Could I claim a minute or two of your time? I have a great favour to ask of you."

Mother looked most gratified to be singled out for such attention, particularly as it could be noted by so many people leaving the station. They walked along the pavement together towards the doctor's car, he talking all the while and she listening intently and nodding from time to time. Jennie and The Girls walked a respectful distance behind, trying to overhear the conversation nevertheless, but failing. Emily soon gave up and began to imitate the doctor's important walk instead, shoulders back, stomach out, and her chin thrust down into her neck in just the way his rather jowly folds sat upon his wing collar. Jennie began to giggle but Laura tugged at her sister's sleeve in embarrassment.

"Stop it!" she hissed. "They'll see you!"

"Well, he's so pompous! And Mother thinks he's so wonderful!" Emily exclaimed, straightening up just in time as the two adults came to a halt beside his car.

"Friday afternoon then," Mother was saying as the three girls came alongside them. "I'll try to get as many ladies as I can to be there." She turned slightly, her face rather flushed and her eyes gleaming. "Come along, children, we have a lot to do!" – which made Emily angry so that she raised her head haughtily and swept past the doctor without looking at him. Child, indeed! But Laura lowered her eyes demurely as he raised his hat again in farewell before climbing into his car and driving off in the opposite direction.

The encounter had put Mother in a high good humour, and she raised no objection to Jennie accompanying The Girls around the town.

"But I want you to meet me in Wilding's in one hour," she told them. "I must get some new liberty bodices for Jennie."

Jennie's heart sank. How could Mother be thinking of horrible, itchy, restrictive liberty bodices in the middle of summer! But Mother always operated at least half a season ahead lest the items she wanted should be gone by the time they were really needed, and liberty bodices were donned at the end of September, whatever the weather.

The three sisters watched for some moments as Mother walked up Cross Street, a neat figure in her summer coat of lilac linen and matching small-brimmed hat. She moved swiftly but was never jostled by the crowd. She possessed an ability to stand still for a fraction of a second and look eloquently and pointedly at whoever barred her way so they immediately stepped aside with a murmur of apology as she continued unassailed. At the corner of Monk Street she met an acquaintance and entered a shop selling bed and table linen.

"Come on," said Emily, "if we hurry we can get to Fulgoni's for an ice-cream before she comes out again."

Mr. Fulgoni himself served them, speaking in an impossible accent of mixed Italian and Welsh and making them giggle when he called them 'Young ladies, innit, eh?'

They sat near the front of the ice-cream parlour, from where they could see the comings and goings of everyone else. The shop was long and narrow, with much of one side taken up by a long polished mahogany counter with large mirrors behind it advertising Fry's chocolate in curly, flaking gilt letters. Laura and Emily whispered together as they ate their ice-cream, but Jennie sat in silence, intent on concentrating all her senses into enjoyment of the unexpected treat.

Afterwards they wandered down Frogmore Street to the War Memorial, then crossed the road and sauntered back up the other side. They stopped to look in Stacey's Shoe Shop, which claimed to have the 'Latest London Footwear for Ladies' displayed in the window, which was incongruously surrounded on the outside by pair upon pair of stout men's working boots. They also gazed in the window of Fenella Modes, which sold ready-made dresses – skimpy and vulgar in Mother's estimation, the height of fashion to The Girls – but hurried past the gunsmith's because he always had rabbits hanging outside in summer, and pheasants in winter, which upset Jennie despite her country upbringing.

They arrived early at Wilding's, 'the major' (because it was the only real) department store in the town. "Let's look at Jewellery, before Mother finds us," Laura suggested, and she and Emily spent some time looking at rings and necklaces in large glass cabinets and discussing the merits of brooches set in gold rather than silver, as if they could afford either. Jennie was content to watch the assistants, who fascinated her. They seemed to have been hand-picked to match the luxury goods which they sold, and were tall and slender with fashionably shingled hair and white faces which were remote and unapproachable. They wore the regulation black-dresses-with-white-collars with a certain dash that somehow stopped them looking like uniforms.

Upstairs in Ladies and Childrenswear, where Mother was waiting for them, the middle-aged assistant was made of stouter stuff. Her hair was scraped into an uninteresting bun, and the same black dress bulged in unexpected places, the hem drooping uncertainly at the back. She wore a tape measure around her neck and had a small pincushion crammed full of pins attached to the belt of her dress. She was indisputably Welsh, smiling kindly at Jennie through small round spectacles and calling her 'my lovely' as she measured her chest.

After four of the dreaded liberty bodices had been purchased Jennie had to stand for a long time and wait whilst Mother and The Girls inspected bolts of material for winter dresses. She passed the time by watching the brass canisters, into which all sales invoices and money were placed by the assistants, being shuttled overhead to the central cashier – who then returned the canister with a receipt and the customer's change – and wondering whether she dared interrupt Mother to tell her that she needed the lavatory.

Eventually, however, choices were made, Jennie was taken to the Ladies' Powder Room, and they all sallied forth to meet Father and Tom outside the Angel Hotel.

"Here they come now," said Laura, just as Mother – who as usual had arrived at the Angel early – had begun to tap her foot impatiently at their tardiness. The town, on market day particularly, was a jumbled confusion of motorised cattle lorries, large impressive cars belonging to the well-to-do, and smaller cars belonging to the more humble (some with dickey seats on the back), all mingling with horses and traps or carts to which many of the country people clung, either out of obstinacy or lack of funds. Most of the shops displayed as many of their wares as possible outside, making the narrow pavements even narrower, so that many people walked in the road with a brave disregard for the traffic around them.

Despite the throng, Father's van was easily recognisable. It was painted in a deep glossy green, trimmed with gold, and the sides were embossed with the words 'E. Davies, Dairyman' – also in gold. Father, through dint of sheer hard work, had cornered the largest share of milk deliveries in the area, but several of his neighbours (who also owned dairy cattle, but were not as successful as he) claimed that he'd built up his round because people remembered his distinctive van. One or two had asked him where he had got the idea for the colour scheme from, but he'd simply chuckled and refused to tell them that he'd copied it from a tin of Tate and Lyle's Golden Syrup.

Father had converted the parcel shelf beside the driver's seat into a passenger seat, and it was to this that Mother was assisted. The doors at the back of the van opened to reveal a shelf down each side on which the milk churns usually stood. These were now placed on the floor in the middle and the four children, rather uncomfortably, sat on the shelves with the various purchases distributed between them. Mother would have liked to own a car like Doctor Moxom's so that she could sit in comfort in the back, but Father had said that they couldn't afford it, so that had been that.

"I'm having a little gathering on Friday afternoon," she told Father now. "We met Dr. Moxom when we got off the train. He wants me to persuade as many ladies as possible to come, so that he can talk to them." She glanced sideways at her husband to see if he had realised what an important ally she was to the doctor, but he was intent on negotiating his way through the busy thoroughfare. "I met one or two ladies in town, and thought perhaps Tom could take some invitations round Goytre tomorrow?" she went on.

"I'm sure he could," Edward replied, resolving privately that he and Tom would spend Friday afternoon mending fences in the bottom field – as far away from his wife's 'little gathering' as possible. He didn't bother asking what the talk would be about, as he knew that Katharine would only make veiled references to 'women's needs', which always made him want to say something rude about what most of the women hereabouts were *in need* of.

"Plenty of business going on in the market," he said instead. "Some poor old boy from Crickhowell was selling up his stock – had some good heifers, too. I'm collecting one of them tomorrow."

Mildred. It would be Mildred. Jennie caught a hint of a wink as Father turned his head slightly towards the back of the van. Mother was scornful of their habit of giving names to the cows, which Jennie was pleased about now. It gave her something that only she and Father would share.

Mother murmured appropriately as Edward continued to talk but her mind was on what she would prepare for tea on Friday, and, just as important, what she would wear.

4

Harry

Coal dust danced in the thin shafts of pale sunlight filtering through the high windows of the shed, scattering and re-forming each time the door opened. The creaking of the door, never remarked upon before, was now a noisy, impertinent intrusion into the hush which had descended not just over the pit but over the whole town.

Harry watched as his father clasped Ivor's broken body to his chest before kissing his son's forehead with a gentleness Harry hadn't known he possessed. He watched as his father laid Ivor back down and nodded to the attendant. He watched as his father turned away and brushed his hand across his face.

Harry didn't know if he was crying himself; the pain in his chest was so great that the rest of him felt numb. This couldn't be right. The world couldn't tip itself on its head in so short a space of time. It couldn't be true that he would never again walk up the Keeper's with the older brother who meant so much to him.

Dad stepped away from Ivor's body with a look of utter bewilderment on his face. The father who had brought all three boys up with a firmness that sometimes bordered on roughness; who had made them strip off and wash in cold water in the back yard every morning of the year; who had insisted on good manners and honesty with a ferocity that belied his wiry build – was suddenly looking lost and diminished.

With a jolt Harry realised that, with Dai away and Ivor gone, it was now up to him to be the man he'd wanted to become.

He forced down the pain that was threatening to make him physically sick, and stepped over to his father. "Da," he said gently, "it's time we went home. We need to let them know before they hear it from someone else."

His father turned to him with unseeing eyes. "What am I going to tell Mary?"

Bill was waiting for them with Harry's uncles. They stopped talking as soon as Harry and his father appeared, and silently the small group made its way back down towards the town. At the bottom of High Street the uncles shook Dad's hand and set off to tell their own wives what had happened.

Four pairs of female eyes were raised to theirs as they entered Nan's living room. Harry's Mam looked steadfastly at his Dad, who simply said, with a choke: "Our Ivor ..." and then shook his head.

With an anguished cry Mam flung herself into her husband's arms as, over the top of her head, his eyes bleak in his white face, Dad muttered, "It should have been me ... It should have been me..."

There was anger amongst the miners who went to pay their respects to weeping widows and mothers over the next few days.

"They should've put steel props in ages ago, like they promised, not kept those old wooden ones," the men muttered amongst themselves, but it was muted because there were too many men already unemployed to risk bringing the anger to the boil and call for a strike. Instead there were heated debates between the managers and Federation representatives, with more promises made, and more distrust generated. In an effort at appeasement the managers promised to carry out full repairs to the damaged colliery, pledging that it would help maintain employment in the town, and with that the Federation had to be content. No mention was made of the intention to close Milfraen completely, as relayed to the family by Maisie.

"It'll still happen," she said. "They'll use this as an excuse to say they've done a survey and the mine has to be closed."

Harry's Mam and sister Lizzie were consumed by grief over the next few days, while his Dad wore a haunted expression and spent long hours sitting on his own in the cold little front room of their house in Morgan Street. It was left to Nan and Harry to organise the arrangements, to send a telegram to bring Dai back from London, and to field inquiries from well-meaning friends and neighbours, whilst Bill, aware that he was an outsider in this family, quietly kept Nan's shop going.

Long processions followed the hearses up Varteg Hill the following week to the windswept cemetery, where it was possible to believe that loved ones could find peace in a resting place overlooking the whole valley, but difficult to believe they could find warmth in its cold, rain-sodden earth. Afterwards, shunning the crowds, Harry made his way back up through the town, where all the shops were closed as a mark of respect, until he reached the Keeper's pond, and the spot where only days ago he and Ivor had been so carefree. He had relinquished his mantle of manhood willingly to Dai, and here, alone on the mountain, he was a boy again, weeping until he thought his heart would break.

Dai's anger at what had happened simmered just below the surface throughout the few days he was home, only kept in check because of the subdued atmosphere in the house. Always the argumentative one in the family, he had left the town in disgust that Ramsey MacDonald's Labour Government, a General Strike and the Miners' Federation had achieved nothing, either singly or together, to help the working man in Blaenavon. Harry wondered whether Dai would come home for good now, and take up the fight, but he was intent on returning to London.

"Found myself a girl there," he told Harry. "Can't give her up, can I? And there's nothing for me here. It's lucky you've got the job at the Cworp, 'cos our Mam won't want you going down the pit now."

Deep down Harry had known that this would be the case, but there was something about Dai's attitude that irked him. It was easy to be full of righteous anger from a distance. He had never been as close to Dai as he'd been to Ivor, and now he found himself wondering if he would have minded so much if it had been this brother who had died.

Somehow the tragedy of that night was gradually absorbed by the town. It wasn't to be forgotten, or its profound consequences for those directly affected underestimated by the renewed rhythm of daily life, but the earning of the daily shillings and the sheer hard work it involved were too urgent and demanding for there to be too much time to stand and reflect on the losses that were an inevitable hazard in the grim industrial microcosm of the valleys. Day by day the town crept back to normality, the disaster still providing fodder for corner-shop gossip until slowly it was superseded by the more pressing concerns for a sick child or an elderly relative.

At Harry's parents' house in Morgan Street the family rallied round, more aunties than Harry remembered having turning up with plates of food, and staying to sit with his Mam for as long as she seemed to need them. Harry visited daily, but shied away from suggesting he returned to live. At the moment he felt he would be a poor substitute for Ivor.

Harry was there when Wyn Hopkins came to the house to apologise to Mam for the accident that had taken her son.

"It was my fault!" he kept saying. "I told him to sit there... I didn't mean him to come to no harm... trying to look out for him I was...

and the others…. I should have got them out … it was my fault …!"

Gradually the full story of what had happened emerged. Ivor had been Wyn's young 'butty', his mate, working at the coal face under Wyn's direction. They'd stopped for their break, and Ivor had settled himself down in a corner to eat his bread and cheese. "That prop doesn't look too safe next to you there," Wyn had said. "Best sit over the other side, if I were you."

Ivor had moved to the other side, while Wyn took a closer look at the pit prop. As he did so, the prop where Ivor was now sitting gave way and Ivor was buried under a ton of coal and rubble.

Wyn took to coming to the house every few days, reiterating his guilt. "Never made a mistake like that in all my years… I should have seen it… thought I was looking after him! Can't sleep now, keep seeing the prop give way … seeing him crushed…"

Most times Mam heard him out, pity for the man causing her to hold back her own grief until he'd gone. But finally it was too much. Memories of her firstborn as a child had filled her head all day; the feeling of a small hand clasped confidently in hers had been so real that she hadn't been able to stir from the chair. The image of a shy smile beneath a mop of tousled curls was ever-present when she closed her eyes; the memory of the emotion which swamped her body when she'd held her beautiful baby in her arms for the first time had overwhelmed her. She suddenly screamed at Wyn to stop, to go away, to leave her with pictures of her son as he had been, not as he was when they finally pulled him out, and once she started screaming she couldn't stop.

Harry's Dad told Wyn he wasn't to come again, and after that they heard that he'd left Blaenavon and gone to live at Mountain Ash.

The family closed ranks again, until their Mary gradually began to surface from her grief, while her husband kept his burden to himself. And Harry learned to accept that for now, at least, he was stuck in the Cworp and would have to find some other way to become a man.

5

Jennie

The house was a hive of activity on Friday morning. Laura was instructed to give the already immaculate parlour a thorough polish, and Bessie and Jennie had to clean the dairy, with the door propped open so that Mother could issue frequent reminders of what was required from the kitchen where she and Emily were busy preparing food.

The kitchen was exceptionally large, with a range and bread oven taking up most of one wall and a huge dresser, which had been built along with the house so that its top corners disappeared into the join between wall and ceiling, took up another. There were doors in three corners: one led into the hall, one to the back stairs, and one through to the washroom and dairy. In the fourth corner stood Mother's pride and joy: a Valor stove. This enabled her to make sponge cakes and other delicacies that were impossible to achieve if one only had a range to cook on. Only Mother used the Valor stove, because anyone else was bound to make it dirty or scratch its enamel surface. It was much in use this morning and by eleven o'clock a Victoria sandwich, a batch of fruit scones and a tray of dainty almond biscuits were cooling on the table in the middle of the room.

Dinner was a rushed affair for everyone because, although the ladies weren't expected until three o'clock, Mother wanted everything ready by two. For once Tom wasn't upbraided for bolting his food, while old Stan the cowman, eating his meal afterwards with Bessie, was fixed with a steely glare for taking so long to chew each mouthful (on account of having no back teeth). He didn't appear to notice, though, and seemed to take even longer – deliberately, Mother decided, to annoy her.

"Lovely, missus," he said, as he always did when he finished, and leaned back in his chair as if to linger over a cup of tea. When this wasn't forthcoming he appeared finally to understand the need for urgency.

"I 'spect you'll be wanting me out from under you so's you can be ready for your tea-party," he said amiably to Mother as he shambled to his feet and lifted his cap from the back of the chair. But Mother was so agitated with him by this time that she couldn't look at him and busied herself with jam in the larder until he'd gone.

Emily had expected to be included in the afternoon's activities and was surprised when Mother told her to prepare a picnic with Laura.

"I want you both to take Jennie out from under my feet. And it's a lovely day – you could go across to the woods at Penperlleni."

The suggestion was issued as a command.

"But I'm not a child, Mother!" Emily protested. "I've left school! Laura could go with Jennie – they don't need me there!"

"And I don't want you here!" Mother's tone was firm, but she looked slightly embarrassed. There was a pause and then she said quickly, "Dr. Moxom only wants to talk to *married* women."

Emily opened her mouth to ask why, and to point out that if it was anything to do with babies then shouldn't she be there if she was going to be helping to care for a baby in a few weeks? But Mother had turned slightly pink and began to talk about what to take on the picnic, so Emily knew it was futile to go on.

M arie Stopes!" Tom said when he came across the girls as they trudged across the bottom field to the gate.

"Who?" asked Laura.

"Marie Stopes," he repeated. "That's who the talk is about."

"What do you know about it?" said Emily sharply, wishing he wouldn't stand there with a stupid grin on his face. Tom had an amazing capacity for knowing everything that went on, despite being out in the fields all day.

"Well, I delivered the invitations, didn't I? And I just happened to look inside one of the envelopes."

"That's sneaking!" exclaimed Jennie, but Emily immediately shushed her. Tom would refuse to tell them anything more if they upset him, and Emily, as the oldest child and *almost* a woman, felt quite definitely that she ought to know as much as Tom, if not more.

"I expect she's just some doctor who tells women how to bring up their babies," she said casually, but watching Tom carefully.

"Not how to bring them up," said Tom slowly, pausing then for maximum effect. "How *not to have them* in the first place!"

Laura blushed to the roots of her hair. "I don't think we should be discussing this… not with Tom… and Jennie – she shouldn't be listening…" Thoroughly flustered, she appealed to Emily. But Emily, even more intrigued, decided to call Tom's bluff.

"It wouldn't have said that on the invitation – you're making it up!"

"No I'm not!" he replied hotly. "It said that there would be a talk about Marie Stopes and her book called *Wise Parenthood,* which deals with the subject of 'Family Planning'. And in case you didn't know, big sister," he continued in a jeering tone, standing very close to Emily, "that means doing things so that you only have babies when you want to!"

"But what sort of thi—"

"*Emily! Please!*" Laura was writhing with embarrassment. "Let's talk about this later, when…" She nodded her head meaningfully in Jennie's direction.

But Jennie, who had appeared not to be taking much notice of the conversation, suddenly shouted: "It's not true! You can't not have babies if you don't want them, because –"

She stopped before she could blurt out the real truth; that if there had been a way, then Mother would not have had her! Instead she took to her heels and bolted through the gate into the lane.

"There! Now look what you've done!" Laura was sufficiently full of righteous indignation to make Emily feel guilty, and both girls hurried after their young sister. But Tom just stood and watched with an expression of disgust on his face. Girls, and especially very small sisters, were incredibly annoying!

Then he thought of the girls he saw walking to the High School in Abergavenny in the mornings when he was returning from the milk round, and a grin spread over his face. Perhaps not *all* girls were annoying.

That seemed to go very well!" Dr. Moxom stood rubbing his hands together in a satisfied way as Mother returned to the parlour from seeing the last lady out. "And an excellent tea you laid on, I must say! I am most indebted to you."

"Thank you." Mother received his compliments in an unusually demure manner, a faint flush colouring her cheeks, and she cast her eyes down coyly.

She really is a fine-looking woman, Dr. Moxom thought. *Seems too young to have a daughter of sixteen. Pity she's a patient…*

Mother raised her eyes to find the doctor's admiring glance still upon her. She began to collect the cups and plates on to a tray.

"Would you like more tea, Doctor?"

"No, thank you. I must be on my way soon. But perhaps… ?" He waved his pipe inquiringly.

"Of course," said Mother, who didn't normally allow smoking in the parlour.

She was aware that he continued to watch her as she moved about the room, making her feel clumsy, but excited too. Thank goodness he's a doctor, she thought. It was exhilarating to know of his interest in her, but reassuring too to know that it would never go any further. She wondered what it would be like to be married to a doctor and live in a smart town house instead of a farm in the back of beyond, and have everyone treat you with due deference because you were a doctor's wife. Yet Dr. Moxom's mousy little wife seemed blithely unaware of the eminence that was hers, and made no attempt to become a leading light in Abergavenny society.

Her reverie was interrupted as Dr. Moxom, having performed the ritual of lighting his pipe to his satisfaction, began to talk.

"I think, in view of the success of today's little gathering, that I might hold a clinic – just once a month perhaps, so that ladies might come to seek advice... of a particular nature, so to speak." Now that they were alone it was difficult to mention the matter other than obliquely.

B ut the afternoon hadn't been quite as successful as the doctor thought. Two of the ladies, quite shocked at the frank way in which female sexuality was explored by Mrs. Stopes, and further embarrassed by the fact that a man, albeit a doctor, was explaining these issues to them, told their husbands about it. They, in turn, were furious, and laid the blame at Mother's door.

However, Mother's haughty demeanour at church on Sunday was too much for them, and they were unable to confront her, although they did their best to cold-shoulder her. But as Mother was a past master of that particular craft it had little effect. So they accosted Father on market day, when Mother wasn't with him because the weather had turned and it was pouring with rain. Father, in his quiet, amiable way, listened politely and then took the wind out of their sails by agreeing with them.

"I know my Katie gets some funny ideas in her head," he said, ruefully, "but she don't mean no harm, you know. You just take no notice and it'll all blow over. Anyway, your wives didn't have to stay as long as they did if they didn't like what they were hearing, did they?"

But he was thoughtful as he drove home with Tom. What was Katie playing at? She didn't even like sex any more – hadn't let him anywhere near her since Jennie had been born, so what was she doing talking to all these other women about it? He remembered their early, passionate days. She hadn't needed any instruction then. He sighed at the emptiness of their life together now, and decided not to say anything at home – it would only precipitate a row, and roused passions of any sort these days made his enforced celibacy even harder to bear.

His resolve weakened, however, by the evening, when the persistent rain of the last few days had worsened his wife's temper because the washing hadn't dried and she was 'behind' with everything. Looking forward to an evening indoors after bedding down the animals for the night, he entered the kitchen to find Katie at loggerheads with Emily.

"She only dropped it because she was nervous – and she only gets nervous because you keep telling her off!" Emily was saying in a voice as near to shouting at her mother as she dared.

"And when you've had some experience of bringing up children, you might be entitled to tell me what to do with mine!" Mother's voice was loud and hard. "And if you can't speak civilly to your parents, you had better go upstairs as well!"

"Gladly!" Emily retorted, flinging wide the door to the hall and clattering noisily up the stairs.

"What was all that about?" Edward asked as his wife gripped the back of a chair tightly, her face set in anger.

"Jennie again, of course," she said with bitterness. "I told her not to wipe the large dinner plates because they are too heavy, but she insisted on helping the others, and then of course she dropped one, so now we haven't a complete set any more! It's always the same – no matter what I do with that child, she thwarts me! She's either under my feet, or can't be found when she's wanted... and now The Girls are home she's getting an insolent way of looking at me. And then they spoil her, no matter what I tell them! We had hysterics from her tonight, just so that they'd feel sorry for her..."

"Katie, Katie!" Edward caught hold of her hands and held them firmly in his, making her turn to face him. "You must stop all this – Jennie is just a child! You expect too much of her at times, probably because the others are so much older..."

The fire in her eyes as she looked at him sparked an answering fire in his belly. How lovely she still was, all the more so when roused – either to passion or anger. A growing desire for her made his voice catch in his throat.

"Emily has a point – you are too hard on the child," he went on, but at this she pulled her hands away from him.

"Oh, I might have expected you to side with your precious daughters! You have no idea what it's like for me... no idea! Stuck here day after day – everything to do... no life ..." She moved around the kitchen, lifting things unnecessarily from one place to another, putting distance between them as she continued her litany of grievances.

For once Edward didn't make his customary retreat. He couldn't; he wanted her too much. His earlier reminiscences of what their young life had been like spun round in his head.

He strode across the room and caught her by the shoulders. Her body was rigid with emotion.

"What more do you want?" His own voice had risen now, edged with frustration. "I try to give you everything I can. You have a beautiful home, four lovely children, as much money as I can make – all for you!"

He stopped. There was something in the depths of her gaze that he couldn't fathom. Need? Desire? How long was it since that flame had burned?

"You could have a wonderful marriage," he said, slowly and deliberately. "*Married loving* – wasn't that what your Dr. Moxom was talking about? Where has ours gone, Katie?"

He moved to enfold her in his arms, to kiss her, ease the tension in her, but she wrenched herself away from him.

"Oh, that's always what it comes down to in the end, isn't it? Animal instincts! Never mind what the woman wants – just get her in the bedroom!"

Fighting the urge to pick her up and carry her there, protest though she might, Edward leaned forward so that his face was near to hers.

"There was a time," he said angrily, "when you were perfectly happy to be there!"

She stepped back as if he'd struck her, furious that he'd dared to refer to the baser side of her nature which had mortified her so all these years.

"I know better now," she hissed, her face contorted with rage. "I spent my youth tending to my parents' mistakes, and the best years of my life dealing with my own. I'm never going to put myself in the position of making any more and –"

"Don't worry!" he interrupted, "I shan't be asking you to, ever again!"

She seemed about to say more, but suddenly straightened herself, and he watched as she fought and succeeded in regaining control of her emotions. Taking a deep breath and squaring her shoulders, she turned and walked swiftly to the door, the only hint of distress showing in the way she bit hard on her clenched fist as if willing herself not to give way as she left the room.

Edward lowered himself into a chair at the kitchen table and sat motionless for a long time.

Persistent November rain had left rivulets of water running down each side of the lane which led down to Goytre Hall on the main road. Jennie watched the different trails they made as she trudged up the lane after school. As was her habit, she spent the lonely mile pondering the insoluble question of Mother.

She'd tried in so many ways to get into Mother's good books over the last few months, but it had been harder than ever. It was easy with Father; he never seemed out-of-sorts, just got on with everything in his steady methodical way – glad of your help if you were offering it, but just as happy with your company. But Mother's moods couldn't be anticipated. Jennie had taken to watching her, trying hard to read her face and then eagerly offering to do this or that, like the ever-alert farm dogs who followed at Father and Tom's heels. But it seemed that was wrong too, as more often than not Mother snapped at her to go and find something to do.

"But I want to help you," Jennie had tried to remonstrate, only to be told, "You'll be more of a help if you get out from under my feet."

It was nearly dark when Jennie reached the farm gates and the welcoming glow of the farmhouse lights at the end of the drive. She found herself wishing for many things as she fastened the gates carefully. She wished they could be a proper, happy family, so that she didn't have to wonder whether the inside of the house would be as welcoming as the outside appeared. She wished it was still summer, with The Girls at home, so that the light evenings could be spent out in the fields.

There'd been some highlights to the summer, despite the agony of discovering that her mother didn't want her. Like when Tom had been allowed a rare day off to accompany his sisters to the top of the Sugar Loaf; a longed-for treat that lived up to all Jennie's expectations. Tom had enjoyed the freedom from the daily grind and for once proved to be excellent company, chasing Jennie on the lower gentle slopes and swinging her round when he caught her; tipping her up over a stream that tumbled down the mountainside and threatening to drop her in until she squealed for mercy; telling her the names of the birds they saw, and suddenly holding her still when a buzzard appeared on a rocky crag ahead of them.

At the top he'd taken out his penknife and carved all their names into the large flat piece of rock on which they could stand and feel on top of the world, looking across and down at the Skirrid, the Black Mountains stretching out behind them and Abergavenny laid out in miniature in front of them. They sat eating the food they'd brought with them whilst they tried to outdo each other in recognising landmarks, and Jennie felt that she had the best family in the world, and her bruised little heart began to heal a little.

She also wished, shamefacedly, that Aunt Eunice could be her mother.

Towards the end of August, Aunt Eunice and her husband Frank had come to visit for the day. "Hello my darlings!" Eunice had exclaimed as she swept into the hall and tried to embrace the three girls together, ignoring the sour look on Mother's face because her visitors hadn't given enough warning of their arrival.

Eunice, Mother's youngest sister, was her complete antithesis. Where Mother was serious, she was light-hearted; where Mother was methodical and house-proud, Eunice lived in a perpetual muddle in a large untidy farmhouse, and thought nothing of stopping in the middle of a boring chore and sitting down to play the piano instead. But her natural vivacity meant that no-one else, except Mother, minded or even noticed the chaos that existed at Llanover Farm.

Much to Mother's annoyance, Eunice had married a much wealthier farmer than Father, despite Mother's prophecies throughout her girlhood that her flibbertigibbet ways would lead to a sticky end. Eunice had laughed at Mother then, as she laughed quite often now, a pretty tinkling sound that had entranced and excited her older husband.

But even Mother's disapproval thawed after a few hours in Eunice's company, and by the evening Eunice had the whole family assembled round the piano in the parlour.

"Let's have a sing-song before we have to go!" She played with a certain amount of talent and a lot of enthusiasm and knew all the popular songs of the day.

"Come on Katharine, your turn!" Father urged after everyone else had sung – even Tom, who'd managed the first verse of *To Be a Farmer's Boy*, which was all he knew.

"No, I don't think so," Mother demurred in a tone that would have silenced her children. But Father persisted.

"You've got a beautiful voice. You always used to sing. Do it for us now."

For a moment the crease in the middle of Mother's brow appeared, and Jennie held her breath, waiting for the sharp words which would put an end to the idyll. But Father held Mother's eyes with his, until she was the first to look away.

"Very well."

She sang *Room With A View,* a recent favourite, in the clear sweet voice that the children rarely heard except in church, and by the end of it Jennie had found tears welling up.

Why can't the family always be liked this? she wondered. *Why does it need someone like Aunt Eunice to come along to make us all nicer to each other?*

The others must have been thinking similarly, because after Mother finished there was a lull where everyone became very quiet. Father was still gazing unwaveringly at Mother as she brushed away praise for her fine voice with unusual modesty, until Aunt Eunice began *The Laughing Policeman* and insisted that "all the youngsters join in the chorus and see who can laugh the loudest!"

But those happier summer days seemed long gone, and now there were only the cold dark days of winter ahead, when she'd probably be under Mother's feet more than ever. Jennie sighed as she trudged down the path and round through the yard. She hoped Mother would be sufficiently distracted this evening not to insist that Jennie did her piano practice. Not that she minded learning to play – it was Mother's reaction to her playing which jarred her nerves lately.

Mother insisted that Jennie leave the parlour door open as she practised. Then, whenever Jennie made a mistake, Mother would exclaim: "Ah!" from wherever she was in the house, in harsh, impatient tones sufficient to unman Jennie completely, and she would have to begin the piece again.

I'll have to make myself become more like Emily, she decided as she opened the door into the kitchen, *and toss my head and not mind every time Mother finds fault.* But then, Emily knew that deep down Mother loved her, and perhaps that made all the difference.

It was as if by thinking of Emily she'd managed to conjure her up, because there sitting at the kitchen table was her big sister, sipping tea as Mother busied herself at the range.

With a cry of delight, Jennie flung herself into Emily's arms and then pulled back. "Your hair – you've had it cut!"

"Do you like it?" Emily turned this way and that to show off the neat, glossy bob.

"It's far too short," Mother exclaimed before Jennie could answer, "and makes you look too old. What on earth must Mrs. Talbot think of it?"

But Emily was unperturbed by Mother's disapproval. She had quickly become aware that having a job away from home kept her out of Mother's jurisdiction. "Actually, Marjorie – she asked me to call her by her first name – thought it was an excellent idea because it stays so much tidier when I'm with the children. And it will be better like this when I'm nursing." Said with just the sort of nonchalance Jennie longed to emulate.

Mother could find no easy argument in the face of both logic and

47

Emily's employer's approbation, so contented herself with a grumble that Emily was still under age and her parents should be consulted in matters of her well-being – and this was one of them. Emily let her grumble on, knowing that she'd won on points, and winked at Jennie when Mother wasn't looking.

"I've got a whole weekend at home – the family have gone away – so we can have some time together," she told her little sister, whom she thought was looking even more woebegone than usual.

By the next day Ernest Gronow had somehow heard that Emily was home, and invited her to a supper dance at Goytre village hall. To everyone's surprise Emily accepted, and Ernest arrived promptly at seven, his starched collar looking as if it was strangling him. He sat on the edge of the chair in the parlour waiting for Emily, reddening every time he replied to Mother's polite conversation. When Emily finally entered the room, tall and slender in a blue wool dress with a dropped waist which no-one had seen before, he stood up so quickly that the bowler hat perched on his knee fell to the floor. He blushed all the more as he stooped to retrieve it and tried to say hello at the same time, so the word came out as a sort of hiccup.

Emily saw Mother eyeing the short hem of her dress disapprovingly. "Marjorie gave it to me – she said it suited my colouring," she said, as she grabbed Ernest's arm and ushered him out of the door, her proximity rendering him completely speechless.

It wasn't Ernest, but a different young man who escorted Emily home, which didn't please Mother.

"You'll turn out just like your Aunt Eunice if you're not careful," she said waspishly.

"And if I do I'll end up with a wealthy husband like Uncle Frank who dotes on me, so you'll have nothing to complain about, will you?" Emily flashed back.

Mother pressed her lips tightly together and for once said no more.

6

Harry

Harry turned up his jacket collar and thrust his hands deep into his pockets against the bitter November wind which hit him as he rounded the corner from Broad Street into Lion Street. He liked to walk up through the town on his way home from work, knowing there'd be plenty of people to pass the time of day with, including pretty shop girls to whom he could call a greeting with a bravado in the dark that deserted him if he met them in daylight.

He crossed the road to look at the pictures of forthcoming attractions outside the Coliseum Cinema. Ron Attwell – proprietor, manager, doorman – stood in the entrance.

"Charlie Chaplin on tomorrow night, Harry. Coming with the girlfriend, are you?"

Harry turned to him with a grin. "Nuh. My girl likes Bottom Hall better. Says the seats are more comfy. Tarrah!"

'Bottom Hall' was the other cinema inside the Workmen's Institute at the bottom of the town. The Coliseum being nearly at the top of the hill was known, therefore, as 'Top Hall', in the same way as the two Cworps were differentiated.

Harry hurried on up Lion Street before Mr. Attwell could say anything more. He really must find a girl to ask out, he decided; a conclusion he'd reached many times recently but had been unable to act upon. After all, he was sixteen, had been at work for two years now – which made him almost a man, so it was time to start acting like one and acquire a girl. And he wasn't bad looking: average height for a Welshman, which perhaps was a bit on the short side really, but then he still had time to grow a few more inches. His dark hair and blue eyes were a bit more unusual, he wasn't covered in spots like some of his friends, and his teeth were good.

The trouble was, in a town like Blaenavon everyone knew everyone, and working in the Cworp made him particularly well-known.

And, like every other small valley town, people would comment the minute they saw a girl on his arm, and he would prefer to do his courting more privately – at least until he'd had a bit of practice.

He turned into the pitch-black gully that led to the back of Nan's house. This same alleyway had been home to bogey-men and hideous nameless monsters when he was a little boy, so that he'd been too frightened to go down it unless Nan had left the back door open, letting a shaft of light shine through. Those fears had gone now – only the fear of making a fool of himself with a girl was left.

"Nan! It's me!" he called as he entered the back kitchen, anticipating the tea that Nan would have ready for him as soon as he took his jacket off. But the house was unnaturally quiet, and there was no Nan in the kitchen, straightening up from the range, the blackened kettle in her hand to fill the tea-pot.

Harry went through to the shop at the front of the house. That too was empty except for Bill, who sat behind the counter reading the paper. He looked up as Harry came in.

"Your Nan's gone over to Morgan Street, Harry. Your Mam's been taken bad. Lizzie came for your Nan. She said to –"

But Harry was gone before he could finish, back up the gully and running hell for leather across the town.

What could be wrong now? Surely to God Mam hadn't done something stupid?

It had been over a year since their Ivor had died, and for months Mam had been like a stranger, going mechanically through the basic motions necessary to go on living; just! – saying little, noticing less, as she grieved for her eldest son. Sometimes she'd sat for days on end looking into the fire, neglecting the house of which she had been so proud, and its other inhabitants. Once or twice these long silences had culminated in prolonged paroxysms of weeping, everyone hoping after each one that she would be better able to cope once she'd 'got it off her chest'.

Gradually, though, Mam had begun to get better. Not the Mam they all knew, chatting and laughing as she did six jobs at once, but at least she'd started to talk again, and show a bit of interest in what was going on. It was even longer, though, before she began to pick up the reins of the household again.

Which was why Harry still spent most of his time at his Nan's, so as not to worry his mother.

He slowed down now as he crossed Market Street, feeling hot from running – and from the prickles of guilt that ran up and down his spine as he thought about his mother. *I didn't need to have stayed away this long,* he owned to himself. But, having always been Nan's favourite, it was much more comfortable to stay in her warm, bustling home than return to the house in Morgan Street, which had no warmth left in it since the day his brother died.

And I was thinking of going back soon, he argued with his conscience – and Mam had been much better lately, even put a bit of weight back on, and was livelier round the place what with making plans for Christmas. *Perhaps whatever's wrong is nothing to do with our Ivor.*

He reached the front door of the small terraced house. The doctor's car was parked outside and several small boys had gathered to inspect it. Their mothers came out from time to time, ostensibly to check that the kids weren't damaging the car, but really to see what was going on at Number 37 that necessitated a visit from the doctor.

Taking a deep breath, Harry opened the door and stepped straight into the front room. His father stood in front of the fireplace – unlit, because this room was never used except on special occasions – the anxiety on his face lifting a little when he saw his son; but before either could speak there was a clatter on the stairs as Ceinwen James, who delivered babies and did the laying out, came heavily down them.

Did the laying out! – Harry turned a horrified face towards his father, but Dr. Freeman had followed Ceinwen down the stairs and was already speaking.

"I think that's all we can do for the moment, Mr. Jenkins. I've given your wife something for the pain and she should sleep soon. Plenty of rest she needs now, for a few days, and nothing to worry about." He rested his hand on Harry's shoulder. "I'm sure this young man and his sister will help all they can."

"Very grateful, Doctor. Very grateful indeed," Harry's father muttered as he fumbled in his pocket, his eyes not meeting the doctor's. Harry suddenly realised the cause of his embarrassment. He dug his hand into his own pocket.

"Thank you, Doctor." He pressed the half-crown into the doctor's hand. He sounded as if someone was strangling him. "My Mam –" he forced himself to say, "is she…?"

"Your grandmother's with her," said the doctor, "and I believe your sister is making her a cup of tea. Why don't you take it up to her? Just stay for a minute, mind, but you'll see that she's alright."

Harry went into the kitchen as his father saw the doctor and Ceinwen out. He glanced at the clock on the mantelpiece. Only half past six. Plenty of time for Ceinwen to go round the doors and tell everyone what was wrong with his Mam.

Lizzie came towards him, her face white and tearstained, and rested her head on his shoulder. She was a year older than him, but smaller and rounder, although they shared the same facial features.

"Poor Mam!" she said. "And that poor, poor little baby."

"*Baby?*" Harry pushed her away from him slightly so that he could look at her face. "What baby? What are you talking about?"

"Our Mam, silly! She was having a baby!" She stared at his incredulous expression. "You mean you didn't know? Seven months gone, she was," she continued when he didn't say anything, "and seemed to be getting on fine. And then suddenly she started – but it was much too small, wouldn't take a breath… poor little mite!"

Tears welled up in her eyes again, as the kettle began to sing on the hob. She busied herself making the tea as Harry stood there, dumbfounded. His mother had been expecting a baby and he hadn't even realised. And hadn't been around enough for anyone to bother to tell him. Not that it was something that was talked about very much, except by the women when the menfolk were out of the way.

I should have noticed, he thought. *I should have cared enough to see that she wasn't just putting on a bit of weight.* But then his parents seemed so old; he hadn't even been sure that they still did things… like that!

His mother looked older still when he took her tea in. Her hair was loose around her shoulders and he saw streaks of grey running through it that hadn't been there a year ago.

Nan gave him a grim smile. "I told Bill to make sure you stayed where you were. No place for men and boys at times like this."

His eyes were on his mother. "Seems like I've stayed away a bit too much." He stepped nearer to the bed. "I'm sorry Mam."

She thought he was referring to the baby and patted his hand. "The doctor's idea, it was," she said. "Thought it would help me get over our Ivor. Time I did, I know." She smiled wanly at him. "Don't look so scared! A few days in bed, and I'll be back to normal – *really* back to normal, you'll see."

Harry didn't know what else to say. He stood in the cramped room, unusually warm from the small fire burning in the grate, and felt awkward in the silence that followed. He wanted to tell his Mam that he loved her, wanted her to be well again; that he'd been frightened she was going to die … but those weren't the sort of things you said out loud once you were no longer a child, and you only said them then if you were sure no-one else could hear.

His grandmother broke the uneasy silence. "I think it's time you walked me home, Harry. Bill will be wanting to shut up the shop, and Maisie will be in by now."

His Mam turned her head and smiled at her own mother. "Thanks for coming – and thanks for the sheets."

A visit from the doctor, too expensive to request except in cases of real emergency, was treated with great respect, and any housewife worth her salt worried lest he think she was slovenly in her habits. So the urgent message carried by Lizzie that her Mam was losing the baby was accompanied by a desperate plea for clean sheets, which at the time was as much an anxiety for her mother as the premature labour that was wracking her body.

Nan studied the worn features of her eldest daughter, for whom she'd wanted so much. She herself had shed no tears when Doctor Freeman had been unable to breathe life into the tiny mite that had slid silently into the world, but she wanted to weep now. She kissed her daughter's brow, which felt cold and clammy despite the heat of the room.

"Lizzie will see to you tonight and I'll be along in the morning. You get some sleep now. Tarrah, love."

Downstairs her son-in-law was eating a meagre supper of bread and cheese. He got up too quickly from the table and was immediately wracked by a fit of coughing, so that he had to hold the edge of the table to steady his thin, bowed frame. The skin was stretched tight over his cheekbones and, Harry noticed, it had a yellowish tinge to it.

When the coughing was over he wiped his face with a handkerchief and then began to speak as if nothing had happened. As Harry and Nan were leaving, he gripped his son's hand. "Thanks for … you know, the doctor…"

"That's alright, Da. Payday in a day or two. I've got enough till then."

When they'd gone Albert Jenkins went up to see his wife, but she was asleep, her head back on the pillows so that a slight whistle escaped from her mouth as she breathed. He watched her for a moment or two and wondered for the first time whether the baby they couldn't have afforded to keep properly if it had lived had been a boy or a girl.

Harry and Nan walked back across the town, quiet now that most people had gone home from work.

"I think your Mam needs you back at home, Harry. Be better for her to have more people to fuss round again. In fact I think both your parents could do with your help."

"I cough up my pay every week, except for my bit of pocket money," Harry declared, rather defensively lest his grandmother think he wasn't prepared to do his bit. "And if I go back, where will I sleep? Lizzie's in the back room now – I can't share with her."

"You wouldn't have to," said Nan. "Lizzie can sleep in with your Mam. Your Da's been sleeping downstairs on the couch for months now – he coughs too much if he goes upstairs in the cold."

Something else he didn't know. Harry felt the needles of guilt creeping up his spine again. When had his parents changed from being the reliable cornerstones of his life to the frail people he'd seen tonight? *Before Ivor's death,* he told himself. The strikes, that's when the rot really set in; long winters with little to eat and little to warm themselves with, and what they did have going into the mouths and on the backs of their four children. He remembered the bowls of food when they came in from school, made from all sorts of odds and ends, but tasty just the same, and Mam always saying she'd eat hers later.

Nan's voice broke into his thoughts. "The baby was going to give your Mam something else to think about, help her to stop dwelling on losing Ivor. And it doesn't look as if Dai's coming home just yet, so you're the only one who can fill the gap."

"I'll talk to Dad tomorrow night about moving back in," Harry said.

Nan's house seemed full of relatives: Maisie; Bill, who was considered family now even though he had still got nowhere with Maisie; Uncle Fred, Nan's eldest son and the only one who seemed to be prosperous; and his wife. They all began to speak at once when they saw Nan and Harry, having sat around the fire for the last half-an-hour speculating as to what might have happened to their Mary, and thus keyed up to hear the worst.

"She's alright," said Nan, quieting them all with a wave of her hand and plopping down onto the horsehair couch that ran along one side of the room, "and I'm saying no more until I've got a cup of tea in my hands." Maisie hurriedly topped up the pot from the kettle that sat permanently on the hob.

"C'mon Harry lad, you have a cup too – by here; you look cold." Fred, noticing Harry's pale drawn face, pushed him down into a fireside chair.

Nan took a long slurp of tea and then began to speak, her voice matter-of-fact and not for a moment betraying her own anxiety.

"Mary's lost the baby, which is sad in one way, I suppose, because a life has been lost, but if you ask me it was a bloody silly idea in the first place – our Mary was too old and in no fit state to carry another child. Thought we were going to lose her as well at one point, but I've got to be honest, Dr. Freeman was very good, and she's going to be fine." She drank some more tea. "And I suppose Ceinwen James was good in her way," she went on, with a sniff, "once she'd had a good look round to see what Mary had in the house."

They were all quiet for a moment, and Bill used the occasion to pat Maisie sympathetically on the shoulder. Then Nan began to marshal them, not giving them time for unnecessary sentiment, setting Maisie to help get supper ready, asking Bill questions about the shop, and indicating with her eyes to Fred that he should absorb Harry in conversation.

Nevertheless, Harry was glad to get to work the next day. Two more of his uncles had called round with their wives during the course of the evening, and inevitably conversation had dwelt on the plight of his mother, the state of his father's chest which made finding work so difficult, and what, if anything, they could all do to help.

Maisie and Bill were sitting at the table in the living room, finishing their breakfast, when he hurried downstairs seeking the warmth of the fire after the freezing cold of his bedroom. Nan, who only ever sat down in the evenings, was moving about the room, tidying, taking dishes out into the back kitchen, and urging Maisie to hurry up. Maisie's job in the colliery office meant she didn't start until eight thirty, and also meant that she was excused from helping too much in the mornings, as she had to keep herself tidy for her work.

"I'm going! I'm going!" she exclaimed, cramming a last piece of bread into her mouth and jumping up as Nan's voice from the back changed from encouraging to threatening.

"You look peaky," she said to Harry, giving him a hug as she passed him – which she knew would make Bill wish he looked peaky, too.

Nan came back into the living room and glanced at Harry.

"There's porridge ready," she said. "Sit yourself down while I get it."

"I don't think I'll bother –" Harry began, but she interrupted.

"*Porridge!*" she insisted. "You're not going all day with nothing in your stomach." Her words were gruff, but there was an underlying kindness in her tone. She bustled back out into the kitchen to fetch a bowl, and then stood by the fire ladling steaming spoonfuls from the big pot on the hearth.

"Fancy the pictures tonight?" asked Bill. Despite being a few years older, he and Harry were firm friends; on Bill's part because he was friendly with everyone, and on Harry's because Bill had a devilish sense of humour which erupted into fiendish pranks when he'd had a few. They had become closer during the last year, which helped to fill the gaping void left by Ivor's death.

Harry was about to say yes when he remembered the half-crown he'd given to the doctor. He'd been jaunty about it to his father, but it was all he had until payday, and today was only Wednesday.

"I'll be visiting our Mam," he said instead. "I need to talk to her and our Dad about moving back over there. Why don't you ask

Maisie?" he added quickly, before Bill could say anything about him leaving that would make him wish he didn't have to.

"I might," said Bill, deliberately casual because he liked to believe that no-one else knew of his passion for her.

Harry set off down High Street, which was nearly all residential apart from the obligatory pubs and chapels, and a couple of corner shops, and quiet at this hour. The miners still lucky enough to be in work had started the early shift several hours since, and the more industrious housewives had already been out whitening their front doorsteps as the first part of their daily battle to keep the dirt and grime of the collieries out of their homes.

High Street was flanked on both sides by rows of terraced houses, stone-fronted and dropping down every two to accommodate the steep hillside on which they were built. Because of this they varied slightly in size, some having three small bedrooms instead of two, but they were all the same in the paucity of facilities: a cold water tap in the scullery, and a toilet in the backyard. Things had improved slightly though, since the beginning of the last decade, in that all the houses now had mains drainage – although the only means of flushing the toilet remained a bucket of water. Some of the rows of tiny cottages in the middle of the town still had several houses sharing one badly drained toilet, and in these streets constipation was endemic amongst young girls, who preferred to ignore the call of nature rather than suffer the ignominy of responding to it whilst their next door neighbour stood outside waiting his turn.

Harry reached the bottom of the street and turned the corner past Horeb Baptist Chapel, of which all of his family were stalwart members. It was a plain building on the outside, as befitted a nonconformist chapel which eschewed the fripperies of the Roman and Anglican churches, but inside the simplicity was enhanced by the U-shaped upper floor supported on pillars, the warm glow of the highly polished wooden pews, the rich dark wood of the raised pulpit, and the magnificence of the pipe organ above it. At the back of the chapel were several small rooms, and a larger one used for every occasion for which a tea-party was a suitable accompaniment.

Harry tugged at his cap and put his head down against the bitter wind that whipped round the corner. If November was anything to go by, they were in for a hard winter.

The Cworp stood on the next corner and a narrow alleyway ran between it and Horeb, leading to a yard housing the bake house, the slaughterhouse, a room for making sausages and pie fillings, and a stable for six horses. So, depending on the time of day, your nostrils could be assailed by the smell of new bread, fresh blood, or horse manure, or at times a noxious concoction of all three.

This morning, though, the bake house had a head start. Harry hurried down the alley and, breathing in appreciatively the aroma of fresh bread, went into the little store room that doubled as a cloakroom, took off his cap and jacket, and donned a long white apron. Then he walked through the main large storeroom and into the shop, where the other members of staff were already engaged in preparing for opening. One of the girls was polishing the long mahogany grocery counter that ran down one side of the store, while another scrubbed the provisions counter on the other side. A cousin of Harry's was scrubbing the big marble slab that was used for cutting butter and cheese, and at the back of the shop the glass-fronted bakery counter was being stacked with loaves of bread and, on display, custard slices and other cakes and fancies.

"'Morning, Mr. Pugh," Harry spoke respectfully to the stern looking gentleman with a Van Dyke beard who was overseeing operations, and waited for his instructions.

"Rice and sugar need topping up," Mr. Pugh said. "Last batch of bread is nearly ready, so then you can make a start with the deliveries."

With a brief hello to his workmates, Harry went back into the storeroom and began measuring out rice and sugar into paper bags – dark blue for the sugar, grey for the rice – and folding the top of each one precisely into an envelope shape, with the corners neatly tucked in. When he'd first started he'd made a dreadful mess, especially with the sugar which was so difficult to sweep up, but now he was quite an expert and rarely spilt any.

He took the packages behind the grocery counter and stacked them on the tall mahogany fixtures until the appropriate shelves were full, then stood back to check that all was in order, appreciating the symmetry and neatness. Three large japanned bins were attached at intervals to the fixtures, and he lifted the lid of each to see if they were full. They held the different types of tea, which were supposed to be blended according to the customers' tastes, but in these difficult days two of the bins contained the cheaper Indian tea, while only the third contained the more expensive Mazawattee.

Dilys, who was in charge of the grocery counter and had been re-stocking the row of biscuit tins that stood in front of the counter, came up behind him when he'd finished and slipped a paper bag into his pocket when Mr. Pugh wasn't looking.

"Broken biscuits," she whispered, "for when you're out later on. And don't go giving them all to that old horse."

Despite having worked at the Cworp for two years Harry was still the youngest employee, the taking on of more school-leavers having been suspended as business slackened and the takings dropped – which meant that Harry still had to undertake the more menial tasks, even though he'd become quite proficient at counter work. Dilys, in particular, tended to feel sorry for him and wanted to mother him, especially in bad weather when he had to be outside driving the delivery cart.

But Harry, with no more thought now of going down the mine, was grateful to have a job and worked at making himself as indispensable as possible, just in case there was any talk of laying off. He'd already learned to drive his Uncle Fred's car, in readiness for the time when the carthorse would be replaced by a motor van, as other big stores were already doing. And he enjoyed the variety: delivering the bread each morning, stocking up and making up orders at the beginning of the week when things were slack, then helping on the counters at the end of the week when most people did their main shopping.

Today he was particularly glad to be out and about, even if it was bitterly cold, as he knew that Ceinwen James would have done a good job in spreading the news about his mother as far and wide as possible and it would be the topic of conversation amongst many of the women who came into the store.

He went back through the store to the stable yard. "Hello boy," he said to the large piebald, who whinnied at his approach. He fed him a handful of oats and then put his bridle on, talking to him all the while.

"Fed up I am, today, Major," he explained. "Our Mam's poorly, our Dad doesn't look much better, I'm skint, and I haven't got a girlfriend!"

Major nuzzled his nose against Harry's neck as he led the big gelding out of the stable. Harry smiled. "Understand every blooming word, don't you?" – to which the horse snorted in reply.

Harry turned him round and backed him between the shafts of the cart, where the old horse stood patiently as Harry loaded up with the deliveries. Then they were off, Harry hardly having to twitch the reins as the gentle animal plodded along the route he'd been travelling since long before Harry had taken charge of him.

They headed out towards Cwmavon road, where a long row of large terraced houses had been built at the turn of the century, when Blaenavon was at its most prosperous. Beyond the terrace were several grand detached houses set in their own gardens, where the doctor, a bank manager, and the works estate manager lived. The road led out of Blaenavon down through the valley towards Abersychan and Pontypool, where the trees in summer and autumn hid the squalor of the cottages dotted about, and made the valley beautiful.

Major stood quietly while Harry delivered the bread to each house on his round, sometimes moving on before Harry reached him, to stand patiently at the next house on the route. They zigzagged back across the town, up and down the steep hillside and along the narrow streets, until they went back past the Cworp and the bottom of High Street, and along Church Street. They passed the little Church School where May Dando had been the sole teacher for nigh on twenty years, taking all the children together in one room heated by an old stove in the middle, on which Miss Dando's wet handkerchiefs gently steamed throughout the winter.

The town was busy now, local delivery vans and carts doing their rounds, and larger lorries travelling up and down from Abergavenny and Pontypool. Women were out doing their daily shopping, a serious business when a little had to be made to go a long way, and on many of the street corners stood huddles of unemployed men and boys.

Harry turned off Church Road and went up into the 'Park', a wooded area of land upon which, in elevated positions in keeping with their status, were two large houses – the bigger being the home of the Blaenavon Company owner, Mr. Lumley-Jones, and the other having been built to house his general manager, Captain Jackson. Little was seen locally of Lumley-Jones, his steel and coal empire enabling him to live the life of a gentleman and concern himself only with matters brought to his attention by his various managers.

Harry's sister, Lizzie, worked in the Company house under its housekeeper, and sometimes there'd be a quick mug of cocoa smuggled out to Harry if there was no-one about.

Today, though, Harry didn't even see Lizzie, and he didn't hang around. A pale wintry sun was shining in a blue sky, but it was bitterly cold. "C'mon Major," he said. "Up to Big Pit now, for the sawdust," and he urged the horse back through the Park, out past the lodge gates and on up the road that led to the colliery.

Each Wednesday, when his deliveries were complete, Harry took the cart up to the big carpenter's workshop where the pit props, railway sleepers and the like were made, and collected large sacks of the sawdust which was spread each morning on the newly-swept Cworp floor. The colliery, the steel works with its ever-pounding hammer, the tyre factory, the railway, and all their associated workshops covered the lower slopes of the Coity mountain, facing the hills on which Blaenavon was built, so that wherever one was in the town the activity of the Works, and the three huge coal-tips to one side, dominated the view. Above these the Coity rose, long and flat on top, patiently enduring the assault on its belly, whilst below the road to

Pontypool threaded its way between the two hillsides, following the course of the river, Afon Llwyd – the 'grey river', bereft of the trout that once swam in its clear waters; nothing more now than a filthy trickle since man had begun to burrow and despoil its banks.

From the town all that could be regularly heard of the Works were the bass beat of the big forge hammer and the brassy clatter of the railway, but once up the hillside and amongst the buildings the noise swelled to a full orchestra. The violin squeaks of the pit wheel turning, the double bass sawing in the carpentry shop and the 'cello whining of machinery made up the strings; the faster tenor beat of the hammers in the blacksmith's forge and the stamping of horses' hooves provided the rest of the percussion, whilst men's voices, shouting to be heard, made up the recitative.

"Be with you in a minute Harry!" one of the carpenters called as he pulled up in front of the workshop. "How's your Mam?"

"Not so bad," Harry called back, and received a nod in reply. Somehow it was alright when men asked questions like that; they asked, you answered, and that was that. None of the fishing for gory details or the endless speculating on what had been or what might yet be that women seemed to enjoy so much.

Harry climbed down from the cart and gave Major the biscuits from his pocket. He leaned against the horse's warm flank and studied the view. From here all Blaenavon could be seen, spread-eagled on the opposite hillside – row upon row of terraces in varying degrees of repair, from the very old rubble built cottages of Stack Square to the better quality tiers, mainly around the perimeter of the town. Ten thousand men, women and children lived here, most of them dependent on the Company and its associated businesses for their livelihood, and few of them ever straying further than Cardiff.

The road at the top of the town led out over the Blorenge towards Abergavenny, over moorland which had been thick with purple heather a month or two previously and upon which Mr. Lumley-Jones enjoyed grouse-shooting parties with his friends.

To an outsider the moorland horizon looked bleak and uninviting, the town a drab grey scar with no visible redeemable features save the architecture of the Institute and one or two of the more grandiose Victorian chapels. But Harry looked upon it and loved it all. Every twist and turn held memories of his childhood, and his dreams for the future encompassed no more than a desire to enjoy the best that the town could offer.

He liked to stand, as now, and pick out the landmarks of his childhood: the steep road that ran from the top to the bottom of the town, down which he and his friend Arthur had ridden the scooters they'd been given one Christmas, terrifying themselves and anyone who got in their way because they were unable to stop until they reached the bottom; the Drill Hall near the old Army barracks where the well-to-do of the town held balls, and where he and Arthur would peer in through the window to watch them and then perform a grotesque parody of their dances on the grass outside; the bakery and warehouse in Hill Street where they found a load of dead rats and had taken their tails to school to claim thruppence a tail during the rat epidemic, convincing old Miss Dando that they'd killed the rats themselves; the Rolling Mill pub where his Dad had taken him when he was very small and he would stand on a table to recite a poem for the men which began, 'There was a bloody spider ran up a bloody spout ...' and be given pennies, until his Mam found out and put a stop to it.

"Six sacks, is it, Harry?" The carpenter roused him from his contemplation, and together they loaded up the cart.

One of the Chapel women left some tickets in the shop this morning, for the Avonia Players. She said she'd seen you looking a bit down and thought it might cheer you up," Bill told him as soon as he got in that evening. "*Kith and Kin* they're doing next week. I said you might go with a young lady."

Nan straightened up from the range and put a steaming plate in front of him. "What young lady is this, then?" There was a teasing gleam in her eye, which made Harry redden, so he put his head over the plate and hoped that the steam would get the blame.

"Dreaming he is," he said, ignoring Bill's wicked grin at his discomfiture. "I haven't got a 'young lady', and if I did have I wouldn't take her to that old thing. I'll ask Da if he wants to take our Mam."

But when he went over to Morgan Street he found his father sat in the chair by the fire, his mouth set in a thin line, reluctant to chat. Harry thought he knew why. It was the day when Lewis the Coal delivered to Morgan Street, bringing the "Lowance Coal' as it was known – the coal that each Company worker was allowed as part of his wages. It was tipped outside the front of the houses and guarded jealously by each housewife, lest a kick or two might send some of it across into the neighbour's pile, until their menfolk arrived home and could carry it shovel by shovel down the gully that separated every few houses, and into the coal shed. Only, of course, there'd been no coal delivered outside the Jenkins' house; instead his Dad had stood at the front window, weak and impotent, and watched as others had taken in their load.

"How's our Mam?" Harry asked.

"Better," his father replied. "Plenty of people in and out all day to see her. Been like a bloody circus here at times – never seen so much tea drunk."

His mother smiled when he went into the bedroom, and there was a hint of colour in her cheeks.

"I'm fine," she told him. "Well enough to get up, really, only nobody'll let me. All the family's rallied round, as usual. Have you had your tea? Lizzie will be getting something for your Dad when she gets in – working late tonight, she is; there's a 'do' up at the house."

He smiled back, pleased to see her looking better. "I had tea at Nan's before I came over. I've been thinking…" He began to twist his cap around in his hands, saw Mam watching and stuffed it in his jacket pocket. "I'd like to come and live at home again… here, with you and Dad and Lizzie… if you think there'd be room…"

There! He'd done it, and her smile lighting up her eyes made it worthwhile.

"Of course there's room. Come back tonight if you want! Or perhaps… Saturday might be better. Give Lizzie time to sort out her things, then she can come in here with me… I expect you know your Dad has to sleep downstairs now?"

She spoke so easily and laid plans so readily that he knew Nan had already paved the way for his return. He nodded. "Saturday, then. I'll tell Nan tonight. Lots of people asking after you today," he went on. "In and out of the shop all afternoon they were. And Mr. Pugh heard, and even he said he hoped you'd soon be better."

Harry had had to help on the provisions counter during the afternoon, a job he normally enjoyed but one he'd hoped to avoid today.

The women who were genuinely concerned had merely said things like, "Sorry to hear about your Mam's trouble," or: "Give her my best – tell her I'll pop in to see her when she's feeling better." But Mrs. Hughes, crony of Ceinwen James and similar in build, so that they waddled down the street together like a pair of squat bookends, had come in when the shop was quite full and fired a barrage of questions. "Better today, is she, your Mam?" Then, before Harry could answer, she was away, talking to those around her: "Terrible time she had – *haemorrhaged*, Ceinwen said. They had to send for Dr. Freeman!" Then back to Harry: "'Course she was never properly over the other business, was she? Still fretting over your Ivor – awful shame that was… I'll have a quarter of tea while I'm here."

Harry had fetched the tea while Mrs. Hughes, sure of her audience now, continued. "Awful time to have another, mind. What is she now, Harry – forty, your Mam?" She shook her head sagely and folded her arms under her sagging bosom. "Difficult age for a woman."

Dilys had seen the angry glint in Harry's eyes and called over: "Was that your Janet I saw in Top Hall last night, Mrs. Hughes? Well-built girl for fourteen, isn't she?" – and was rewarded by Mrs. Hughes spending the next five minutes defending her wayward daughter's dubious honour to anyone who would listen.

As if reading his thoughts, his Mam's voice became anxious, timorous, and her fingers plucked at the edge of the sheet. "Did anyone... were they... you know, did anyone say anything... well, critical, like?"

She looked so defenceless and pathetic, and suddenly so young, despite the greying hair, that Harry felt a surge of protective love for her. He sat himself on the edge of the bed and stilled her hands with his own.

"Critical? Of you nearly dying and losing a baby into the bargain? Of course not! Everyone wished you well! And Mr. Pugh said you're a fine woman and I'm lucky to have such a beautiful mother!"

"Ooh, go on with you!" She pushed him away with both hands, laughing, but he could see she was pleased. A faint flush spread over her face, and for a moment she was the mother of his childhood.

Suddenly they heard the front door open and slam shut again, and Lizzie's voice raised excitedly.

"Whatever's up with Lizzie?" said Mam. "Go on down and find out, and if it's anything interesting, tell her to come up. Bored to tears I am, sitting here doing nothing!"

But Lizzie didn't go up to see her mother for a good half-hour, until she'd composed herself and discussed with her father and Harry whether it was wise to risk upsetting her. By this time Mam was hammering on the floor and threatening to come downstairs if someone didn't tell her what was going on.

"There's been an awful tragedy, Mam." Lizzie perched on the side of the bed, her round, normally cheery face pale and troubled. "I was coming from the House, down through Park Street, and I saw this commotion going on at the top of the street. So – nosey-like – I went to have a look what was going on. Wished I hadn't when I got there!"

Lizzie screwed up her face in an effort to stop the tears flowing. "It was outside Elwyn Rees's house – you know, he married Elsie Jones. Such a pretty girl she was. Well – he's killed her, Mam! Shot her and then gassed himself!"

Her resolve weakened as her mother gasped, and she flung herself into the older woman's arms. "Terrible it was. They'd taken the ... bodies ... away, but the families were there, all crying, and you could still smell the gas. I wish I'd never gone to see what was happening!

Why ever did he need to go and do something like that?"

The answer was to come at a packed inquest a week later. It seemed that, in the euphoria of newly-wedded bliss, Elwyn had run up huge debts to provide a home for his wife, and short-time and a poor head for figures had left him unable to see any way out of his financial predicament. Rumour had it that he'd been so appalled at the mess he'd made of his wife's pretty face when he shot her that he'd been unable to turn the gun on himself, and so had turned the gas taps on instead. No-one ever discovered how he had come by the gun.

7

Returning to live in Morgan Street as planned, Harry found more turmoil. Elwyn Rees's mother lived next door, and she was inconsolable at the loss of her son.

"Why did he do it?" she wailed. "If he was in trouble he only needed to say, and we'd have got by somehow!"

She insisted on following her son's coffin to the cemetery, a practice frowned upon by the Chapel elders, who feared it too harrowing for a woman to withstand – and their fears were justified when she tried to follow the coffin into the ground and had to be dragged away screaming.

In the end Mam was the woman's salvation, and unwittingly her own, too. Up and about now, and unable to bear the sounds of grief that could be heard through the wall, echoing her own of a year ago, she'd gone next door and gathered the distraught woman in her arms and talked until the sobbing ceased. What she said no-one knew, but Elwyn's mother would have nobody else from that moment, and it seemed that as she daily found words of comfort for her neighbour, Mam finally threw off the mantle of her own grief.

By the end of the following week Harry had had enough of doom and gloom, and began to think of the free tickets for the Avonia Players. Although he'd scoffed at the time, their plays were usually good, and it seemed a shame to let the tickets go to waste. He tried in vain to think of a girl to ask out, but the ones he really liked were either already spoken for, or were so attractive that he couldn't pluck up courage to ask them. Lizzie was going to the cinema with Maisie, to enjoy a good weep over Rudolph Valentino, so eventually he suggested to Bill that they both cut their losses and go to the play together.

"Aye, alright then," said Bill. "At least we can have a good laugh at everyone we know dressed up and trying hard to look like someone else. And p'rhaps we can run to a bag of chips each afterwards."

Their seats were good ones, half-way back in the stalls, and it being the last night there was a packed house. The play turned out to be a period musical, with Madame Howells, renowned teacher of Pianoforte and Theory of Music, playing the piano energetically to the left of the stalls. She was a large lady, dressed grandly – if rather tightly – in black sequins, with a turban affair on her head from which a feather stood up, bobbing in time to the beat as her plump arms rippled up and down the keyboard playing a medley of what was to come.

"She looks like something from Ali Baba," whispered Bill. "You sure we've got the right play?"

The lights went down. "Ssh!" said Harry. "They're starting. Have some of these." He offered a bag of sticky dark toffee donated by Nan.

Towards the end of the first act, Harry suddenly leaned forward in his seat. A girl of about his own age had stepped to the front of the stage and begun to sing. She lifted her head and sang out to the far reaches of the hall, and Harry was struck by the purity of her face, which matched the purity of her voice – a mezzo-soprano showing promise of maturing into a full-bodied richness.

Her light brown hair was swept back at the sides, and then tumbled in loose curls to her shoulders, displaying a graceful arched neck and fine bone structure. Her lips, artificially red in the stage lights, curved upwards at the corners, as if she couldn't help smiling despite the sad song she was singing. As her voice rose to the last notes of her song, her body rose slightly too, so that its slender outline could be seen faintly through the long dress she was wearing.

Applause broke out as she finished. Harry nudged Bill. "Who's she?" But Bill had his mouth full and just shrugged.

When the lights went up for the interval, Bill looked at Harry shrewdly. "You liked the look of that little girl, didn't you?"

Harry didn't meet his eye. "I just wondered who she is. I haven't seen her before – and with a voice like that I'd have thought she would've been better known before now."

Bill smiled and then said, "Wait here."

He rose and ambled out of the hall, heading for the refreshment room, leaving Harry wishing he'd bought a programme so that he could at least find out the girl's name.

Bill returned just as the lights were going down again. He slid into his seat. "Megan Powell – just moved into Elgam Avenue, 'cos her father's died. Party after this – we're invited. You can meet her then."

Harry stared at him incredulously. "How did you find all that out?"

He could sense Bill grinning in the dark. "Gladys on refreshments. Known her a long time. Bit keen on me she is."

Harry opened his mouth to ask more, but a woman in front wearing a hat like an upturned flower-pot turned round and fiercely whispered, "Ssh!" at them, so he had to wait.

He didn't take much notice of the second act, except when Megan was on stage, although she didn't sing on her own again. On reflection he wasn't so surprised that Bill had managed not only to glean some information about her, but also to get them both invited to the party. Bill was a tall, lean young man with a soulful face and easy-going charm which many a young lady found irresistible. Except Maisie, of course. But then, Bill carried such a torch for her that his charm and dry wit always deserted him when she was around, so that he appeared staid and dull.

Harry began to wonder what he would say to Megan, if he could manage to talk to her at all. He felt his palms grow sweaty at the thought. He would probably be as stupid as Bill always was around Maisie. He joined in the thunderous applause at the end of the show, stood for the National Anthem – played with such energy by Madame Howells that he could see the piano begin to rock – and then turned to Bill.

"This party ... perhaps we'd better not go. Bit cheeky of us really, when we've not been properly invited."

"Are you daft? Miss the chance of a free do? Anyway, it's all arranged – I'm going as Gladys's young man, and you're with me."

They went to help Gladys clear up, so that the party, held in the room behind the stage, was in full swing when they got there. Jugs of beer and cider had been brought in from the Waun Tavern across the road, and there was sherry or lemonade for the ladies. A long table at one end of the room groaned under platefuls of sandwiches, Welsh cakes and fruit cake, provided by the Avonia ladies, each one determined that her culinary skills should not be outshone by another.

At first Harry couldn't see Megan, and he stayed close to Bill and Gladys in case anyone asked him how he came to be there. But nobody seemed to mind and gradually he relaxed, aided by the glass of beer that Bill silently handed him, and began to chat to people he knew. Then he saw her, standing alone by the food table, looking awkward and uncertain. Feeling awkward and uncertain himself, he nevertheless made his way across the room until he was standing beside her.

He stood looking down at the food. He could smell her perfume – something far more exotic than the lavender water his mother and Nan used. It made his skin tingle, and he looked at the food without seeing any of it. *Say something, you fool,* he told himself, *or she'll move away!*

"This loo—" Too high-pitched. He cleared his throat and tried again, half an octave lower. "This looks good. All that acting must make you hungry."

For a moment he thought she wasn't going to reply, and he wondered in panic what he should do next. But then she turned to him, and he raised his eyes and saw that she was smiling – a lovely smile that produced dimples in her cheeks and made her eyes crinkle at the corners.

"I'm starving!" she admitted. "But I can't see anyone else eating, so I didn't like to tuck in!"

He suddenly felt manful and in control.

"Well, perhaps if we make a start the others will join in."

He handed her a plate, and was rewarded with another smile that made his heart thud. For a few moments they were both busy selecting food, although suddenly Harry didn't want to eat. It would be just his luck to spit crumbs at her, or spill something down his front.

"I thought you were very good," he said as she began to nibble delicately at a sandwich. "Lovely singing voice, you've got."

She didn't simper or try with false modesty to disagree with him, but looked straight at him and said, "Thank you. All the women in our family are musical."

"Haven't seen you around before – new here, are you?"

She nodded, her mouth full of Welsh cake. There was a tiny crumb on the edge of her lip, and he watched in fascination as she licked it away with a small pink tongue. He decided to risk eating something himself to keep her company.

"We moved here a few months ago from Brynmawr – after my Dad died. There's only me and my two sisters left now. We've moved in with my auntie, but at first we kept going back to Brynmawr – for the choir, and everything. But it's hard to keep going there – you can't always get a bus, and … well, it gets a bit expensive, too."

Her face had fallen a little, whether with thoughts of her father, their old home, or their lack of money he wasn't sure. He was wondering whether to offer his condolences when her face brightened again.

"Then someone suggested we join the Avonia Players, so here we are. We've joined the Bethel Chapel choir too."

There was a pause. *Think of something else to say,* he told himself, *before she goes off!* But before he could think of anything she gave a little laugh, a delicious low gurgly sound, and leaned forward slightly and touched his arm. The light pressure of her fingers burned through the cloth of his jacket.

"But listen to me going on, and I don't even know your name."

"Harry Jenkins," he said, "Blaenavon born and bred."

She stepped back a pace and held out her hand. "How do you do, Harry Jenkins, Blaenavon-born-and-bred?" Her voice was solemn, but there was laughter in her eyes.

He took her hand in his, wishing he could surreptitiously wipe his palms in his jacket first. "Pleased to meet you," he answered, just as solemnly, then they both laughed.

Now, he thought, *ask her out now!*

"Do you... have you... would you ever...?" he stammered, feeling hot and cold at the same time, while she looked at him in amusement.

His stumblings were interrupted by a call: "Meg! Come on, time to go!"

"My sisters," she said. "They're a bit older than me, and think they have to take care of me all the time." She turned to go, and then turned back, her eyes twinkling, and her lips twitching provocatively. "We're singing up at Pwlldu the Saturday after next."

And then she was gone, moving swiftly across the room, her brown curls bobbing on her shoulders. She joined two women waiting at the door, their coats and hats on, making polite good-byes. Harry could see the family resemblance; they were handsome women with the same colouring and bone structure, but they were a good ten years older than Megan.

He looked around for Bill, but could see no sign of him. *Perhaps he's in the Gents',* he thought, and set off to find him, needing to tell him of the many virtues he'd already discovered in Megan. But Bill wasn't in the Gents' Room either.

Harry was wandering back down the corridor towards the party room when he heard a muffled giggle. The noise came from a dark side-passage, full of rails bulging with costumes. Harry peered into the dark, and as his eyes became accustomed to the dimness he glimpsed a flash of white thigh and a man's large hand caressing it. The hand moved around the leg, fingers sliding inside the top of smooth silk stocking, then roaming upwards, disappearing under folds of skirt hitched up above the exposed thigh.

The giggle came again, and Harry felt the blood course through his body.

"Hush! Someone will hear us, and then I'll have to stop doing this... and this... and..."

The voice was whispering, but there was no mistaking it. Bill was there, taking all sorts of liberties with Gladys, and she was obviously enjoying it.

Harry suddenly became aware of his voyeuristic situation and quietly scurried back into the party, wondering if anyone would notice if he helped himself to another glass of beer. He felt in need of it. What if someone else should hear the two of them? What if Bill got

Gladys into trouble?

The beer was all gone, so he helped himself to a large glass of lemonade and found a chair in the corner. Two middle-aged women nearby, customers at the Cworp, smiled at him benevolently.

"Didn't know you were with the Avonias," said one.

"No, no – I'm here with a friend… he knows someone… his girl-friend," he stammered. They nodded understandingly, and to his relief turned to one another again.

He sat examining the dregs of lemonade in the bottom of his glass for some time, and then suddenly Bill stood in front of him, looking, Harry thought, inordinately pleased with himself.

"Did you speak to Megan?" He glanced around the thinning room. "Where's she gone? Frightened her off, did you?"

But Harry didn't want to talk about Megan any more. He stood up. "You took your time! What are you playing at? I heard the two of you down the corridor, and God knows how many other people did, too!"

But Bill was unperturbed.

"Gladys is just getting her coat. Then I'm going to walk her home. You coming?"

"No I am not! I don't want to play gooseberry," Harry said sourly.

"Don't be daft!" said Bill. "It's not like that. Gladys and me, we just have a bit of fun together, that's all."

"And what about Maisie?" said Harry, his voice high with right-eous indignation. "I thought she was the one you cared about!"

Bill had started to walk towards the door, but now he turned and faced Harry squarely, an expression of amused exasperation on his face. "So she is," he agreed. "But I can't spend all my life waiting about for someone who doesn't seem to know I'm there." He leaned his head nearer to Harry. "And what you have to learn, boyo, is that some girls do, and some girls don't. Gladys does, for which I'm extremely grateful, but she's not the same as Maisie."

He straightened up again. "Now, are you coming?"

But Harry shook his head, and set off on his own, leaving Bill to go in search of Gladys.

He walked briskly across the town, his hands thrust deep in his pocket and his breath forming clouds in the frosty night air. He tried to work himself up into an outraged huff on Maisie's behalf, but images of Gladys's white skin kept intruding, and he knew that deep down he was envious of Bill's prowess. Besides, Bill was right, he couldn't hang around waiting for Maisie to give him an encouraging word. Perhaps it wouldn't hurt Maisie, though, to know that other girls found Bill attractive.

He turned his thoughts towards Megan and pictured her pretty face smiling at him. Was her body as white and enticing as Gladys's? He resolved to go to the concert at Pwlldu; she must have wanted him to, or she wouldn't have mentioned it. And possibly if he hung about the top of the town, near Elgam Avenue, he might see her again before then.

He began to whistle softly as he turned the corner of Morgan Street.

He did see Megan again. He was helping to serve on the grocery counter the following Friday afternoon, always the busiest of the week, and there was a queue of people waiting to be served. Over on the provisions counter Mr. Pugh was serving Harry's Aunt Catherine, in the unctuous manner which he always reserved for a relative of one of the staff. Aunt Catherine, like many of the older women, loved to be attended to with this sort of deference, and always made the most of it.

"What's the American cheese like today?" Harry heard her ask. Mr. Pugh handed her a sliver to try, and then waited while she chewed it thoughtfully. "Yes," she said at last, "I'll have a pound of that," as if she didn't buy it every week. Then: "And what sort of butter do you have this week?"

"Well …" said Mr. Pugh, considering, pursing his lips so that his little goatee beard quivered and jutted out. "We've got the salted, here, which perhaps you might find a bit *too* salty, and we've got the unsalted – a bit milder, that one." He waited, until Aunt Catherine thought she should try a bit of each, just to be sure, just as she did every week, while across the shop Harry willed her to hurry up. Mr. Pugh's servility only lasted as long as it took to satisfy the customer, and Harry knew he would have some caustic comment to make later.

Sure enough, as they passed one another on the way to the till, Mr. Pugh hissed at Harry: "I don't know why we don't just make her a bloody sandwich and be done with it!"

Dilys overheard, and grinned. She nudged Harry. "Cheer up! Your old nursemaid's just come in!"

Harry looked towards the door, and his heart sank. Waiting in the queue, and nodding and smiling at him, was old Fanny Pearce. When Harry was a baby she'd helped Nan in the shop, and because Nan often looked after Harry, she'd helped with him as well. She'd been old all Harry's life, but now she was completely decrepit. Shrunken and wizened, she hobbled on legs made uneven by rheumatism, her wasted body wrapped in an assortment of garments whose only matching feature was that they were all none too clean.

Harry smiled perfunctorily at her, and then, to his horror, he saw Megan enter the shop behind her.

"Tea, sugar, tapioca, rice?" He churned out the practised litany, intended to jog the memory, to the next customer, and tried to concentrate his efforts into serving her, whilst all the time he was aware of the queue shortening, and Megan's place in it.

Finally Fanny was next and Dilys was free to serve her. But Fanny stepped aside, and turned to Megan.

"It's alright – you go next, my lovely. I'm waiting for my boy here to serve me!" She pointed a thin, horny-nailed finger at Harry and gave a cackle, exposing a few worn brown teeth. "Used to nurse him, I did, when he was a baby! *Beautiful* baby, he was!"

Harry squirmed. His seventeen-year-old raw self-absorption didn't see a pathetic old woman living only on past memories. All he saw was the Beast, come on purpose to embarrass him, whilst Beauty stood beside her. He felt no pity, only an intense desire to be rid of the old woman. He served her next, tersely and rapidly, his head bent to his work, ears deaf to her reminiscences of his childhood, which was all she had by way of conversation. And all the time he was aware of Megan, could feel rather than see – because he didn't dare look at her – her kind glances towards the old lady.

Megan left before Fanny had completed her few meagre purchases; gone, and he hadn't even acknowledged her presence!

"Tell your Nan I'll be up to see her one of these days," Fanny said, as she made to leave. Harry mumbled a reply, his thoughts engrossed in how he could make up to Megan for the awkwardness of the situation and his lack of courtesy.

There was a lull in the shop now. Dilys stood facing him squarely as he turned from the counter to check the shelves, and she refused to move until he was looking her in the eye.

"Must be terrible to be old like that, and lonely, mustn't it?" she said softly before moving past him towards the storeroom, nothing but contempt on her face, and he squirmed again, this time in shame.

The weather the following week turned even colder, and by the weekend the first snow had fallen. Determined still to go to the concert, Harry borrowed his father's thick overcoat and set off early for the couple of miles' walk up the mountain to Pwlldu. A small hamlet perched on top of the Blorenge, and thus able to enjoy the benefits of atrocious weather for most of the year, it had originated when ironworks and quarrying had prospered a century earlier, and now existed thanks to a small amount of open-cast mining. It consisted mainly of two rows of houses, imaginatively christened Long Row and Short Row, the vital pub, a tiny chapel, and a school-cum-welfare hall.

In the summer the views over the deep valley below were breath-taking, and then Pwlldu attracted energetic walkers from both sides of the mountain, but for the rest of the year its inhabitants were left to share their lives with the wild mountain ponies and numerous scraggy sheep. The women, of necessity, were square and sturdy, and would walk down to Blaenavon on Friday market-day carry-ing large baskets, their infants cocooned in thick shawls wrapped Welsh-fashion around both them and their mothers. Their shopping complete, they would then make the long trek, heavily laden, back up the mountain.

Harry trudged on up the Abergavenny road, and was soon joined by others equally determined not to be put off by a spot of cold weather. As they walked, however, snow began to fall again, and by the time they reached Pwlldu a strong wind was driving it into drifts.

He was glad to reach the warmth of the schoolhouse and find a seat near one of the oil heaters strategically placed around the room in an effort to off-set the draught from the ill-fitting door.

"Hello, Harry. Haven't seen you for a long time!" A young girl Harry didn't immediately recognise slid into the seat next to his. She laughed. "You don't remember me, do you? Ivy – Ivy Miller!"

His eyes widened in surprise. At one time Ivy and her parents had lived next door to Nan, and they'd often played together as chil-dren. Then the family had moved to Forge Side and Harry had rarely seen them.

"Ivy!" he exclaimed. "I wouldn't have known you! You've... grown. Changed!"

She fluttered her eyelashes. "For the better, I hope!" And Harry saw that indeed they were changes for the better; she'd grown into an attractive girl.

"What are you doing here?" he asked.

She pouted prettily. "A lad from along our street invited me – there's a busload here from Forge Side – but then we fell out, and I thought, blow it, I'd come anyway. What about you?"

"Oh, you know, something to do," he replied awkwardly, and was glad when the MC stepped forward and announced that the concert was to begin.

Megan sang just before the interval, along with a group of ladies from her chapel. Harry watched her intently, hoping she might see him as she sang. Once again her voice soared, carrying those of the other ladies, and her face looked lovelier than ever. He clapped fervently when it was over, and turned to Ivy to see if she had enjoyed it, to find her watching him with a knowing look in her eye.

There were refreshments during the interval. Harry hung around the table, hoping that Megan would be feeling hungry again. After some minutes his patience was rewarded, and she made her way towards the food, but this evening she was flanked by her sisters and they seemed happy to chat amongst themselves. Harry stood miserably nearby, and then, aware that the interval would soon be over, he screwed up his courage and coughed loudly then smiled as three heads turned towards him.

"Hello again. Another good bit of singing!"

"Thank you. I'm surprised so many people've turned up in this weather." Did her voice sound a shade cool? He searched her face, but her expression was pleasant enough. He thrust his hands in his pockets to stop himself fidgeting and wondered what else he could say, but she began to speak again.

"I don't think you've met my sisters. Phyllis and Edie, this is Harry Jenkins – he was at the party after the play."

"How d'you do?" They both shook his hand and then all four stood waiting for someone else to speak.

"Do you live in Pwlldu?" Phyllis, the elder one asked him.

"No, no – down in the town. Morgan Street." He wished the sisters would go away but they continued to stand, sipping tea genteelly. Finally he turned to Megan.

"I'm sorry I didn't get chance to speak to you in the shop the other day. There's a lot to do on Fridays."

She gave a delicate little shrug. "I didn't think you'd seen me. You were very busy serving people." He looked at her eyes; brown-green with dark flecks in them. They looked amused, but was she sympathising with him or laughing at him? He began to understand how Bill felt with Maisie.

She was wearing a crisp white blouse with a wide lacy collar and a dark skirt, matching the other ladies in her choir, but her body seemed impossibly slender. He wondered what it would be like to put his arms around her fragile waist and kiss her shapely lips, and then he grew hot in case she could somehow divine what he was thinking.

Edie put her cup down on the table. "Better be going," she said. "Our choir's singing next. We should get ready."

They all said goodbye and moved off. Then Megan glanced back over her shoulder and said, "Be seeing you!" – which gave him a glimmer of hope for the future as he stood and thought of all the things he could have said to keep the conversation going.

Ivy came up to him. "It's still snowing out there. You could have a lift back in our bus if you want. There's a spare seat as I came on my own." She looked sufficiently wistful for him to sense her loneliness.

"That would be nice. Thanks."

He regarded her more closely as they resumed their seats. She hadn't grown into a bad-looking girl. Not a beauty like Megan, of course, but her heart-shaped face had an engaging honesty about it, and her dark auburn hair, cut short, waved prettily enough about her face. Her clothes had a well-pressed neatness about them that indicated they were probably the one good set she possessed.

The concert wore on. Harry began to be bored by it, after his lack of success in talking to Megan. His thoughts were meandering as a slightly built man began to sing in a thin reedy tenor, when he felt a sharp dig in the ribs. He turned to Ivy and she motioned towards the door. Snow had been blown through the gap between door and floor, and was beginning to pile up and the people near the back were huddled well down into their coats. Ivy tilted her head back towards the little man who was extolling the virtues of *Lilacs in Springtime,* and her shoulders began to shake. Harry began to smile too, and soon they were trying hard to stifle the giggles that had beset them when they were children.

It had stopped snowing when they left the hall, but the cold air stung their cheeks as they made their way towards the bus, their voices loud in the muffled stillness all around them. They talked companionably as they trudged through the snow, but once seated on the bus they fell quiet. Fortunately the wind had blown a lot of the snow away from the road and the driver had been running the engine for some time, so they had no trouble setting off, but the snow hid the many dips and ruts in the poorly-made road, and the bus lurched and swayed from time to time as it encountered them.

Then, when it gave a particularly severe jolt, Harry and Ivy were thrown together, and her hand flew out and clutched his leg. She didn't move it once the bus righted itself, but began softly to caress the inside of his thigh, whilst looking straight ahead, as if her hand were working independently of the rest of her.

Do something! he told himself, but while his insides contracted with pleasure at her touch, his exterior appeared paralysed. Eventually he covered her hand with his own, and immediately she carried his hand to her own lap, and pressed it down so that it made a cleft in the thick material of her skirt, and he could feel the inviting softness of her.

The heat of her body seemed to transmit itself up Harry's arm, intensifying as it travelled, so that his whole being felt on fire. Was

Ivy a 'girl who did', he wondered, and if so, did that mean *he could*, with impunity? And still they sat, staring straight ahead, saying nothing. All around them in the dark people talked and laughed animatedly, but they seemed a long way off. All Harry was aware of was the nearness of her body, and its promise, and he felt overwhelmed by his own ignorance and desire.

Suddenly she spoke. "We've gone too far!"

Harry jumped in alarm, until he realised that she was referring to the distance the bus had travelled. "You should have asked the driver to put you down in Market Street," she went on, as the bus trundled on to the bottom of the town and began its ascent up the opposite hill towards Forge Side.

"It doesn't matter," he said, trying to sound firm and manly. "I think I ought to walk you home – it's very late."

He sensed her smile in the dark. "That would be good of you," she said primly, and firmly replaced his hand between her legs.

Forge Side consisted of four long tiers of houses, one behind the other, built steeply into the hillside so that the front of one row looked down over the backyard of the row below. They had been hurriedly constructed alongside their namesake fifty years ago, the owners being more concerned with filling them with workers than with their aesthetic qualities, so that they hadn't even been given names and were merely referred to as A, B, C and D rows.

"We'd better go round the back," Ivy said as they headed towards C Row, her arm tucked cosily inside his. "Mam will have left the back door open for me."

They fought their way up the wet, slippery side street, clinging on to each other and chuckling as they lost their footing from time to time, so that they were both out of breath by the time they reached Ivy's back gate. They stood for a moment, gasping, facing each other.

"Come in here," Ivy said, suddenly pulling him through the high gate into the back yard. "Her over the road often watches through the front bedroom window." She leaned against the back wall, still holding on to his coat. "And I wanted to thank you properly for bringing me home."

Before he could reply she reached up and kissed him, not a polite peck, but long and lingering; an experienced, promising kiss. It was easy to respond, more easy than he'd even dreamed. He pulled her closer to him, pressing his lips against hers until they parted, and he could explore her mouth with his tongue. And it was just as easy to take control, to press his hard urgent body against hers, and let his hands slide down until they felt the fullness of her breasts.

They continued to kiss, but now his mind was on the discoveries his fingers were making as they roamed her body, fumbling clumsily with buttons and fastenings that tantalisingly enclosed her warm softness. Suddenly she pulled away from him slightly with a throaty chuckle.

"There's keen you are, boy!" She began to straighten her dishevelled clothes, and then, relenting, nuzzled into his neck. "Too cold for all that, tonight!"

"When, then?" he answered desperately, his voice thick with thwarted desire. Then he realised how brusque he must have sounded. "I mean, when can I see you again?"

She drew back from him once more, smiling in the dark. "Well, that depends. On all sorts of things. Like whether you can think of somewhere I might like to go. And whether you can afford to treat a girl..."

He knew she was laughing at him, exulting in the power she'd just displayed, and that probably it was all just a game to her – one she knew how to play far better than he. It didn't matter, though. At the moment he wanted her to teach him the game more than anything else in the world.

Before he could say any more there was the sound of a door banging from within the house, and a light appeared in the downstairs room.

"Quick! My Dad!" she cried, a frightened girl, all vestiges of womanly allure gone from her voice as she began to push him towards the gate. Then, just before he left she grabbed the lapels of his coat. "I always go to Top Hall pictures on Thursday nights." She planted a kiss on his mouth and gave him a final shove through the gate.

He trudged home, oblivious to the singing of the cold air in his ears, his mind reeling with the sudden upturn his life appeared to be taking. He was nearly at the bottom of the town when he remembered Megan. Having daydreamed about her for the past few weeks, it was difficult to relinquish her as the object of his desires, and he pictured her sweet face as she sang, and how her eyes could change from soulful to merry in a flash. Yet it was difficult to believe that she would be capable of the earthy excitement which Ivy had engendered this evening.

He let himself into the house and tiptoed quietly to his room, anxious not to disturb his father. The bedroom was icy cold and he was under the sheets in minutes, his feet finding the heated stone bottle put there by his mother. But sleep eluded him as he re-lived the evening, and it was the early hours before he drifted off, dreaming of Megan's face superimposed upon the delights of Ivy's body.

8

There was already a queue outside Top Hall when Harry got there, but he could see no sign of Ivy. He wandered around for a while, reluctant to join a queue for a film he didn't particularly want to see on his own. He was feigning interest in the contents of Dean and Jones's Ironmongers' window, further along the street, when he felt a light tap on his shoulder. He turned and there was Ivy, wearing the same outfit as before, but with a hat tilted saucily over one eye.

"Are you coming in?" she asked, nodding towards the picture house. "They've opened the doors."

He smiled and was about to offer his arm when he realised that she wasn't alone.

"This is Peggy," she said quickly, noticing his look of dismay. "We always go to the pictures together in the week. Do you two know each other?"

Harry knew Peggy by sight: a plain pear-shaped girl with a pudgy face surrounded by frizzy curls.

"Hello Harry," she simpered. "Remember you from school – and see you in the Cworp sometimes."

Harry nodded ungraciously, his heart sinking as they moved forward. But Peggy seemed to have been primed beforehand, and dropped behind them as they reached the ticket booth, so that Harry doggedly paid for himself and Ivy only.

Ron Attwell was standing in the foyer. "Thought your girl preferred Bottom Hall, Harry!" he said with a sly grin.

Harry drew himself up to full height and squared his shoulders. "Didn't say there was only one girl, did I?" he replied with a deliberate wink, in the hope that Ivy would be impressed with this evidence that he was a man of the world.

Ivy whispered in his ear as they made their way to their seats. "Sorry about Peggy, only we always come out together on a Thursday, and I didn't know for certain that you'd be here."

Harry had been walking in front of the two girls, and turned now, a caustic comment about Peggy's presence on his lips, but as he did so he caught her eye, peering anxiously over Ivy's shoulder, and he managed to turn his disappointment into a tight-lipped smile. But the evening was spoilt as far as he was concerned. Peggy sat the other side of Ivy, clutching her bag on her lap, her heavy features staring rigidly at the screen, but Harry was constantly aware of her presence. He wanted to hold Ivy's hand but felt too inhibited, and knew that he would feel dreadfully embarrassed if Ivy responded enthusiastically. So all three sat, each finding it difficult to concentrate on the picture.

Like the three bloody wise monkeys, Harry thought, wishing he'd brought some of Nan's toffee.

His spirits revived, though, when he discovered that Peggy lived only a short way from the cinema, and quite cheerfully saw her safely to her door.

"Goodnight Harry, goodnight Ivy," she said, giving her friend a significant look. "Mind how you go!" And she made a sound between a giggle and a snigger as she opened her front door.

"Jealous, she is," Ivy said, tucking her arm companionably through Harry's as they set off down Broad Street.

The snow had gone, but there was a sparkle of frost on the road and pavements and their breath came in clouds as they walked. Quite a few people were about, couples who had also been to the pictures, and men going in and out of the pubs. Their boots clattered in the quiet night, and voices carried clearly on the crisp air as no-one passed another without some sort of acknowledgement. Many people greeted Harry by name, which clearly impressed Ivy.

"Don't you know a lot of people!" she exclaimed.

Harry chuckled. "I think I'm probably related to most of them one way or another, my family's been in Blaenavon that long. Or else they're customers in the shop, or on my delivery rounds." He began to reel off the names and addresses of those they'd met, and then included the names of their next door neighbours so rapidly that Ivy began to laugh.

"Stop! You'll be telling me next what they all order and how much they pay!"

"Not allowed," he said seriously, and then dipped his head closer to hers. "Mind you," he whispered confidentially, "there's one or two round here that has visitors when their man's on nights and don't realise that the bread boy knows. Just as well my old horse Major can't talk!"

Ivy chuckled and then sighed. "I wish my job was more exciting. I spend most of my time in the back room and hardly ever see anyone. Wasting my youth away, I am."

Ivy worked for a small laundry run by a frightened rabbit of a woman and her husband, who had an ungainly limp and a very uncertain temper – both acquired in the mud-baths of France during the war.

"Plain nasty he is, sometimes," Ivy told Harry. "And other times he just sits poking the fire with a big black poker. No wonder she creeps round looking scared all the time."

Harry squeezed her arm consolingly. "Perhaps something better will turn up for you soon."

She glanced up at him coquettishly from under the brim of her hat. "Barmaid I'd like to be. Plenty of people to talk to, and I think I've one or two assets that would be useful!"

"Wouldn't your Mam and Dad mind?" he asked, thinking what the reaction of his parents would be if Lizzie announced her intention of working in a public house.

Ivy laughed. "My Dad's in one or other pub most nights, so I reckon he could keep an eye on me! And you know our lot – nothing's too bad as long as you go to confession on a Saturday and mass on a Sunday!"

Harry had forgotten that Ivy's family was Catholic – part of a surprisingly large contingent scattered about among the ardent Chapel-goers, and many of them living in Forge Side, direct descendants of the Irish workers who'd sought employment when the ironworks were at their peak. Unfortunately the Catholic Church and Presbytery were sited at the very top of the town, about as far away from Forge Side as you could get. Father Ignatius – or 'Father Good Gracious', as Harry's Mam insisted on calling him – would often be seen scurrying from one end of the town to the other trying to round up his errant flock, with as little success as the farmers who owned the sheep that roamed unchecked over the mountain.

The priest was a shabbily dressed, scrawny figure compared to many of his nonconformist counterparts, whose girths seemed to spread in direct relation to the size of their congregation, but nevertheless the Catholic Church continued to flourish – due, it was thought, to the largesse of the Italian Ice Cream Parlour proprietors, relatives of the Fulgonis of Abergavenny.

"Where's your Dad tonight?" asked Harry as they began the climb up to Forge Side.

"Night shift," said Ivy. She paused for a moment and then added: "So I don't need to worry about being in early. Mam will be too tired to wait up for me."

Harry felt emboldened by this. He stared up at the sky, thick with stars. "It's a beautiful night. Fancy a bit of a stroll on the mountain?"

Ivy feigned a shiver. "At this time of year? It's freezing!"

Harry moved closer and put his arm around her waist. "I'm sure we could think of something to keep warm!"

"I can think of somewhere better than a cold old mountain." She grabbed his hand and led him down the mean little street which held Forge Side's only shops. The one at the end was empty and boarded up, its entrance deeply recessed.

"No-one'll come down this way," she said, moving to the far corner nearest the door. "Quite private, it is."

Harry needed no further bidding, and spent an enthralling half-hour learning more about the intricacies and excitements of the female anatomy.

"I want you, Ivy," he whispered hoarsely when his explorations had heightened his senses to such a degree that he was prepared to throw all caution completely to the wind.

Despite her most agreeable sighs and little groans in response to his lovemaking, and the very satisfactory knowledge she seemed to possess of how best to tease and arouse him, she'd obviously kept her head better. With a few swift movements she was able to disentangle herself and adjust both their dishevelled clothing.

"Mustn't be too greedy," she said, her voice calm and affable, "and anyway, my back's hurting against this door frame."

She picked up her hat from where she had placed it carefully on the floor, and he realised that the romantic interlude, for tonight at any rate, was over.

For Harry the next few weeks sped past, and before he knew it everyone was busy preparing for Christmas. With over half the workforce unemployed, the main concern for most people was whether they could provide any sort of festivities for their families. Those who shopped regularly at the Cworp anxiously awaited the 'divis' – the cash returns they were given according to how much they had spent in the shop over the last few months, which would help to provide one or two little treats, and possibly even some toys for the children. Those still in work did their best to help relatives who had nothing, and out-of-work fathers tried their hand at making toys out of bits of wood for children who'd spent weeks pressing their noses against Briggs' Toy Shop window and dreaming futile dreams.

Mam was determined to make this Christmas a better one than the last as she continued to grow stronger, and had been hoarding pennies whenever she could to add to the dividend from the Cworp. Harry's father stayed out of the house as much as possible, more than ever aware that he was under his wife's feet as she scoured the house from top to bottom.

"I thought cleaning was supposed to be done in the spring," Harry complained when he and his Dad had been commissioned to move the heavy sideboard in the front room so that Mam could clean behind it.

"So it is," agreed Mam, "but you can look on this as last spring's do, as I never got round to it, and it'll give you a taster of what to expect next spring!"

In between cleaning Mam joined the queue of other women who took their Christmas cakes and puddings to Kennard's, the town's public bake-house, where for a small charge the big bread-ovens could be used by the public to cook items that were too large for the wall-ovens set beside the range in most homes. Occasionally a dispute would break out if a housewife felt that her cake had been too near the side or back and had therefore been over-cooked, but most were happy to take their chances.

Lizzie was often working late up at the Lumley-Joneses, as they were not only expecting a houseful of guests for Christmas but had also arranged pheasant shooting parties every other weekend up on the Blorenge mountain. Lizzie had worked with a will in order to keep in with the cook, in the hope that she might be given a bit extra when the unofficial Christmas 'bonuses' were handed out. These were the result of the cook's careful editing of the housekeeping books so that a staff kitty could accumulate, to be distributed every six months according to rank and length of service.

"A step towards fairer distribution of wealth for the workers!" claimed Matthews, the chauffeur, an ardent (if furtive) trade-unionist. It certainly motivated everyone to work hard, and Mrs. Lumley-Jones was able to congratulate herself that she ran her household like clockwork, and so would not be tempted to employ a housekeeper who may not agree with the views of the rest of the staff.

Consequently Lizzie arrived home late in the afternoon of Christmas Eve with the end of a ham and a bagful of fruit, all edible but too marked to grace the Lumley-Jones's dining table, and enough spare shillings for Mam to be able to buy a large chicken. She was in high spirits, as Christmas Day was on a Friday and she was due her weekend off anyway, so she had three whole days' holiday to look forward to, which she'd guarded jealously and steadfastly refused to give up – even when the cook had dropped heavy hints about how busy the household would be, especially on Boxing Day.

It was nearly tea-time when Mam and Lizzie staggered in through the front door with last-minute purchases, many of them bought cheaply just as the shops were closing.

"Ooh, put that kettle on, Liz, and let's have a quiet cup of tea before your Dad and Harry get in!" Mam plopped down into an armchair while Lizzie obediently swung the kettle on its hob over the fire and then began to unpack their baskets. As she did so there was a knock on the front door.

"Stay there Mam, I'll go," said Lizzie as her mother made to rise from the chair.

"If it's next door, tell them I'll go through a bit later on!" Mam called after her, and then rose hurriedly when she heard Lizzie give a welcoming cry of pleasure. Unexpected visitors, and the living room in a mess! She hurried through the door so that she could keep whoever it was in the front room, and then gave a squeal of delight when she saw who was standing there.

"Dai! Oh, Dai!" She rushed forward into big strong arms that lifted her off the ground and swung her round. Tears began to fall as he set her down again. She held his face for a moment or two between her hands. "There's lovely you've come home to us for Christmas!" she said softly. "Missed you I have."

He laughed gently, a little embarrassed by her emotional welcome. "Well, if I knew it was going to upset you so much, I'd have stayed in London! And I've brought you a visitor, too!"

Mam gave a start as he stepped back and she saw standing quietly behind her son a slightly built girl, very pale except for deep red lips, and with short blonde hair which curled improbably onto her cheekbones.

"This is Bridget," said Dai, with a note of pride in his voice. "Lives next door to us in London, and I've told her so many things about you all that I thought she ought to come and see for herself!"

Mam waited for a fraction of a second for Dai to say something more about his relationship with this girl, but when nothing more was forthcoming she quickly held out her hand in welcome.

"Hello, Bridget! I didn't see you there for a minute. There's stupid you must think I am, crying over this big lump here! Come on in, you must be ready for a drink! Lizzie, make that tea for us, there's a good girl – I expect they're both parched! How long can you stay? Mind you, I don't know where we're going to fit you both in!" She wrinkled her brow in thought whilst ushering them both into the living room.

"Don't worry Mam," said Dai, "I'll go and see if Uncle Fred can put me up, and there'll be room for Bridget at Nan's, I expect."

Harry and his Dad arrived home a little later to find them all still sitting over tea and Welsh cakes, the groceries ignored on the table and Mam, Dai and Lizzie talking nineteen to the dozen whilst a bemused Bridget looked on, unable at times to follow the rapid Welsh lilt as they hopped from one subject to another to catch up on all the news.

"Hello, Dad! Back like a bad penny!" Dai rose to greet his father, his voice loud in the crowded room, and his large healthy frame making it impossible to believe that he'd been fathered by the shrunken man whose hand he now gripped. Harry caught a glimpse of pity in his eyes before he turned and introduced Bridget.

"You back for good, or just a visit?" Dad asked, as yet more tea was brewed.

"A few days, that's all. Back to work then."

"Thank God for that!" said Dad. "Nothing for you down here, boy! Waste of bloody time and footwear, all that marching we did!"

Harry groaned inwardly. Dai and Dad had always been for putting the world to rights. He hoped that wasn't going to be the tone of things over Christmas. He felt a tug on his arm, and Lizzie was pulling him into the back kitchen where she was putting away the shopping.

"What do you think?" she hissed in a stage whisper, as soon as the door was shut.

"What about?" he said, knowing full well, but liking to aggravate Lizzie.

"About *her*, of course! *Bridget!*"

"What should I think? She's hardly had chance to open her mouth yet."

"I think she's lovely," breathed Lizzie. "Her hair's been beautifully cut, and she's wearing make-up! Lipstick, and I think she'd got something on her eyes – her lashes can never be that dark naturally – I've been looking at her!"

Bridget immediately went up in Harry's estimation if she'd been able to withstand the sort of scrutiny that Lizzie and Mam would have subjected her to.

"I expect Mam'll have something to say about that," he said.

Make-up was frowned upon by both his parents, thereby convincing Lizzie that the wearing of it was the height of sophistication and the only sure way to attract a man.

"Her clothes are smart." Lizzie went on, "Did you see the coat she was wearing? Ever so slim she is, too."

"Bit too thin for my liking, and a bit too pale," said Harry, thinking of Ivy's voluptuous curves and Megan's dark enticing looks. "Not a patch on a nice Welsh girl, but Dai never was a very good judge."

Lizzie gave him a push. "Ooh! You're just saying things to be annoying. I think he's deeply in love with her, that's why he's brought her home – and they'll probably get engaged, and – "

She stopped suddenly as the door opened and Bridget stood there, cups and saucers in her hands, and Harry saw more clearly for himself the red lips and sooty lashes.

"Can I do anything to help out here?" she asked in her flat, rather nasal London voice, which Harry privately admitted was the only truly unattractive thing about her. "Dai and Mr. Jenkins are talking politics." She pulled a face and then grinned conspiratorially at Lizzie, enslaving her completely. "I'd rather do the washing up!"

Women in the back kitchen and politics in the living room! Harry decided to escape out the back way and go over to tell his cousins that Dai was home.

Mam surveyed the front room with satisfaction. The drop-leaf table had been opened out to its fullest extent and covered with a snowy-white cloth and now, with two extra chairs borrowed from next door, took up most of the room – but that wouldn't matter once they were all sat down. A small fire burnt brightly in the hearth beneath the tall mantelpiece, which had been polished until it shone. In the middle of the mantelshelf was a Westminster clock, which didn't always tell the right time but had a fine wooden casing. It was flanked by two china dogs, which in turn were flanked by a pair of large black vases with pink roses twisting round their pot-bellies. The ornaments were Mam's pride and joy, the only objects in the house that she felt were worth anything, and even in the hardest times she'd steadfastly refused to allow them to be taken to old Snell's pawn shop.

The front door burst open, interrupting her reverie, as her two sons, her husband and Bridget came in, stamping their feet and clapping their hands together to warm themselves. They'd been on a brief tour of the family to introduce Bridget, and to get out from under Mam and Lizzie's feet as they prepared the dinner. They were in high good humour, some of it brought about by the whisky they'd consumed at Uncle Fred's, and appreciative of the rich smells emanating from the kitchen.

Their good spirits continued throughout the meal, Dai regaling them with stories from London which indicated he was prospering nicely. He and an aunt had set up a second-hand clothes shop, Aunt Brenda having become a dab hand at knocking on the doors of the wealthy and persuading them to part with unwanted garments. Dai ran the shop, helping with the sponging and pressing of the clothes so that they looked as good as new, and then outrageously flattering the women and girls who sought to buy them. Harry privately thought it sounded a funny way for a man to make money, but there'd been presents for them all that morning which had certainly cost a bob or two, and there seemed to be plenty of money jangling in Dai's pockets.

Dai leaned back in his chair when the meal was over and stretched out his arms. "It's good to be back with my family! And my compliments to the cook!" he said, smiling at his mother.

"Our Lizzie did as much as me," she said, smiling back. "Good little help, she is, in the kitchen."

"And most of the food courtesy of the Lumley-Joneses, in one way or another," Lizzie laughed. Her round face, like her mother's, was pink from her exertions in the kitchen and the warmth of the little front room, and her eyes sparkled with fun.

Dai's features became still. "Shame we have to rely on bloody hand-outs from them instead of jobs though, isn't it?" He leaned forward and opened his mouth to warm to his theme, but caught his mother's eye and an imperceptible nod towards his father, and subsided in his chair.

His mother rose from the table. "No politics today, boy. There's many in this town with nothing on the table at all. Be thankful for what we've had, is it?"

In the evening the whole family congregated in Nan's house: all her children, *their* own children, her elderly brother and sister, Aunt Catherine, and a few neighbours and friends for good measure. Bridget's eyes widened when she saw how many people were squeezed in. "I thought we were keen on a good knees-up where I come from," she said, as Nan urged them into the sitting room and started to introduce her to members of the family she hadn't yet met, as 'Dai's-young-lady-from-London.'

Several of the men eyed her appreciatively. Her blonde hair, with its two immovable kiss-curls, shone round her head like a halo, and she was wearing a dress of pale pink in a silky material which shimmered slightly when she moved.

One of the men nudged Dai as he helped himself to a glass of beer. "Nice little Christmas cracker you've got there, butt!"

But the older women, dressed respectably but sombrely in mauve, dark blue and maroon, heaved their ample bosoms whilst uttering words of welcome and scrutinised her more carefully, noting the fashionable clothes and make-up which would be the subject of much murmured debate and covert whisperings at the first opportunity.

Overtired children ran in and out of the room, some clutching precious Christmas presents. The air became thick with pipe and cigarette smoke, and voices grew louder as the men downed beer and the women drank shandy or tea. Dai was soon the centre of a circle of young men taking it in turns to out-do one other in making the others laugh. Loudest and funniest of all appeared to be Bill. Harry saw Maisie watching him speculatively.

"Coming out of his shell, tonight, isn't he?" Harry nodded in Bill's direction.

"It's probably just the beer talking," Maisie replied.

"No, no!" Harry shook his head emphatically. "Like that all the time, he is, when we're out together. The girls like him, too. Never short of a girl when he wants one. I reckon one of them'll hook him good and proper before too long."

He looked out of the corner of his eye to judge the effect of his words, but Maisie was looking straight ahead, and said no more.

Nan stayed on her feet all evening, squeezing her ample proportions in and out of the room and between chairs and tables, passing plates of sandwiches and cake around. The affection felt for her by her children was evident, her sons teasing her gently about her size, to which she responded with good-natured chuckles, while their wives offered to help but were told to sit down and enjoy themselves.

Eventually the young children were put upstairs to bed, while two small babies were handed round to be cooed upon by all the female relatives until they too escaped into sleep. Then the lid was lifted on the piano and one of Harry's aunties sat down to play.

"Come on, Gareth!" several voices urged. "Give us a song!"

A cousin stood up and squeezed his way through to stand beside the piano. Small and plump, his face red and glistening from the beer he had already consumed, he stood with glass in one hand and cigarette in the other, and sang *Myfanwy* in a full-bodied pure baritone.

"That was beautiful!" Bridget exclaimed, after everyone had applauded and one of the women had wiped an eye, and Gareth's glass was refilled. "Do you speak Welsh?"

"No, my lovely," he answered, plopping down beside her on the sofa and resting a hot plump hand on her knee. "Only sing it. Can't understand a bloody word!"

Aunt Catherine said that she used to speak Welsh when she was a girl, and began to repeat some of the words she could remember. "Don't listen to her!" Dai shouted across the room. "She can only remember the swear words!" Everyone laughed, more so when she shouted back: "There's one or two I could think of to use on you!"

More singing followed, some in Welsh, some in English, until everyone declared themselves worn out. Harry saw his mother and father looking relaxed and happy, and noticed that Maisie was standing next to Bill during the singing, both of them leaning against the sideboard at the back of the room, and she made no objection when Bill's arm slid round her shoulder.

During the lull that followed, Uncle Fred called across to Dai: "Still play a bit of brag, these days, butt?"

But before Dai could answer Nan spoke up. "There'll be no cardplaying to-night. It's the same as the Sabbath!"

"When do you have to go back, Dai? Sunday, is it? Right then."
Uncle Fred winked at Dai. "My house tomorrow night." He turned
to Harry sitting beside him and lowered his voice. "You can come as
well if you like, only don't let your Mam know!"

Around midnight the party broke up, with everybody arranging to walk everybody else home until they all left in one big group,
spilling out of the doorway into a night of rare quiet. No sound from
the Forge or the Pit, and no-one else seemed to be about. Harry was
staying the night at Nan's so that Bridget could have his bedroom.
He stood on the doorstep amid all the goodbyes and stared up at the
Coity, looming dark and still above the town, the three black slag
heaps to its right for once blending into the skyline. The colliery itself
was in darkness, its sullen presence barely outlined in the faint lights
that shone from Forge Side.

Harry suddenly felt immeasurably sad; sad for his family for
whom this one day of jollification was over for another year, and sad
for the town, the place that he loved, preparing to face another year
which held even less promise than the one soon ending. He turned
and watched Dai and Bridget going arm in arm around the corner
into Lion Street, and wished for Ivy's warm body.

With a sigh he turned back into the house, just in time to see
Maisie give a surprised Bill a swift kiss on the lips before running
lightly up the stairs.

Ivy had invited Harry to tea on the Sunday after Christmas Day,
and although he was eager to see her, he viewed the visit with
some trepidation. An invitation to Sunday tea with the family was
tantamount to declaring that you were 'going steady', and keen
though he was to prolong his association with Ivy, he didn't want
anyone to think that theirs was a serious liaison.

The front door was opened by an eager nine-year-old, who took
one look at Harry and then yelled: "Mam! 'E's 'ere!" at the top of
his voice.

A thin, faded woman came bustling forward, pushing back a
straying hair that would have once been the same colour as Ivy's.
Her eyes were tired, but welcoming, as she held out her hand.

"Hello, Harry! Remember you from High Street! Come on in.
Ivy'll be down in a minute."

The wind blowing across the Coity had been raw, but there didn't
seem to be a lot more warmth inside the little house in C Row. Like
his own home, the front door opened straight into the sitting room,
but there the similarity ended. There was no linoleum on the floor,
merely bare draughty boards inadequately covered with a couple

of rag rugs. A pitifully meagre fire burnt in the grate, but that was obviously a tribute to the occasion, judging by the patches of damp creeping up the walls. A small sagging sofa with one foot missing sat drunkenly under the window, and against the opposite wall was an old-fashioned tall settle, the back of which could be pulled down to form a bed. A battered round table and one hard-backed chair completed the furniture in the room, which was bereft of any sort of ornament or picture.

Harry stood awkwardly, cap in hand, surveyed by a bevy of Ivy's younger brothers and sisters who had rallied to the cry of the nine-year-old.

"Did you have a nice Christm—?" He and Ivy's Mam began to speak at once, stopped, and smiled at one another. Then Ivy came clattering down the stairs, talking rapidly. "Stop gawping you lot! Let's have your coat, Harry! Mam, let's forget about being posh and go in the other room – it's freezing in here!"

She ushered everyone through the door into the back room, which served as a kitchen and living room. A stone sink stood in one corner, beneath a window which had a large crack in one pane and a tiny piece missing, through which the wind whistled. A deal table stood in the middle of the room, and around it was an assortment of chairs in varying states of disrepair. A scuffle broke out between two of the children as they sought to pull a chair to the fire for Harry.

"Quiet now! You can go in the front room, if you behave!" said their mother. She turned to Harry apologetically. "I can't send them upstairs, I'm afraid. It's a bit too cold. They'll calm down when we have tea."

Harry, Ivy, and Mrs. Miller sat round the fire making strangled attempts at conversation. Ivy did most of the talking, her mother's attention being constantly distracted by the children, who were running in and out with a few toys that looked too old and scarred to have been Christmas presents. She turned back each time and gave a tired, distant smile, having completely lost the thread of the conversation. For his part, Harry was unutterably depressed by his surroundings, despite the house being little different from those that many of his friends and relations lived in. He was also not looking forward to meeting Mr. Miller, whom he knew to be a man of considerable bulk and temper. It seemed that he wasn't expected, however, and tea was to proceed without him.

Ivy was different at home. As talkative as ever, there was a feverish note of anxiety in her speech, she was less relaxed and her features took on a taut, sharper look. When it was deemed time for tea she insisted on preparing it, slapping the children away when they crowded round the table and almost scowling as she reached up into the cupboard beside the fireplace for the bits and pieces of mismatched china stored there.

It was already dark when tea was over and Harry unblushingly made to leave with the excuse that he had to go to evening chapel, thankful that they weren't Baptists or they would have known it was a service he rarely attended. The meal hadn't been a success. Thick slices of bread with plum jam, which was pounced upon as a treat by the children, a fruit cake carefully cut into thin slices, and tea made with condensed milk, which he didn't like but made valiant efforts to drink. He'd taken his lead from the two women, who ate little so that there was more for the children, a ploy he recognised from his own mother when times were hard.

"I'll walk with you to the end of the row," Ivy said as he thanked Mrs. Miller for her hospitality.

They trudged along in unaccustomed silence. He took her arm. "Gone very quiet, you have. Didn't say anything to give offence, did I?"

"Don't be silly. Of course you didn't."

"What's the matter, then? *Some*thing's wrong with you."

She turned to him with no hint of the womanly wiles which so attracted him, but with a look of painful honesty in her eyes.

"I wish I hadn't invited you! It made everything seem so... so..." She made a little despairing noise, half-way between a hiccough and a sob, as they turned the corner.

Harry pulled her into the shelter of the gable end wall.

"What are you talking about?" He could feel anger rising. "Are you ashamed of me, or something?"

She pulled back from him. "Don't be daft! Ashamed of *you?* Of course not! Ashamed of everything else, more like... back there..." She jerked her head in the direction of her home. "Not up to much, is it? Never bothered me too much, before, either. But I kept thinking, remembering... When we were little and I used to come into your Nan's place, and she'd be putting the tea things on the table... everything matched, nice little delicate cups and saucers, and the room was cosy, with all your Nan's things around. And proper nice armchairs by the fire, and everything all polished... And then I looked round our place today, and there was nothing like that... and it made me think about what *you'd* be thinking when you saw it, and ..."

Her voice petered out on another hiccoughing sob. Harry put his arm around her and pulled her back towards him. For the first time he felt a wave of tender love, mingled with pity, for her, and for once did his best to ignore the other urges that the nearness of her body always produced. At the same time he thought of the meagre suppers he usually shared with his father. Cosy, yes, but often not very much to put on the table.

"There's silly you are," he told Ivy, offering her his handkerchief. "I didn't come to see what you've got, I came to meet your family – and lovely they were too. And don't forget," he went on as she made snuffling noises into his handkerchief, "my Mam's still got two wages coming into the house, and not as many mouths to feed." He thought it better not to talk about his Nan's house, which did indeed seem almost luxurious after the sparseness of C Row.

"Huh! There's two wages coming into our house most weeks," she said bitterly; "except nearly all of one is usually thrown away on drink! And then our Dad comes home on a Saturday night and starts knocking everything about! That's why there's nothing on the walls or shelves, you know! Mam got fed up long ago with trying to put it all back together again."

"Well then! Need a medal, the pair of you, I think, for coping as well as you do!"

But she wasn't to be cheered, and after a brief goodbye he watched as she went disconsolately back along the Row. He wanted to go after her and try to comfort her more, but the depression that had fallen upon him within her home made him understand only too well how she felt, and words to the contrary held only a hollow ring.

Strange, he mused, as he trudged down the hillside, how poverty was so comparative. The children wearing clogs were better off than the ones who were barefooted, those wearing daps were better off again, whilst the wearers of shoes were definitely considered as comfortable. He'd always thought of his own family as having to scratch to make ends meet, and there was many a time he'd come home from work to find his mother sitting in darkness, waiting for someone to come in with a penny to light the gas. Yet he'd never known the grim, utterly defeated poverty of the little house he'd just left.

He quickened his pace, eager to return to his own home, thankful that Dai, with his politics and his dire warnings that worse was yet to come, had left for London that morning.

His Mam smiled as he entered the living room. "You're early, Harry! Not fallen out with your young lady have you?"

"'Course not," he smiled back. "Just wanted to be back with my old Mam, that's all!" He leaned forward to hug her, in an uncharacteristic display of affection.

"Go on with you!" she cried, giving him a playful push but looking pleased all the same.

"Didn't get a good enough tea, more like," and she bustled out into the back kitchen, unaware of how true her words were.

Part Two

1939 ~

9

Jennie

Jennie gazed critically at herself in the cheval mirror in her bedroom, turning this way and that to see how the dress fell, trying to get a view of her profile. Not given to spending much time in front of a mirror, she felt quite pleased with what she saw. The flowery chiffon dress was well cut, clinging to her body and then falling in folds from her hips. It flattered her slenderness, and the little gathers each side of the V-neckline gave her more bust. She turned her attention to her hair, newly permed, which surprisingly Mother had approved of. More grown-up, Jennie decided, but it still felt very strange when she put her hand up and felt the curls.

She decided she would do, and moved across to the window to check that the April day was maintaining its early promise of sunshine. No point in going across the landing to Laura's room; Mother, having made herself ready hours ago, would doubtless be there, making Laura even more nervous than she already was by chivying her lest she be late. She'd been like that on the morning of Emily's wedding too, a year ago, although Emily, being Emily, had of course taken no notice whatsoever and blithely arrived at the altar twenty minutes late.

Jennie lowered the sash window and leaned on the sill, drinking in the fresh Spring air and scanning the mountains. She could just make out the dots of lambs on the lower slopes of the Sugar Loaf, whilst higher up the trees were beginning to show the faintest halo of green about their bare branches. She sighed with satisfaction, as she'd done since childhood whenever she surveyed this view. Forever changing with the seasons, yet changeless. Impossible to think that the country could soon be at war.

She wondered what the mountains would say if they could communicate. Would they laugh together at men who still seemed to have learned nothing during all the years that they'd been watching over them? Would they remember the futile battles they'd already witnessed through the centuries, when hardy Welshmen had sought sanctuary in their secret places because the castles built to keep out the English had been overpowered? Would they smile indulgently at the foolish antics of men who swarmed like ants around their base, knowing that they would still be here when even the giant ants had been forgotten?

She was roused from her reverie by a knock at the door, and Emily entered, wearing a flowing green wool coat which did much to conceal her advanced state of pregnancy.

"Ernest and I are ready to take Mother now, so she can make her grand entrance before the bride! And the bridesmaids' car is here, so you'd better come down too."

She turned to leave before Jennie could answer, her movements still brisk despite her encumbered size. Then, as an afterthought, she turned back and looked her sister up and down.

"That dress suits you," she said with a nod. "In fact, you look really pretty! Especially if you add a smile or two!" She winked and grinned at her younger sister, so that Jennie was forced to smile in response, and then they went downstairs together.

Ernest Gronow, Emily's husband now despite bearing a name that she still couldn't stand, was waiting for them at the foot of the stairs. Or rather, waiting until Emily told him what she wanted him to do next. He bestowed on his wife the same doting look that Jennie remembered when he'd first begun to court her sister almost ten years before.

Emily had been scornful of him then, and had led him a merry dance over the years until suddenly capitulating and agreeing to marry him. Now she treated him in the same way she would a faithful shaggy dog; rather absentmindedly, with more overt displays of affection when she remembered. Jennie wouldn't have been surprised if she came across Emily scratching him behind his ear when they were sat together reading, and she didn't think Ernest would mind. He seemed happy enough with the scraps Emily fed him, and was content to walk in her shadow, especially when they visited the farm, where he was still completely in awe of Mother.

The other bridesmaid, Muriel – a friend of Laura's since schooldays – was also in the hall, and the four of them made desultory conversation until Mother, resplendent in dove grey with a picture hat, descended the stairs.

"That girl's nerves are in a shocking state!" she declared with grim satisfaction to no-one in particular, as they trooped out behind her to the waiting cars.

Katharine Davies looked around at the guests enjoying the wedding breakfast. The speeches were over, the toasts had been given, and the guests were beginning to drift away from their tables, waiting for the dancing to begin.

She finally allowed herself to relax a little. She really was very pleased with Laura's choice of husband. An eloquent, upright young man, Cyril had already shown his devotion to his country by joining up; not, to his great disappointment, as a pilot in the RAF, because of his poor eyesight, but she knew he'd soon make his mark behind the scenes.

Katharine nodded and smiled benevolently at one or two of the guests, distinguished looking people on Cyril's side. She liked Cyril's family too. Hereford people with a bit of money in the bank – enough to see that Cyril had made a good start in the insurance world, and doubtless enough to see him right again once this silly business with Germany was sorted out. And Laura would make him a good wife – you only had to watch her to see that she doted on him. Yes, they would go far together.

It was a good wedding party, she decided. Sufficiently tasteful to show any of the guests that the Davies family was far from being common farmers. Very different from her own wedding, she reflected. That had been a quiet, hasty affair with her stomach so tightly corseted, lest anyone discover her guilty secret, that she could hardly breathe. They'd been happy, though, at first. She felt herself grow hot as she remembered those early passionate times when she would have let Edward do anything – anything to assuage the desperate physical craving that took over her body and demanded to be satisfied.

She pushed those memories away; they were always accompanied by a sense of disappointment and failure. *But we haven't failed otherwise,* she told herself fiercely. *We've come a long way; we're successful, respected. This wedding proves it.*

Her attention was distracted by a high-pitched laugh from one of the long tables leading down from the top one, and the corners of her mouth were pulled down as she looked with distaste upon the owner of the laugh.

Nancy. It had to be, of course.

She wondered for the hundredth time what had possessed Tom to marry such a frivolous young madam, from a family in Abergavenny renowned for producing highly-strung daughters. She wasn't going to last five minutes as a farmer's wife. But then, she reflected, Tom had never been one for listening to advice from other people, least of all his own parents. He'd treated his father with growing contempt as he steadfastly refused to adopt the modern farming methods that Tom was so keen on, until one day he'd announced that he was going to find somewhere of his own, and in no time at all it seemed he'd found a smallholding to rent, and had married this silly girl.

Katharine looked away from them, irritated that they had broken into her reflections – and found herself being scrutinised by a pair of dark brown eyes belonging to the best man, Charles Keating, who had slid into the seat next to hers.

He smiled engagingly. "Your daughter is a beautiful bride. You must be very proud of her!"

Katharine knew that Laura was too heavy to be considered beautiful, but she accepted the compliment graciously. She was intrigued by this tall, good-looking man whom she'd heard about but never met. Puzzled too; they were supposed to be old school friends, yet this man seemed several years older than Cyril.

"I gather you and Cyril were at school together?"

He smiled again, showing strong, even, white teeth.

"Sort of. I was at the top end of the school when he came there as a timid little ten-year-old. I used to coach junior cricket, which he was awfully keen on but dreadfully bad at. Came on a lot, though, which he insists was down to my coaching, but frankly I think it was more to do with his acquiring some decent spectacles!"

Katharine smiled politely. "But you kept in touch?"

"Now and then – Old Boys' matches and the like. Didn't really renew the friendship until we both started at Howard and Renshaw's. It was good to see a friendly face then, I can tell you – both of us wanting to make a good impression, but neither of us too sure of what we were doing! Been firm friends ever since, so it made sense to join up together."

She studied his face as he spoke. Well-bred, she decided, definitely well-bred. Clean features, a rather aquiline nose, and a very slightly haughty look, until he smiled. And that confident, clipped way of speaking. She wondered what he'd done before he went into insurance, and what his family was like, but didn't want to ask too many questions.

But she didn't need to ask, he seemed happy to carry on talking. "First chance I'd had to settle into a career. I'd been too busy before then, sorting out the family estate – my parents died within a short time of each other."

She murmured conventional words of sympathy, which he acknowledged with a slight nod. "I was a late child. I suppose I'd always known that I would lose my parents while I was still quite young."

She watched his long fingers open a slim silver case, extract a cigarette, and tap it nonchalantly against the back of the case. There were dark hairs on the backs of his hands and curling around the white cuffs of his shirt. She had a fleeting image of his naked chest, with the same hair curling thickly across it. Suddenly aware of his closeness, his masculinity, she felt her body stirring.

"Do you mind?" He held up the cigarette enquiringly.

She lifted her eyes to meet his deep brown ones, her rigid self-control giving no indication of her thoughts. "No – no, of course not. If you'll excuse me, there are one or two guests I must speak to before the dancing begins."

She made to rise out of her seat and he rose too, holding the chair as she stepped back from the table. He leaned forward slightly. "I hope you know that the best man always demands a dance from the bride's mother?"

She gave him a small smile before moving off towards some of Cyril's relatives.

Charles blew a small cloud of smoke into the air as he watched her go. A good-looking woman, he decided, although she must be in her mid-forties at least. Kept her figure well, too. He watched her incline her head graciously towards an elderly man who seemed rather deaf. Just the sort who'd be a right little firebrand beneath that carefully correct exterior, in his experience.

He smiled inwardly. He was very, very experienced.

Jennie sat on a chair and eased her left foot out of its shoe. She loved Father dearly, but it had to be said that he was no dancer. Three times he'd trodden on her feet, each time catching the place where the narrow satin shoes had already begun to rub. She wiggled her toes out of sight under the chair for a few moments, then painfully squeezed the shoe back on. She would sit for a while longer and watch the dancing, rather than risk further agonies from elderly uncles who liked to think they still cut a bit of a dash on the dance floor.

Mother was moving about the room, a regal smile fixed firmly on her lips as she basked in everyone's appreciation of the wonderful do it was, while also managing to keep an eagle eye on everything so that events proceeded to her complete satisfaction. *It's poor old Father who has to pay the bill, though,* Jennie thought – and a reception like this, at the prestigious Llanover Hall, would have set him back considerably.

In contrast to his wife, Father was standing near the refreshments table talking quietly to Aunt Eunice and Uncle Frank. The younger people were all dancing, Emily laughing as she tried to hold herself close to Ernest but couldn't because of her 'bump', and even Tom had erased the dour expression that usually overcame his features when he was with his family, and was smiling down at Nancy as they whirled with more exuberance than expertise around the floor.

That's probably what being in love did for you, Jennie decided. Tom was definitely a nicer person since his marriage, despite what Mother said about Nancy, and Laura positively glowed at the mere mention of Cyril's name, and always wanted to hold his hand or cling onto his arm whenever they were together. Jennie wondered if her parents had ever been in love in that way. There was certainly precious little evidence of it now, although Father never treated Mother with anything other than kind consideration, even when she was at her most waspish – which was ever more frequently lately. But they never touched, and had never even shared a bedroom as far back as she could remember.

Laura danced past with Cyril, and smiled at Jennie. Was she looking forward to her wedding night, Jennie wondered? Emily dealt with such matters in her usual robust way, and had declared to Jennie after her honeymoon that it was all 'great fun'. But Laura had always been rather fastidious, and had frowned at Emily for talking so frankly to Jennie. Nevertheless, she'd purchased all sorts of pretty, delicate underwear and nightwear to 'look nice for Cyril', and her eyes had twinkled as if in anticipation of his response when he saw her in it, so she must be looking forward to the intimate side of marriage.

Jennie sighed. It must be nice to be in love; having someone with whom you could really talk, and who cared about how you felt.

She saw Charles across the room, murmuring something to a cousin, who laughed in response and looked at him with flirty eyes. He was very handsome, Jennie decided. She'd just finished *Gone With The Wind*, read avidly in the privacy of her bedroom late at night just in case Mother disapproved. (Mother hadn't read the book herself, but often disapproved of something for no particular reason, and the fact that she didn't like Americans would be enough.) Charles was definitely a Rhett Butler, Jennie thought; sophisticated, charming, and far too worldly to be interested in a young girl who helped on her parents' farm.

"Come on, old girl! Can't have the chief bridesmaid skulking in the corner! Time for you to be dancing!"

Cyril was urging her to her feet. Since joining the RAF he had adopted the enthusiastic phrases of the pilots with alacrity, but with the slight Hereford burr to his voice Jennie thought his 'come on, old girl' sounded more like her father coaxing the cows to milking.

"I wasn't skulking," she said firmly as she stood up, "I've already been dancing with Father, but I sat down because I was feeling warm."

Cyril's face was the colour of a ripe tomato beneath his sandy hair. He ran his finger round the inside of his collar. "Know what you mean. Dashed hot in here! Still, everyone seems to be having a jolly time. Come on! Laura's told me how well those nuns taught you to dance. Let's see what you can do with the foxtrot!"

He led her into the dance. He was extremely light on his feet and she quickly matched her steps to his, and was able to ignore the heat of his hands through her dress and the beads of sweat on his brow. She wondered if Laura minded him kissing her when he was all sweaty like this.

As the dance ended, Charles approached them. "Time you were making a move, Cyril. Your train leaves in half-an-hour."

Cyril glanced at his watch. "Lord! You're right. Better have a quick word with my folks before we do the formal goodbyes. Look after Jennie, will you Charles? She's a cracking dancer!"

But Jennie didn't want to dance with the tall, suave man who had already made her feel gauche and tongue-tied when they'd accompanied each other out of the church.

"No!" she cried, making to follow Cyril. "I must go and help Laura change – if you'll excuse me…"

But Cyril stopped her. "It's all right. Muriel disappeared upstairs with her. Must be all but ready by now. Stay and keep Charles company – I'm sure he's had enough of being polite to all the old fogies!"

He grinned at his friend and moved away. Charles smiled down at her indulgently. "Looks like you're stuck with me, I'm afraid. Would you like to dance, or would you rather sit this one out?"

"Yes – no! I mean, yes please, I would like to dance." If they sat it out they would have to talk, and she'd probably make a complete fool of herself. "And I'm sorry, I didn't mean to sound rude. It's just that I thought I was supposed to help Laura and I didn't want her to be waiting for me … that's what I did last year when Emily got married… helped her, I mean, not made her wait for me – "

Oh, this was terrible! Why did she have to gabble like this? Why couldn't she be gay and amusing like Emily when men were around, or at least gravely polite, like Laura?

"They're starting a waltz," he said, still using that tone which obviously meant that he found her very young for her eighteen years. "Would you care to?"

She nodded, and then found herself in his arms. He was an even better dancer than Cyril, and led her expertly around the floor.

"Cyril was right; you dance very well," he commented, with sufficient admiration in his voice for her to glow at the compliment. "Do you dance a lot?"

She shook her head. "Not since I left school. There aren't many places nearby to go dancing, and –" she didn't want to say that Mother wouldn't let her go without a male escort, and she'd never managed to secure one – "and, well… it's just a bit difficult, living on the farm," she finished lamely.

"So what do you do to amuse yourself?"

"I read a lot… and I belong to St. Peter's Ramblers. We meet most Sunday afternoons." The rise in popularity of rambling clubs over the last few years had been a godsend for her, getting her out of the house during the dreary hours while Mother rested, and giving her the only opportunity to meet other young people. Much to Mother's disgust she'd bought a pair of shorts and had insisted on wearing them, despite the caustic comments. Striding along in shorts and shirt and humming *Waltzing Matilda*, which had become the ramblers' anthem, she was never happier.

He listened politely as she told him about the club, but as she spoke she was aware of sounding dreadfully provincial. She cast about feverishly for something more interesting. "And… I play tennis with Ced Griffiths' sons. They're our nearest neighbours, and they put up a grass court in the summer."

"But you can't persuade them to take you dancing?"

She gave a spurt of laughter as she pictured Ced Griffiths' burly sons – who only tolerated her tennis playing because she was good and usually available – squeezed into respectable suits and sedately tripping around a dance floor. "They're over there." She indicated two strapping lads standing to one side and eyeing the dancers with distaste. "As you can see, it's not quite their idea of fun!"

He followed her gaze and then laughed with her, and she decided that she could like him very much indeed.

The dance came to an end, and he gave a small inclination of his head. "Thank you. That was most enjoyable." But he immediately moved away and she realised that he'd merely been doing his duty as best man. She turned her head and caught Mother watching her, with a strange combination of her usual disapproval and something else which Jennie couldn't analyse. Probably she'd laughed too loudly when talking to Charles, or stood too close to him in what could be construed as a brazen way by somebody as keen to find fault as Mother.

She shrugged inwardly. She was so used to Mother's unpredictable vagaries that they only bothered her now when they became extreme. For the rest of the time she took a leaf out of Father's book and simply acquiesced quietly, because that was what made life easier. It didn't seem to make Mother any happier, though. Somehow the more Jennie and her father agreed to Mother's whims, the more things she found to become dissatisfied with.

"They're off now!" somebody shouted. Everyone surged to the door to wave to the happy couple; Laura full-bosomed and beaming in a maroon costume with a peplum waist and a perky little matching hat, and Cyril in a stiff suit with a faint chalk-stripe, looking a little cooler now.

Laura threw her bouquet which, to Jennie's horror, headed her way. She purposely fumbled at catching it so that it fell to the floor, where it was pounced upon by Muriel and held aloft triumphantly. Jennie joined in the teasing and speculation which followed, relieved that the attention hadn't been focused on her. She'd already suffered the comments of aunts and uncles that she was now the only one still at home, and when would wedding bells be ringing for her? – and the indignity of having to admit that there was no-one whom she could claim was the least bit interested in her.

A rosebud from the bouquet was still on the floor. She stooped to pick it up, and stood for a few moments considering it. How marvellous it would be for someone to come along and sweep her off her feet. Someone who'd take her away from Mother's constant criticism and tell her instead that she was wonderful!

Looking up, she found Charles Keating's eyes boring into her. A smile played upon his lips – a smile of condescending sympathy; a smile which acknowledged the futility of her hopes and dreams. She blushed and turned away, grateful for once to hear Mother's voice imperiously demanding her attention.

*W*e've finally *finished the harvesting,* Jennie wrote to Emily at the end of June. *Early this year, of course, because the weather has been so good. I'm as brown as a berry, which Mother doesn't like – she thinks it looks common – but I expect you are, too, living by the sea.*

Emily and Ernest had moved to Plymouth, where Ernest was involved in something terribly complicated to do with ship-building. Their son, Philip, was just two months old.

I hope I shall be able to come down to see you soon, although Mother says we'll be much too busy. She's made Father open up the cellar so that she can store things down there – you wouldn't believe what she's squirreling away. If there isn't a war we won't need to buy anything for years! At the same time, if anyone mentions the war she insists that Hitler deserves to be given another chance, because he's done a lot of good in Germany and made the trains run on time! Father tells people who come to the farm not to say anything to Mother about the war as it upsets her, but it's really because there's no telling what she might say. Honestly, Em, if it wasn't for being able to escape to Laura's every now and again, I think I'd go mad.

She paused at this point and chewed the end of her pen. She sat at her little table beneath the window in her room, staring out at the blue-hazed mountains that seemed more distant in the evening sun. She wouldn't be surprised if she did go mad eventually; not dramatically mad with lots of seizures and foaming at the mouth, but quietly strange as the years passed, then decidedly eccentric, and finally completely dotty. She'd seen it before in spinsters of the parish who'd reached a certain age and never left home. She sighed. She still loved her home, but it was pretty obvious that she was going to be stuck here for the rest of her life. Mother simply expected it of her, and made sure that there was little opportunity for anything else, while Father had come to rely on her more and more around the farm; particularly since Tom had left.

And none of it would seem so bad, she decided, if Mother showed even the slightest sign of mellowing. Rather, her moods and contrariness were getting worse, despite the fact that her life was more comfortable than it had ever been. But, somehow, none of it was as she wished. When Father became Chairman of the local Farmers' Club, as she'd wanted, it was suddenly only a *tuppenny-ha'penny concern*, and it would be far better if he tried for the parish council.

When the Milk Marketing Board had been established, Father had increased the herd and sold the surplus milk to the Board, leaving it in gleaming churns perched on a beautifully constructed bench at the end of the drive. The money earned had been used to purchase a brand new Ford, thus releasing Mother from the demeaning necessity of travelling in the milk van, which should have pleased her. On the contrary, the MMB was dismissed as a ruse by the government which would ultimately render dairy farmers destitute, and the car was grudgingly allowed to be an improvement, but still not up to the standard of Dr. Moxom's – although she made the best of it by insisting on sitting in the back, which was far more ladylike than keeping her husband company in the front.

Jennie sighed again. Perhaps Mother would go mad first, and then they could keep her hidden away upstairs, like Mrs. Rochester, and she and Father could do all the things they wanted, when they wanted, like reading the newspaper first in the mornings instead of waiting till Mother produced it from under the chair cushion when she'd quite finished with it herself. Or sit in the parlour in the evenings with their feet on the fender and listen to plays on the wireless. And Father could wash and shave in the bathroom instead of in the icy washhouse. Or perhaps Mother would become sweetly senile in her dotage, bestowing gummy beatific smiles on Jennie and telling her what a wonderful daughter she was every time she did her a small kindness ...

She forced her attention back to her letter.

Cyril's still stationed at Cheltenham, so he's often home at weekends. He's become ever so involved in Monmouth life, but at the moment Laura doesn't feel like doing much, so I often go with him, and when he can't come home Laura likes me to go over to keep her company.

Laura and Cyril had settled into a small townhouse in Monmouth, where Laura, in a more benign imitation of her mother, had decided she'd like to make a mark on the local society – to which Cyril, much given to social climbing himself, wholeheartedly agreed. He had immediately joined the tennis club, the golf club, and Rotary. Unfortunately their plans had been thwarted somewhat, not only by the threat of war, but also by the inconvenience of Laura becoming pregnant on her honeymoon and thence suffering from every minor ailment imaginable and, Jennie thought in her less charitable moments, several unimaginable ones too.

Jennie knew she was being made use of, but she didn't mind. She would experience an overwhelming sense of release whenever she stood at Nantyderry Halt on a Friday evening, waiting for the train that would take her the couple of stops to Monmouth. If Cyril was at home he'd meet her at the station and talk very seriously as they strolled back to the house, telling her all his views and feelings about the fraught state of affairs the country was in; views that he wouldn't express in front of Laura for fear of worrying her in her 'delicate condition'. At other times he would travel down from Cheltenham in Charles Keating's sleek car and Charles would stay for the weekend too, which would make Laura flutter around, determined to play the hostess, so that invariably by Sunday afternoon her ankles would begin to swell and her head to ache, and she'd have to retire to bed.

Jennie had mixed feelings about the weekends when Charles was there as well. She'd hope each time that he was going to be, and then feel desperately disappointed if he wasn't, or be tense and nervous if he was. His presence seemed to imbue the other two with a sense of being gay, dashing young things – he would flatter Laura outrageously, and Cyril would become even more 'RAF', twirling the ends of the moustache he'd been painstakingly encouraging his fair skin to grow, and saying 'wizard' unnecessarily often. Jennie longed to feel that she too was one of the moths fluttering round Charles' flame, but he didn't treat her in the same way as he did Laura. Usually he insisted on taking her back to the farm in his car, when he would talk to her in the same avuncular manner he'd used at the wedding, while she suffered agonies at not being able to think of one witty rejoinder that would make him look at her with a modicum of interest.

Mother has taken quite a shine to Charles Keating. She always insists that he has a drink with us – or rather, with her. Father retires to the corner with the paper after he's done his butler's bit with the sherry bottle, and she usually finds me something to do so that I don't stay in the room. Not that I mind. She positively simpers when he's there. 'And what do you suppose Mr. Chamberlain intends to do next?' she asks him, sitting there with her head on one side, waiting for his reply. I think she's trying to play the help-less female. Little does he know!

She chewed her pen again. Perhaps she was being unfair to Mother – perhaps Mother was simply attempting to be a good hostess to a personable man.

But then she remembered their exchanges just last weekend.

"I don't know what we'll do if it really does come to war," Mother had said, after Charles had intimated that there was little doubt in the minds of the top brass with whom he seemed to mix. Jennie had been on the point of escaping to the kitchen for a quiet cup of tea alone, but had caught Mother's expression as she looked at Charles. She had been openly admiring of him, and he in return had looked straight into her eyes as he patted her hand and told her that he was sure she would manage wonderfully. Jennie's stomach had churned; his voice had been almost a caress, and by the time the kettle had boiled she found that she no longer wanted a cup of tea.

But she couldn't find the words to describe this properly to Emily. *It's just sour grapes,* she told herself. *What you'd really like is for him to look at you like that. Well, he's not going to, and the sooner you accept that, the better.*

She finished her letter and changed back into the old trousers she wore around the farm. It was time to do all the evening chores. She resolutely turned her back on any more thoughts of Charles Keating.

But she couldn't stop him invading her dreams, where he would hold her tightly in his arms and caress her in such a way that when she woke next morning she would be riven by unfulfilled longings and hopeless desire.

10

The imminence of war continued to dominate every news bulletin on the wireless and every conversation on market day, but Jennie's life proceeded undisturbed. Somehow it was impossible to believe that anything could disrupt the quiet, rhythmic harmony of farm life, and it was easy to turn her back on the gloomy forecasts of those who could remember only too well the grief and hardship meted out twenty years earlier by the 'War to end all wars'. For the first time in her life she had some semblance of social life, away from Mother's dictates, so while Hitler plotted and schemed and Chamberlain appeased, she lived only for the weekends when she could get away.

Emboldened by the upturn in her life, she made plans to visit Emily at the end of July, when farm life could be said to be at its quietest. Father, delighted to see the daughter that had become his refuge and his strength blossoming into a young woman, encouraged her.

"You go, m' girl, while you can, and get a bit of sea air. I daresay I can get a boy in for a couple of weeks to give me a hand, and Mother can manage to get the tea herself for a little while." This last was a daring jibe at Mother's insistence that whatever Jennie was doing, she had to leave it and be in the house at four-thirty to prepare tea. For once, though, Mother simply set her lips in a grim line and said nothing either for or against Jennie's arrangements.

The following weeks flew past as Jennie made her preparations. The swimming costume that had been alright for the odd day at Southerndown Sands with Laura was now deemed too old, and a smart new red one with ruching down the front was bought from Wildings, along with a strappy sundress that would also double for evenings if the opportunity of a dance arose. Jennie was unsure about the dress when she got it home, and spent a long time holding it up against herself in front of her bedroom mirror. It was a rather daring departure from the shirtwaister style that she normally wore, and which she knew suited her.

I expect Emily will encourage me to wear it, she decided, smiling at the thought of Emily's high spirits which hadn't seemed to diminish with motherhood, judging from her letters. *But I don't think I'll show it to Mother.*

She glanced at her watch. Heavens! Nearly dinner time, and she'd promised Father she'd help with moving the sow into the freshly prepared sty where she would stay until she produced her litter.

She was running across the yard when she heard a clatter from up the drive, followed by a shout – Father's voice, loud and urgent. She ran through the gate and hurried up the drive, where she could see the tractor and trailer near the farm entrance.

"Father!" she cried. "What's wrong?"

As she reached the tractor she could see for herself. Father was lying on the ground, his face ashen, with one wheel of the trailer planted firmly on his right leg and an empty milk churn lying on his left.

He spoke in gasps. "The trailer pin … has snapped! The beggar … rolled back on me … when I was lifting the churn up. No! Don't move it!" His voice rose sharply as Jennie knelt beside him and made to lift the churn. "It's the only thing … stopping the trailer … moving back further. You'll have to … get a rope … and fix the trailer back … onto the tractor, so's you can drive it off me."

Jennie had turned almost as white as Father as she surveyed the situation. "The ground's sloping too much here – I might not be able to start the tractor without it rolling back a bit first. That'll hurt your leg more."

She stood up and looked vainly about in the hope that she could see someone else, although she knew full well that Mother was the only other person on the farm, and there was rarely any passing traffic on their quiet country road. She turned back to Father, who was sitting up leaning on one elbow, his face contorted with pain. There was a thin line of sweat on his upper lip.

She grabbed a piece of sacking from the trailer. "Lie back on this," she told him, bunching the sacking into a pillow. "I'll try to pull the trailer off myself. It's empty, so it's not heavy. Can you bear it?"

He nodded, his eyes closed, his hands gripping his right leg around the thigh. He spoke hoarsely. "Take it steady. Don't want you injured as well."

Jennie moved round to the front of the trailer and caught hold of the broken shaft with both hands. She braced herself and began to pull on it, gently at first and then gradually exerting more pressure. It began to move, then settled back on itself, making Jennie wince at the pain it must be inflicting on Father, but he didn't utter a sound.

She tried again, cursing the slope of the track, which one didn't notice unless one tried to cycle up it.

Very slowly, agonisingly slowly, the trailer began to move. She kept a steady pull on it until Father gave a shout of pain and triumph as his leg was freed.

Jennie swung the trailer round until it faced across the track and then pushed it so that it ran into the hedge and came to a standstill. She turned back to Father, lifted the milk churn off his left leg, and sent it careering drunkenly and noisily down the drive as she knelt to examine his legs. The left one seemed alright, and he was able to move it cautiously, but his right foot lay at an odd angle to his leg and he was unable to move it at all.

"I won't touch it," said Jennie. "It isn't bleeding, but it looks broken. Will you be alright if I go for help?"

He nodded. "I'll be fine. Fetch Ced. He'll help. Don't go fetching the Doctor, though. Ced will sort everything out" The tightness of his lips belied his words.

Jennie fled down the drive and in through the open front door, yelling to Mother as she went. Grateful for once that Katharine had insisted they have a telephone installed – although no-one used it without asking her first – Jennie was already dialling Ced's number as Mother appeared from the kitchen.

"What on earth are you shouting about…?" Words of rebuke died on her lips as she heard Jennie breathlessly explain to Ced Griffiths what had happened.

It was as if, Jennie thought later, Mother had known all along that nothing would come of her plans. Late that night she sat in the kitchen with Mother, drinking cocoa, the day's chores finally finished. Father had been installed on a narrow camp bed in the dining room, where Mother could minister to his needs but he wouldn't be under her feet, and he wouldn't be making a mess in the parlour. The lower part of his right leg was encased in still-wet Plaster of Paris; his left leg was swollen and badly bruised, while his mind was still fuzzy from the sedation he'd been given as his leg was set.

"You'll have to write to Emily first thing," said Mother. "Tell her you won't be coming. She'll only get it a day before you were due there, but that can't be helped."

Jennie waited for her to say what a pity that the holiday was not to be, or offer words of encouragement that she could go as soon as Father had recovered, but she said no more about it. Instead she carried the empty cups to the sink and began to wash them up. She had determined to be noble in giving up all thought of a holiday, wanting to be cheerful about it for Father's sake, but now she found herself bitter, cheated, and felt again the force of Mother's indifference to her feelings and her needs.

And so ended the summer for Jennie. The balmy days, unusually hot, when by midday the whole world seemed to be drowsing, were lost on her as she struggled to keep the farm going and to cope with Mother's incessant demands to help with Father.

As storm clouds gathered over Europe, a similar cloud settled over Jennie. Gone was the opportunity for the first real holiday of her life; gone were the weekends of escape with Laura and Cyril. She rose earlier each morning to get the milking done, slipping out of the house without so much as a cup of tea because Mother disliked her bringing the range to life before she herself was down, and forbade her completely to use the stove.

Jennie couldn't lift the churns to take them to their appointed place at the end of the drive, so the driver from the Milk Marketing Board agreed to back his lorry down to the yard gate. By the end of the first week deep ruts had been scored in the dirt track, which gave Mother her first topic of complaint for the day and which usually continued throughout breakfast.

"Let me get a lad to help me from the village, then," Jennie said in exasperation. "It's what Father would've done if I'd gone away."

"There's none to be had. I've checked." Mother replied shortly, so that Jennie didn't know whether she was telling the truth. "Besides, your Father wouldn't really have got someone to help, he was only saying that to make you feel better."

"But he wouldn't have had to help in the house as well," Jennie muttered as she followed Mother out of the kitchen to help change the beds, too tired to stand up to her any more.

Father watched in alarm as Jennie became thinner and thinner and dark circles appeared beneath her eyes. In the end he put his good foot down and insisted that Ced Griffiths be approached. Ced sent his youngest son for the best part of each day, for which Jennie was grateful, but she couldn't add to Father's worries by telling him that the extra work on the farm was only part of the reason for her haggard looks.

The other reason was, as usual, Mother. As the days wore on her temper became fiercer and more uncertain. Each visit from Dr. Pritchard, a country bumpkin in Mother's opinion, brought forth from her first a diatribe on the trials she had to bear, and then pronouncements that Father would never be able to work properly and they would have to sell up – despite Dr. Pritchard's insistence that the leg was healing well. She conveniently forgot that many a time she'd hankered after a nice, detached villa in the town, and dwelt instead upon their uncertain future, since no-one would want to buy a farm with war looming.

Her vitriol about this and a dozen different things each day was heaped upon Jennie. Mother watched with a critical eye over everything she did in the house, and none of it was right. Consequently Jennie became still more nervous and jumpy in her presence and clumsy in her actions, giving Mother even more opportunity to pour scorn on her ineptitude.

"You'll have to help me with the poultry tomorrow," she told Jennie one hot afternoon towards the end of July, an afternoon when Jennie had been filled with resentment because she should have been spending it relaxing in Devon. "I've six to get ready for Goytre Hall – they've a wedding on this Saturday."

Jennie continued laying a tea tray to take into her father. She hated having anything to do with the poultry once they were killed – hated the feel of clammy chicken skin after it had been plucked, and the smell of blood and innards as they were cleaned out. Normally Mother preferred to do the work herself, taking a pride in this one aspect of farm life with which she chose to be identified, but she was determined on this occasion to prove that the current demands being made on her were too great.

Jennie backed herself out of the kitchen carrying a large wooden tray and headed for the dining room. Father had progressed to an armchair, with his foot supported on a tapestry stool covered by a linen cloth to protect it, where he sat and fretted – his only view of the farm being the front garden and drive where, of course, no animals were allowed.

Jennie forced herself to smile as she entered the room, and was rewarded by seeing Father's face light up. She knew that he relied on her almost entirely to relieve the monotony of his day, his wife rarely entering the room except to perform nursing duties. She nodded towards the window. "Aren't the roses looking beautiful? No sign of greenfly." She set the tray down on a small table. "I'll deadhead them tonight after supper."

"I'll be able to potter about out there myself soon, when old Pritchard lets me use a stick. How's Susie?"

Susie, the old sow, had kept Jennie up for hours the night before, delivering her litter. Jennie had been fearful lest Susie roll on the piglets as they were born, but the animal was far more experienced than her carer, and as Jennie worked herself up into a lather of anxiety Susie had calmly produced a litter of ten hardy piglets.

"Mother and babies all doing well," Jennie told her father now, "but the midwife is feeling a bit jaded! Early night for me tonight."

He scanned her face as she leaned over to pour the tea for him. "Is everything alright otherwise?"

"Of course." She refused to mention Mother. If she began to complain about her she'd have difficulty stopping, and she was determined that her father shouldn't worry. She patted his shoulder. "Everything's under control. It will all be there waiting for you once you're up and about."

"I didn't mean the farm – I meant ..."

"The war?" She made a face. "You listen to the news more than I do – it's all looking a bit grim, isn't it? Which reminds me – Mother wants to buy more hens at next week's market. It's all part of her stocking-up policy, so there'll be more chicken sheds for you to build once you're fit."

He ran his eyes over the brittle form of his daughter, tense despite her cheerful words and fixed smile, but didn't know what else to say. He gave up and matched his tone to hers. "You'd better see if you can get some creosote and wire for me if you go with Mother, then. Perhaps it's time we did a bit of stocking up as well. Are you going to stay and drink some of this tea with me?"

"Better not – I'll come back later and help you into the parlour so you can listen to the wireless."

Next morning Mother commandeered her as soon as the morning chores were done and Jennie had come into the kitchen for elevenses. Bessie's most recent successor, a timid young girl named Alice, looked up from scrubbing the larder floor and gave her a watery smile.

"Mrs. Davies wants you over in the chicken sheds as soon as you're ready."

She ended with a loud sniff, a perpetual habit which meant that her days as Mother's helper were already numbered. Jennie wasn't sure whether the girl was chronically adenoidal or whether the sniff had developed as a result of being permanently on the verge of tears since her employment at the farm. Any attempts to find out had been met with the assertion: "I'm fine, thank you. Quite alright." *Sniff, sniff.*

Which is what all of us say rather than upset the status quo and therefore upset Mother, Jennie thought as she quickly downed a cup of tea. *She's got us all exactly where she wants us and she's still not blooming satisfied.*

She found Mother busy separating the next batch of chickens to be fattened up to replace the ones she'd already slaughtered and bled. Jennie was grudgingly forced to admit that in this, as in so many other things, Mother was ruthlessly efficient. There were special enclosures where the chickens to be fattened were put so that they would be given extra corn feed for the next couple of weeks. When she thought no-one else was about Mother might be heard talking and crooning to them, but then would quite calmly catch one, hold it by the neck and insert the knife down its throat to kill it.

She turned as Jennie approached. "We can take the six I've done into the wash-house now. I want to be finished plucking them by dinner time. You can singe them and clear up the feathers, and then we'll clean them out."

Mother's slim, capable hands made short work of plucking each bird. Jennie fetched a taper, lit it, and ran it over each body, burning the hairs that were exposed on the plucked skin. The smell of chicken flesh, blood and burning hair made her want to go outside and gulp in great mouthfuls of clean air, but Mother seemed not to notice. She hummed softly as she worked, an indication that for once she was in a better mood. She spoke little, seemingly lost in thought, until Jennie was sweeping up the last stray feathers and she was about to begin gutting the birds.

"I'm going to finish dressing these tomorrow morning. They can go into the cold larder overnight." Her hands were spattered with blood as she placed the chicken livers, which were always kept, into a bowl.

"Couldn't we finish this afternoon? I could take them to Goytre Hall in the morning then when I'm out in the van anyway. It would save me some time."

Mother turned towards her from the sink, the humming and her preoccupation ended, her eyes glittering dangerously. "And I've got other things *I* want to do. Ced's boy can always take them in for me – we can't run this farm totally for your convenience, you know!"

She turned back to the sink before Jennie could protest, and pounced on the next bird with vigour. *Here we go,* Jennie thought, *another diatribe on everyone else's selfishness and her martyrdom.* But to her surprise Mother's next words were softer, almost conciliatory.

"I believe Charles may be calling in this afternoon to see your father. I can't be out here doing all this messy business when we have a visitor."

So that was it: Charles. Arriving yet again supposedly to see Father. Which he would do, of course. He would sit with him for a certain length of time in the dining room and discuss events in Europe and what Mr. Chamberlain may or may not do next. But he would sit even longer afterwards with Mother, drinking tea and discussing... what? Jennie didn't know.

Charles had become a frequent visitor to the farm since Father's accident. He was no longer stationed with Cyril at Cheltenham, but had been moved to Brecon, where reconnaissance exercises were being carried out over the Beacons and Charles, apparently, was indispensable in organising the ground crew and admin staff. Nevertheless he managed to find considerable opportunities to travel across to Goytre. Jennie had been delighted at his frequent appearances at first, but as he invariably found her with unwashed hair, wearing disreputable corduroy breeches and smelling faintly of dung, she now preferred to stay out of the way.

She looked across at a chicken lying drunkenly across the wooden draining board, its head lolling over the edge. Tomorrow, when Mother had finished her ministrations, the chicken would be wedged plumply onto a tray surrounded by parsley, its head sitting perkily on its breast, its comb and beak bright red, slices of chicken liver decorating its back, and it would be hard to believe the bloody mess that had to be gone through to achieve this aesthetically pleasing result.

Just like Mother, Jennie thought gloomily. Charles will arrive this afternoon and she will be charm itself, putting herself out to be the perfect hostess, impeccably groomed, smiling at his pleasantries and even – Jennie ground her teeth together at the thought – becoming quite skittish when he pays her a compliment. And he'll have no idea how much of her is dressing, and just how bloody she can be underneath.

Katharine Davies lifted her working dress over her head and hung it on the inside of the wardrobe. It would do to wear again tomorrow. She peeled off her thick lisle stockings and reached for her silk ones, stretching her toes daintily as she put them on, while making a mental note that she should buy plenty more while there was the chance. Her thoughts were full of what else could be done to fend off the day-to-day unpleasantness that war would undoubtedly bring, until she stood up and surveyed herself in the dressing table mirror.

Her petticoat was trimmed with lace and fell over a figure that was still as neat as it had been twenty years ago. She stood sideways, admiring her upright carriage, and ran her hand over her stomach, pleased that despite four children it was only slightly rounded. Her palm moved upwards as she turned back to face the mirror and cupped her breast, pressing it upwards and feeling its fullness. Her thoughts turned to Charles, and she felt her nipple harden under her fingers. He would probably be here in under an hour. She felt her insides contract with pleasure, and she knew that she wanted him.

She moved her hand down to her side and leaned forward to study the face in the mirror. Her hair, which was still swept up on top of her head as it had been since she was a girl, had lost some of its lustre but still showed little sign of grey. Her skin was still good and there was no sign of a double chin – thanks to the carriage that she prided herself on. She smiled slightly at her reflection to lift the corners of her mouth and release the cleft that tended to appear between her brows when she was tense. She didn't think she looked her age – perhaps she could take off five years, even ten depending on the light. She tried to be honest with herself, but she wanted the mirror to tell her so much more.

She reached for a clean dress and sat on the edge of the bed doing up the small buttons that ran down the bodice, and wondered what it would be like to feel Charles's hands upon her. It was so long since she had let Edward anywhere near her ...

Edward.

She tried to recall how she'd felt when they were first together, but the memory was gone. She had striven for so long to bury the urgings of her body that now, as far as Edward was concerned, she'd succeeded. There was nothing left except bitterness and blame, which she'd readily heaped upon him for every little thing that had happened in their lives. She'd blamed him for their hasty necessary marriage, blamed him when she had craved him day and night to bring her to the same heights of ecstasy that had only happened once, with such disastrous results. And carried on blaming him when two more children arrived in quick succession – and had punished him, and herself, when she'd insisted on separate bedrooms after Tom's arrival.

She closed her eyes as memories she had tried so hard to suppress came flooding back, and she heard her own mother's voice explaining with much circumlocution that true ladies endured what only men could enjoy.

Thoughts of Charles enjoying her body inflamed her, and while there was no passion left for Edward, she could remember that feeling of wanting, wanting ... and she heard her own voice, the voice of a hoyden, pleading with him to satisfy her, to rid her of this craving. She remembered the shame that would course through her the morning after, and the look in Edward's eyes which could only be disgust at her behaviour.

And finally she faced the memory of some six years later when her sister Eunice had married, and wine had flowed freely at the reception. Edward had come to her bed, had whispered words of love and longing to her that had made her relent and take him in her arms. She had found fulfilment then, had cried out with joy and felt complete for only the second time in her life.

She opened her eyes and stared at her reflection, her mouth set in a grim line. She'd paid for it, of course, as her mother had warned her that all women pay in the end. It had begun again, the craving, the disappointment, and eventually the complete disgust when she found that she was pregnant once more. Her fury at her body's betrayal had re-fuelled the piety that she'd cloaked herself with before, and which she now wrapped around herself again, to warm the cold empty nights with her God as her bedfellow.

But no matter how she tried, God continued to be an exacting taskmaster, and to punish her however she attempted to appease Him. She realised now that He'd known the dark side of her nature even before she had recognised it. He'd punished her when her parents died and she had struggled to keep the family together; and now there they all were, all better off than she, all prospering and happy – just look at Eunice!

Then there had been the struggle to raise her own family, to make something of them, and now they were all poised to get on in the world while she remained at the farm, still being punished, the possibility of the life she'd truly wanted receding as the years advanced.

And all the while there had been Edward's eyes, reproaching her, wanting something that she refused to give any more – and Jennie's eyes, her very presence all through childhood reminding her of her own shameful desire, so that at times she couldn't bear the child to be in the same room with her.

She tried to pray now, to pull the pious side of her nature back into line and push away the awful thoughts that were filling her head. But pictures of Charles kept breaking through – the noble line of his profile, his dazzling smile, the sheer masculinity of his presence that made her want to swoon towards him whenever he stood close to her, the hands that enclosed hers when he took his leave; smooth, gentleman's hands that conveyed a world far away from the farm.

"You're too old for this," she told the face that stared back at her. She clutched the crucifix that always hung in front of her dress. "God, give me the strength to turn away from all that is evil!"

She reminded herself that Edward would be there; that it was Edward he was coming to see.

Her body took no notice of her mind. Tingling with anticipation that Charles would soon be here, it carried her downstairs to meet him.

11

Laura's face broke into a wide smile as the train drew in and she saw Jennie standing patiently on the platform. It was just like the old days when Jennie would be there, waiting for Emily and herself to return from school. She stepped heavily down onto the platform and gave her sister an enormous hug. Gracious, the girl was thin! Or was it that she herself, only just half-way through her pregnancy, had become so large?

"This is a lovely surprise!" she exclaimed, moving back from Jennie and surveying her critically. "I didn't think you'd be able to escape from the farm to meet me."

Jennie gave a small shrug. "It's not so bad now. Father's getting about with a stick, doing much too much, of course, but he's determined to prove that his leg is better."

They left the station and began the familiar walk along the lane past the ten-acre field. "No cartwheels these days?" Laura asked.

Jennie grinned and for a moment the tiredness left her eyes. "I could still do them – especially when I'm wearing my working breeches. But you should feel honoured – I've put a skirt on especially to come to meet you!"

"How is Mother? Pleased that Father isn't under her feet any more?"

The shutters came down on Jennie's face. She looked resolutely ahead at the mountains in the distance. Her voice was tight and controlled when she spoke. "She's the same as ever. Father's accident gave her plenty to complain about – that and how badly off we'll all be when the war starts." She smiled thinly and turned towards her sister. "She's quite convinced that there will be a war, now, and doesn't say so much about Hitler, but I think she may still have a grudging admiration for him – they're quite alike in some ways, after all!"

Laura smiled back at Jennie's words, but she was worried, a worry mixed with guilt. Her sister's appearance quite shocked her; there was none of the carefree girl about her that had begun to emerge earlier in the summer. Perhaps she should have come over to stay when Father had his accident – at least she could have helped in the house, and possibly soothed Mother a little.

They walked in silence for a few minutes as Laura tried to stifle her conscience. At the time of the accident she'd been suffering from morning sickness and that had seemed sufficient reason to stay away. She hadn't appreciated how much of a burden had fallen on Jennie.

"Why don't you come back with me this evening?" she cried, suddenly inspired. "You look ready for a break, and Cyril's coming home for a couple of days – we could all have some fun."

Jennie turned towards her, a hungry look in her eyes, whilst immediately finding reasons why it would be impossible. "I'd love to, but I couldn't. Father still can't manage on his own – and young Alice isn't much help to Mother. And I don't want to spoil your time with Cyril – you haven't seen him for – "

"Nonsense!" Laura broke in robustly. "Everyone deserves some time off, and you look as if you haven't had a single day in weeks. And Cyril will be bursting with energy and wanting to go off and play tennis, or whatever." She glanced down at her burgeoning figure with a rueful smile. "And I can hardly partner him, can I?"

Jennie opened her mouth to protest more, but Laura patted her arm and hushed her. "I'll deal with the parents, don't you worry. They can't keep working you like this, or you'll be the next one who's ill."

She dealt with them very skilfully, explaining over lunch that she was hosting a coffee morning next day for the Conservative Ladies of Monmouth, hinting that it was her way of boosting the family's significance in the town while Cyril was away.

"I'd be so grateful if Jennie could come to give me a hand – I'm still so ghastly in the mornings. I don't know what possessed me to agree to do it, except that when Mrs. Carter starts organising things, no-one dares say no!"

"Of course Jennie can go," Father said straight away, just as Mother opened her mouth to object. "Ced's boy is still coming over – Ced's only too glad to keep him busy. Stop him from joining up, he hopes. We'll manage fine."

Laura and Jennie exchanged a small triumphant smile, while Mother struggled with her emotions. Should she play the martyr, as her wishes hadn't been considered, or be magnanimous in order to assist her second daughter's social advancement? She chose the latter, especially as her daughter's increased social standing might also enhance her own.

Jennie worked like a Trojan for the rest of the day, impervious to her weary limbs, and entered the kitchen at tea-time whistling tunelessly.

"Do you have to make that racket?" Mother demanded shrilly. "I have the most dreadful headache."

An afternoon spent listening to Laura extolling the virtues of her husband, town life, and the society within it, in that order, far from making her happy for her daughter's happiness, had indeed resulted in her head aching unbearably. That Jennie should be going to share in that life, if only for a couple of days, filled her with a sour envy.

"Shall I fetch you some aspirin?" Jennie stopped whistling immediately and set about slicing bread for tea, at the little side table expressly designated for that purpose.

Mother ignored her question and glared at her instead. "You'd better cut that bread a bit thinner, it's all we have until I bake some more. There now!" she exclaimed triumphantly as the next slice, cut too thin, fell apart. "Now you've wasted it completely!" She elbowed Jennie out of the way. "Go and take that teapot off Alice – you know what she's like, she'll spill boiling water everywhere! Alice! You see if Mr. Davies is coming in to tea – and that boy, if he's still here! No Laura, Alice can go. You're the visitor today – there's no need for you to help if only these two would pull their socks up!"

Laura watched as Jennie became a fumbling dolt under Mother's lashing tongue. Alice crept miserably about the kitchen, often stopping in mid-sniff when she caught Mother's eagle eye. Laura wished one of them would stand up to Mother, shout back at her unreasonableness and challenge her authority, but she knew that they wouldn't, just as she herself wouldn't if Mother's wrath was directed at her. Alice would doubtless leave as soon as she could persuade her family to find her another position, or Mother would simply send her away one day. And Jennie? What would Jennie do? Her only escape from the farm would seem to be marriage – she was completely untrained for anything else – and if the war lasted as long as the last one she wasn't going to find it easy to meet a prospective husband. Laura shook her head sadly, and was relieved when her father came into the kitchen.

By the time they all sat down to tea, Mother's head was pounding so that she could barely speak. The rest of the family took her to be merely in one of her bad tempers, and sat subdued. No-one asked her how she felt, which only increased her sense of being badly done by.

Father pushed his chair back from the table and hoisted himself up on his stick as soon as he'd drunk his tea. His leg ached and he would have liked to sit and rest it, but he knew there would be no rest inside the house when Katharine wasn't feeling herself. Much better to be out in the sunshine, and put up with the discomfort.

He turned at the door. "Oh! I nearly forgot. I saw Tom this

morning. He's going to call over this evening with Nancy."

Mother's face turned purple. She jumped up from the table so that the pain throbbed fiercely in her temples. "You knew this morning? Why didn't you tell me earlier?" She began to issue orders as she swiftly put on her baking apron. "You girls will have to clear up in here! I'll have to get some cakes made. Laura, I'm afraid you'll have to help as well!"

Laura opened her mouth to protest at the tone of Mother's voice and remind her that she'd already offered to help earlier, but she thought better of it.

Father limped across the room and put his hand on Mother's shoulder. "Katie, Katie! Don't fret so! It's only Tom and Nancy. I thought you'd be pleased that they were coming over."

She shrugged his hand away. "But it didn't cross your mind that they would expect to stay to supper and I might not have enough food prepared? Or did you think it would be alright to give them bread and cheese?"

Father thought bread and cheese would be fine, but decided now was not the time to say so. He sighed heavily and retreated. Mother watched him through the window as he crossed the yard. His halting progress, far from engendering her sympathy, made her only want to blame him all the more for everything that was wrong with her life. If only he was stronger, had more drive to *be* someone, they would have made more of an impact in the community. She wished he would be tougher in his business dealings, more ruthless, so that people respected him more.

And, deep down, part of her wished he would stride back into the house, take her forcefully into his arms, and carry her upstairs…

Jennie and Laura stayed to see Tom and Nancy, and then escaped on the last train back to Monmouth. They strolled through the quiet twilit town, the air tangy with the hint of autumn not far away, and the nostalgic regret of a late August evening. They talked about the coming baby, and giggled together as they suggested more and more preposterous sounding names to each other, but by an unspoken agreement they didn't mention the fear of war, or the other taboo subject: Mother.

By the time she'd unpacked her few things Jennie could hardly keep her eyes open, but Laura was determined to sit up and wait for Cyril to arrive, so Jennie left her with a supper tray and the wireless, and was asleep before her brother-in-law came in.

She awoke early next morning, from habit, with a pale sun peeping invitingly through a chink in the bedroom curtains. She stretched luxuriously and lay for a few minutes, revelling in the knowledge that today she wouldn't have to do anything she didn't want to. Which immediately gave her the energy to do plenty of things that there normally wasn't time for: a leisurely breakfast, a stroll round the shops, perhaps, or a walk along the river ...

She crept down to the kitchen in her dressing gown and put the kettle on. A ridiculously small freedom, but one which didn't escape her. As she stood waiting for it to boil she was aware that part of her was listening for Mother's footsteps and a cry of, "What are you doing *now?*", and a tut-tutting and unnecessary rubbing at imaginary marks.

She carried a kitchen chair out into the little courtyard at the back of the house, and sat drinking her tea and listening to the town awake. Noises that one didn't hear in the country – the clatter of the milk van, the rumble of delivery lorries and buses; doors slamming as husbands left for work, snippets of conversation as people passed along the pavement on the other side of the courtyard wall. She wasn't sure that she'd like town life, but nevertheless it intrigued her; so many people so busy, so purposeful. Were they happy, she wondered? Did they have time to dream as they rushed about? Did they take trips into the country at weekends and grow wistful for some rural idyll?

It could be idyllic, she knew. Demanding, relentless, repetitive, very often cold and dirty, but so filled with beauty at times that one could cry. She didn't want any other way of life, but could she continue to stand it as it was?

The noises around her faded into the background and her tea grew cold as she thought hard about what she really wanted. *Freedom,* she decided at length. *Not freedom to do anything else, but freedom to be myself, to say what I want to say, to feel what I want to feel. I want to be like Aunt Eunice, with a husband who adores me and lets me run the household on my own terms.* She knew that she could be a wonderful farmer's wife; that her ambitions would run no further than that, but with a man she loved she could do it all so well.

And therein lies the rub, she thought, pulling the corners of her mouth down in wry exasperation. Where would she meet any man, never mind one prepared to love her, when her life was so circumscribed? Any day now war would come, and all the young men would be taken away. No-one knew how long it was going to last, but she hadn't heard any foolhardy claims, as in the last one, that it 'would all be over by Christmas'. The men who had come back from France the last time rarely talked about it. Their lives before the war and their lives after the war could bear recollection, but the memories of those four awful years were buried, too painful to contemplate. How many golden young men would give their lives this time, or return with their bodies and minds shattered?

She leaned back in the chair, raising her face to the warmth of the sun, and forced herself to think of other things. Stupid to dwell on what she couldn't have, and what might be, when she had this day to enjoy.

Cyril, coming to look for her, stopped dead in the doorway and caught his breath. Before him was an attractive young woman – no longer his wife's kid sister, to be slightly patronised and admired only for her youthful energy. Her hair, which had been too short and tightly permed at their wedding, had grown into lustrous dark waves that framed her finely-drawn features. Her dressing gown was open, displaying the lean contours of her body through the thin material of her nightdress, and leaning back, eyes closed, her face healthily tanned, she was a picture of sensuous abandon – far removed from the fraught, put-upon creature that Laura had told him about the night before.

She lifted an arm to brush a stray lock of hair from her brow and, opening her eyes, caught sight of Cyril watching her. She jumped up, colouring prettily, and wrapped her dressing gown tightly around her.

"Sorry. Didn't mean to disturb you," said Cyril, equally flustered. "I didn't think you'd be up yet. Laura said you were looking pretty tired."

She picked up her teacup. "I was. But it's such a lovely morning, I was enjoying the prospect of not having anything to do except enjoy it. Shall I take Laura a cup of tea?"

"No, no – she's already up. Rather an urgent call to the bathroom, I'm afraid." He grinned, suddenly looking ridiculously young in his crumpled pyjamas, despite the now more luxuriant moustache. "Tell you what. I'll go and throw a few clothes on and then I'll cook us all one of my breakfast specials. Then we can set about deciding how to make the most of the next couple of days. How does that sound?"

"We'll have to show our faces at this coffee morning, I'm afraid," said Laura later, as they tucked into scrambled eggs, bacon, and mushrooms.

Jennie savoured her cup of fresh coffee, never drunk at home. "I thought that was all a ruse for Mother's benefit."

"Oh no, it does exist, only Mrs. Carter herself is hosting it – she'll be full of : 'It's time we let Mr. Churchill run the country!' more than likely, but she's a very useful person to know, and she's got a beautiful house we can have a good gawp at. Then we could do some shopping on the way home, if you like, and then, my dear, the rest of the day is yours –" still in her dressing gown, she spread her hands over her stomach – "because I shall be resting."

She turned to Cyril. "What did you want to do, darling? Golf, while we girls go off for the morning?"

"I think so, yes." He turned to Jennie. "Have you brought your stout shoes? I fancied a walk up the Kymin this afternoon. Been sat in an office for far too long recently, and I'm not sure –" he was going to say, 'when we might get another chance for a while', but hastily amended it – "whether this weather will hold out much longer. Like to come with me?"

"I'd love to," said Jennie. "That was a wonderful breakfast, thank you. I'll clear away while Laura's getting ready, if you want to get along to the golf course."

"No, no, no," he protested. "You're here for a bit of a break from all of that." But she could see he was keen to be off.

"Nonsense!" she told him, beginning to gather up cups and plates. "Believe me, it will be a pleasure to have the kitchen to myself."

Mrs. Carter was a tall, aristocratic-looking woman, well-dressed in an understated way, with long elegant hands and feet. She held herself very upright and carried an air of quiet authority that made her a natural leader. She spent much of the coffee morning exhorting the ladies to join the WVS, and spoke of forthcoming war as if it was already a foregone conclusion, so we might as well get on with it – so that Jennie felt quite depressed as she and Laura strolled back through the town. She gazed about her and became aware of an air of purposefulness around the place that she hadn't noticed before. People appeared to be going about their business in a more determined fashion, as if already bracing their shoulders for what was to come. It had all seemed a rather distant possibility until now, almost like the First Aid techniques she'd learned with the rambling club; reassuring to know, but highly unlikely ever to be put into practice.

Laura didn't appear to share her sense of disquiet, however, or if she did she made a very good job of disguising it. Preparations for the arrival of her baby and her future as a good wife and mother so filled her conscientious mind that Jennie hadn't the heart to share with her the thought that was now uppermost in her own head: What would they all do if Hitler continued his relentless sweep across Europe, until he eventually swept across the British Isles too?

"Is it going to be very bad?" she asked Cyril later, as they sat at the top of the Kymin. Below them lay Monmouth, stretched out on each side of the river, shimmering slightly in the afternoon sun. Behind them the wooded hillsides of the Forest of Dean held its mysterious secrets.

Cyril didn't reply for so long she thought he hadn't heard her. Then he said, slowly and deliberately, "I think it's going to be far, far worse that any of us can imagine."

He was silent again. All around them was quiet and still, so that his words hung in the air.

"Can we... Is there nothing...?" she faltered.

He didn't look at her, but lifted his head as if to address the few puffball clouds that drifted overhead. "Germany has succeeded in re-arming herself while we've all refused to recognise it. We're hopelessly unprepared. We all had that big scare a year ago when it looked like war, which we should've learned from, but Chamberlain and all his lot are still dithering about trying to remain gentlemen and are still convinced that Hitler is going to respond like a gentleman, which he patently isn't. Every bit of paper I've pushed round my desk in the past few weeks shows that the men who *really* know all about it are very worried indeed."

They sat for some minutes, hugging their knees, watching a group of young boys rowing a boat erratically down the river. A small breeze blew up, cooling the air and bringing with it the first hint of autumn approaching, of summer ending. Jennie wondered what else about their ordered, comfortable lives was also about to end, and shivered involuntarily.

Cyril, as if reading her thoughts, suddenly stood up. "Come on!" He pulled Jennie to her feet. "Enough of this. Whatever happens won't be for us to decide, and we're supposed to be cheering you up, not piling on the doom and gloom. Are you here tomorrow as well? Good. Then we can fit in a game of tennis."

They chatted inconsequentially as they made their way back down the hillside, Cyril determined to remain lighthearted. But as they stood on the step about to enter the house, he turned to Jennie with a look of utmost seriousness.

"If anything should happen – you know, to me, when I'm away... you will look after Laura and the baby for me, won't you? You're really the best one I can ask."

Jennie returned his look steadily. Pompous at times he might be, and a keen social climber, but he was completely sincere in his feelings for Laura, and Jennie had developed an affection for him that she'd never felt for her own brother. It wrung her heart to think that a young man with a promising future should have to make contingency plans for there being no future at all. She reached up and kissed him tenderly on his cheek. "Of course I will."

They smiled trustingly at each other, and then a movement

further along the pavement caught Cyril's eye.

"I say! Here's Charles!" To Jennie's private amusement he immediately adopted his best RAF voice as he pumped Charles' hand. "Hello, old boy! Sneaked a couple of days off as well? Come on in! Laura will be delighted!"

Charles appeared strained and distracted, Jennie thought, barely returning Cyril's enthusiastic greeting or her own welcoming smile. Perhaps he, too, knew more of what was about to happen and couldn't stop worrying about it.

But Cyril hadn't noticed his friend's restraint. He had already bounded into the house, calling for Laura to come and see who had just turned up.

12

Charles had suffered a maelstrom of emotion during the last two days. Nothing had happened as he'd anticipated. Yesterday's train journey to Paddington was interminable. Charles had thought that there were plans to evacuate as many civilians as possible from London, but there appeared to be no end of people eager to head for the capital. Admittedly there were quite a few servicemen on the train. A boisterous quartet of young Welshmen was in his compartment, going to Reading. He'd watched them saying goodbye to their wives and girlfriends on Newport station quite happily, safe in the knowledge that until war was actually declared, they would remain in Britain. They talked in rapid, almost incomprehensible snatches, interspersed with guffaws of laughter, leaning forward, resting their arms on spread knees. Every now and then they'd go out into the corridor to smoke, cupping their cigarettes in their hands to prove that they were men.

He leaned back in his seat and wished that he'd travelled First Class after all. At least he could have had a decent cup of coffee without fighting his way to the buffet car, but funds were pretty low at present. It would have been better to drive to Surrey, but he didn't want Sylvia to see that he possessed a car. He thought of her letters, neatly folded in the inside pocket of his jacket. He didn't know how the devil she'd managed to find him, but find him she had, and her letters had become increasingly insistent, until he knew that he must return and try to sort everything out.

He had difficulty getting a cab at Paddington, so that by the time he'd bought a ticket at Victoria he had to run to the platform, and only just made the train for Leatherhead. Once there, he had to wait again for almost twenty minutes until a battered taxi trundled up the station approach, driven by an elderly man who then took him along the Dorking road with painstaking slowness.

It was mid-afternoon by the time he reached Headley-on-the-Hill, and the lack of lunch was doing nothing to improve his temper. He paid off the taxi-driver, ignoring his meaningful stare at the meagreness of the tip, and strove to rearrange his emotions. It would probably take all his charm to keep Sylvia sweet.

Sylvia had heard the taxi, and was now at the front door of the large white house with mock Tudor beams on its upper storey. "*My dear!*" she exclaimed. "It's just *wonderful* to see you again!"

She leaned forward and he returned her embrace, but managed to turn his face slightly so that their lips didn't quite meet.

"You look very dashing in your uniform, I must say!" she told him as she led him into the drawing room.

"And you look as beautiful as ever!" he replied gallantly.

She rang a small hand bell. "What will you have, darling? Tea? Or something a little stronger?"

"Tea will be fine, thank you. And a sandwich would go down well. It was a hellish journey – if I'd stopped for lunch I would have missed the train from Victoria."

She gave orders to the maid who appeared in answer to the bell, and then sat beside him on the sofa. "Poor darling. Are they working you *frightfully* hard down there in wherever it is? You do look rather tired."

And you, he thought, *are looking a bit … old.* Dressed as stylishly as ever, and perfectly made up, there were nevertheless some telltale little lines around the mouth and eyes, and the beginnings of a crêpey look around the neck. But then, blue-eyed blondes did seem to fade early, in his experience.

"Not working too hard to be unable to come to you when you said you needed me." He made his voice velvety smooth, but she pouted so that the lines around her mouth became furrows, and glanced at him from under her lashes.

"You took a while though, didn't you darling, even though you knew I would be missing you *desperately.* It doesn't do to leave a girl too long on her own, you know."

He took her hand between his own. "They've moved us around no end, I'm afraid. Never a minute's respite. This is the first time I've been able to wangle more than a day off in I don't know how long." He inclined his head closer to hers. "I've missed you too, you know. I tried to phone you whenever we were on the move again," he lied, "but you were always out. I hope you weren't enjoying yourself *too* much while I've been working so hard?"

She ran a finger lightly down the lapel of his jacket, and opened her mouth to speak, but the door opened and the maid reappeared with a laden tray. Sylvia began to fuss around, moving small tables nearer to the sofa. There seemed to be an edginess about her, although she appeared pleased enough to see him. She's going to ask me for her money back, he decided, and she's wondering how to go about it.

He leaned back and surveyed the room. It looked as though she'd been re-decorating again; many of the furnishings were different since he had last been here. Which meant she still must be alright for a bob or two, so why did her letters say that she had to talk to him urgently?

He watched as she poured the tea, leaning forward so that the silk wrap-over bodice of her dress gaped slightly and he could see the swell of her breast. But it failed to move him; *she* failed to move him as she had once done.

It had been seven years since he'd first met her; widowed, child-less and wealthy – and nearly fifteen years his senior. But it was through her that he'd come to realise that he held a certain attraction for older women. She'd been a natural flirt, whiling away her time keeping up with fashions and beauty regimes, and making sure that she had a suitable escort when she wanted to go out in the evenings. Her style was extravagant, from her rather flamboyant dress sense to the extra-long cigarette holder that she toyed with, and the over-emphasis of her adjectives when she spoke. But behind her flirtatious exterior he'd been quick to sense a certain desperation; a need, not for marriage again, but for the assiduous attentions of a young man.

Charles had never been in love, but he enjoyed seeing the light that sparkled in her eyes whenever he danced with her, and her responses as he became bolder, and when they had finally consum-mated their relationship he was intoxicated by the sense of power he felt as she lay in his arms.

She'd been extremely generous in her appreciation, and Charles, nothing loath to live the life of a gentleman without having to work for it, had made sure he kept her happy and thus willing to finance the schemes that he told her about in a vague but very enthusiastic way.

That had only been the beginning, of course. When he began to feel a little stifled by Sylvia's adoration, he'd seen to it that his schemes necessitated a degree of travel, and he'd found it relatively easy to find other lonely women who were all too easily flattered by a young, good-looking man. And for his part he became adept at oozing worldly charm while objectively assessing how quickly and how much he could benefit from a liaison, while the sexual re-awak-ening of a middle-aged woman who thought she was long past all that sort of thing became the best aphrodisiac he'd ever known.

Somehow, though, he'd always come back to Sylvia. As each new triumph palled, or became less lucrative, he returned, charming as ever, full of apologies for his absence and reasons why each venture hadn't been quite as successful as he'd hoped – to find Sylvia only too ready to have him back at her side.

Now Sylvia lit a cigarette and sat opposite him, watching as he ate a sandwich. "So tell me, darling – what have you been up to, apart from lots of *drilling*, or whatever it is they make you do when you first join up?"

She made her voice sound girlish and breathy, but as his eyes met hers he saw a guardedness that he hadn't noticed before. It was going to be harder than he thought. He'd obviously made a mistake in staying away too long.

"Not too much drilling, thank goodness, but it's all frightfully boring at times. I've ended up on the admin side; they said that's where my best skills lay –" no point in admitting that he had no interest in becoming a pilot and risking his life if he could possibly avoid it – "and now they've got me doing all sorts of things that are a bit hush-hush, I'm afraid."

He looked away, deciding that the sun streaming in through the drawing room window really did nothing for her, and took a drink of tea. Suddenly everything seemed wrong: Sylvia, over-dressed and overdone; the house re-furbished to the point of vulgarity – the chairs were modern, angular affairs; the walls were washed in a pale green that made one feel cold rather than cool, and adorned in Picasso prints, while various modern *objets d'art* screamed for attention from every surface.

He thought of Katharine Davies, sensually demure but oozing good taste. He knew that she wanted him, and the thought excited him more than Sylvia had excited him for a long time. Perhaps he ought simply to cut his losses and make a clean break from Sylvia – but of course, there was the small matter of the money she'd lent him and the return that he'd consistently promised her over the years.

She came and sat beside him again, but on the edge of her seat, so that she could look at him properly. "There's something I have to talk to you about, darling, which I think perhaps you won't be very happy about. You see –"

He decided to pre-empt her. "If you're worried about your investment, you needn't be. Of course the financial markets are all a bit jittery at the moment, so it would be the worst possible time to sell, but if we can just sit tight until all this is over, business should boom. I've made all sorts of good connections in the insurance world late –"

She lifted an immaculately-manicured hand to his face and placed a red-nailed finger to his lips. "*Darling!* That's not what I'm trying to talk to you about! You know I trust you *implicitly* with all that side of things." She ran her hand reluctantly down the side of his face. "It's more personal than that. I – we …" She faltered, biting the corner of her lips, painted to match her nails, and cast her eyes down in an unusually coy gesture which didn't really suit her.

Then she lifted her head and spoke in a rush. "As I said, I've been feeling pretty lonely, and had no idea even where you *were* half the time, never mind *when* I would see you again … The fact is, darling, I've been offered a proposal of marriage – not that I was expecting it – it came as quite a surprise. But the more I think about it, the more I think I should accept. After all, none of us knows what is likely to happen, and – well, a girl needs to feel she has someone to take care of her. And I know you're not ready to settle down, especially now that you've joined the RAF – and besides, I'm not getting any younger …" She hesitated here, to give him time to be gallant about her age, but he said nothing.

"Oh darling, you *do* understand, don't you? Please say all the right things to me. I couldn't *bear* it if you were to take it badly. You'll always mean such a *lot* to me, you know."

But his silence had been simply relief. He couldn't believe that she was letting him off the hook so lightly. He tried to think quickly how best to play things. Let her know that he was willing to make sacrifices for her happiness, so that she'd feel a tinge of regret. After all, the chap might be pretty well off, and he never knew when he might need Sylvia again in the future.

"I don't know quite what to say," he responded, truthfully for once. "This is all a bit of a shock."

He got up and stood by the window, so that she could admire his profile and be reminded of what she was giving up. "This man, who is he? Is he going to care for you properly?"

"His name is Graham Jarvis – he's a widower. He's semi-retired now, but he still writes lots of clever papers on something to do with plants, I think. He's really quite a sweetie – and he says that I bring out all his protective urges." He'd also said, when breathing rather heavily on her neck during a tea dance, that she brought out the beast in him, but she thought it best not to tell Charles that.

Sylvia rose and went to stand next to Charles. "It won't be like – what we've had together, darling." Her voice was small and slightly sad. "He's a lot older than you, and not nearly so much fun, but if we *are* going to have a war, then at least he's going to be here for me all the time, and that's really what I need." She reached up and kissed his cheek. "Please tell me I'm doing the right thing."

He put his arm around her shoulder and drew her to him. He sighed deeply, and to his surprise, experienced a genuine wave of regret. It would be a bit of a shame not to have Sylvia there in the background, ready to boost his morale with unstinting admiration whenever he needed it – not to mention boosting his wallet.

"I want you to do whatever will make you happiest," he said nobly. "And as I can't give you any sort of security at the moment, I quite understand that you should seek it with someone else. Only –" he looked down at her and gave her his most winning smile – "don't ask me to come to the wedding, will you?"

He'd spent the night in a little bed-and-breakfast near Paddington. Sylvia had urged him to stay and meet Graham, but he wanted time to think. She had made no further mention of the money, and for the first time in ages he felt curiously free, although he hadn't been conscious of his obligation to Sylvia burdening him.

By the time he'd boarded the early train to Newport that morning, his plans had been made. He was good at the work he was doing, and he knew his manners and apparent breeding had already made him popular with his superiors. With a bit of luck he could sit out this war safely behind the lines, and do himself a bit of good as well.

And for as long as he was within easy reach, there was Katharine.

They'd spent a lot of time together while Edward had been laid up, and it had been amusing to watch her fight not to succumb to his charm. He'd been aware of the covert glances she'd given him, and the tension in her body if he had touched her shoulder, or patted her knee, but he'd been unprepared for the discovery that he wanted her as much as he knew she wanted him.

As soon as he got back to camp he would freshen up and then go to see her, he had decided. It was time to take the relationship a stage further, and the prospect exhilarated him.

He smiled inadvertently at the passenger opposite him, a pug-faced woman in a stove hat, who glared back at him and gripped her large black handbag more tightly on her lap as if to protect herself.

The farm had seemed very quiet when he got there. He parked his car in the drive and strolled round to the back. He could see Katharine through the kitchen window, baking with Alice, her face prettily flushed from her exertions. He tapped on the window and then entered through the washroom, by which time her look of surprise had changed to one of pleasure.

"Charles! How unexpected! I'm afraid we're not prepared for visitors, as you can see." She rinsed her hands at the sink, removed her apron, and patted her hair into place, all in one fluid movement as she spoke.

"I hope I'm not considered a 'visitor' after all this time! To tell you the truth, I've got a few days' leave and I'm at a bit of a loose end. I had some business to attend to in London, but it didn't take me as long as I'd expected... so... I thought I'd just pop in and see how you all are. I hope it's not inconvenient?"

Katharine smiled widely. "Of course not! Let me make you some tea." She lifted the kettle to the tap.

Alice, who had been on the sharp end of Katharine's tongue just before Charles arrived, stood and gawped at the transformation in her mistress. Without thinking she sniffed, which instantly attracted Katharine's attention.

"Finish clearing up all of this, Alice," she said sharply, "while I make the tea for Mr. Keating. Then there'll be the floors to do from here through to the dairy."

Charles took the tray from her so that she could lead the way into the parlour. He set the tray down on a side table, and looked about him with satisfaction. The room, as always, was immaculate, the furniture polished to perfection, the dull rose of the heavy curtains blending harmoniously with the carpet and upholstery. Very different from the room in which he'd had afternoon tea yesterday, he decided. He looked at Katharine, standing beside him pouring the tea. *And a very different lady.*

"Do sit down, Charles," she said as she handed him a cup and moved to an armchair. Her fingers were cool as they touched his. She was wearing a simple blouse and skirt, her hair caught up in its familiar style, and she sat forward in her chair, her back very straight. She was probably older than Sylvia, but she looked a lot younger. Her skin was smooth and soft, and her body looked trim but supple. He felt his own body stir as he imagined undoing the tiny pearl buttons of her blouse and discovering that the rest of her skin was just as soft.

Her outward repose belied her inner feelings. She was aware of Charles scrutinising her, and wished she'd been able to change her clothes. What would he think of her in her serviceable skirt and lisle stockings? *Just another middle-aged housewife going about her mundane chores.*

A silence grew between them, an uncomfortable, awkward silence. They both tried to break it at once.

"How did you — ?"

"Has Edward — ?"

She smiled and her shoulders relaxed a little. "I'm sorry. You first."

"I was just going to remark upon how quiet it seems here, especially after London. Is Edward out and about now?"

She nodded. "He's away across the fields somewhere with a

man from the Ministry of Agriculture. They're making big plans for re-organising the farmland so that we can grow more crops, but there's some worry about the drainage, or something."

"And Jennie?"

"Oh! Jennie!" A disparaging note crept into her voice. "She's gone away for a few days ..."

It seemed as if she was going to say more, but she stopped and the silence returned. She lowered her eyes and when she raised them again, found his fixed intently upon her face.

Before she could stop herself she said, "There'll be no-one in before teatime."

For several seconds he still said nothing, and then, quite softly: "You're very beautiful."

She flushed in confusion. No man but Edward had ever said that to her. She stood up abruptly and moved across the room, and began to speak in a voice that was too loud, and too effusive.

"Of course, I'm desperately hoping that Edward's plans won't interfere with the garden. It always looks its best at this time of year, and it would be such a pity to lose the roses, but these Ministry people are quite demanding..."

Her voice tailed off as she felt him stand beside her.

He lifted a hand and tenderly replaced a straying tendril of hair. "I wish I could see you with all this loose, down your back."

She turned to face him, and as his eyes held hers, he ran his hand down one side of her body. Her nipple was already taut against the thin stuff of her blouse. He kissed her then, gently at first, his lips exploring hers, but then more urgently as he felt her respond, forcing her lips apart with his tongue. He put his hand on her buttocks, pressing her against him so that she could feel his hardness. Her body quivered in response, and he began to savour the heady sense of conquest that he knew would soon be his.

Katharine's first emotion was surprise that he'd made the move that both of them had been anticipating for some time. It was what she'd dreamed about every time she made herself ready for his visits. But surprise was rapidly overtaken by stronger emotions. As he moved against her, her body leapt in response and she was consumed by wave after wave of physical desire. All thoughts of Edward, of propriety, were banished. She wanted to feel his hands explore every part of her; she wanted to unbutton his trousers and force him into her body, to feel him inside her, to satisfy the craving that was so familiar but so long suppressed.

His lips moved away from hers and covered her face, her throat, her neck, with kisses. She heard a long low moan, and didn't realise that it came from her. His mouth covered hers again and he pressed her tightly to him once more, so that the crucifix around her neck dug painfully into her flesh.

She moved away from him fractionally and raised her hand to the crucifix. As her fingers closed round it she felt the outline of Christ's body, the arms stretched out in agony upon the cross, and suddenly every Bible story of sin and mortification of the flesh came flooding back to her. The God she prayed to and bargained with every night, whose wrath at wrongdoing she had instilled into her children, was watching her and would sit in judgement upon her adulterous act.

She tried to break away, but his kisses became only harder, more insistent as his hands moved over her body, squeezing her breast, stroking her thighs, and to her increasing shame she felt herself continue to respond.

"Let me take you upstairs," he murmured, as his fingers deftly began to undo the buttons of her blouse.

"No – no! I can't!"

But his head was buried against her, kissing her neck where the buttons were undone. She groaned, and for a moment clasped his head against her, her senses on fire; until his searching lips reached lower, where the crucifix nestled in the cleft between her breasts.

With an agonised cry she tore herself away from Charles, and gripped the back of the sofa, her body shaking with unspent passion. She sought refuge in anger as her mind tussled to overcome her physical weakness.

"This is wrong! We mustn't! You shouldn't have!" Her hair had loosened so that it framed her face, making her more attractive than ever.

Charles stepped towards her. *"Katharine! Katharine!"* His voice was a caress. "Don't be frightened! This was bound to happen between us. You must know how badly I want you – and you feel the same way, I know it."

Yes, yes! her body cried. *I want you so much I can hardly bear it!*

But it's wrong, her mind replied, *you know it's wrong.*

Charles lifted his hand and stroked her arm. "Katharine!" he said again, softly, seductively, as his fingers burned through her sleeve.

"Don't touch me!" she cried. "You shouldn't have taken advantage!" She would have to blame him if she was going to find a modicum of peace in the long tortured nights that she knew lay ahead. "It was wrong of you to stay when I'm alone in the house!"

He stood and stared at her for a long, silent moment. She averted her eyes away from the lean athletic figure and tried hard to stop herself from rushing back into his arms and begging him to take her there and then.

"I think you'd better go!"

But he didn't go. He leaned closer to her, so that his face was level with hers, forcing her to look at him. His eyes held a steely glint. "There's a name for women like you," he said softly. "You've flirted with me for months, so don't try to tell me today wasn't what you wanted."

Suddenly he grabbed her hand and pressed it against his trousers. He gave a grim smile of satisfaction as he saw the light of desire leap into her eyes, even as she tried to pull her hand away.

"I'm good," he said, letting go of her hand. "*Very* good. We could have had something very special together. Now ... you'll never know."

He moved across the room and picked up his hat. At the door he turned. "But you're going to spend a long time regretting that you turned me away."

He left the room, and a few seconds later she heard the front door slam. Purposefully and sedately, her head held high, she crossed the room into the hall and began to ascend the stairs, ignoring the tears that were trickling down her face.

In her bedroom she poured cold water from the jug into the bowl on the washstand, and very slowly began to take her clothes off. She picked up a cloth and scrubbed at her skin, muttering incoherently through stifled sobs.

Lord, wash away my iniquity. Cleanse me from my sin!

He had driven blindly, his mind seething, anger overcoming passion. He'd wanted her, really wanted her, and he'd never before experienced not getting what he wanted. His anger was mixed with the petulance of a small child denied a longed-for toy ... except that as a child he'd never been denied anything.

Images of his mother and grandmother came into his mind. They were standing in the living room of the claustrophobic little house they'd all shared outside Guildford, both smiling encouragingly at his winsome ways, dotingly eager to compensate for the father who had died early and heroically in the War, Charles' hazy recollections of him kept alive by the photograph proudly displayed on the mantelpiece.

He thought of his mother now, still in the little house, the hidden reason for his occasional departures to sort out the 'family estate'; pathetically pleased to see him and proud of his apparent prosperity. Irrationally he turned his anger towards her, towards his grandmother, towards every woman he'd encountered during his adult life. They'd all made it so easy! A winning smile here, a smouldering glance there, the turning on of the charm that came so effortlessly to him – leaving him totally unprepared for rejection from, he was now convinced, the only woman he'd ever fallen in love with.

He found himself in Monmouth and parked his car near the river. He knew that he would probably end up at Laura and Cyril's; there was nowhere else to go except back to camp and besides, as yet he was reluctant to give up all association with the Davies' family.

He walked along the riverbank, oblivious of his surroundings as he struggled to regain his composure and reassess his plans. There were tedious times ahead, and the farm with all its comforts, and an affair with Katharine that could have continued indefinitely, would have been a wonderful haven to which to escape whenever he could.

He gave little thought to Edward; it was obvious from Katharine's treatment of him that the marriage was a pretty empty one, and the man seemed content enough to devote all his time to the farm.

He turned towards the town and headed for Cyril's house. He felt more composed, and his natural optimism began, cautiously, to lift its head. Something would turn up; it always did. *And,* he thought, *sooner or later there will be an opportunity to make her regret that she turned me away. I just have to bide my time* Nevertheless he was still in a more thoughtful mood, his head down, his jaunty step less so, as he rounded the corner into Cyril's road.

He looked up and came to a standstill.

Ahead of him, Jennie was reaching up on tiptoe to kiss Cyril.

His jaw dropped. Although her body was more slender, her profile was Katharine's – the tilt of her nose, the curve of her cheek, the colour of her hair, its waves falling over her shoulders as she reached up – just as he'd imagined Katharine's would.

It was too much. He cursed himself for not realising that Jennie would be here!

He made to turn away, but it was too late. Cyril had seen him and was greeting him with alacrity. There was nothing for it but to go on.

Cyril was already in the house, calling for Laura, but Jennie waited for him at the door. She smiled. Katharine's eyes, but deeper and less challenging, looked at him. He said hello brusquely, and didn't smile in response – and saw a flicker of disappointment shadow her face before she moved ahead of him into the house.

Jennie paused in the act of putting her few clothes into her case, and crossed over to the window. Her room was above the front door, and she gazed down at Laura talking to the butcher's boy as he made his delivery. She envied Laura these little domestic details which running her own home entailed. They gave Laura's life an air of completeness, of having the few things that Jennie desired: the freedom to run her life herself, with a man who clearly loved her, and a home of their own.

She returned to her packing. The short respite had come to a premature end with the news that Germany had invaded Poland. Cyril, making plans to return immediately to his unit, had urged Jennie to stay longer for Laura but, infected by the increasing urgency of the situation, Jennie had stressed the need to return to the farm and help Father.

"Can you run Jennie home, and then cut across to Brecon, Charles?" Cyril asked.

Jennie had felt embarrassed as Charles had hesitated before agreeing, and had attempted to say that she would catch the train. But Cyril, already squaring his shoulders as if to take command, would have none of it, and eventually Charles made a gallant effort to hide his reluctance.

Charles had puzzled her throughout his brief visit. Gone was the bantering, avuncular manner, which should have pleased her, but in its place was a quiet preoccupation, as if he had something on his mind that he ought to share with someone else but couldn't bring himself to. She almost convinced herself that, like Cyril, he knew far more about what was really going on than he chose to admit, and that it was worrying him, but several times she caught him watching her speculatively, and when she'd given him a tentative smile he'd continued to gaze for a few seconds before politely returning it.

The short journey to Nantyderry was a quiet one. Despite her love for her home and her father, Jennie was aware of a tightening of her stomach, a growing tension the nearer they came to the farm. For his part, Charles seemed in no mood for idle conversation.

"Do drop me at the top of the drive," she said, as they turned off the main road into a narrow country lane. "I know you need to get away."

"If you're sure," he answered, his eyes on the sharp bends of the lane.

Soon the car had pulled up on the grass verge alongside the dusty track that led down to the farmhouse. Jennie climbed out as Charles fetched her case from the boot.

"Thank you for bringing me home," she said formally, as she took the case from him. Then, more diffidently, "I hope everything goes alright for you – you know, with the war and – everything… if you're posted away, or whatever…" she found herself floundering under his direct gaze.

To her surprise he leaned down and kissed her on the mouth, a mere brushing of the lips that made her skin tingle.

"You're very sweet," he said, but with no sign of condescension. "Take care of yourself. I'm sure I'll see you again soon."

She watched as he drove away. It was the first time any man had kissed her, however fleetingly. Then she walked slowly down the drive, wanting to keep the feeling of his lips on hers alive, reiterating his words in her head. *It meant nothing,* she tried to tell herself sternly. *These are emotional times; he was being no more affectionate than Cyril is towards you!*

Nevertheless, her heart continued to give a little skip as she mentally re-played the scene.

As she neared the house she composed her features. It didn't do to let Mother see that you were feeling particularly happy, or had had a good time.

Mother, however, was deep in conversation with an officious-looking woman carrying a clipboard, and barely noticed her arrival.

"But Mrs. Davies," the woman was insisting, "I know that you have at least three spare bedrooms here, and you must be aware that we are all being asked to make available what space we can for evacuees."

Mother was wearing her most formidable expression. "And I have told you, *Miss Lloyd,* that all our spare rooms are spoken for. *If* we go to war, which Mr. Chamberlain has yet to decide, my husband is going to need extra full-time help on the farm – he's already been badgered by a dreadful man from Min Ag – and I shall be having live-in help for the house and dairy, as my current girl is leaving next week. In addition my married daughter is returning to live here until after the birth of her baby, and as she is in very poor health, she may need considerable nursing. *Not* that our domestic arrangements should really be any concern of yours!"

Jennie smiled inwardly. You had to hand it to Mother; she was adept at thinking on her feet and could intimidate absolutely anyone. As far as Jennie knew there were no plans afoot for any of the things Mother had just outlined but, listening to her, even Jennie felt convinced.

But Hetty Lloyd was not easily put off. As a young woman she'd been in the Red Cross during the Great War, and had had a wonderful time. She'd thrived on organising people, arranging supplies and doling out cups of tea and heavy-handed comfort to returning heroes, and had had to fight hard to hide her disappointment when it was all over. The years since, with their stultifying routine and lack of men – especially men who would find a dumpy woman with thick calves attractive – had been achingly dull. So when it was obvious that hostilities were imminent again, she'd donned with alacrity her fitted tweed suit, with her ample bosom straining against a man's shirt and tie to make it look more uniform-like, and promptly volunteered for the role of Billeting Officer.

Now, with an official armband on her sleeve and her clipboard balanced in the carrying basket, she cycled from village to village, displaying a vast amount of *directoire* knickers under the tweed skirt as she went, persuading all with more than the most modest dwelling that they should find a place for the poor city children whose lives were soon to be in mortal danger.

"What about attic rooms, or storerooms?" she persisted now. "They could be made quite serviceable with some curtains and a couple of camp beds."

"The only additional space we have is a windowless cellar, which we have been advised to prepare as an air-raid shelter. There are no other rooms attached to this house which are not already fully used for some purpose or other." Mother's voice had become dangerously cold. "Of course there are the chicken sheds – perhaps you'd think that they could be made quite serviceable, too?"

Miss Lloyd ignored the jibe. She thrust out her chest. "In my capacity as Billeting Officer I am supposed to inspect each property I visit and account for the available space."

She waited expectantly, but Mother stood resolutely in the front doorway. "But as I have explained that our house is soon to be completely full there is no need for you to waste your time, is there? Unless, of course, you question what I have told you?"

Miss Lloyd opened her mouth to reply, but then thought better of it. She made a few pencil marks on her clipboard. "I shall have to report this, you know."

Mother smiled at her with saccharine sweetness. "And I shall be happy to tell your superiors exactly what I have told you. Now, if you'll excuse me, there is very little time on a busy farm to stop for idle chit-chat."

If Jennie hadn't been waiting to enter the house she would doubtless have closed the door in Miss Lloyd's face. As it was she turned her attention to her daughter, ushering her into the house as if she'd been away for weeks, leaving Miss Lloyd no alternative but to return to her bicycle.

Once inside the house, however, Mother showed no interest in Jennie's brief holiday other than a fleeting enquiry about Laura. Jennie decided that now was not the time to tell Mother that Charles had brought her home, and went straight upstairs to change into her working clothes before going outside to seek out her father.

Over the next couple of days the memory of Charles's kiss wouldn't go away, no matter how hard Jennie tried to think of something else. When – *if* – he came to the farm again for one of his little chats with Mother, she would avoid him completely, in case he saw that a mere friendly gesture on his part had had such an effect on her. But as the days passed, despite her resolution, she grew increasingly disappointed that they had heard no more from him.

It was more than a week before his car bowled down the drive. Jennie was in the house for the afternoon tea ritual and heard him call out, "Hello! Anyone at home?" – and felt her insides contract.

For once Mother didn't come through at the sound of his voice, so Jennie had to go into the hall.

"Hello," she said, "You've timed that well, we're just about to have tea." She indicated the parlour and walked back through as she spoke, aware that he was following her. "I don't know where Mother's got to," she went on, before he could say a word. "She was here a minute ago ..."

He was standing in the doorway, looking impossibly handsome in his uniform. She wouldn't be able to look for Mother in the rest of the house without brushing past him, so she turned to look out of the window instead, as if Katharine might be hiding in the front rose bushes.

"Actually, it's you I've come to see." She could feel that he had crossed the room and was standing beside her.

"Me? Why?" Surprise made her sound sharp. "I'm sorry, that was rude – it's just that I'm not usually here when you visit, and Mother knows far more about what's going on these days – so does Father, come to that – to chat about, I mean, whereas I ..."

Her voice petered out as she turned towards him and faced his amused gaze.

"You're blushing!" he teased. "It suits you!"

Jennie tried hard to think of icebergs or anything else cool which would make the tell-tale pink die down. "I'm prattling," she said, "which always ends up with me saying things which sound worse than I mean them to... why did you want to see me especially?"

"Because with everything at sixes and sevens at the moment, there's a feeling that one should have a good time whilst one can, so there are lots of dances and so on going on all over the place. And I thought – what a good idea. And then I thought – but I don't have a pretty young lady to take with me. And *then* I thought of a very pretty young lady who I know quite well, and would like to know even better, who might be persuaded to accompany me to a dance in Monmouth on Saturday. Particularly one whom I seem to remember dances very well indeed."

"Oh," she managed, in a small voice.

He gave a wry smile. "Well, I must say, I've had more enthusiastic responses to an invitation!"

"Oh!" she said again. "No... I mean, yes... I would love to be your dance partner. I just wasn't expecting ..."

He was asking her to a dance! And he remembered dancing with her at Laura's wedding! She glanced at the door, fearful that Mother would come through and spoil the moment. But there was no sound from anywhere else in the house.

Charles took a step nearer, so close that she could smell the brilliantine on his hair. "This is very rushed, because I shouldn't really be here, and I'll have to go in a minute. I'll fetch you at seven on Saturday, if that's alright?"

She nodded, not trusting herself to do more.

"Oh, and just one more thing," He had partly turned to go, but now he came back. "I hope we'll end up as a little more than *dance partners*."

He tilted her chin with his hand, and bent forward to kiss her again. This time there was more pressure from his lips, and the kiss was longer, with just enough time to show Jennie that if you kissed back, it was even more pleasurable.

"Give my apologies to your mo— to your parents that I couldn't stay longer," he said when he drew away. "See you on Saturday."

He'd only been gone a few minutes when Mother appeared in the parlour, a deep scowl on her face. Jennie was still standing in the window. "You've just missed Charles," she said.

"I was sorting that silly Alice out. Not everything can stand still the minute that man walks through the door, you know."

"He's asked me to a dance, on Saturday night," Jennie told her.

But if Mother heard her she gave no indication, and turned abruptly and left the room with no mention of the afternoon tea that had dragged Jennie indoors.

Jennie gave a mental shrug. There was time enough for that battle. For now, she would savour the fact that she had been asked out on a date. A proper date! With a man who gave her butterflies every time she thought about him.

Perhaps there had been an ulterior motive to all his visits to the farm, and to Laura's when Jennie was there, after all, and Jennie had been too inexperienced to read the signs and lead him on. And now that war had been declared there was greater urgency on everyone's part to sort their relationships out.

She recalled as many of his visits as she could where she had

had any sort of conversation with him, and found it wasn't hard to imbue the little half-smile that often played around his mouth, and the comments he had made, with a different significance.

The tea remained untouched as Jennie returned to her chores, her head full of what she would wear on Saturday night, and whether, if he was posted away, she might become 'Charles's girl', writing romantic letters to him like they did in the last War. For the first time, she felt herself to be young and giddy, with things to look forward to, and she found that she liked that feeling very much indeed.

Charles saw Edward and Tom in the distance as he drove back up the farm drive, but there was no sign of Katharine, which didn't surprise him. But he was also relieved, as it had made his chat to Jennie that much easier.

Rather gratifying, actually, to see that look of delight on her face.

He would have liked to have seen Katharine's face when he asked Jennie out, though.

He gave a little inward smile. And he would like to be a fly on the wall over the next few days to hear what would be said about Saturday night.

13

Harry

A biting wind was blowing across the top of the mountain, as he'd known it would, but he didn't care. Turning up his collar and thrusting his hands deep inside the pockets of his black overcoat, he began resolutely to pick his way around the edge of the Keeper's pond, for once oblivious to the beauty of his surroundings. In front of him stretched the panoramic view across the valley, wherein lay the villages of Gilwern and Govilon and the town of Abergavenny, to the Black Mountains, dominated by the Sugar Loaf – all as stunning as ever. Behind him, the scarred sprawl of the town he loved, and to his left Pwlldu. Memories of his youth, in every direction.

But Harry, head down, glanced at none of it. He wasn't sure why he'd come up here, except that he'd had to get away from the sympathetic glances and the careful clucking of the womenfolk. He'd done the same when Ivor had died – his first encounter with the loss of someone he loved – and again when his beloved Nan went; but this was far, far worse. This time he didn't know how he was going to get over it.

He reached a large, flat rock and recognised it as one they had sat on, on a day just such as this. The wind had whistled around them then, too, but they'd wound thick scarves around their heads to stop their ears from ringing and had sat on the rock, making plans for the bright, long future that was to be theirs.

He looked at the rock with contempt. They had been pleased with it. A perfect place to sit and feel that the whole world was spread out below them. They'd laughed and held each other and made their plans …

And now Megan was gone, but that stupid lump of rock was still there.

He walked past it, but then turned back. Frowning, he lowered himself onto the rock and closed his eyes very tightly.

It was just as he thought. There was nothing of her here, just an empty space beside him.

He opened his eyes and stared unseeing out towards Gilwern. Cupping his hands round the flame, he lit a cigarette and drew deeply on it.

Perhaps just for today he would remember … remember his Megan…

Megan - 1931

A new decade had brought little cause for rejoicing to the inhabitants of Blaenavon. Promises made by the Company at various meetings with the South Wales Miners Federation were swiftly broken, and then Milfraen Colliery, the one that was going to ensure continued employment, closed down, with little hope of any of the men finding work elsewhere.

The glorious Call to Arms by Mr. J. Caulfield of four years earlier had become a sorrowful memory. He'd mustered the miners of Blaenavon to join the marches to London: "Down to the *Horniment* at Abergavenny, boys, that wonderful *Horniment* that marks the sacrifice of our fallen brethren! Remember it, boys, and take heart from their steadfastness! Join up with our brothers from across the valleys! *And for Gord's sake, boys, stick together!"*

They had stuck together; they had sung together, they'd been cared for along the route, and they'd returned together to square their shoulders to an even bleaker future than they'd faced before.

The Lumley-Joneses, perhaps finally aware of their increasing unpopularity, retreated to London permanently, leaving management of the Works in the hands of Captain Jackson, who seemed never to flinch in the face of the men's animosity. The Company House became a hospital, depriving Lizzie of her job as kitchen maid, but, undaunted, she soon found a job as companion to an elderly lady, Miss Lewis, who lived in faded splendour in Abersychan.

"Bored to tears you'll be, in five minutes," Mam predicted. "Always looked like she'd bitten on a wasp, she did, even when she was a young woman. Small wonder she never married."

"It's a job, Mam, and a roof over my head, at least for now." Privately Lizzie shared her mother's view, but underneath her sweet, soft exterior was a steely determination not to add to her family's worries.

In the event, Lizzie found a distraction in the form of a young carpenter who worked for a nearby undertaker – one of the few businesses continuing to flourish, and whose premises were owned by Miss Lewis. Imperiously summoned by Miss Lewis one day to mend a sash window, he was immediately smitten by the young lady who couldn't hide a dimpled smile as her employer gave precise instructions as to her expectations, and then stood by to observe that they were accurately carried out.

He worked in embarrassed silence, glancing sideways now and again to catch a glimpse of the dimples, until he sliced into his finger with a chisel and had to be taken to the kitchen by the young lady for the wound to be tended.

As she dabbed at his finger with a cloth dipped in bicarbonate of soda and water, he gazed down at her shining nut-brown hair and tried desperately to begin a conversation. Miss Lewis's old dog, a pug with a wrinkled face not unlike its owner's, padded into the kitchen at that moment and gave him inspiration.

"Haven't I seen you taking this old thing for a walk in the park behind the school?"

Lizzie studied his face and decided that she liked the honest expression as well as frank admiration that she saw there.

"I take him every day, about twelve o'clock, so long as it's not tipping down." She leaned forward conspiratorially and jerked her head towards the sitting room. "It gets me away from the other old thing through there for half-an-hour!"

He grinned. "I eat my sandwiches in that park on nice days. Perhaps I'll see you there again."

She looked up from tying a bandage round his finger and smiled, sealing both their fates. "My name's Lizzie – and I already know yours."

Harry missed Lizzie when she moved to Abersychan, and felt slightly envious of her when she returned on her afternoons off, glowing with happiness and making her parents laugh with wicked impersonations of Miss Lewis and her idiosyncratic ways.

One Sunday afternoon she brought Archie Harris with her, and the reason for her high spirits became apparent, sending Mam into a fluster and into the scullery to find the tin of plums she'd been keeping, while Dad tried his best to be gruff and intimidating towards the young man who may have been considering taking liberties with his only daughter.

Before long, though, it was accepted that Lizzie and Archie were walking out together and it was understood that it was only a matter of time before they'd be making wedding plans. Preparations for a 'bottom drawer' and the ingenuity needed to acquire the necessary items when there was so little money to spare occupied Mam a great deal, while Dad continued to look for work, going out early and not returning until late, because anything was better than sitting at home.

Mam's determination to keep going seemed to grow as their circumstances became ever more straitened, but she rarely complained. Only twice did Harry see her cry. The first time was when Dad came home to say that he'd been set on at the tyre factory for the next few days. The second was next morning as she sawed slices of bread off a loaf held close to her chest.

"What's the matter, Mam?"

"Going off to work he is, after all this time, and I haven't even got tuppence for a bit of cheese to put in his sandwiches!"

Whenever he could Harry contrived to be in Megan's company, and he knew a lot more about her now. Her sister Phyllis worked as a teacher-helper at the new Hillside Infant School, and her other sister Edie worked in a sweet shop in King Street. It had puzzled him for some time as to what Megan did, until he discovered that she stayed at home and looked after her Aunt, who was now quite frail.

Invariably, though, he only met her at social gatherings, where her sisters always kept a weather eye on her, and he still hadn't plucked up courage to ask her out. She had a way of looking at him which told him she knew exactly what was going on in his mind, but that the most impression it made on her was one of faint amusement.

His affair with Ivy had fizzled out long since, but it had given him enough confidence to ask one or two others out. There had been one girl called Eileen with whom he thought he was smitten for a while, but eventually he could no longer bear the smell of paraffin that she carried about with her from the hardware shop where she worked. So when he wasn't mooning about after Megan, he spent much of his spare time with Bill or Uncle Fred.

Bill had made some headway with Maisie, but she continued to lead him a dance, raising his hopes one minute and dashing them the next, and he would seek Harry out then, and concoct some wild scheme to take his mind off her. Being Bill, he was able to wriggle out of the consequences of escapades that left Harry bathed in sweat. Funny then, how the only one Bill couldn't consistently convince was Maisie. With a sudden flash of insight, Harry realised that Maisie's hot and cold response to Bill was probably carefully calculated to ensure that Bill, to whom charming others came easily, was always kept on tenterhooks and therefore always interested.

By the same reasoning, perhaps, Megan could well be more interested in Harry than she had so far shown. A comforting thought.

What little traffic there was on a Sunday afternoon was completely halted as the crowd outside the Workman's Hall swelled. Every church and chapel throughout the town was represented and, opposite the dignitaries who took pride of place on a small raised platform, the chapel members were arranged in orderly groups behind their ministers, fanning out around the corner of High Street and Church Street.

The men were in their Sunday best, which had doubtless seen service for several years, as evidenced by the odd shiny patch and new buttons on jacket fronts. The women held themselves very erect, betraying only by sidelong glances their need to see whether their new hat, or collar, or, at the very least, new scarf, was meeting with the envious approval of their sisters. No-one was satisfied, of course, as every woman present had scrimped and saved and counted Cworp dividends to be able to produce something new for the big occasion, and was determined not to acknowledge a better outfit on someone else. Those not belonging to a chapel formed a ragged mass at the back, reaching almost to the rear of the Cworp, with some of the children clambering onto the railings of Horeb Chapel for a better view, until hissed at to get down by a parent – not necessarily their own.

The murmurings and mutterings of the crowd were hushed when the clock at the top of the newly-erected monument chimed the hour for the first time. As its third chime faded, the Mayor stood up.

"Ladies and gentlemen, honoured guests, Captain Jacks – " His voice was lost to the crowd as he turned to acknowledge the privileged and wealthy of the town, then returned: " – llow councillors," as his voice swung round again. "I am truly honoured to be standing here amongst you and to be given the opportunity to open the celebrations to mark the erection of this wonderful memorial to those brave Blaenavon men who gave their lives in the Great War.

"It has taken us many years of patient endeavour to build this memorial, but I'm sure you will agree with me that every penny we've dug deep into our pockets to give to this cause will have been given gladly to the memory of those loved ones – good honest men, many of them cut down in the flower of their manhood."

Here he paused and extracted a large white handkerchief from his pocket with which to wipe a tear from his eye – caused not by the pathos of his oratory, but by a biting wind that whipped round the corner of Church Street. A clever place to put the Memorial, Harry mused, standing near the corner with the Horeb contingent. Guaranteed to produce tears from even the most hardened, every Armistice Day for years to come.

The Mayor resumed his speech, but the wind took most of it up the hill, so that only those assembled on the lower slopes of High Street could hear what he was saying. Harry began to fidget, and wished he could turn up his jacket collar, but he knew Mam would see and frown at him or, even worse, reach out and tap his arm.

He carefully scanned the crowd until he found Megan amongst the Bethel Chapel group. She appeared to be listening intently to the Mayor's words, but as he continued to stare at her she turned her head.

For a moment their eyes held, their expressions intent, perhaps saying more to one another than they ever had in the stilted conversations that had taken place between them during the last couple of years. Then Megan's face broke into a smile – slowly at first, a mere prim twitch of the lips; then, as Harry smiled back, a widening, coquettish, beckoning smile which made Harry want to break ranks and rush to her side and take her in his arms.

Their attention was distracted as, speeches over, the male voice choir stepped forward to lead the singing. The choirmaster raised a pitch pipe to his lips, and a gentle hum was heard as each section found its note. Then he raised his arms and the first notes of *Guide me, O Thou Great Redeemer* issued forth, pure and too strong to be carried away by the wind. The men were in excellent voice, those in work strengthened by the hard physical tasks they performed, and those out of work strengthened by the hours they had free to practise.

Prayers followed, each minister and preacher eager to add his supplication to that of his fellow brethren. Then more singing, the whole crowd joining in this time, for *Jesus, Lover of My Soul* and finally *Abide With Me,* accompanied by many a genuine tear from those for whom the sense of loss they had borne nearly a decade and a half ago returned to overwhelm them again. At the end, the poignancy of *The Last Post* rang out, the notes lingering in the air over a profound silence which continued even after the notes had died away.

The crowd remained still until the Mayor stepped forward once again to signal the end of the official ceremony, and it was only then that men replaced their hats and discreet chattering broke out as people began to move off to their respective chapels, where tea parties had been laid on.

Harry scrutinised the crowd once more until he found Megan's eyes again, apparently searching for his, and he saw in them a warmth that he was sure hadn't been evoked by the sentimentality of the occasion. He made his way towards her, wanting to shout with happiness and celebration and the joy of being alive after the solemn commemoration of the dead.

She stood, murmuring to this one and that, but not moving away with the rest of her party, and he knew she was aware of his approach. Once face to face, he felt the old constraint creeping over him again, so badly did he want to impress her. Then he was reminded of Bill, of his own impatience with his friend's ability to charm everyone but the girl he truly loved, and he forced himself to speak.

"I thought we might have had a hymn from the ladies' choir as well. Quite disappointed not to hear you sing."

"We weren't allowed," she replied, in a faintly mocking tone. "Men fight the wars while women knit socks, so it's only the men who should sing at memorial services."

He jingled some coins in his trouser pocket. "I expect there'll be some people walking down Cwmavon Road tonight, now they're all in their Sunday best." He cleared his throat. "Do you ever...?"

She glanced demurely downwards and then looked shyly at him through her lashes. "I'm not allowed without an escort."

His spirits soared. The coins in his pocket jangled fiercely. "Well, would you like to... with me... tonight?"

She looked up and dazzled him with a smile as, out of the corner of her eye, she saw one of her sisters advancing towards them.

"Seven o'clock – 32 Elgam Avenue," she muttered urgently, before hurrying away.

Elgam was a council estate whose streets spread like capillaries up the hillside towards the Blorenge. Built in the early twenties, it was still considered a new development, and each house was eagerly sought after – if only for the much-prized bathroom. The estate itself was pretty gloomy; the houses, built in pairs to a standard box shape, each fenced in by tall wire mesh much given to rusting, had walls stuccoed in a delicate shade of dirty grey – perhaps the planners' idea, in order to blend in with the open-cast mining that took place further up the hillside.

Much to Harry's relief, Megan herself opened the door when he presented himself at Number 32 and, plopping a pert little hat on the back of her head, came straight out to join him.

As they set off down the street she gazed up at the sky and breathed deeply. "Don't you love the smell of a spring evening?" She turned to Harry, her brown eyes shining, with a vitality that caught and excited him, and an enthusiasm for her dingy surroundings that pleased him.

"My favourite time of year," he said promptly, never having really given it much thought, but realising as he said it that he meant it. The winds of the afternoon had blown away, leaving a pale blue sky with little scuddy clouds already tinged with pink as the sun began to fade.

They cut across the town, Harry jauntily wishing "Good evening" to as many people as possible, so they would see that he was with this beautiful girl. Once they reached Cwmavon Road, however, he gave her all his attention. As he'd suspected, there were many people walking the length of the road, and he was determined that she wouldn't be dazzled by anyone's charms but his.

"We used to come down here and play when we were kids," he told her, pointing to a steep-sided inlet gouged away from the side of the road. "Old stone quarry it is – they used the stone to build the cottages for Varteg Forge. Then, when we'd had enough, we'd run across the road, down the bank and across for a paddle in the river. Mind you, the river's always been so full of coal dust, we were dirtier coming out than going in!"

He felt a slap on his shoulder. "What you doing, talking the hind leg off an old donkey to a lovely girl like this, butt?"

It was Arthur, his old school friend, on his own and looking very smart in a black overcoat. He smiled at Megan, and nodded his head towards Harry. "Been telling you some old rubbish, I know."

"Geography lesson," Megan replied solemnly, so that Harry's spirits plummeted. Seeing his face she relented, and leaned towards him. "And a very interesting one it was, too."

"We were just out for a quiet stroll," Harry told Arthur meaningfully, but Arthur ignored the implication and fell into step on the other side of Megan.

"Just the evening for it," he agreed, and turned his full attention on Megan. "This boy here hasn't bothered to introduce us, but I'm Arthur. And why haven't I noticed such a pretty girl around the town before?"

Megan dimpled at the compliment. "My sheltered upbringing I expect. I'm Megan, Megan Powell. Do you work with Harry?"

Harry glowered as the two of them proceeded to chat like old friends. He walked along beside them, hating his pal for being several inches taller, broader of shoulder and full of easy conversation which made Megan look up at him and give a little tinkly laugh. He tried to remember the witticisms he'd rehearsed since the afternoon, but there was no need of them – Arthur was supplying enough for them both.

"How far are you going?" Arthur asked. "Thought I'd walk on down past Westlakes tonight."

Harry stood still and held Megan's elbow lightly. "We're only going as far as the Coffee Tavern. Stopping for a drink there, we are, so you'll have to go the rest on your own."

There was a firmness to his voice that at last Arthur recognised. With a jaunty shrug and a "Tarrah then!" to Megan, and a "See you tomorrow!" to Harry, he went on his way.

The Coffee Tavern, a small converted house at the side of the road, was just a few yards away. Judging by the people milling about the doorway it was doing good business; mainly in providing cups of tea, despite its name.

"Would you like a cup of tea?" Harry asked, hoping anxiously that she wouldn't want lemonade, because that was dearer and the coins jangling in his pocket didn't actually amount to very much.

"I'm sorry. I promised I would be home by half-past nine, so we haven't really got time to stop."

Harry didn't possess a watch, but judging by the failing light he knew she was right.

"Come on, then." He turned about, completely dispirited by the way the evening was going, so that he almost didn't wait for her to catch up with him. His failure to enchant her sat like lead on his shoulders, and he couldn't heave it off.

They walked for a while in an uncomfortable silence.

"Arthur seems a nice lad," she said at last. "It's good to keep up with old friends."

"He's alright." Harry replied ungraciously. He knew that he was making things worse, but he couldn't overcome his feelings of disappointment. Megan obviously found Arthur more entertaining. What if Arthur asked her out? How could he then bear to see him around the town? He'd been a fool to think that he had anything better to offer. He saw all his hopes of the last two years swiftly dashed by his inability to impress her when he had the chance.

As they neared the middle of the town they bumped into one of Megan's neighbours.

"Hello, Megan my love! Out for a stroll tonight, is it? There's lovely you look, too. Put a bit of colour in your cheeks." She barely paused for breath, but looked Harry up and down and tried to place him. He'd already placed her. Mrs. Watkins, 46 Elgam, always asked for half a pound of streaky, then had a slice taken off when she was told the price.

Megan didn't introduce Harry but stood and responded patiently to Mrs. Watkins' string of fatuous remarks. "How's your Auntie? And how's your Phyllis?" – as if she didn't have the opportunity to see for herself every day of the week.

The new monument clock struck the quarter hour. Harry coughed.

"We'd better be going, Mrs. Watkins," Megan said. "Bye for now."

"Nosey old woman," she muttered as soon as they were out of earshot. "She was dying to know who you are."

"Why didn't you tell her, then?" he asked, ready, in his present mood, to be offended by Megan not wanting to acknowledge him.

The smile that always did such terrible things to him appeared. "What! And spoil her pleasure when it dawns on her in the week when she's queuing up for her groceries?"

As they turned into Megan's street, Harry stopped and faced her. "Did you really have to be in by half-past nine?"

"Of course!" It came to her then, as they walked on, that he thought she was curtailing the evening deliberately. "I wouldn't have come out with you in the first place if I thought I wasn't going to enjoy myself."

Mollified, Harry began to curse himself for his sullenness. "Not much of an evening out, though. Sorry."

They were nearly at her door. "I could probably stay out until ten o'clock on Saturday." There was only a slight smile on her lips now, but her eyes looked promising.

Harry's heart sang. "You could? And you'd want to? I mean, would you like to go to the pictures or something?"

"Pictures or something would be lovely. Seven o'clock again if you like. I'd better go – I've seen the curtains start to twitch."

He wanted to grab her, kiss her, tell her how he felt, no matter if both her sisters were watching, but before he could open his mouth she was through the front door and he was left to wander home, completely bemused at his good fortune.

His good fortune continued all week. He beamed at customers and workmates alike, and even began to whistle behind the counter, until a frosty glare from Mr. Pugh stopped him mid-note. His plans for a special evening out with Megan grew more and more fanciful as the week progressed, hampered only by the nagging doubt that he would be able to finance it adequately. He tipped up all his money to Mam on a Friday night and she gave him five shillings back to last the week, but as his plans for an evening out became ever more grandiose, he knew that it wouldn't be enough. By Wednesday he decided that his only hope was to strike it lucky in a game of cards at Uncle Fred's.

It was a mid-week event among the men of the family, to gather in Uncle Fred's small front room and spend a long evening playing cards. The numbers varied according to who was on night shift, but the regulars always included Uncle Joe, Bill – who had long since been considered one of the family – and, lately, Harry. He'd discovered that all the calculations he did in the shop had trained his memory, so that he could easily recall which cards had already gone from the pack, or which player had laid or discarded a certain card.

Surprisingly Uncle Joe, not known for his brains, also played a mean hand, especially at brag, where his strangely immobile face gave nothing away and one could never be sure when he was bluffing. Harry had managed to keep half of his pocket money for the game, and had changed it into coppers before he left work. They only ever played for pennies, but it was still possible to be a shilling or two up by the end of the evening, if you were lucky.

It wasn't to be his night, though. Increasingly desperate as he saw his pile of pennies get smaller instead of larger, he became reckless and tried to bluff on hands that were really no good at all. He hung on until the bitter end, and succeeded in recouping some of his losses, but was still sixpence down by the time everyone declared they'd had enough.

"Not your night tonight, butt?" said Uncle Joe as he pocketed a large pile of coppers. "Don't think you were concentrating hard enough!"

Harry considered telling him how much he could do with a little extra, but decided against it. Kind-hearted Uncle Joe would have handed all his winnings over if he thought Harry needed it more, but Harry knew he would be looked down upon by the other men present if he traded on Joe's simple nature.

He walked home thoughtfully through empty streets. The card games always went on into the early hours, but Mam never worried when he was with the family. Head down, he pondered his finances. If he cut down on cigarettes for the week – he'd recently taken up smoking, although hadn't yet found the courage to light up at home – and didn't go out for a drink with Bill or Arthur, he could spend freely on Saturday, and not feel the pinch too much.

He locked the front door behind him and pulled the chenille curtain across to keep out the draught as quietly as he could, but nevertheless Mam heard him. She might go to bed, but she was never asleep when he came in.

"Don't forget to bolt the door! And mind the lamp!" Her voice hissed down at him, as it always did. He'd tried before to point out to her that she was silly to worry about burglars *after* he came in, but not before, but she just smiled at him and left it as it was.

Not that there was anything worth taking, he reflected. The clock, perhaps, or Mam's vases, or the incandescent lamp that she was sure he was going to break if she didn't remind him of its presence.

"It's alright, Mam," he hissed back, a smile in his voice at her idiosyncrasies. "Goodnight!"

What do you fancy, Top Hall or Bottom Hall?" he asked Megan as they walked along Elgam Avenue.

She gave a small grimace. "Have you seen what's on? *City Lights* with Charlie Chaplin, or James Cagney in *Public Enemy*. Can't say I'm mad about either of those. I think I must be one of the few people I know who doesn't like Charlie Chaplin."

Harry had privately hoped to see the Cagney film, but relinquished it with good grace. "What would you like to do, then?"

She stopped walking and put a gloved hand on his arm. "Do you know what I'd really, *really* like? I'd like to have fish and chips and stroll along somewhere pleasant eating them. Phyllis and Edie don't approve of eating in the street, you see – if we go to the fish shop we have to have them wrapped and wait till we get home. I've always wanted to eat them outside, straight out of the newspaper."

"Are you sure?" he asked incredulously. Four pen'orth of hake and chips hadn't exactly been what he had in mind to impress her with. "What about a dance? Would you like to go to the Drill Hall? There's usually a good band on Saturdays."

"I do like dancing – love it, in fact, but... well, to tell you the truth, the only shoes I can dance in have got a hole in them. That's why I'm having to wear these old things." They both glanced down at her sturdy brown footwear. Definitely not for dancing. "So until I get them repaired or can afford some new ones, dancing's out."

Her eyes held his, candidly. "Hoping that I wouldn't have to tell you that, I was. But if I'd pretended that I didn't like dancing you might never ask me again."

"I'm glad you did! Puts us both in the same boat. At least you've got two pairs of shoes." He pointed at his feet. "These are my one-and-only."

He was buoyant now, with her shared confidence and the implication that she wanted him to keep asking her out. He grabbed her hand. "Come on! Bottom fish shop's the best! Gherkin, as well, you can have if you want!"

They carried the fish and chips down past the railway station and followed a path alongside the river, blowing on the hot chips and biting them gingerly as they went.

They fell to talking about their lives. "Don't you ever get fed up," Harry asked her, "staying at home all day?"

"Not really. Auntie Jane is very poorly now, so she needs me, and by the time I've seen to her and the house, the days go quite quickly." She spoke with a determined lightness. "And my sisters can earn more than me, so it makes sense for me to stay at home – not that what they bring in goes very far around four of us." She sank small white teeth into a chip. "Of course, all the singing helps – gets me out and about a bit."

She popped the last morsel of hake into her mouth. "Delicious! I just knew they would taste better out of the paper." She extracted a fine lawn handkerchief from her pocket and wiped her hands before replacing her gloves, which had been stuffed into the other pocket.

"Wait a minute!" said Harry. "You've got some grease on your chin."

She stood demurely as a schoolchild as he pulled out his own large handkerchief – thank God for Mam and her clean white hankies! – and carefully wiped her chin. He drew the cloth tenderly to the side of her mouth, and then, slowly and deliberately leaned forward and brushed her lips with his.

She looked steadily at him, her mouth curving in the slightest hint of a smile. "We seem to have come a long way. I think we had better start back."

At the bottom of the town a crowd of people had gathered, listening to the impassioned speech of a little man. He had the bulbous nose and veined face of a hardened drinker, but tonight there was no slurring of his words and his bloodshot eyes blazed with a convert's zeal. Nearby stood members of the Salvation Army, surrounded by a variety of musical instruments.

"Alleluia Lamppost," Harry told Megan. "The Sally Army hold repentance meetings here every Saturday night. Old Danny there repents regular as clockwork once a fortnight, when he's got no more money and his wife's threatening to throw him out!"

"Brothers! Sisters!" the little man was crying, swaying on bandy legs, his arms gesticulating wildly. "I have seen the light! You see here before you a man who was the worst sort of sinner! My family went hungry, I brought them nothing but shame – but all that has changed! The demon drink will have me no more! Alleluia!"

Megan and Harry watched as Old Danny and a motley group of similarly reformed sinners each took up an instrument and lined up behind the Army band.

"You watch," said Harry. "Likes the big drum, Danny does, and it's nearly as big as him!"

Sure enough the little man selected the big bass drum, lifted it up, slung the strap over his shoulder – nearly overbalancing in the process – and proceeded to bang it for all he was worth, with far more enthusiasm than rhythm.

Megan and Harry followed, with the rest of the crowd who had gathered to hear Old Danny's passionate oratory, as the band marched up Broad Street – Old Danny at the rear, unable to see where he was going, but marching on regardless. Halfway up, the steep street split into two, Broad Street veering slightly to the left and

Hill Street slightly to the right. The band was snaking up Broad Street to the rousing strains of *Fight the Good Fight,* when Megan suddenly grabbed Harry's arm.

"Look!" she cried, her face alight with amusement.

Still banging his drum for all he was worth, and now singing at the top of his voice too, head thrown well back, Old Danny had drifted to the right, and was making his solitary way up Hill Street, still able to hear the sounds of the band in the parallel street, and oblivious to the fact it was no longer in front of him.

Most of the crowd had noticed, and stopped to laugh and see how long it took Danny to realise he was on his own, and several young boys ran after him, crying: "Danny! Danny! You're going the wrong way, man!" But he was making such a din that he couldn't hear them.

Harry and Megan subsided onto a seat outside Bethlehem Chapel, doubled-up with laughter. Harry straightened up first, watching as she found the fragment of fine lawn again and applied it to her streaming eyes.

"Oh!" she groaned, holding her sides. "Who needs to see Charlie Chaplin when Old Danny's around!" And she began to giggle anew.

The shared laughter somehow strengthened their companion-ship as they resumed their walk, and it seemed perfectly natural for Harry to catch her hand and hold it tightly in his.

They discovered that Old Danny had finally been alerted to his predicament and had scuttled along a side alley, the enormous drum banging against his knees. He caught up with the band as they turned the corner into Lion Street for their final destination – Lion Square, where several more hymns would be sung before exhorta-tions to the Lord above would be made just as vehemently as those to His sinners below.

Instead of following the crowd, Harry and Megan continued to walk up Broad Street, quiet now before the cinemas, dance halls and pubs began to empty. The deepening twilight gave them both confi-dence, and they began to talk of their hopes and ambitions. She told him of the dark days of losing both her parents and finding herself in new surroundings, and admitted that an anxious Aunt and two fussy sisters placed constraints upon her which she often felt compelled to fight against. In turn, Harry found himself telling her of his turbulent emotions when his brother died, and his fears when he thought he'd been going to lose his mother as well – deep, secret feelings that he hadn't shared with anyone before, lest he be thought less of a man for having them.

"One of the hardest times for me was leaving Brynmawr with

both my Mam and my Dad buried there, although it was some time after my Mam died. It was like I was deserting them, somehow, putting them behind me with that part of my life," Megan told him. "And then I sometimes think of all the things I'll probably do in the future – things that they might've been proud of, but –" she gave a little shrug – "they'll never know, and I can only guess what their reactions would be."

"It must help, though," said Harry, "having your sisters there to share everything with. All girls together so to speak."

He felt her smile break through in the deepening gloom. "They would be very flattered to hear themselves called *girls*. 'Sensible-women-doing-their-best-for-their-deprived-baby-sister-God-Bless-Her,' is how they see themselves. And they take their roles very seriously, I can tell you! I don't think they'll ever see me as anything else until I'm properly grown up and have found somebody to marry."

On impulse he pulled her into the shadow of a doorway. His words came out in a rush. "*I* want to marry you, Megan. I love you!"

He felt her bristle with indignation, standing very tall with her shoulders stiff, and he cursed himself for his impetuosity.

"I wasn't fishing for offers, you know! I just said it as a general remark. Besides, we hardly know each other!"

What to say now? If he retracted his offer it would sound like he hadn't meant it, but to blunder on would show him for a fool if she felt she couldn't care for him.

He went all sorts of hot and cold. "I know, I know. But... I mean what I say ... Perhaps it's too soon to say it..."

He could see her clear brown eyes staring steadfastly at him in the dusky doorway. There was nothing for it but to soldier on.

"Look, I've been in love with you for over a year now, ever since I saw you with the Avonias. Oh, I've had lots of other girlfriends since then –" he hoped she wouldn't ask for details another time – "but I can't get you out of my mind. I know I want to spend the rest of my life with you!"

There. He'd done it now. Never mind the romantic evening he'd envisaged; he'd declared his love for the girl of his dreams at the wrong time and in the wrong place, and not even very articulately. In his idle moments he'd foreseen himself impressing her with sweeping declarations of his undying affections while not for a moment reducing his masculinity: a sort of cross between Valentino and Gary Cooper. And now ...

He waited on tenterhooks for her to say something. She made as if to speak, but noises in the distance of people heading towards them made her quickly step out of the protectiveness of the doorway and continue along the street. Harry fell into step beside her, carefully studying his shoes as he walked.

As they neared her house he became completely desperate. "It's not bad wages at the Cworp, you know." He tried to keep his tone conversational, as if it really didn't matter. "Twenty-five shillings a week I'm on now, and rising every year. Goes up a lot when I'm twenty-one, too – getting on for three pounds, I'll have then – and an extra two-and-six if I work on the provisions... have to do all the cheeses then, see, and know how to cut a side of bacon..." Why was he talking to her about cutting up a pig? Doubtless Arthur would have done it so much better.

She turned to him abruptly in the yellow arc of the gas lamp that stood sentry outside her gate.

"Did you mean it, about loving me?"

He faced her squarely. "Of course. I think you're the most beautiful girl I've ever seen."

She nodded twice, her expression giving nothing away, then walked the few steps to the front door. Uncertain, he stayed where he was, until she tilted her head to one side in invitation.

Close together on the doorstep, she held his lapels lightly. "Love me for another two years, and then we'll see," she said, a glimmer of a smile on her lips.

He was about to answer when the hall light was switched on, illuminating the front step through the fanlight above the door. Then footsteps could be heard.

Still holding his lapels, she gave him the briefest of kisses. "Same time next week?" she asked, but didn't wait for a reply, opening the front door and sliding round it in one easy movement.

Afterwards, he was always surprised at how smoothly their romance had progressed. They met just once a week at first, on a Saturday night, and soon discovered that if the evening was chilly then the back row of the cinema was an inviting place, no matter what film was showing. Sometimes they would go dancing, and Harry would marvel at the lightness of her as he held her in his arms. Occasionally they would meet during Saturday afternoon and take a bus to Pontypool, or even the train to Newport, and stroll in the parks or look round the shops, despite having no money to spend.

Harry would often be fired up with frustration on the way home, bemoaning his lack of funds and listing all the things he would buy her if he were rich. But Megan only laughed and engagingly told him that she was more than happy with what she had. And it was true. There was a serenity about her that enabled her to view her life, with all its shortcomings and deprivation, with equanimity, and, although she was as pleased with pretty clothes and trinkets as the next girl and took great pains over her appearance, she never hankered after things it would be unrealistic to hope for.

Not that she lacked imagination. They soon discovered a mutual love of reading, and frequently met 'by accident' in the lending library of the Workmen's Institute. Megan proved to be wider-read than Harry, and gradually weaned him away from thrillers and detective stories and introduced him to authors such as Wilkie Collins and George Eliot, although he drew the line at Jane Austen, which had far too much feminine appeal for his liking.

As the evenings drew out into summer they began to meet on Sunday evenings as well, providing Megan wasn't singing with the choir. If she was, Harry would troop along to whichever chapel or hall they were performing in, and soon knew the choir's repertoire by heart. These evenings were more frustrating, because of the limited time they had together, and invariably Megan would be flanked by Phyllis and Edie, but by this time Harry was so smitten that any time spent with this lovely girl was better than none.

On free Sunday evenings, however, they became a regular sight along Cwmavon Road, so much so that if Harry was seen alone he would have to face a barrage of teasing from his mates: "Come to her senses at last, has she?" – "Frightened her away, have you, butt?"

Sometimes she'd come into the Cworp, and the teasing would increase. "Young lady waiting to be served, Harry!" Mr. Pugh would call from the other side of the shop, so that all eyes would be on Harry as he took Megan's order and everyone would listen to their stilted conversation.

Arthur would rag him the loudest but, alone together, he congratulated Harry on his good fortune. "Beautiful girl you've got there. You'd better look after her, mind, or I'll be stepping in and taking over!"

His father echoed a similar warning when at last he took Megan home for the ritual Sunday tea. "She hasn't got a Dad of her own to look out for her, so you mind and take care of her."

Mam, always able to read him like a book, and having watched his eagerness to be at Megan's side over the last few months, simply said, "Lovely little girl, she is. I think she'll do for my boy," and then took her glasses off and poked at her eye with the corner of her apron, muttering something about smut from the fire.

There had to be a tea-party then, of course, at Megan's home, although it wasn't too daunting since he was already on fairly familiar terms with her sisters. He had yet to meet the now bedridden Auntie Jane, though, who'd been asking to see the young man who'd been putting a bloom in her niece's cheeks.

She was nursed on a couch day and night, beside the fire in the main living room, and it was here, on a low table next to her, that the tea was laid out. As soon as Harry entered the room he was overcome by two things: the immense heat in the room from the banked-up fire despite the mild summer weather, and a sickly-sweet aroma that pervaded the room and lodged itself in his nostrils. It conjured up unpleasant pictures of all the undignified aspects of chronic sickness, overlaid with something he couldn't place for several days, although the smell seemed to stay with him. (Later, walking along the back of the Cworp one afternoon, it came to him: the same odour emanated from the dustbins outside the butchery. Putrefying meat.)

Interred beneath a mound of blankets topped by a sleek fur rug was the wasted body of Auntie Jane. Her face was tiny, drawn and grey, almost the same shade as the fuzzy hair surrounding it that had probably once been lustrous curls. Yet her eyes remained sharp; a faded blue, they missed little, and her voice when she spoke was firm, with nothing of the querulous invalid.

"Hello, Harry. I'm sorry I can't get up to greet you." She extended a thin, almost transparent hand towards him.

"No, no, that's quite alright... Don't worry ... Pleased to meet you," Harry stumbled, uncertain how to treat an invalid.

He needn't have fretted, though. Unlike Phyllis and Edie, whose conversation seemed restricted to the social niceties, Auntie Jane had a thirst for what was going on in the community of which perforce she was no longer a part, and Harry, with his knowledge of the majority of the town's inhabitants, was a most welcome guest. Soon they were chatting almost to the exclusion of everyone else.

Nevertheless, Harry was thankful when it was time for Megan to see him out. The hothouse atmosphere together with the sadness of a lively mind incarcerated in a rapidly failing body depressed him unutterably.

"How on earth do you cope every day and stay cheerful?" he asked Megan.

She shrugged. "She's no trouble, and she's been so good to us. And she sleeps quite a lot during the day, so I escape out into the garden."

'The garden' was a euphemism for the narrow strip of grass that ran around the outside of the house, that even the hardiest of mountain sheep would be hard pressed to find appetising.

From then on Harry made a point of calling in at the house on his free Thursday afternoons, chatting with Auntie Jane over a cup of tea and then taking Megan out for an invigorating breath of fresh air over the mountains. Sometimes they climbed to the Keeper's pond on top of the Blorenge, and at others they strolled up Llanover Road until they were well out onto the mountain to the East of the town, and could look down over the Usk valley as far as the Severn.

On sunny afternoons they would throw themselves down on the soft tussocks where whimberries would later appear, and enjoy the privacy that they were unable to find anywhere else. Their evening jaunts always ended with Harry depositing Megan on her doorstep at the appointed time, although as their romance progressed her sisters displayed some discretion by lengthening the time allowed to say goodnight, before turning on the light and making very obvious noises in the hall.

Even alone on the mountain, though, Harry held himself carefully in check. Megan had none of Ivy's boldness or experience and try as he might he had not yet succeeded in persuading her to admit to a love for him. But when he enfolded her in his arms and felt her body nestling against him and her lips tentatively responding to his, he knew that he'd wait forever if that was what she demanded.

Years later, whenever he looked back on that summer, he saw it as a glorious time of happiness brimming with expectation. No matter that the dole queues lengthened, men gathered defeatedly on street corners, and children became thinner and more ragged; or that shops and businesses closed and women took longer and longer to do their shopping as they tried to make their meagre housekeeping stretch still further. People died, babies were born, some to a better welcome than others, and one man gave up the unequal struggle and drowned himself in the Mile Pond. But afterwards Harry could pinpoint nothing except that it was the summer when he knew he'd fallen in love.

14

Harry wasn't certain whether it was the iciness of the wind or the bleakness of his memories that had turned the waters of the Keepers pond a deep, stark black. Looking over the valley, his fingers idly traced deep grooves in the rock on which he sat; initials carved there years ago by – who? What had happened to them since? Had they, too, known pain?

But Harry knew that there was no pain as deep as his, and never would be, that any other human being could experience.

1934

"**Two more** weddings! Thank goodness our Harry's will be the last for a while!" Mam leaned her elbows on Nan's table, her teacup held between her hands.

"Strange to think we'll both be seeing off our youngest within a month or so of each other," said Nan, stirring sugar vigorously into her cup. "Still, I suppose we must be thankful that our Maisie finally said 'yes' – I don't think I could've stood much more of her and Bill under my feet all day!"

Her eldest daughter regarded her searchingly over the top of her teacup. Her mother's round rosy face seemed a bit too florid at times, and her movements, never ungainly, despite her bulk, had developed a slow purposefulness recently, as if it cost her much to make the effort.

"Are you going to be alright once Maisie and Bill are wed? You can't rely on finding someone to be as much of a help as Bill."

"We're both going to notice a difference when there's fewer round the table of an evening," Nan replied, avoiding a direct answer to the question. "Still, I expect Lizzie will be calling in on you often enough, especially once the baby's born."

Lizzie and Archie had married the previous year and had found a house to rent further along Morgan Street, with Lizzie becoming pregnant almost straight away. Archie had acquired an old bone-shaker bicycle which he pedalled steadily to Abersychan and back each day, his carpenter's bag slung over his shoulder, whistling softly through his teeth on the way there but needing all his breath for the uphill slog at the end of the day.

Mary smiled. "I see more of Lizzie now than when she was working for Miss Lewis – I'm still not sure about becoming a grandmother, though, especially when my little sister is only just getting wed."

Nan chuckled. "I think it was our Lizzie and the baby that spurred Maisie on. I don't think she fancied being a spinster great aunt! Time she got on with it too – she'll be thirty next birthday! I'd had five of you by then! And don't you worry about being a grandma – you'll soon get used to it!"

Mary poured herself another cup of tea. "Looks like I'll have to – there's another one due in a few months time, seemingly."

"Dai and Bridget?"

Mary nodded, her face clouding over slightly.

Nan studied her for a moment and then rose to prod at the fire with a crooked black poker, before swinging the kettle on its hob back over the glowing coals.

"It's my belief," she said as she sat herself heavily back at the table, "that your trip to London didn't go as well as you'd have us all think."

Mary stared intently at Nan's chenille tablecloth, whose plush red had faded to a sort of autumn russet. She was aware of Nan's gaze steadfastly upon her, silently inviting her to share whatever was troubling her. *When did your mother stop being a mother?* Mary wondered. Would she herself still be worrying over her daughter when Lizzie was in her forties and she in her sixties?

"You're right," she said at last, as Nan waited, patient as ever. "I don't think our Dai really expected us to go to the wedding." She gave a small smile. "Come to that, neither did we! And ... all that talk about how well he'd being doing... well, talk's all it was, I think. I'm sure he only wanted us not to worry about him, but..."

Dai had written early in the year to say that he and Bridget were getting married. His parents had thought no more of it except to tell the rest of the family, but they had decided amongst themselves that Mary and Albert should travel to London to see their eldest child marry. For Mary, whose horizons had only stretched as far as a rare trip to Cardiff and the odd charabanc outing to Barry, it was a particularly daunting prospect. But the hat went round the family until enough money had been collected to send them both off to

Paddington, with a bit to spare.

"Only for one night, mind," Albert had insisted. "I saw all I want to see of London when we went on the marches."

So before they knew it they were on the early morning train at 4:30. Dai was on the platform at Paddington to meet them, and took his mother's arm as she looked around in bewilderment at the noise and confusion, even at this early hour of the morning.

"Glad you haven't brought too many bags," he said, picking up the cardboard suitcase that held both their belongings. "There's a couple of buses to catch from here back to our place. Got plenty of time, though. The wedding's not till two, and I think I'm better out of the way!"

The 'couple' of buses turned out to be three, giving Mary ample time to find out more about Dai's marriage plans, which had been very hazily sketched in his letter.

"You know me, Mam, never one for writing much. But everything's taken care of. Wedding at St. Elphege's, then back to Bridget's house for a bit of a do."

"St. Elphege's?" Mam's voice and eyebrows rose simultaneously.

Dai avoided her eye. "Catholic family, see, Irish background and all. Not allowed to get married anywhere else."

"There's Protestant Irish, as well," Mam replied tartly, and then relented a little when she remembered that she didn't want to spoil her son's day. "But I suppose it's only the Catholic ones that come over here."

There was a pause as they all seemed intent on studying the streets through which they were passing. Dai began to point out landmarks, until his father interrupted him.

"So you'll have had to 'turn', then?"

Dai shrugged. "No choice, I'm afraid. It was either Bridget and be a Catholic, or no Bridget."

They were silent again as his parents digested this information, and the air seemed tense between them until Mam reached out and patted his hand. "Just as long as you sing in Horeb when you're down with us," she said, with one of her special small smiles.

The third bus took them through a jumble of ever narrower and meaner streets, until finally they arrived in the heart of Whitechapel.

"It was all so drab," Mary told her mother now. "No better than this place – well, worse really, 'cos at least we can get out and have a bit of fresh air. But it was just row after row of houses up there – no sunshine at all getting into some of them, just shadow all day."

Aunt Brenda's house stood on the corner of one such street,

where she'd lived throughout her marriage and where she continued to live after the demise of the Londoner she'd wed. Its bay window displayed the second-hand garments that were for sale within, and Aunt Brenda had turned the upstairs into living accommodation for herself, with a small back bedroom for Dai. She was a large, energetic woman, nothing like her brother Albert; indeed, it seemed as if they had each received the physique intended for the other. Her hair was a suspiciously rich brown, swept back off her brow, making her appear even more statuesque. She had an imposing bosom, but, restrained into a sort of hard shelf by the rigid corseting that ran from neck to thigh and creaked when she leaned forward, there was nothing soft or yielding about it.

Her appearance totally belied her manner, however. Copious tears were shed over the brother that she hadn't seen for so many years as she clasped him to the well-supported shelf, followed by entreaties to tell her all about the family – although she hardly stopped talking for long enough, as she fussed about them, for them to fit in a reply.

"Given you my room, I have, seeing as it's got the double bed – and I'll go in Dai's old room for tonight," she told them in a curious hybrid of Welsh and cockney accent. "I've only done soup and sandwiches for dinner – all my lot are on their way round to see you, so I thought it would be better than trying to cook a meal as well."

Her 'lot' consisted of the four burly children she'd produced before her husband had died, possibly worn out by her exuberance. All her children were married and lived with families of their own in the rabbit warren of neighbouring streets, and by early afternoon most of them had crowded into Brenda's rooms.

Mary thought she was going to drown in tea by the time Dai, resplendent in a navy suit, squeezed his way through to them.

"Come on, I'll take you next door to meet Bridget's family!"

But next door was just as crowded, and here the accents were mixtures of London and Irish brogues which Mary and Albert could barely understand. There was a difference in the atmosphere too. Everyone seemed to shout at the tops of their voices, and several of the men had already started on the beer intended for later. Bridget, whom Mary remembered as such a quiet girl in contrast to the brashness of her family, was ensconced upstairs with her sisters, but both her parents and numerous aunts and uncles eagerly greeted their Welsh visitors and Bridget soon came down to join them.

One or two of the men made incomprehensible remarks to Albert before jabbing him in the ribs and throwing back their heads with laughter, so that he felt bound to attempt an artificial chuckle, which sounded more like a snigger, not to give offence.

"The wedding service was alright, once you got used to all the kneeling and standing," Mary told Nan now, "but afterwards... well, I know our family can drink, but it just seemed ... different, somehow. The men all stayed in the front room, and the women were out in the back, except for Bridget and her sister, who went between the two; and I think the men were having a race to see who could get drunk the fastest."

No attempt had been made to tidy the room where the women sat. The mantelpiece was covered with a layer of coal dust, a clock which no longer worked, two broken combs, some hairpins, a lipstick, a lidless jar of petroleum jelly which had melted slightly in the heat from the fire, and two dirty, cracked tea-cups. The window had no curtains and the sill was covered in similar rubbish, so that Mary itched to sort it all out.

She searched for words to explain to Nan how the men had become increasingly belligerent as the evening wore on, taking no notice of the remonstrances from their womenfolk, until a fight broke out in the sitting room, which eventually spilled out on to the pavement. The priest, who'd been drinking with the best of them, waded in and separated the antagonists, but no-one seemed to know what the fight was about.

"I'd have been so *ashamed* for that to have happened at my daughter's wedding," Mary declared, "but everyone went back inside and carried on as if nothing had happened!"

Except for Albert, who, despite being dwarfed by the sturdy Irishmen, refused to have anything more to do with the celebrations. He marched into the back room, rigidly upright, which made him seem a good six inches taller, and told Mary and Aunt Brenda that they were all to return next door.

The next morning they'd gone in to Bridget's family to say goodbye, and Mary had been shocked to discover that Bridget's older sister, husband and two children also lived in the narrow little house. They were all in the back room, which was still in considerable disarray from the previous night.

"Where are you and Bridget going to stay?" she managed to hiss at Dai as they waited for Bridget to fetch her coat in order to see them off.

"In the front bedroom. Bridget's sister's got the back two, and her Mam and Dad are sleeping downstairs. Her little brother is going to sleep in my old room round at Aunt Brenda's."

"I don't suppose it's any worse than many you get round here," Mary reluctantly told Nan. "And Bridget did look a picture in the church – Aunt Brenda got her a lovely dress from somewhere; all lace it was… It's just that, from what Dai had said, I thought he was doing really well – you know, would get a little house for the two of them, maybe set up a bit of business of his own. But life is just as tight up there, so he might as well've stayed home, and at least then we'd have known how he was getting on. And where are they going to put a baby when it comes?"

Nan remembered how she herself had wanted so much more for her firstborn child, who now sat in front of her careworn and old beyond her years, and said nothing.

Mary stood up. "Time I was going." She turned back to her mother as she put her coat on. "You won't let on, will you – that it wasn't all we cracked it up to be?"

Nan patted her arm. "Of course not. No need, is there?"

Before she opened the front door Mary turned to Nan again, and this time Nan knew she was going to tell her what was truly on her mind.

"I don't think Bridget will go the full nine months."

"Just as well they're still up in London, then, isn't it?" said Nan, "No-one down here will be counting that closely. And as long as Ceinwen James doesn't find out, we'll be alright!"

E die! Phyllis! Auntie Jane! You'll never guess!"
A flushed and excited Megan burst into the room where the three ladies sat listening to a play on the wireless. Her shining chestnut curls bobbed on her shoulders and her deep brown eyes danced. Behind her Harry stood, more quietly, but he too was beaming.

"We went to the Cworp whist drive! Packed it was… and we won! A brand new bedroom suite! Isn't it wonderful?"

She plopped down on the end of Auntie Jane's couch to catch her breath; they'd run all the way along Elgam Avenue.

"Wonderful indeed!" Auntie Jane agreed. "What a wedding present!"

Unable to sit still, Megan jumped up again and went to fill the kettle while her sisters, equally pleased, asked Harry more about it.

"Oak, it is – nice quality too. Must be worth over fifteen pounds. Two wardrobes, a chest of drawers, dressing table, and a bed."

"So all we need to get is a mattress," Megan added as she came back into the room and put the kettle on the range. "They'll deliver it for us, too, as soon as we want."

The whist drives were held about once a month in the function rooms over the Cworp, and had become so popular that excellent prizes were now to be had.

Harry chuckled. "We're going again next time – see if we can get a three piece suite as well!"

"No need for that," smiled Auntie Jane. "Pass me my bag, Phyllis."

The voluminous handbag of worn and cracked black leather was kept permanently by her couch, stuffed full of precious papers, certificates, and goodness knows what. She rummaged in it, and pulled out a large brown envelope.

"You ought to have this now," she said, handing it to Megan. "It would've been there for you when I'm gone, but it looks like I'm going to be hanging on for a bit longer, and it will help you to set yourselves up."

The envelope contained a wad of money. "You can count it later," Auntie Jane told them, as they gasped in shocked surprise. "But there should be enough to get you a mattress and a few chairs or whatever."

From the look on their faces it was obvious that Phyllis and Edie had known of their aunt's intentions, and they sat nodding their approval.

"Oh, Auntie Jane! You shouldn't have!" Megan declared, throwing her slender body across the fur rug and hugging her aunt.

"It's small reward for what you do for me," Auntie Jane told her, with such feeling in her voice that Megan's eyes began to glisten, and she got up to busy herself with cups and saucers.

"Thank you, Auntie Jane," Harry moved forward to plant a kiss on her shrivelled cheek. She reached up and placed a clawed hand, cold as ice, each side of his face.

"Just be good to her," she said quietly, her gimlet eyes, giving the lie to her wasted body, holding his.

"I will," he said simply but just as intently.

Strolling home that night, Harry hummed softly. The words of *Love is the Sweetest Thing,* a popular song of a couple of years ago, kept playing in his head. He'd waited the two years, as Megan had asked him, and eventually he'd known that she returned his love. In four weeks Megan would at last be his, and the time, for both of them, could not go quickly enough.

The desire to marry had become more urgent of late for more pragmatic reasons, too. The Cworp was beginning to feel the bite as unemployment in the town continued to go from bad to worse, and there'd been much heated wrangling in the Co-operative movement as to how the essentially Trade Unions-orientated Society could justify adding to the unemployment figures, when their long-held boast had been that they were there to protect and support the common man.

Harry and his colleagues were well aware of the rows, and he knew that the single men would be laid off first if the Society felt forced to rescind its policies. *Just let us be married before anything happens,* he pleaded to the Almighty when he was in Horeb, *and have our week's holiday.*

The Cworp had been the first employer in the town to give holiday pay. If you worked for the Company there was no such thing: any holidays, even Bank Holidays, were unpaid, so that those lucky enough to be in work couldn't afford to take the time off, and those who were unemployed, with nothing but time on their hands, couldn't afford to go anywhere.

For the last year, Harry had stopped saving with the Sunday School Club, which ensured that members had a day at the seaside once a year, and had put the money away separately. There wasn't enough for a full week's holiday, of course, but he now had a tidy sum, augmented from time to time by winning at cards, and he'd persuaded Megan that they should have one night at Weston-super-Mare to celebrate their marriage.

Their only disappointment was in not having somewhere of their own to live. Unlike Lizzie and Archie, they hadn't found a house to rent, and it looked as if they were going to have to fall back on Megan's family's offer to share the house in Elgam Avenue.

"It won't be so bad. We'll have a bedroom and the front sitting room to ourselves," Megan had tried to assure Harry, "and I'd want to go on looking after Auntie Jane anyway, so perhaps it's for the best."

Desperate to have Megan as his wife, Harry reluctantly agreed.

Maisie and Bill were married two weeks before Harry and Megan. Bill had suddenly announced one day that he'd come into some money, left to him by a relative in Hereford. His unexpected good fortune had changed him overnight into an assertive individual who sat Maisie down one evening and gave her an ultimatum: he would buy a coal delivery business that was currently available in the town and they could settle down together in reasonable comfort, or he would go back up Hereford way and set himself up in something there.

"I'm not waiting about any longer – and you shouldn't be either," he told her, in the most unromantic fashion.

But it worked. All Maisie had wanted was to be swept off her feet, and here was Bill, who'd tried every other way to secure her affections, doing just that. Within weeks the business was bought, along with the lease on a little house in William Street, and a wedding date fixed.

June, 1934

C ome on, you two, time we were on our way to Newport!" Uncle
Fred's voice cut across the chatter in the front room.

"Ready when you are," Harry replied, thankful to get away from
the tea drinking and dainty sandwiches. He turned to Megan – his
wife! "Better go and find your hat and say goodbye to Auntie Jane."

"That's it, Harry!" called out one of his cousins in a loud voice
that made Phyllis wince. "Tell her what to do! Start as you mean to
go on, boy, and show her who's boss!"

"Some hope!" Harry laughed back. "Had me twisted round her
little finger, she has, since the first day I set eyes on her!" Sounding
thoroughly content to be a beaten man, he went to say his goodbyes
too, and to thank both Megan's sisters for the wedding breakfast
they'd put on.

"Hang on!" cried another cousin as they were about to leave the
house. He pushed ahead of them out onto the narrow path leading up
to the front door. "That's it! Just stand there and smile!" He'd acquired
a box camera by saving matchbox cards and had announced himself
official photographer at the recent spate of family weddings.

The photo taken, many of the family spilled out on to the pavement to see them off, as if they were going away for a month rather
than one night. They squeezed into the back of Uncle Fred's bull-
nosed Morris while he persuaded Nan to sit in the front.

"I don't need you to take me home!" she protested. "It's walking
up the hills that takes my breath away, not down them."

"Don't be silly," said Uncle Fred, starting up the engine. "Gets
you out of the washing-up this way."

Uncle Fred drove the newly-weds to Newport, from where they
took the paddle steamer to Weston. It was a glorious afternoon, so
they stayed on the deck watching the sun glinting on the water, which
shimmered where it met the sky. Megan, holding on to the large hat
which she'd bought specially, leaned against the railing into a light
breeze that sprang up as the steamer increased speed. Harry moved
beside her and whispered his longing for her, which made her laugh
so that other people looked across and couldn't resist smiling too, at
sight of the pretty girl.

Harry's heart swelled with pride. He wished he could properly
convey to her the depth of his feeling, which ran so much deeper
than a simple 'I love you' or jokey innuendoes about his physical
need for her could ever impart. But somehow the words, which
sounded fine when read in a book, weren't able to trip off his tongue.

And, however garrulous his family could be, they kept expressions of endearment for those under ten – or else for the bedroom, whispered in the dark.

That was something else that made him feel cold, despite the heat of the sun. What if everything went wrong tonight? What if Megan, despite the warmth of her response when he held her in his arms, failed to enjoy what was to happen between them?

He grabbed her hand, to ward off thoughts which only made him nervous. "Come on, Mrs. Jenkins – let's go inside and have a drink."

The boarding house was on the sea front, ruled over by a sharp-nosed little woman who looked at them suspiciously, with none of the welcome that they had hoped for. But when Megan smiled at her winningly as she signed the dog-eared book the woman produced, and said: "It's the first time I've signed my new name – we were married this morning," she relented slightly and said, "I hope you'll be very happy, I'm sure."

And with a sniff which seemed to signify that she wasn't very sure about it at all, she led them up to their room, which was large but very plain. The double bed looked old, with a dip in the middle, and was covered with a slippery satin quilt whose pink colour had obviously run in places when it was washed. In one corner stood a sombre wardrobe; in another, where it caught no light at all, was a dressing table, its mirror spotted with age. A small empty fireplace stood cheerlessly between the two.

"Bathroom and lavatory down the landing," their hostess recited. "Tea is at six o'clock, and the front door's locked at eleven sharp."

Despite the warmth of the late summer's afternoon Megan shivered and, noticing, the woman said, "I'll see that there's a fire lit in here this evening – it's often a bit chilly in early June."

Her lips twitched as if she was going to say something more, possibly about their newly-wed status, but she thought better of it and left the room abruptly.

Harry slid his arms round Megan's impossibly tiny waist as she raised her arms to remove her hat. He wondered if they could… if they should… here, now, this afternoon. Then he pictured the ferrety-faced woman, who would probably hear them, and thought better of it. He moved away from the allure of his wife's body, to the window.

"Not much of a room, but at least there's a sea view. The tide's right out – do you fancy a stroll along the beach?"

"That would be lovely, but I'll have to change – I don't want to ruin this outfit on the sand."

An awkward silence fell between them. Their intimate moments throughout their courtship had been confined to caresses amidst the heather on the mountain top, or long goodnights on the front doorstep. Neither had seen the other undressed.

Their eyes met, their thoughts converged, and a slow blush rose from Megan's throat and suffused her face. She turned and began to unbuckle her suitcase, while simultaneously Harry cleared his throat and made for the door. "Think I'll go and wash my hands – freshen up," he muttered, and swiftly left the room.

He took as long as he could, splashing water on his hot face as he tried not to think of Megan shedding her clothes. Eventually he walked back along the corridor with a firm tread and cleared his throat again before entering the room.

Megan was tidying her hair, lifting it off her face with two tortoise-shell combs, so that her curls tumbled down her back. She'd changed into a pale lemon short-sleeved dress with tiny flowers on it.

"Ready when you are," she said, "but – don't you think you should change out of that suit?"

At the stricken look on his face she burst out laughing and the tension between them was broken. "Don't worry! I'll put our things in the wardrobe! Promise I won't peep until you're finished!"

He wanted to say it didn't matter, and strip off in front of her there and then, but he couldn't pluck up the courage somehow, so he perched on the far side of the bed and quickly replaced his good suit with his everyday trousers, while Megan clattered about, putting away their meagre belongings with considerable industry.

As they left the room his spirits soared. Somehow tonight would be alright, the sunshine outside was beckoning, and he had the most beautiful wife in the world!

On impulse he stopped at the bottom of the stairs and knocked on the landlady's door. "We won't be requiring tea this evening," he told her grandly. "My wife and I will be eating out."

"Can we afford it?" his wife asked anxiously as they crossed the road to the promenade.

"Of course," he answered with more confidence than he felt. "It's still our wedding day – I don't want to have our first meal together with old ferret-face watching us."

They walked down a flight of steps onto the beach. "A mile of sand when the tide's right out," Harry said. "Uncle Fred told me that when I was a nipper, and I always wanted to come here and run right across it, and then build a huge sandcastle."

"Well, I don't know about the sandcastle, but last one to the pier's a sissy!" Megan cried, and she was off, gaining a good head start before her words had registered. Then he was after her, catching up fast, so that she turned her head and shrieked as she saw him, and redoubled her efforts.

But they were both winded long before the pier was reached. They stood, holding on to each other as they caught their breath and laughed with the sheer exhilaration of being on holiday, and in love.

"Come on!" said Megan, when they'd recovered from their sprint. "Shoes off! I'm not coming all this way without a paddle!" She threw herself down on the beach and began to untie the straps on her shoes, and he saw that she wasn't wearing any stockings.

He joined her on the sand, quickly removing his socks and shoes and rolling up his trouser legs. "I thought we were supposed to be all grown up now we're married!" he grinned.

"Grown up things come later!" she answered provocatively, and then she was off again – down to the water's edge this time, to gasp as a wave splashed over her toes, so much colder than it looked.

It was 10:30 when they returned to the boarding house, after a fish-and-chips supper (at Megan's insistence, a romantic reminder of their first proper evening out together) and a variety show at the Pier Theatre.

They didn't see the landlady, but true to her word she had lit a small fire in the grate and the room seemed more cosy and inviting. Some of their earlier awkwardness returned, and by unspoken consent they took it in turns to change whilst the other visited the bathroom.

While she waited for Harry, Megan climbed into the bed, which to her dismay groaned and creaked with every movement. She didn't know if there were people in the room next door, but she did know that the thought of it would inhibit Harry. So far the day had been perfect; she didn't want the night to be a disappointment for either of them.

On an impulse she jumped out of bed, turned out the light and dragged the slippery quilt down onto the floor in front of the fire. She had just settled herself on it when Harry came through the door. He stood still at the sight of her, kneeling before him, her eyes luminous in the fire light, her face lifted trustingly towards him.

He dropped to his own knees, eyes holding hers. Slowly, tremblingly, he reached out to the ribbon tying the gathered neckline of her nightgown. Her hands moved up and undid the buttons, and with a shrug of her shoulders the gown fell to the floor.

The light from the fire flickered over her naked body, her breasts fuller than her slight body suggested, her hips as slim as a boy's. He groaned at the urgency of his need for her.

"Oh, Megan! I love you so much!"

Her response was blotted out as he took her in his arms and

crushed her mouth with his.

Afterwards, they lay in front of the glowing embers, the pink quilt wrapped around their entwined limbs. "I hope I didn't hurt you – I meant to be gentle; shouldn't have rushed at you like that – couldn't wait…"

Megan placed her fingers on Harry's lips to still his stumbling words. She nestled her body closer to his. "If that old fire will only keep going long enough to keep us warm, you can do it all over again …"

15

Harry's thoughts were briefly interrupted by a bird, flying free and high in the distance on a course that crossed his eyeline. Too far away to identify; close enough to sense the joy in its flight. Like the innate joy that had sparkled in his Megan ...

1935

Mam wiped a duster fondly over the three small framed photographs, lifting each one so that she could dust the sideboard underneath. They'd all been taken by the cousin with the box camera. He'd made a good job of it too, and Uncle Fred had had the snaps framed as a present for his sister. Both couples – Lizzie and Archie, and Bill and Maisie – had been taken on the steps of Horeb Chapel, Lizzie smiling shyly while Archie stood straight and self-conscious, and Bill looking both triumphant and relieved to have finally slipped a ring on Maisie's finger.

But the photo of Harry and Megan, taken outside Megan's house, was the one Mam liked best. A large rose willow-herb weed had sprung up beside the front door, but in the photograph it looked like a climbing plant, giving the impression that they were somewhere more countrified than the grey-fronted house in Elgam Avenue. Megan's lustrous beauty and happy dancing eyes shone out even though the quality of the picture was poor, and Harry seemed to glow with pride.

In many ways life had become better during the past twelve months. After endless years of unemployment, Albert finally had a job. Morris the butcher had started him off some time ago, taking care of two pregnant sows on a stony bit of waste land up Llanover Road. Albert had taken a sow and a couple of piglets in payment so that he could carry on claiming dole, until he'd been able to build up a small piggery of his own. With all his time to devote to them, he became adept at raising porkers, up to seventy pounds in weight, before they were sold to the butchers in the town. It didn't bring in much more than the dole, but Albert had his valuable self-respect back, he was out in the fresh air, which was working wonders on his weak chest, and there was always half a pig to be hung in the cold larder in the back kitchen.

"I'm going to wake up one morning and find my feet have turned into trotters!" Harry had declared when he was still living at home, after yet another meal of bacon and potatoes. But he'd only been joking; he too had seen how his father walked with a lighter step and held his head up when he joined his friends for a pint in the Rolling Mill.

"I don't know what he finds to do up there all day, mind," Mam confided to Harry. "Must be the best-kept pigs in Wales!"

But Harry had seen his father when he and Megan had strolled up Llanover Road on Thursday afternoons, cursing the pigs affectionately as he made shelters for them out of old bits of wood and corrugated iron, or sitting on a makeshift bench consisting of a plank on two boulders as he put the world to rights with a crony over a pipe of tobacco ...

Mam studied the photos again as she replaced them on the sideboard. There'd been happy times lately. Maisie and Bill, making a go of the coal delivery business, with Maisie doing the books at home now that she no longer went out to work, and keeping a careful eye on every penny; Lizzie giving birth to baby Bethan, in their cramped front bedroom with Mam and Nan in attendance, and proving to be a born mother ... she still had the extra pounds on her from carrying Bethan, and there was already another baby on the way, but there was a cosy roundness about her that suited her. Must have been what Nan was like as a young woman, Mam mused, and then wondered if Lizzie was also going to follow her grandmother in the number of children she would end up producing.

A frown darkened Mam's brow as she thought about grandchildren. She saw Bethan nearly every afternoon, but wondered if she would ever see her other granddaughter. There had been a letter from Dai to tell them that little Annie had been born, six months after the wedding as Mam had predicted, but there'd been no news since. She sighed, replaced Harry and Megan's photo, and returned to her chores. At least *they* seemed happy enough and she had no doubt from the way Megan's gaze fell on Bethan that they would be the next ones to produce a grandchild.

Harry strode home from work with a jaunty step, feeling happier than he had done in weeks. He wouldn't tell Megan straight away; he'd get her out of the house first, without telling her family where they were going.

Despite his love for Megan, he could no longer pretend that he was happy with their living arrangements. He hadn't realised before their marriage what a quiet, well-ordered existence the two sisters led; had mistakenly believed that the decorum displayed when he went to tea had been laid on for his benefit – just as his Mam would nudge him and say, "Best behaviour, mind," when they were expecting company. But he soon discovered that the whole of their lives were conducted this way – a stultifying round of polite conversation and impeccable manners, as if they were all only distantly related, and a complete lack of imagination when it came to Megan and himself.

Only Auntie Jane, from her prone observation post, saw the frustration Harry was experiencing at being surrounded by straight-laced females with whom he would never feel so at ease as with the comfortable women in his own family. But her own attempts to afford the young couple more time to themselves were invariably thwarted by the more dominant Phyllis, who had no intention of allowing the reins of the household to slip through her fingers merely because a young man – and one who probably wasn't good enough for her youngest sister, truth be known – had come amongst them.

The couple would escape to their own sitting room in the evening, after the mandatory family tea which Megan prepared, only to be disturbed by a timid knock on the door from Edie to announce: "Phyllis says to tell you that she's making a pot of tea and do you want a cup?" Or: "Phyllis says that if you want to listen to that programme on the wireless, we've got it on too, so we may as well listen to it together."

No-one else ever entered their bedroom though, to which they would often retire at an early hour, and their new bed gave none of the squeaks or groans of the one in Weston, but Harry heard Phyllis's heavy tread on the staircase so often when he was feeling at his most romantic that now, no matter how engrossed he became in the delights of Megan's body, there was always a part of him that waited for it, like a dog with one ear cocked for danger whilst apparently sound asleep. He would urge Megan to keep still until the sisters' bedroom doors were firmly closed, but she, less in awe of her family, would giggle and move her body provocatively to tease him.

He knew now why his parents had urged them all to Sunday School every Sunday afternoon when they were young, and why his father had been so affable on their return. Harry and his brothers had shared a big double bed in the back bedroom throughout their childhood, with Lizzie on a little bed in their parents' room; it had never occurred to him then that his parents may have longed for more privacy, but he understood it now.

After today, though, things would be different. Harry wanted to be like his other recently-married relatives, men who could walk into their house after work and feel master of their own home, and swing their women into their arms if they wanted to, without feeling that they still had to seek permission from an older guardian of her virtue.

He waited until they'd all finished their meal. "You won't mind if Megan doesn't help with the clearing away tonight, will you ladies? We have to go out – some business to attend to."

Megan had already begun to stack the dishes, and looked up sharply, but quelled the question on her lips when she saw the firm expression on his face. "I'll just get my coat," she said.

"Come on then, what's all this about?" she asked as, minutes later, they were walking down the road at a brisk pace.

Harry pulled a bunch of keys out of his pocket and jangled them in front of her. "How would you like a home of our own?"

Megan's eyes widened in delight. "Where …? How…? *Really?*"

"Yes, really, if we want it. A flat, in Mountfield Place – the big house on the corner of Greenfield Terrace. Mr. Pugh at the Cworp told me about it. His brother-in-law, Jonas I think his name is – only he's always been called Nelson on account of only having one eye – it's his house, but he lives down Cwmavon Road with Gwillym Probert's widow (they used to keep the Rising Sun up King Street) – married to her of course, so he's turned this place into flats. Funny little man, he is – I don't know how he lost his eye… don't think he was in the war…"

Megan was by now used to Harry's potted histories of the people of the town whom he knew so well, even when she'd no idea who they were, and usually listened patiently, but now she broke in.

"*And?*" she asked. "Which one are we going to look at?"

"Oh, sorry! The top one. I don't know anything else about it – Mr. Pugh got the keys for me. All he told me was that it's six bob a week."

The 'flat' was really just a couple of rooms off the top landing, each with a big square bay window looking out over the street. There was a fireplace with a wall oven in the larger room, and leading off it was a narrow kitchen with a sink and a gas ring, which overlooked the side road. There was a toilet on the half-landing which was shared with the flat below.

Harry flicked a switch on the wall. "Electric light! Dad won't like that!" Electricity had just reached the town, but Albert steadfastly refused to have it in the little house in Morgan Street, and no argument could persuade him that it was safer than the flickering gas lights he was accustomed to.

Megan moved about the rooms carefully, saying nothing: opening cupboards at the side of the fireplace, inspecting the oven, while Harry watched her, willing her to like it.

"Our furniture will fit in a treat!" he encouraged. "And I can bring coal up for you in the mornings before I go to work – I expect there's a shed for it out the back." He followed her gaze to the scuffed and torn brown linoleum that covered the floors. "It'll look better once there's furniture in, and we can cover the worst bits with some rugs."

She walked over to the window and looked out. She could see over the rooftops of the smaller houses opposite; above them rose the Coity, its green slopes dotted with sheep if you looked straight ahead, and scarred by the workings of men if you turned to the right. To the left could be seen the outline of the cemetery on Varteg Hill.

"These windows will take some covering," she said, "but I expect I can get some remnants from Pontypool market, and run them up on Edie's machine."

"You mean you like it?"

Megan turned to Harry's eager, hopeful face. "I think it's fine – even if we do have to carry coal up two flights of stairs and share the toilet with strangers!"

He hugged her with relief, and then they walked round the rooms again, deciding what they would put where.

"Do you think," Megan said at last, "that there would be room for a baby here? Oh – not yet!" she added hastily, seeing his eyes widen, "but soon, perhaps – you never know…"

"Shouldn't be a problem. Plenty of space down in the hall to keep a pram, and a nice bit of grass out the front there for when the weather's nice … Come on, let's go and tell the others!"

As they toiled back up the hill, Megan became thoughtful. "I'll have to keep looking after Auntie Jane, you know. There isn't anyone else to do it, and she's used to me now. I don't think I could let her down."

Harry thought about this for a moment.

"It wouldn't be too difficult," she went on, "After all, the flat's not that big, it wouldn't take a great deal of looking after."

She waited, but still he didn't speak. Truth to tell, he hadn't considered this side of things in his desire to have their own home, and he wasn't sure what he thought about it. Auntie Jane was family, after all, and therefore was entitled to be taken care of, but whatever she thought now, Megan would have her hands full virtually running two households at opposite ends of the town.

"Phyllis and Edie will have to help out more," he said eventually, "and they mustn't expect you to go running over there at weekends as well."

"Of course they won't," she said confidently, although she suspected that Phyllis would be none too pleased to lose her. "And don't worry," she teased as she tucked her arm in Harry's, "I'll have your tea on the table as soon as you get in from work!"

"Anyway," she went on, as they both continued to think about it, "you never know – if that baby we were mentioning earlier turns up I'll *have* to stop at home, won't I?"

But nothing, thought Harry grimly as he shifted his weight on the hard granite, had lived up to the high hopes they'd both had. Nothing.

1936

"**That's it,** then!" Megan came out of the kitchen to see Harry fling his cards down on the oilcloth-covered table in the corner, before throwing himself into the armchair by the side of the fire, his mouth set in a bitter line. She said nothing, but fetched him a cup of tea and placed it beside him on the fender before perching on the opposite chair.

"Twenty-seven shillings! That's all we'll get a week from now on! After nearly ten bloody years! And nobody doing anything about it except bickering! There'll be nobody left in this town soon, I tell you – only the old people and the useless. Everyone else'll be off out of the valley to find something decent!"

Bitterness and strife had run deep in the Co-operative movement, and the local Labour Party was riven with argument, but in the end could do nothing to prevent the laying-off of men in the one work-place that had pledged to support them. And it wasn't just young boys. Harry, despite his married status and length of service, had had to go too.

Megan continued to sit quietly, staring into the fire. When at last she spoke her voice was subdued. "Thought I might have a bit of good news for us today. Almost positive, I was, but – well, it's not going to happen after all. Not this month, anyway ... So!" She glanced up and raised her voice to an artificially cheerful level. "We'll manage. Plenty of others have to, and at least we've only ourselves to feed."

But he saw her eyes cloud as she spoke, a reflection of his own anguish but for a different reason, and the anger went out of him.

Over two years married, and no sign of a baby. It was beginning to play on her mind. He'd seen the wistful expression on her face whenever she held Lizzie's babies, which Lizzie seemed set to produce effortlessly each year, and the quiet way she'd greeted the news that Maisie was now expecting. She no longer responded, either, when inevitably some member of the family would nudge her and say, "Your turn next!"

The lines of bitterness left his face as he looked at her, trying hard to be resilient when there was little at the moment for her to look forward to, either.

"Come here," he said softly, and she obediently rose from her chair and nestled on his lap, her head on his shoulder.

"It's probably all meant to be, you know," he said with a confidence he was far from feeling, absently stroking her thigh as he sought for words to make them both feel better. "Time I was leaving that old place, anyway, and trying something else. I've thought for a while it was coming – almost a relief now. And I know enough people in Blaenavon – if there's anything going, I'll get to hear of it, I know I will."

She nodded into his neck, neither of them voicing the fact that there was rarely 'anything going' these days.

"I see the little ones from Hillside School, sometimes, when I'm coming back here." Her voice was muffled. "At dinner times. Being taken by the teachers, they are, up to St. Paul's vestry for a bit of food – carrying a mug each for their cocoa, poor little mites. And our Phyllis says that more than that go without, because their parents won't let them have charity. Pitiful to see, it is. Made me vow that *our* child, when we have it, won't go without!"

She sat up straight on his knee and attempted a wobbly smile. "So perhaps we'd better wait for that baby a bit longer – make sure it won't need charity when it does arrive."

He took out his handkerchief and smoothed away a suspicion of wetness around her eyes. "Just you see. I'll get another job, and before you know it there'll be so many little ones running around us that you'll be dying for a bit of peace!"

Her smile became a little firmer, but she didn't answer him directly. "That tea's gone cold," she said. "I'll make a fresh pot."

By September, two months after losing his job at the Cworp, Harry's prediction that he'd soon find something else was becoming less and less likely. He'd managed to keep himself more or less busy during the warm summer months – helping his father with the pigs, or walking all over the town to see people he knew who might have a use for him. During August he borrowed Bill's coal lorry and drove a party of Horeb lads to Builth Wells for the summer camp that they saved pennies all year for. In previous years they'd often walked the whole way, pushing their camping gear on a hand-cart and arriving at Builth in the early hours of the next morning. But this year it was a relief to many of them to have a ride, even if it was a dusty old lorry; somehow the energy just wasn't there to face such a long walk.

Harry's dead brother Ivor had gone on such a camp the year before he died. Mam still had the postcard he'd sent: *Arrived 4:30 this morning. Having a wonderful time...* He tried to picture Ivor when they reached the camp, doing all the things that he saw the boys now doing, but found that he couldn't recall Ivor's face clearly, and he was glad to turn the lorry round and head for home again.

Most of the time he stayed out of the flat during the day. Megan continued to care for Auntie Jane, but the flat was always spick and span before she left in the mornings. He knew that if he stayed out she'd have dinner with Auntie Jane, and then there'd only be tea to get in the evening.

As soon as he entered the flat after another fruitless afternoon wandering about the town, he stoked up the fire and put the kettle on in the hope that Megan would soon return, and wondered what he should do next. It still seemed unnatural to be at home during the day, and to sit down and read the paper he'd bought seemed an indulgence. Being a proper Valleys man, though, it didn't occur to him to begin to prepare the evening meal.

He turned with relief from contemplation of the Coity as he heard footsteps on the stairs. Megan was home; they'd talk and laugh together and he could push away the anxieties that crowded in on him when he was alone.

But it was Phyllis outside on the landing; stern-faced and purposeful.

"Megan's out," Harry said straight away.

"I know. That's why I've come. It's you I want to see."

A rare visitor to their home, she walked into the living room, her eyes darting into all the corners, and sat herself down, ramrod straight, on the edge of the sofa.

"Would you like some tea?" Harry attempted. "I've just put the kettle on."

"No, thank you. I won't stay long."

Harry couldn't recall ever having spent any time alone in Phyllis's company, and her grim demeanour reinforced the feeling that she'd never really approved of him, although he knew not why. He could feel resentment of her censorious presence building up inside him, but he did his best to quell it.

"Well then," he said in an over-hearty manner, just stopping himself from rubbing his hands together. "What do you want to see me about?"

Phyllis inclined her body slightly so that the round black hat, which looked like a bowler with the brim turned down, shaded her eyes.

"I want to know what you're going to do about our Megan!"

Harry's attention sharpened. He'd no idea what she was talking about. "What do you mean?"

Phyllis gave a satisfied snort of derision. "I thought as much. You probably haven't even noticed have you? Letting the poor girl carry on, wearing herself out!"

Harry felt his temper, voice, and resentment begin to rise. "I don't know what you're on about!"

Phyllis lifted her head high, so that her eyes, dark and penetrating, peered out from under the hat.

"Losing weight, she is! Going as thin as a stick. Auntie Jane's noticed. Picks at her dinner, Megan does, not eating enough to keep a sparrow going. Then she's rushing out of here every morning, rushing back in the afternoon. Doing too much, she is! I said it was a daft idea, moving down here when you could've perfectly well stayed with us."

Prickles of anxiety ran over Harry's scalp. Megan hadn't been eating much in the evenings, he had to admit, but she always said it was because she ate such a big dinner with Auntie Jane.

His fears made him defensive. "She says she eats too much at your place – and she's always been thin…"

"Huh! You're the one who can't keep his hands off her, and you've not even noticed!" Her eyes accused him of every lascivious thought he'd ever had about his wife, her lips bloodless and grim, bringing out a forcefulness in him that surprised him as much as it did her.

"You're quite right. It's obviously too much for her, so she'd better stop! You or Edie will have to look after Auntie Jane from now on, and Megan can stay in her own home!"

He could see from the startled look on Phyllis's face that this wasn't what she'd expected him to say. "But Auntie Jane… she's used to Megan now… she'll miss her! She can't manage on her own, and Edie and I are out all day…"

Harry wavered a moment as he thought of Aunt Jane, but thoughts of his wife urged him on. "Well, one of you will have to start being in all day. I know that means you'll have to manage on one wage, but we're all having to tighten our belts at the moment."

"Don't you think Megan ought to have a say in this? She might prefer to come back to our house instead of being up here at the top of this old building. And I know you're hard up – it would save you some money!"

She was standing facing him now, and he was glad that he was taller than her. "Of course I'll talk to Megan about this, but she's my wife now, and we have a life together. Auntie Jane is *your* responsibility – or ought to be – not Megan's."

"Grateful enough to have her money, though, weren't you, when you were getting wed! Toadied up to her nicely, you did then!"

Harry's face flushed a dark red and his voice became dangerously flat and quiet. "You know as well as I do, that money was no more than Megan deserved! What sort of life was it for a young girl, looking after an invalid all day? As for Auntie Jane, she doesn't need '*toadying*' to. As far as I'm concerned she's the best of the lot of you, and it's a terrible pity that she's the one lying on a couch all day!"

Phyllis opened and shut her mouth like an angry goldfish, but no sound came out. She picked up her handbag and made for the door. "I knew it would be a waste of time talking to you," she cried as she wrestled with the doorknob that would only turn if it was held a certain way.

Harry watched her, making no effort to help. "You're not disappointed then, are you?" he answered.

The door suddenly opened faster than she was expecting, so that she nearly overbalanced. Harry would have laughed if he hadn't felt so furious with her. But his anger evaporated a little when she turned to him at the top of the stairs, her indignant expression becoming something more ageing and uncertain.

"Only worried about our Megan, I am, really. Always been the one to worry about her – just want what's best for her."

"And do you think I don't?" Harry replied softly.

He was glad Megan hadn't bumped into Phyllis on her way home, so that he could explain the situation in his own words.

"We all think it's too much for you," he finished. "So you won't need to trek up to Elgam Avenue any more – one of the others is going to look after Auntie Jane."

Megan eyed him suspiciously. "You had words, didn't you? You're not telling me everything about this, Harry Jenkins!"

"No, we didn't!" But he saw the 'you can't fool me' expression on Megan's face. "Oh, alright then – I suppose we did get a bit worked up with each other. She wants us to go back up there to live, see. Thinks we'd be better off, with me not working and so on, but I think it was just a way of getting you back full-time to take care of Auntie

Jane."

"And I suppose you told Phyllis that?" Megan sounded half amused and half exasperated.

"Sort of," he admitted with a wry smile. He leaned across the table where they were sitting after tea, and smoothed a tendril of hair from her face. "I told her that I was worried about you, too, if you're not taking care of yourself, but that I thought we're happy as we are... You *are* happy, aren't you?"

In a moment she was in his arms. "Of course I am! And I think you're all silly to get in such a state about me. I'm absolutely fine!"

But Harry could feel the sharpness of her shoulder blades as he caressed her, and cursed the truth of Phyllis's words. "No, your sister's right," he said. "That's probably why I got cross with her. Time you had a break and stayed at home – unless you *want* to go back to the other house?"

"You know I don't. And I'll do as you say, seeing as how you seem to have it all arranged between you anyhow. But I'll still be going up there to see Auntie Jane, you know, and it will be difficult not to lend a hand, especially if Phyllis or Edie are about and not doing it all properly."

"I'll come with you," he promised, pleased that she'd acquiesced so easily. "After all, there's damn all else for me to do at the moment."

But their combined visits were not a success. Edie had been the one designated to stay at home, as she earned less than Phyllis, and she fluttered around them in such an embarrassed way that Harry knew Phyllis had done a good job of painting him as an unfeeling wretch. He also couldn't bear to see the comprehension in Auntie Jane's eyes that she was the cause of distress in the family, no matter how hard they all tried to pretend otherwise. He gradually stopped going, so that at least Megan could enjoy a return to her old relationship with her sisters, but he sensed her anxiety when she came home, and wondered if he'd been right to insist on them staying where they were. As for Megan, she didn't look so tired, but she didn't seem to gain any weight either, and he worried that the physical strain she'd been under had simply been replaced by a mental one.

In the end Auntie Jane solved the situation by dying quietly in the middle of the night, so that Edie screamed when she came downstairs next morning and found her cold, rigid body.

Megan moved back into the house for a couple of days then, to help Phyllis, as Edie had completely gone to pieces, and it wasn't until they were back in the flat after the funeral that she wept.

"I'm not crying because she's dead," she told Harry as he tried to comfort her. "I'm crying because of the wasted life she had. All those years spent inside a useless body! Only one chance we get, and hers has been and gone – not much of a life at all."

It was soon after this that the night sweats began. The first time it happened Harry awoke to find Megan sitting bolt upright in bed, her breathing coming in shallow gasps.

"What's the matter, love?"

"I – I'm not sure. Bad dream, I think."

He moved to put his arm around her. "What's this? Megan, your nightdress is soaking! Whatever's wrong?"

"I told you. A bad dream – must've frightened me more than I realised. And it's very warm in here. I expect this nightie's too thick."

But by this time she was beginning to shiver. "Stay there and I'll get you a clean one," Harry told her. "You'd better have a hot drink, too."

He watched some colour creep back into her face as she sipped the cocoa he'd made. "Doctor's for you, tomorrow, I think."

"What! Spend half-a-crown for him to tell me that I've got a touch of 'flu? I'll take a couple of aspirins with this drink, and I'll be fine – you'll see."

And certainly next morning there was no indication that their night's rest had been disturbed. If anything, there was more colour in Megan's cheeks, and she looked brighter than she'd done since Auntie Jane died.

Reassured, Harry forgot about it until some weeks later, when he woke to hear Megan moving stealthily around the room. "Only been to the toilet," she said to him, before he spoke. "Go back to sleep."

Nan eased her considerable bulk down into the chair opposite Harry, pleased that he'd popped in. Life was much quieter now that she no longer ran the shop, and she didn't go out as much as she used to.

"Best thing you can do is get her to the doctor," she told Harry now. "You just worrying about her won't do any good."

Just ten minutes in Nan's company had been enough for her sharp eyes to see that something was bothering her favourite grandson, and it had taken only five more for her to wheedle it out of him.

"The trouble is, she won't admit that anything's wrong. I've lost count of the times she's got up in the night now, because she's sweating like I don't know what. She won't talk about it, so I lie there pretending I haven't heard her get up, and she pretends not to know that I'm awake, and next morning we both pretend that nothing happened."

Nan didn't reply, but simply sat nodding her head a little.

Harry shifted uncomfortably in his seat. "I was wondering... well... if it might be some sort of ... *woman's* problem."

He could feel himself reddening. This wasn't the sort of thing you talked about, but pragmatic Nan, who knew him almost better than he knew himself, was just about the only person he could broach the subject with.

"You know," he persevered, "she's desperate for a baby, but nothing seems to be happening in that direction, and I just thought – well – she could be getting herself all wound up about it, couldn't she? Inside, like, and it's making her poorly?"

Nan remained thoughtful for a moment. "And her monthlies? Nothing wrong there?"

Deeply embarrassed now, Harry could only shake his head.

"I expect it's just a mixture of everything, then," Nan went on, ignoring his discomfiture. "Not been an easy time for her lately, has it? What with you out of work, and her Aunt dying." She sniffed eloquently. "And I don't expect either of those sisters are much use to her if she's upset – one won't say 'boo' to a goose, and the other with a face like a forty-shilling pot."

Despite his anxiety, Harry had to smile at his Nan's summary dismissal of his in-laws.

Nan smiled back. "Get Megan to come here, if you can. We'll see if your old Nan can have a chat with her – or at least let her know how worried you are. Now give me a pull up out of this chair, so I can see you out."

She huffed and puffed as Harry hauled her upright, then waddled down the narrow passageway to the door, her puffy feet overflowing the sides of her carpet slippers.

She watched him go, until he turned the corner of Lion Street. He hadn't mentioned any cough, so she hadn't liked to remind him that both Megan's parents had been consumptive.

She rubbed the palm of her hand briskly across her chest as she returned to the kitchen. That cake she'd shared with Harry was too fresh, she decided as she reached for the bicarbonate of soda to ease the sudden sharp indigestion that assailed her.

They were just getting ready for bed when they heard heavy footsteps on the stairs, followed by a frantic knocking on the door.

"Harry! Harry! Come quickly!" Uncle Joe's voice urged before Harry could unlock the door.

"What is it?" he asked, as Joe stumbled, breathless into the room.

"Our Mam! Been taken bad, she has, and wouldn't let me go for the doctor. I didn't know what to do! Said I'd fetch our Mary but she got in an even worse state, and she didn't want Fred, either, so I said I was coming for you, and she didn't mind that so much."

Harry was pulling on his trousers as Joe spoke while Megan fetched his shoes.

"You haven't left her on her own, have you?"

"Of course I haven't!" Joe sounded indignant, but Harry was never sure just how competent he was under pressure. "Mrs. Schofield from next door is with her. Lying on the couch, she is, in terrible pain. What shall we do?" Anxious child-like eyes beseeched his nephew, seventeen years his junior, to take care of the situation.

"You go for Doctor Freeman – never mind what Nan's been saying to you, and I'll go over to her."

He turned in the doorway. "You'll be alright?"

Megan nodded. "Unless you want me to come with you?"

"No. I'll be quicker on my own... perhaps later. I'll be back as soon as I can." He hurried down the stairs with Joe.

Megan prodded the fire back into life. No good going to bed till she knew what had happened and she might as well be warm while she waited.

As he ran across the town Harry was reminded of the evening which seemed such a long time ago now, when he'd run in the other direction because he thought that his Mam was going to die. He was filled with foreboding that those fears, this time for his Nan, who was well into her seventies, would be realised.

Mrs. Schofield, wearing a scarf tied around her head and a faded blue candlewick dressing gown, stood up as soon as Harry came in. "She's not good, Harry," she said, clutching the dressing gown modestly across a very flat chest. "I've given her a drop of brandy – always keep it in the house, for medicinal purposes – and it seemed to revive her a bit, but she's bad again now." She lowered her voice and mouthed: "I think it's her heart."

Harry nodded his understanding. "I've sent Joe for the doctor. Thanks for coming in, Mrs. Schofield."

He went over to his grandmother, and Mrs. Schofield, uncertain of what to do next, fell back on the old standby and went to fill the kettle.

Nan's eyes were closed, her breathing hard, and her lips were an eerie shade of purplish-blue. She opened her eyes as Harry took her hand.

"Hello, my lovely. Silly old woman aren't I, causing all this fuss?" Her words came in gasps and she gave a small grunt every time she exhaled.

"'Course you're not, Nan. Dr. Freeman will be here in a minute and he'll soon have you as right as rain."

She shook her head, slowly, deliberately, as if that effort alone was too much. "Not this time. Think this old body's a bit too worn out." She closed her eyes, but continued to keep a firm grip on his hand.

"Heart failure, I'm afraid," Dr. Freeman told Harry and Joe in the front room while Mrs. Schofield, with an air of satisfaction that her diagnosis had been correct, made Nan tidy after his examination. "I can give her some pills to ease the congestion a bit, which will make her more comfortable, but other than that…" He shook his head solemnly.

"Thank you Doctor," said Harry, seeing him out through the door as Joe's face began to crumple.

By midmorning most of the family were assembled in Nan's downstairs rooms, their words hushed and manner subdued as they kept her company while she died. No-one talked about Death; they kept their comments banal and comforting in their familiarity, but they all knew that the Reaper was visiting the house and would eventually claim his victim.

It was easier for the women who, when they weren't taking turns to sit with Nan, could busy themselves with endless tea-making and washing-up and could give each other a quick consoling hug in the back kitchen. The men simply sat in the front room, punctuating their smoking with isolated comments in a sort of verbal shorthand which they all understood.

Just before midday Harry's Mam came to find him. He was out in the back yard, unable to stay any longer within the house's gloomy confines.

"She's asking for you," Mam said. "I think she's failing… could you, you know… be there? Always were her best boy, after all." She gave a little wistful smile, acknowledging the part Nan had played in bringing up this youngest child.

"Of course I will," he replied, pity for his Mother's wan features welling up inside him, and realising with a shock that without Nan, his parents would be the oldest members of the family.

Bad things always come in threes' had been one of Nan's favourite sayings, and she was right, Harry thought, as he stood at her graveside whilst the minister intoned. First my job going, then Auntie Jane dying, and now Nan herself.

191

Not that he could equate the coffin now being lowered into the ground with Nan. Nan dying as he held her hand he could accept; she'd quite simply gone away, in front of him, within seconds of her last laboured breath. So there was no fear or even distress at the time, just an overwhelming awareness that she was no longer there, and a huge affection for the body that had contained her. But Nan inside this wooden box, being put into the ground, was completely unconvincing.

Distress came later, when the memories of his boyhood kept surfacing, all of them intertwined with Nan's loving presence, and the realisation that he could no longer seek her out. Irreverent memories assailed him now, of the Nan who wasn't above cuffing one of them round the ear, or carrying out her threat to sort them out with her wooden spoon.

There was the time when she'd allowed him to keep pet rabbits in her back yard. Eight at the time, he must have been. The rabbits were in a hutch, alongside which were some pipes that the council had left to be laid in the gully, but they'd never come back to do anything with them. Two of his uncles, returning from a day out a bit the worse for drink, had let the rabbits out, and they'd disappeared immediately inside the pipes. Pandemonium had quickly ensued, with the uncles making unsteady and unsatisfactory attempts to rescue the rabbits, while Harry stood in the entrance to the gully howling his head off.

"My rabbits! That's my bloody rabbits! They'll bloody die now and it'll be all your bloody fault!"

Nan had come bustling out. "Hisht Harry! Don't swear like that! Children mustn't swear!" Then she had turned on her sons, her anger rising as she saw the state they were in: "Will you two silly buggers hurry up and find those bloody rabbits, before I bang your bloody heads together!"

Harry smiled inwardly now at the memory of the sturdy little woman sorting out her big lumbering sons. At the other side of the grave was Joe, crying unashamedly for the mother who'd never allowed anyone to treat him with anything less than dignity. Beside him was Dai, who'd come down from London alone, with snapshots of the little girl and boy he now had.

Dai had talked to Harry in hushed undertones while they were waiting for the hearse to arrive. "Staying down for a few days, I am. Want to find somewhere for Bridget and the kids."

"Why? Are you leaving them?" For some reason Dai's presence irked Harry. He guessed that the smooth black overcoat that Dai was wearing had come from Aunt Brenda, and it gave an impression of prosperity that he knew to be false from the conversations he'd overheard between Mam and Nan. But that didn't seem to bother Dai, who'd arrived with the air of one who had generously found the time in a busy life to pay his respects to his grandmother.

"I'm joining up," he told Harry now. "The Air Force. Nobody seems to realise it down here, but sooner or later there's going to be another war – either Hitler or Mussolini will make sure of that, never mind all this trouble in Spain. Best to get in now, I reckon, while you can still choose what you want to do."

"But why the Air Force?"

Dai grinned. "Always fancied flying – all those *Biggles* stories, I expect! See a bit of the world, too." His face sobered again. "And if there is a war, that's where the action will be, mark my words."

"And Bridget? What does she think? Why bring her down here?"

"Because it will be too late if – or rather *when* – war breaks out, and London will be the last place to leave women and children. Better if they settle down here now." He looked at Harry thoughtfully for a moment. "Why don't you come with me? Nothing for you here, is there? And the pay's not bad."

Harry didn't want to admit that he wouldn't leave Megan, in the face of his brother's apparent indifference to being separated from his family.

"No thanks," he said. "Never fancied aeroplanes! I think I'll stick to finding something that keeps me firmly on the ground."

They were interrupted by Albert telling them that the hearse had arrived. Harry couldn't resist one small dig. "I expect Bridget'll find it hard down here, after the life she's used to in London."

He thought he saw a shadow flicker across Dai's face, but he avoided a straight answer. "Mam will be pleased, though, to have the rest of her grandchildren around her."

Which left Harry feeling that somehow his brother had won on points, as he always seemed to do.

The funeral over, the men returned to Nan's house for the tea, but Harry couldn't bear it; it was too much of a parody of the happy family gatherings at Christmas.

"I'm going out for a walk," he whispered to Megan, and she, seeing the misery in his eyes, had recognised his need to be alone.

B een looking for you everywhere!" Uncle Fred came up to the bar of the Rolling Mill, where Harry was trying to make half a bitter last a long time. "Got a job for you, if you're interested. Friend of mine on the Water Board says they need people to oversee the new pipes they're laying, over in Glamorgan. I've already told him about you, and he says he'll see what he can do. What do you think?"

"I think I'll have another beer! And one for you! That's the best news I've heard this year! How do I get hold of this friend?"

In the event, it didn't turn out to be office work after all – those jobs had been snapped up within hours of being made available. Instead, Harry found himself digging trenches to lay the pipes; harder physical work than he'd ever experienced.

"Look at this!" Megan cried at the end of the first week, holding his hands palm-upwards. "You've got blisters as big as acorns!"

"But at least there's a pay packet to go with them," he answered, wincing slightly as she bathed with disinfectant the blisters that had burst. He put his arms around her when she finished. "And think of the muscles I'll build up – regular Charles Atlas, I'll be!"

She smiled and was about to answer when suddenly she pulled herself out of his arms and began to cough. "Sorry!" she gasped. "Just a tickle …"

But the tickle went on and on, developing into a paroxysm that left her breathlessly slumped over the back of a chair.

"Megan?" His voice was as hoarse as if he too were afflicted.

Slowly straightening up, she turned towards him. Their eyes met. Each saw in the other the sure knowledge that Megan was becoming seriously ill, and that there was now a shadow over their future just as surely as there would be a shadow over Megan's lungs.

Just as with the first couple who stood before the Tree of Knowledge, the revelation brought despair and pain, the enormity of which they could not share for the moment, and in silent distress they turned away from each other.

The cold of the stone beneath him began to seep through his clothes. He really didn't want to remember the final years, but some remorseless demon within wouldn't let go.

It all flashed before him now: the endless visits to the doctors and hospital specialists who all shook their heads and recommended prolonged treatment at a sanatorium; the countless nights when Megan's temperature would rise, along with his terror at the prospect of losing her. But still, as her health had deteriorated, she had steadfastly refused to go away to some distant infirmary. Softhearted, pliable Megan, with a voice that soared like a dove but now was quieted because she hadn't the breath to use it, resisted every attempt to persuade her to accept the only treatment available.

"You know and I know that there's no guarantee it will work," she told Harry, "and I'm not going to spend all that time away from you, and then die miles away from everything and everyone that I love."

It was the only time she mentioned dying.

"Lots of fresh air, a healthy diet, that's about all we can offer," Doctor Freeman told him when Harry sought his advice, desperate to hear something that could give a glimmer of hope. "There's some work going on with new drugs," the doctor went on, "but it's going to be some time before we know whether they'll be of any use."

He hesitated, as if considering whether to say more, then looked steadily at Harry for a moment before deciding that he should. "Tuberculosis – it doesn't always just affect the chest, you know. It can attack other parts of the body as well – the kidneys, and the bones, for example…"

"Are you saying Megan has it – everywhere?"

Doctor Freeman patted his shoulder. "Sometimes it's the patient who knows better than anyone just how ill they are. If Megan doesn't want to be sent away, well… let's just say that it will probably be as well to go along with what she wants."

So Phyllis eventually got her own way, too, when they were forced to move back to Elgam Avenue because Megan could no longer manage the stairs. But it was a hollow victory for Phyllis, and one that, to her credit, she made no attempt to crow about. The hostility between herself and Harry was put aside, although not forgotten, so that a united front could be maintained before Megan.

Surprisingly, Bridget turned out to be one of the mainstays of Megan's life as she sank into invalidity. Dai hadn't been able to find anywhere for his family to live, so while he commenced his training they moved in with Albert and Mary, where Mary kept her lips firmly pressed together over her daughter-in-law's more slapdash ways, for the sake of her two little grandchildren.

Still slender despite two pregnancies, Bridget's blonde hair no longer ended in two pert kiss-curls but fell to her shoulders in glossy bouncing waves, slightly obliterating one eye. The face underneath, though, now had a pinched pallor indicative of lack of sunshine and good food, except for the rouged spots on each cheek. But despite her looks going, and despite her husband being away – or perhaps because of it, Harry thought – Bridget's personality bounced along with her hair.

She stepped in where those around Megan had feared to tread, sweeping her off to watch Walt Disney's *Snow White*, and encouraging her to sing the songs for the family afterwards, even though it took Megan's breath away – while she, a good mimic, imitated the American twang of the Dwarfs. Harry would sit and watch the two of them, Megan's eyes shining at her sister-in-law's tomfoolery and two hectic spots of colour appearing on her almost translucent cheeks, to rival Bridget's rouge. She looked, to him, spectacularly beautiful, and he would impress the image onto his mind. *This,* he would tell himself, *is how I must remember her!* – and then his chest would contract as he realised that he was already acclimatising himself to his eventual loss.

The pipe-laying work had ceased after a few months, but was replaced by a succession of other short-term jobs. It was easier, once in this sort of employment, to hear about anything else on the horizon, and as the country gradually woke up to the threat across the channel and reluctantly began to organise itself, the prospects for the unemployed began to improve.

There were often gaps between one job and another and then Harry would borrow Uncle Fred's car and drive Megan out over the Brecon Beacons, or to the coast. He would sit with her, chatting about this or that, or reading to one another, whilst he was ever watchful that she was taking in huge gulps of pure air – willing her to do so; refusing to accept that while this might assist her lungs to get rid of their terrible intruder, it would do little to rid the rest of her body of its pernicious effects.

Sometimes they went to the races at Chepstow. Megan would excitedly place money on the most outlandish horses, despite Harry's best advice, laughing when her horse won and Harry's more carefully considered nag didn't, and then she would tease him about his supposedly superior knowledge of horse-flesh. It would be impossible to believe, then, that the life was gradually being squeezed out of her – until she flagged on the way home, and the dreadful coughing would begin again.

And just as he'd been oblivious to the plight of those around him when he'd fallen in love with Megan, now the frightening events that were being played out as Europe prepared for war were nothing more than a distant rumble, a mere backdrop to the anguish as he watched her die.

The wind – he was sure it was the wind – was making his eyes water. He told himself it was time to go, that he should go back home and tell his mother that he was leaving, but the inertia of grief wrapped itself around him and kept him on the mountain, staring blankly at the vista below.

Sitting on the rock at the edge of the Keeper's, he fingered the papers in his pocket. The words at the beginning of *How Green Was My Valley* came back to him: *I am going to pack my two shirts... and I am going from the Valley.*

He'd bought the book as soon as it was published, and read it aloud to Megan during the last, terrible, debilitating weeks of her illness, and he'd known then that when she died he, too, would be going from the Valley.

He didn't see, now, how he could stay. How would he cope with all the memories, forever crowding in? Bad enough when she was too ill to go out and every step, every street he walked alone held a poignant reminder of days when she'd been well, and a warning that those days would probably be no more.

No, better to put them all away, bury them deep with Megan's thin wasted body, and go far away from the sight of everyone else getting on with their lives as if she'd never been.

God, how he hated funeral teas! The relief in people's eyes which they tried to hide, relief that 'it' was all over, and they could return to their own little concerns, away from the awkwardness and discomfort of loss and grief. The kindly neighbours who'd stayed behind to mind the kettles and prepare the food, pressing cups of tea into the women's hands, and something a little stronger for the men. Women casting a critical eye over the table to see how good a spread had been laid on, and men wondering how much they could tuck into without appearing too unseemly in their greed. All of them careful to keep their voices down and their demeanour sober, but forgetting from time to time when they recognised someone that they hadn't seen since the last funeral.

Harry had watched them all, gritty-eyed, from a corner of the room. Men had come up to him and shaken him by the hand and patted him on the shoulder, and female relatives had planted dry little kisses on his cheek, and then they'd all stood around tensely, wishing he would make it easier for them by saying something. In the end they'd turned with relief to Megan's sisters, who were weeping copiously on the sofa, which at least gave everyone the opportunity to mouth as many platitudes of comfort as they could think of.

When he could bear it no longer, Harry had slipped out through the back door and made his way up the mountain.

He heard his name being carried on the wind, and turned to see Bill coming toward him, but still he sat.

Bill said nothing until he was perched on the rock beside him, shoulders hunched as he passed him a lighted cigarette. "Told your Mam that you were probably up on the Keeper's – remembered that you came up here before; after Nan died."

Inhaling deeply, Harry nodded his head but didn't speak.

Bill glanced around, as if he hadn't walked these same paths a hundred times before, drawing on his own cigarette. "Good place to come," he said, staring out across the mountain-top. "The sort of place you can howl your head off if you want to." He looked sideways at Harry, but he too was concentrating on the mountain.

"I'm joining up," Harry said at last, into the silence. He rummaged in his pocket and handed Bill the papers. "Royal Corps of Signals. I leave tomorrow."

Bill shuffled through the papers as if reading them, but really having no idea of what they said. He wanted to comfort this young man whom he'd always regarded as a younger brother, but words failed him. He'd tried to imagine what it would be like to lose Maisie, without even the burden – or comfort – of a child (depending on how you looked at it) to keep you going, but his mind baulked at the prospect. He could understand Harry's desire to leave it all behind.

"Come on then," he said at last. "Let's go home, and I'll help you pack."

16

Jennie - 1940

The air made the skin on her face tingle as she opened the door of the milking shed, and all around the early morning sun sparkled on the mounds of snow overlaid with yet another heavy layer of frost. There was an unreal feeling to this morning, although so far it had been the same as any other except that she and Father had risen even earlier to get the milking done. The unreality was largely in thinking of what was ahead and the knowledge that the next time she did the milking she would be Mrs. Charles Keating.

Mrs. Charles Keating! She sank down onto a milking stool and savoured the sound of the words.

No-one had been more surprised than she when, after the weekend spent with Laura and Cyril, and that first date, Charles had begun to court her in a serious fashion.

As war was declared and everyone waited for the next few months to see what Hitler intended to do, world events were inextricably linked with the equally dramatic events which were unfolding in her own life. Listening to news broadcasts on the wireless, grappling with the blackout, and coping with the avalanche of dictums arriving from the Ministry of Agriculture, were all intertwined with the feel of Charles's arms around her, and his kisses – often so lingering and urgent that they took her breath away and made her aware of bodily urges of which she'd hitherto had no knowledge.

She'd thought that once war had been declared he'd be sent off to dim and distant parts, but he had stayed throughout the autumn and early winter, turning up at the farm whenever he could and whisking her off to dances at Little Mill or Crickhowell – and, once, to a supper party with his Air Force friends at Brecon, where she'd felt incredibly young and naive. At the dances, though, she'd been proud to walk in on Charles's arm, aware that other girls noticed his sophisticated air and good looks which made the local lads seem callow youths by comparison. Charles would whirl her around the floor, whispering comments in her ear which would make her laugh, or sometimes blush, until she felt drunk with happiness.

Catching sight of herself in a mirror in the Ladies' Room on one such occasion, she suddenly realised that happiness could actually make her look quite pretty.

As she relaxed more in his company she found him increasingly easy to talk to. Confiding her dreams to him, he listened with grave attention, yet with none of the condescension she'd sensed previously. And then he'd taken her dreams and elaborated upon them, painting pictures for her of spots to visit, sights to be seen; telling her of places he'd been to and helping her to realise that there was so much more of the world to be experienced outside this small corner of South Wales.

"Wait until we get this war sorted out," he said. "Then we can really begin to live."

Which had been the first indication that he was considering their relationship in a long-term way.

It was only when she ventured onto the subject of families that he became reserved. "It must have been awful losing your father in the war and then losing your mother as well," she said. "Were their deaths quite close together?"

"No-oo. My mother survived for a little while on her own. But she never really got over my father going."

Jennie would have liked to have asked more about his mother, but his face had taken on a remote expression and he quickly changed the subject.

He hadn't seemed to like it much, either, when Jennie tried to tell him of the difficulties with her own mother, although he couldn't have failed to notice the antipathy between them by now...

"All finished?" Father poked his head around the thick curtain that hung inside the door of the milking shed. Jennie nodded, and they walked companionably across the yard to the house.

"Mrs. Davies is upstairs helping with the baby," Gwyneth told them confidingly, "so I made a start and took them something up." As she placed the tea-pot on the table she gave Jennie a broad wink which said: *If you eat up quickly you'll get a bit of peace!*

Jennie smiled back conspiratorially. Much as she loved babies, she couldn't bear to spend another breakfast time listening to how fractious little Selina had been during the night and how done in by motherhood Laura was.

"You ought to be having yours upstairs, today of all days," Father said now as they sat down. "Doesn't seem right, you getting up to milk cows on your wedding day."

Her smile spread wider to include him. *"Don't you know there's a war on?"* Her mimicry of Mother's voice was so accurate that he gave a throaty chuckle. It was currently Mother's favourite phrase, used whenever she was intent on bending the will of those around her to do her bidding.

Mother hadn't been shamming after all when she'd told Hetty Lloyd that her house would soon be too full to take evacuees – or had she deliberately filled it to make sure that Miss Lloyd no longer bothered her? You could never be sure of Mother's motives. Nevertheless, Laura was duly installed prior to her confinement, a difficult one which had seemed to give Mother a sort of grim satisfaction and plenty of opportunity to point out that men really had no idea of what women had to cope with. Jennie had already heard her tell Laura that she ought to see Dr. Moxom, so it looked as though Selina was destined to be an only child if Mother had her way – as she usually did.

Then Gwyneth had been installed as a full-time maid, occupying the smallest bedroom at the back of the house. Mother didn't like her name because it was too Welsh, but there was little she could find fault with in the girl's work. Despite Mother's efforts Gwyneth remained relentlessly cheerful, accepting all the jobs she was given with a "Right-oh, Mrs. Davies!" – in sing-song tones and often besting Mother by adding another job to the list herself. "Might as well while I'm about it, hadn't I?" she'd say with a smile, before Mother had the chance to reply.

Jennie was filled with a mixture of intense happiness, excitement and apprehension that was doing strange things to the pit of her stomach. Her wedding was to be such a simple affair that she'd given the event itself minimal attention; instead, her thoughts were constantly straying to afterwards. She was passionately in love with Charles, but would her passion be sufficient for such an experienced man? She wondered if she would know instinctively what to do, how to respond – or was it something one had to learn?

If Emily had been here she could have asked her, but with one small boy and being pregnant again, it had been decided that a journey in such bad weather was not advisable. The sense of unreality returned to Jennie; her wedding day was to be so completely unlike that of either of her sisters, she wouldn't have been surprised if someone had shaken her and told her it was all merely a fantasy.

She caught Father watching her over the rim of his tea-cup.

"Nervous?" he asked.

"A bit. No – very!" she admitted. A slight blush spread over her cheeks. "I somehow don't seem grown up enough to be a married woman!"

He smiled at her pretty, open face and inwardly agreed with her. How had the years passed so quickly that now this youngest child of theirs – the 'afterthought' whose arrival had caused such ructions and signalled the end of any true relationship between himself and Katharine – was about to be married?

"As long as you're sure? You could always wait until the next time Charles has leave, you know."

She thought for a moment of all the things she felt *un*sure about. How did one know that this was really *it*, for instance? She would have liked to explain that sometimes, when Charles's eyes changed from cornflower to ice and she didn't know why, she was scared it may all go wrong. That her emotions veered from apprehension when she couldn't fathom his mood, to stomach-churning unadulterated joy when he smiled his special smile at her and held her in his arms. *Was that what every girl felt?* she wondered. *Was that love enough to last a lifetime?*

But she couldn't say anything of this to Father, dear though he was. Those weren't the sort of things talked about in this household, especially not at seven-thirty in the morning and with Gwyneth flitting in and out.

"Oh, I'm sure!" she answered, her voice unwavering. "About loving Charles and wanting to be his wife – besides, we don't know, do we, any of us, what's going to happen over the next months. There might not be another time."

She was unaware that she was echoing the words Charles had used when he'd urged her to marry him quickly, before he was sent away.

He'd arrived at the farm one afternoon in January, when the sky was heavy with snow, the dark clouds obliterating the tops of the mountains. Jennie hadn't known he was coming and flew into the kitchen when she saw his car, to find him and Mother sitting in an uncomfortable silence.

"Could have cut the atmosphere with a knife!" Gwyneth told her family on her next day off. "I never thought Mrs. Davies would agree to them getting married. Don't think she likes him one little bit."

Mother left the room as soon as Jennie entered it, and it had been then that Charles told her he was to be posted away in three weeks' time. "Only to Yorkshire at first," he said, "so I won't get any special leave, and after that, who knows? We chaps who aren't actually flying could be sent all over the place. But I will have a weekend off first, and I think we should be married – then – before I go away."

The words came out in a rush, in the ardent tones of a man deeply in love, and that Jennie savoured every time she re-played the scene as she went about her chores. She'd needed little persuading.

Father's reservations about the gap in their ages had been dispelled by the radiance of Jennie's expression as she hung on Charles's arm, and Laura, full of post-natal emotion, had gone into raptures about the romance of a wedding before the couple were to be parted – 'for how long, no-one knew'. Only Mother had said little, an unusual enough feature in itself, and for a fleeting instant Jennie had wondered if her mother was jealous. Then she'd laughed at herself. Mother seemed to have little time for men these days, and if she seemed cool and uninterested in the hasty wedding preparations, then where Jennie was concerned that tended to be her normal reaction. The only real interest she'd shown had been in the choosing of the venue.

"I think we should just have a quiet wedding here in Goytre," Jennie had said.

"Don't be so ridiculous!" Mother exclaimed. "The church is too small, and there's nowhere half-decent for a reception. Abergavenny will be much better." Jennie had thought that for once Mother was trying to ensure that she had the same as her two sisters, but Mother's next comments quelled that. "Besides," she said, "even if there is a war going on, people will think you've got something to hide if you have some pokey hole-and-corner affair." And she fixed Jennie with a steely stare, as if she almost suspected it herself.

Jennie had carefully broached the subject of families again with Charles when trying to put together a hasty guest list. "Is there anyone we can invite from your side who would be likely to get here at this time of year?"

"Nobody at all, whatever the season, I'm afraid," he'd answered quite cheerfully. "Only child of only children, so there are no aunts, maiden or otherwise, uncles, or cousins we need to be polite to for the day!"

"What about friends?"

"Oh, I'll ask a few chaps from the Squadron to come along to fill up my side of the church." He'd taken the notepad and pencil from her then, and pulled her towards him. "I'm sure they'll all want to come along to see what a wonderful girl I'm marrying." And then he began to kiss her, so that she forgot to ask about any friends he may have had before he joined up.

It was after midday and everyone else was ready, but still Katharine lingered in front of the cheval mirror in her room. It had been snowing again during the morning, and Edward was concerned that they leave in plenty of time to reach St. Mary's in Abergavenny.

Katharine gazed sombrely at her reflection and wondered how she could bear to go through with the rest of the day. The past six months had been agony for her whenever Charles came to the house, and Jennie's cheerful face had filled her with anguish and guilt which twisted itself around in her mind, at times convincing her that this situation was only as it was because Jennie had been such a willing victim to Charles's charms. It was Jennie's fault therefore that Charles continued to be a part of their lives, continued to pierce the armour that she, Katharine, had carefully constructed around herself. If Jennie hadn't thrown herself at him, he would no longer be around! ... At times her feelings ran so high towards her daughter that she could barely bring herself to talk to the girl.

But in the dark reaches of the night, Charles's words would return to haunt her: *You'll spend a long time regretting that you turned me away!* - and then she couldn't hide from the knowledge that Jennie was merely a pawn in his game, a dupe to ensure that Katharine suffered.

She'd tried, once, to talk to him, to let him know that he'd won. They'd been alone together in the kitchen, a situation which she'd avoided up until then. But on this day Gwyneth, having made them some tea, had taken one look at their stony faces and fled upstairs, deciding that turning out the linen cupboard was preferable to the atmosphere in the kitchen, which was even icier than outside.

"There's no need for this," Katharine said as soon as Gwyneth left the room. "Why can't you just accept that we both behaved foolishly and find other distractions somewhere else?"

The smile he'd turned upon her hadn't reached his eyes. "Perhaps I've already found a *better* distraction right here."

She opened her mouth to argue with him, but closed it again. To call him a liar could invite unwelcome comments of how much more attractive he found her daughter than herself, and, true or not, she couldn't bear to hear them.

He had leaned back in his chair, seemingly relaxed, but his eyes glittered dangerously, and try as she might she couldn't hate him.

At that moment Jennie had burst in through the door, her face alight and her dark hair bouncing on her shoulders.

"Hello! When did you get here? I didn't expect to see you again so soon!"

"Can't keep away. You should know that by now!" He leapt up to greet her, brushing aside her protests that she smelled of the farm-yard.

Katharine could stand it no longer and had left the room to take out her feelings on the hapless Gwyneth, but it was no surprise to her when later that evening Jennie announced that Charles had asked her to marry him.

She continued to stare now at the troubled eyes that looked back at her in the mirror and wondered for the thousandth time what she should do. There was still time – just – to put a stop to all this. She could go downstairs now and tell Jennie everything – explain exactly why Charles was pressing for this marriage, which would wipe the silly smile off the girl's face once and for all.

And if you do that, what then? Will you even be believed, or seen as a jealous, vindictive, middle-aged woman who can't bear to see her youngest daughter marry a handsome man?

For Charles had done his work well. His displays of affection towards Jennie in front of the family were completely convincing, and he'd developed a flattering interest in farming matters which made Edward regard him with approval.

If she were to tell all to the family, couched in terms indicating that Charles had made unwelcome advances to her which she'd spurned, there was no doubt in her mind that Charles would retaliate with claims of how she'd led him on – and how would she appear to them all then?

Her pride lifted her chin in the mirror. She couldn't run that risk, and see the framework of an upright God-fearing woman, which she'd spent so many years constructing to compensate for her earlier failings of the flesh, be irreparably broken.

She sighed, shrugged herself into her coat, and wrapped a stony-eyed fox fur around her shoulders. What couldn't be altered must be endured. At least after tomorrow Charles would be going away, perhaps for a long time. Perhaps – to her everlasting shame, she uttered a heartfelt prayer – perhaps he wouldn't come back. He'd already intimated to Edward that once Hitler had been despatched he'd like to settle down to a farming life, and Katharine knew that were it to happen, she would never know a minute's peace.

It was a strange quartet which set off for the church. Father gave all his concentration to the icy roads, while Mother's stern expression was more fitting for a funeral. Jennie, despite being the bride, sat in the back of the little Ford that Father now drove for family outings, beside a fidgety Laura. Having left baby Selina, for the first time ever, with Gwyneth, she was ashamed of feeling relieved to be free of her maternal duties, and compensated by fretting all the more about whether Gwyneth would take care of the baby properly.

"For goodness' sake, that girl knows far more about babies than you do!" said Mother sharply, Laura's repeated 'I hope she'll be alright' exasperating Katharine sufficiently to stick up for Gwyneth for once. Laura subsided into her seat and began to think of how she was missing Cyril, instead. He'd been given leave when Selina was born, but had been unable to make the journey home again for this wedding.

For the first time, Jennie experienced a sense of foreboding, and the feeling of unreality intensified. Surely her wedding day deserved more of an air of festivity than this? She began to worry again about her appearance. Laura's wedding dress had been hastily altered to fit her by a very competent dressmaker from Abergavenny, but even she couldn't disguise the fact that the basic design of the dress was for someone considerably more buxom than Jennie, and unrelieved white had never done much for her naturally pale complexion. She'd fixed her hair into a rather slippery bun under the yards of net veil and was sure now that it would gradually fall undone as she made her vows. There'd been no-one there to help her with it – Laura had been busy giving Selina a last feed, and Mother had shut herself away in her room for hours, getting herself ready.

Only Father had been there when she descended the stairs, and at the time his expression of pride and admiration had more than made up for everyone else's indifference.

"You look beautiful," he said, and she'd known that in his eyes she was. She only hoped Charles would think the same.

Gwyneth emerged from the kitchen then, and tutted and exclaimed enough for three people. "Like Snow White, you look, with your dark hair – off to marry your prince!" And she'd thrust a lucky silver horseshoe into Jennie's hand. Jennie was carrying it now, along with her prayer book, in place of a bouquet.

The recent snowfalls had clothed and re-clothed the countryside in white, and even the main road had deep drifts of snow on it. There was an eerie stillness and quiet about everything, the white landscape merging with the dull grey of a laden sky, blurring the horizon. In the town, puny shop boys had been despatched with spades that overpowered them to clear the snow from the pavements, making huge mounds on the roadside. In places it was impossible to see where the pavement ended and the road began, so the few people who were about walked wherever they could, their feet making no noise in the snow.

They were able to park the car very close to the church gates, and thankfully the path had been cleared of snow. Tom and Nancy were waiting for them in the church porch, Nancy wearing a bold tartan suit, impossibly high heels despite the awful weather, and bright red lipstick. Through the door of the church came the strains of the organ.

Nancy grinned at Jennie. "Why so solemn? Haven't changed your mind, I hope, because he's in there –" she tipped her head towards the closed door – "looking incredibly handsome, and the chap he's got with him as best man is quite a dish too!"

Out of the corner of her eye Jennie saw Mother wince at Nancy's turn of phrase. Nancy noticed too, but it only made her grin all the more. "Besides," she added, "I've brought you these!" And with a magician's flourish she produced a posy of Christmas roses and snowdrops. "We found the snowdrops when Tom was clearing some of the snow from outside the back door, so I brought them in a few days ago, to make sure the flowers bloomed in time."

"Oh, Nancy! They're beautiful! Thank you so much!"

Touched by Nancy's thoughtfulness, the see-saw of Jennie's emotions rose again. It *would* be alright; she'd make sure it was. She was going to be the best wife a man ever had, and once this war was over she and Charles would settle down on the farm together, and doubtless they would eventually take it over when Father became too old. It was all she'd ever wanted or dreamed of, and she was only moments away from the first steps towards making it happen.

She heard her own voice – firm and resolute, despite the freezing cold of the church – making her responses, gaining confidence from the smile Charles gave her as she stood beside him, watched by her family and the small huddle of friends who'd managed to make it to the church. Then they were in the vestry signing the register, Jennie's hand wobbling slightly from excitement and cold. It didn't even seem to matter when Charles told her apologetically that they would be unable to proceed to Singleton's, the photographer's, after the church because snow had brought the roof of the studio down. Instead they went straight to Cushing's Tea Rooms, where a surprisingly good wedding breakfast had been laid on. There was a piano in the corner, which, once everyone had finished eating, Aunt Eunice had pounced on.

"Come on, everyone!" she cried. "This is a wedding, not a funeral!" and she began to pound out familiar songs, while Nancy organised the men to push the tables back so there was a bit of room for dancing. Between them, Aunt Eunice and Nancy infected everyone with a sense of fun and abandon, so that even Laura forgot she was now a young matron and positively flirted with Charles's best man.

There was a moment when Jennie stood alone, the music temporarily halted while Aunt Eunice had a drink and recovered from her exertions, and everyone else was milling about and chatting in small groups. Across the room, Charles had been cornered by Uncle Frank.

"I don't know how the War-Ag expects us to keep up with their demands when we've got all this bad weather," Uncle Frank was grumbling in ponderous fashion. "They make no allowances for the difficulties a bad winter brings."

Jennie watched them for a few moments, admiring Charles's profile and the shape of his lean body as he bent forward slightly towards the older, shorter man. As if he knew she was watching them, he looked up, met her eyes, and smiled; a conspiratorial smile that linked the two of them – and at that moment Jennie experienced a thrill of pure love and happiness. No matter that her wedding was nothing like the grander affairs of Laura's and Emily's. No matter that her mother had hardly spoken two words to her since the day began, or that there would be no photographs placed in a beautifully bound album for her to sigh over when Charles was away, as Laura frequently did over hers. She was a married woman now, one step removed from Mother's overbearing authority, and married to a man who was surely the answer to every girl's prayer.

A cold blast swept through the kitchen as Edward went out to do his final check around the farm. Charles stayed near the warmth of the range and lit a cigarette. "Perhaps you'd like to go on up?" he'd whispered to Jennie a few minutes earlier. She'd smiled at him gratefully. "I think I will." Murmuring a goodnight to her parents, and planting a whisper of a kiss on her father's cheek, she'd left the room.

It had been a good day, Charles reflected. Jennie had been a pretty little slip of a thing in that dress which looked a shade too large for her, and he'd been filled with a feeling of well-being at the good wishes which had surrounded them. He congratulated himself that it had all turned out very well after all.

Marriage to Jennie had never been part of his plan, initially. Seeing her as simply the means to retaliate against Katharine, he'd used her shamelessly during those first few months, revelling in the discomfiture his demonstrations of affection towards her had produced in her mother. But gradually his feelings towards her had changed. He began to like the adoration which glowed from her eyes, and the freshness of her in his arms. He'd never had any sort of relationship with a young girl before and he found it excited him in a way he hadn't thought possible. And under his spell, Jennie was blossoming into a very attractive young woman.

So, as the months passed, his plans changed imperceptibly. He began to see that marriage into this family was going to be far more beneficial than a relationship with Katharine would have been, and the idea of possessing Jennie's virginal body more than a substitute for the excitement of an affair. It also had the added bonus that if he played his cards carefully he could be set up for life. It was obvious that Tom was not going to return to the family fold sufficiently to take over the farm, and the life of a gentleman farmer held much appeal. After this war, which was really a dreadful inconvenience to his plans, he would set about making himself indispensable, and the farm sufficiently prosperous, that he could live the life of a gentleman to which he was sure he'd been born.

He stubbed out his cigarette with a small smile of satisfaction and thought of Jennie, upstairs waiting for him, and the gentle seduction scene he would soon be playing out. Perhaps he should give her a few more minutes. In the meantime, he could check the downstairs rooms, as he knew Edward always did before retiring, and savour the knowledge that from now on this would be his home.

He didn't realise Katharine was in the parlour until he stepped into the room to damp down the fire. She was sitting in an armchair, completely motionless, the only light in the room coming from the fire and a lamp in the corner.

"I'm sorry – I didn't know you were in here. I thought you'd followed Jennie upstairs…"

She said nothing, but simply turned her head towards him. She was sitting very upright, the soft wool of her dress moulded to her body beneath small pintucks at the shoulders, so that the fullness of her breasts was emphasised. The kindness of the lamplight shadowed her face, so that she could have been any age. Regal and outwardly composed, he knew that if he looked into her eyes he would see a turmoil of thwarted desire.

He remembered the feel of her on that one occasion that he'd held her close, and felt his body stir. He remembered the excitement of the imminent conquest that he'd been so sure of. With growing horror he realised that he wanted her still – now – far more urgently than he wanted her daughter lying upstairs waiting for him.

Hating himself he muttered something about locking up for Edward and turned to go.

Katharine couldn't drag her eyes away from him. Very soon he would be in bed with Jennie, holding her tightly, loving her. Would he kiss the cleft of her breasts, the way he had her own last summer? The thought sent waves of longing through her body and she pressed her thighs down very tightly against the chair.

More than anything she wanted to stop him climbing the stairs, and the words came out almost before she knew it.

"You're not the first, you know."

He was in the doorway when she spoke. The words hung in the air between them, but he didn't turn round.

She ran her tongue around lips that were suddenly dry. "Why do you suppose she spent so many weekends at Monmouth last year? It wasn't Laura she was with all the time – it was Cyril."

He remained motionless for some time. The silence between them was broken only by the ticking of the grandfather clock in the hall. He wanted to turn around and stride towards her and shake her until she told him she was lying, but he was afraid that if he caught hold of her, or confronted her in any way, he would betray Jennie in just the way Katharine was suggesting Jennie had already betrayed him.

He heard the kitchen door open. Edward had returned. Without another word Charles crossed the hall and began to climb the stairs. He paused outside the bedroom door, and then headed for the bathroom. He couldn't go to Jennie until he had sorted some of this out in his own mind.

Katharine was lying; of course she was! It was just another move in the game they'd been playing over the last six months. But even as he tried to convince himself of this, his mind flashed up the picture of Cyril kissing Jennie on the doorstep of the house at Monmouth. He'd thought at the time it was simply a brotherly kiss, but now in his mind's eye he saw Jennie's body lean eagerly towards her brother-in-law. They'd spent the afternoon together – was it a kiss of gratitude for what had already passed between them?

Jennie's increasing attraction for him had been her fresh youth, her air of inexperience and guilelessness. For once in his life he was going to have something that was unspoilt, unsullied, and this had brought out a tenderness in his nature that he hadn't been aware he possessed. But now a seed of doubt had been planted in his mind, and, for the second time in a few months it seemed, he was going to be denied that which he had set his mind, if not his heart, upon.

Used to making calculated decisions, he tried desperately now to decide what to do. His first instinct was to walk away from it all, rather in the manner of a small child who throws down his favourite toy because it is scratched, and thus damages it further. But, Charles reminded himself, Jennie was now his wife. *His wife!* It wouldn't be as easy to walk away from this situation as it had been to walk away from Sylvia, and many others before her. And then there were the rest of his plans; should he jeopardise those because a jealous woman had tried to spoil everything for him?

Contradictory thoughts chased each other round his head, until finally he decided that he must ignore Katharine's bitter words. He would go to Jennie now, and love her as gently as he could, and deny Katharine the satisfaction of having ruined his wedding night.

He half hoped, as he entered the bedroom, that she'd have fallen asleep, but she was propped up in the big old double bed which had been installed in her room, wearing a nightgown of finest lawn which showed the slope of her young shoulders, her dark hair forming a halo around her face.

"Hello," she said carefully.

He forced a smile. "Do you mind if I draw the curtains back?" he asked. She nodded, so he moved across the room, pulling the curtains open until a wintry moon could be glimpsed in a clear sky.

"I think we're in for another heavy frost," he said, as he sat on the end of the bed with his back to her and began to undress. Part of him could almost laugh at how unromantic he sounded.

When he was ready he climbed in beside her and pulled the cord above their heads which switched off the central light, but the room was still bathed in soft light from the moon.

Carefully he folded his arms around her. "You looked very beautiful today. I don't think I've had time to tell you that yet."

He saw her smile in the light from the window. "I kept worrying at first that my hair was going to fall down or something else would go wrong, but once I was with you in the church everything felt alright."

He began to kiss her, feeling the softness of her hair and the smoothness of her skin. He moved closer to her, running his hands with practised ease over her body. He felt her shiver and immediately doubts assailed him – was it the nervous tremble of a virgin, or the anticipatory response of an experienced woman? As his hand stroked her thigh, images of Katharine crept into his mind, refusing to go away, until he didn't know to whose body he was responding. He kept his eyes tightly shut, willing himself to concentrate on the young girl beside him, but it was Katharine's face he saw, and now his mother and grandmother were there, swirling around his brain, smothering him with their smiling encouragement; then Katharine again, her hair tumbling tantalisingly down her back, her mouth twisted into a provocative knowing smile.

You're not the first, you know.

All desire left him. He stopped kissing Jennie and moved his body slightly away from her. She became very still.

"Charles?" She moved her hand up to caress his hair, but was stopped by an imperceptible movement of his head. She glanced up at him and saw his face, stern and forbidding. At once she was the plain, gauche girl she'd felt herself to be when first they'd met at Laura's wedding.

"We're both very tired tonight." he said at last. "Perhaps we should go to sleep."

He waited for a moment, but she didn't reply. Dropping a chaste kiss onto her forehead, he turned away from her onto his side.

Jennie lay watching the moon. She'd thought it romantic a few minutes earlier, but now it seemed cold and hostile – a barren planet casting its eerie light on a world that suddenly Jennie could make no sense of.

She had no idea what to do. She'd more or less known what to expect on her wedding night – a lifetime spent on a farm, Emily's glowing recommendations of married life, and even Laura's coy ones, had all convinced her that every bridegroom was supposed to be eager and ardent. What had gone wrong? What had made Charles end a day that had seemed to her to be filled with love and good cheer in such an abrupt manner? Was it something she'd done, or not done? Something that no-one had thought to prepare her for?

She kept her body very still. To move might disturb Charles and make him turn towards her with explanations that she wasn't sure she wanted to hear; neither did she have the confidence to snuggle up to him and try to tempt him again with her womanly wiles ... And as the long minutes of the night stretched into sleepless hours, she became convinced that she possessed no womanly wiles. Both her father and Charles himself had told her that she looked beautiful today, but obviously beauty and desirability were two completely different things.

Her Mother's words, buried for years in the deep recesses of her mind, dormant but not destroyed, ready to flourish again at the least encouragement, came bursting to the surface. *You were never wanted! It was a mistake!*

Over the years she'd tried hard to convince herself that her mother was simply prey to strange passions; had invented all sorts of excuses for her behaviour whenever it threatened to remind Jennie of the vehemence of those words – but now she realised that they were true. She hadn't been wanted; certainly not by her mother, and perhaps even her father had only grown to love her as you do a stray animal if it lingers around for long enough – affection mixed with a kind of pity that makes you nicer to it than you had intended.

And now Charles didn't want her. Not as a woman, anyway.

Another mistake. Mother must have been right.

Ithought you were going to have today off?" Father smiled at her as she squeezed round the milking shed curtain. The shed, with its windows blacked out and lit only by oil lamps, so that it was perpetually night-time within, was bathed in a cosy glow.

She made herself smile back. "I was awake. Force of habit I suppose. So I thought I'd come and give you a hand, and then perhaps we can all take it a bit easier today."

Edward opened his mouth to say she looked tired, but hastily realised what a tactless remark that would be. Instead he said, "Is Charles aw—?"

"He's still asleep," Jennie said quickly. "I slipped out without disturbing him. I don't think even in the Air Force they're used to quite such early hours."

She fetched a stool and moved away to start milking at the other end of the shed. It was comforting to lean her head against the warm flank of the cow, comforting to be back in her old worn trousers and jersey, to go through the same routine as yesterday morning and the one before and the one before that, making it almost possible to blot out, for a while at least, that she was now a married woman in every sense but the true one.

She wondered how they'd be with each other for the rest of the day. Should she try to talk to Charles, ask him what had been the matter? On the other hand, she reasoned, perhaps he genuinely had felt tired, or had been thinking purely of her. Perhaps her calm acceptance of his lovemaking advances had sent out completely the wrong signals.

She only hoped that they could get through the day together without either of her parents, and in particular Mother, realising that anything was wrong.

In the event it seemed that she needn't have worried about that, at least. When she and Father went into the kitchen, Charles was already downstairs, dressed in casual trousers, checked shirt and pullover, with a lock of his ungreased hair flopping forward over his brow in a most endearing fashion.

"Hello, you two! Thought I'd get breakfast going, after you've nobly been up and about so early. Porridge coming up in a minute!"

He smiled at Jennie, the same warm, intimate smile that she was used to, confusing her so much that for a moment she wondered if last night had never happened – or, as she knew it had, whether she was the only one to think it had been unusual.

It was Gwyneth's day off, but she'd been unable to trek to her home through the snow, so was wisely keeping to her room. Rather a pity in one way, Jennie thought. She would have liked Gwyneth to have seen Charles deftly coping with the range and producing breakfast with a flourish, either unaware of or ignoring all Mother's edicts about how her kitchen should be run, so that she and Laura arrived downstairs simultaneously to find the three of them tucking in to poached eggs.

"Good morning!" Charles exclaimed, jumping up from his seat. "How would you like your eggs, poached or scrambled?"

Mother's voice was icy. "We don't usually eat breakfast before church on Sundays."

"I don't think church is going to be possible this morning," he replied, in the same cheerful tone. "Have you seen how bad it is out there?"

"Charles is right," said Edward, passing his tea-cup to Jennie for a re-fill. "It's been snowing again since we got up, and I don't think it's going to stop for a while. The only way we'll get to church this morning is to go on the tractor."

Jennie caught the ghost of a wink, and despite her low spirits couldn't resist a smile at the picture of Mother perched on top of the trailer. Katharine, however, chose to ignore her husband and moved to cut herself some very thin slices of bread at the side table.

And so the day progressed. Charles spent much of it outside helping Edward clear some of the snow, so that either by accident or design there was little time for the newly-weds to spend alone. When they were with the rest of the family Charles's good humour presented a picture of a contented newly-wed man, and infected them all with a sense of bonhomie. He was just as affectionate towards Jennie as he'd always been, so as the day wore on she too felt lulled by his charm, and managed to convince herself that the problem had been nowhere near as big as she'd thought it to be. Charles was obviously determined to put their wedding night behind them, and she would do the same.

That night they entered the bedroom together, and before she could make any sort of move Charles was beside her.

"Not much of a start to married life, is it? Snowed in with your family all around us, and not even a single night's honeymoon!"

He was looking at her so tenderly that she was sure this was his way of explaining the previous night. She wanted him to know that she understood. "It doesn't matter. I thought my wedding day was the most perfect day of my life."

He kissed her then, long and lingeringly, and she pressed her body close to his.

"I'm going to miss you so much when you leave tomorrow," she murmured.

But he seemed not to have heard her. He was intent on unbuttoning her blouse, which he then slipped down over her shoulders, taking the straps of her slip with it. He kissed her again, more fiercely this time, and then she was being carried to the bed, and the rest of her clothes removed with a passionate haste. She made to remove his also, but he brushed her hands aside and tore them off himself. Then he was on top of her, the weight of his body taking her breath away, muttering: 'Jennie, Jennie, Jennie!' in her ear, and it seemed that every part of his body was assaulting hers until, with a spasm of pain that made her cry out, their marriage was rapidly, brutally, consummated.

Afterwards he held her in his arms, kissing her gently, stroking her skin, soothing her, until eventually the soreness of her body eased and she drifted off to sleep.

She was unaware of Charles carefully extricating his arm and moving across to his side of the bed.

There! I think that's everything! I'll leave it for you to lug down the stairs."

In an attempt to stave off the anxiety of when she might see him again, Jennie had carried out the wifely duty of packing Charles's case for him. He turned from adjusting his tie in the mirror. "Thank you."

"My pleasure. Except it isn't really a pleasure because I don't want you to go away!"

She crossed the bedroom to him and reached up to kiss the side of his face, smooth from its recent shave and smelling of the expensive men's cologne he used, which Jennie thought terribly sophisticated – the men in her family using nothing more than good old soap and water.

Despite her sadness at his imminent departure there was a small well of happiness inside Jennie, and she felt a growing confidence. Admittedly last night's physical encounter hadn't been quite what she had been expecting, but she supposed the first time for every woman must be painful, considering how one's body was being invaded. What she recalled now was Charles's urgency, the demanding way his body took control of hers, which must mean that she was desirable, after all. And perhaps next time, whenever that may be, she would learn how to respond so that it would become as enjoyable as Emily evidently found it.

She snuggled against Charles's body now, her arms round his waist. He dropped a kiss on the top of her head. "We really should be going if I'm going to catch that train."

She nodded. "I'll go and start the tractor while you say your goodbyes."

The snow was too deep to walk across the ten-acre field to Nanty-derry Halt, and it seemed the only way was to go by road on the tractor. But at least that meant that Jennie could see him off alone, being able to drive the tractor but not, as yet, having mastered a car.

She stood beside him on the platform, a thick coat worn over two jumpers giving shapeless bulk to her slender frame, and a bright red scarf wound round her neck. The sky had cleared to a brilliant winter blue, but despite the sun's rays bouncing off the snow it was still dreadfully cold, making Jennie bang her gloved hands together and hop up and down on the platform to bring life back into her frozen feet.

She looked, Charles thought, ridiculously young.

She noticed his thoughtful expression and stood still. "Don't the mountains look wonderful? They seem so near today. I used to talk to them when I was little, especially the Sugar Loaf. That's it in the middle, and over there is the Blorenge, and on this side is the Skirrid. It's called Holy Mountain as well, you know, because there's a dip on one side that's supposed to be the Devil's footprint, although why that should make it Holy I don't know..."

Her voice petered out. He didn't seem to be listening. "I'm sorry – I'm gabbling," she said." It's difficult on railway platforms, though, isn't it? No-one ever knows what to say before the train arrives ... What are you thinking about?"

He seemed to make an effort to collect himself and stop glancing up the line to see if the train was coming.

"I was wondering," he said quite truthfully, "how long it will be before I see you again."

Charles leaned back in the seat as the train curved around the first bend in the track, blocking the small figure of Jennie – still waving on the platform – from sight. He let out a deep breath, thankful that he was the only person in the compartment. He could relax now. No need to keep up the cheerful facade of the last twenty-four hours.

His face set into haggard lines. He knew already that he'd made a dreadful mistake and for the first time was thankful that the war gave him an excuse to get away. All the previous day, whenever he'd been in the house, it was Katharine's presence that he was aware of rather than that of his bride. The electricity of mutual attraction and desire was there between them again, as it had been before.

His consummate acting skill, developed from an early age in an attempt to cover up his background and honed to perfection during the years spent as a 'ladies' man', had stood him in good stead. Not by so much as a flicker had he shown anything but proper regard for the woman who was now, ludicrously, his mother-in-law, and he was sure that Jennie hadn't for one moment suspected the truth of his confused feelings. Except for the awful gaffe on their wedding night, of course, but even that had been overcome the following night.

He wanted to push memories of that episode from his mind, but they refused as yet to go away. He took them out and looked at them, acknowledged the fact that it had still been Katharine's face in his mind's eye while he'd been taking her daughter's body, and that he'd done so swiftly and brutally, so that in the end he had no idea as to whether she'd been a virgin or not.

It might have been easier if Jennie had ranted and raved at him in the first place, when he'd turned away from her in such an ungentlemanly fashion. Perhaps then anger would have given him the impetus to push Katharine out of his mind. But Jennie had accepted his behaviour without question, and seemed absurdly happy with things the way they were – rather in the manner of a dog which has been beaten gratefully licking the beater's hand next time it's stroked.

He should've been feeling at least relieved by Jennie's apparent generosity of spirit, but he wasn't. If anything, there was a growing resentment towards her because she was making him feel such a heel. She'd said goodbye to him with unshed tears glistening in her large grey eyes, and had clung to him when he kissed her goodbye. Adoration was one thing, and extremely gratifying, but why did women always become so clingy as soon as you showed them any affection? His mother and grandmother throughout his childhood had clung to him, wanting his affection to fill the barren wastes of their lives. And most of the women he'd known since, who had seemed strong-willed and capricious during the chase, had become soft and demanding once they'd capitulated. It had always been time then to embark on a fresh chase.

It would be the same with this marriage, he was sure.

Would it have been so with Katharine, he mused? Hard to imagine her demeaning herself to ask anything of another person which would in any way give them the upper hand. For a moment he pictured himself making love to her, watching her fight the flame of desire that would be lighting up her eyes, and so fighting his advances, challenging him to overcome her. A response which so far, whoever the lover had been, had proved the greatest aphrodisiac he'd known.

He stood up impatiently as the train pulled into Newport, and dusted his trousers down as if brushing away the suffocating demands of all these women. By the time he caught his London connection he was beginning to feel glad that the RAF would be keeping him for the foreseeable future, and that immersion in a man's world, with perhaps only the occasional dalliance with a willing WAAF, was just what he needed at present.

By the time he reached his station in Yorkshire, he'd got a grip on himself. He'd extricated himself from difficult situations before, and doubtless when the time came he would be able to do so again. In the meantime his marriage, Jennie and Katharine were things he needn't trouble himself about for some time to come.

He pushed them resolutely out of his life.

Monday washing was in full swing when Jennie returned to the house, glad of the warmth of the steamy kitchen. Laura stood at the sink washing the delicate baby clothes, while Mother, thankfully, was seeing to the main laundry with Gwyneth in the wash house.

"Why don't you take your things upstairs and stay out of the way for a while – have a bit of time to yourself?" Laura suggested. "Mother's taking the weather personally because the washing won't dry – nearly bit my head off when I suggested we leave some of it until tomorrow."

Jennie nodded and went heavily up the stairs to her room, wondering if being in love made everyone as emotionally exhausted as she now felt. She seemed to swing from elation to despondency and from confidence to insecurity at the drop of a hat – something she'd not noticed in either of her sisters. True, Laura had been pretty emotional in the early days of her marriage, but Jennie had put that down to the effects of pregnancy. Perhaps, though, she hadn't been as sure of Cyril's affections as she'd always appeared.

She lay on the new wide bed, which seemed out of place in the familiar room and was probably going to be freezing to sleep in on her own, staring at the ceiling and twisting the gold band on her finger round and round.

It had suddenly occurred to her, as she drove the tractor home, that since making their marriage vows on Saturday Charles hadn't once said that he loved her.

17

The hedgerow along Star Pitch looked tired and dusty, parts of it thick with brambles which had straggled away from its neat contours, leaving it in need of a decent trim. The road was dusty, too, where tractor mud had been compounded through the long hot summer by the relentless trundle of army lorries forcing their way along the narrow lane, carrying armament parts for the factory at Glascoed, or troops for the camp at Llanover.

But for now there were no lorries, and the road held an afternoon stillness made more so by the lack of breeze. The voices of the two young women carried in the quiet as they breasted the hill, the pram squeaking and bouncing in front of them, the baby lulled to sleep by the motion.

They talked animatedly as they walked, their steps easing off on the downward slope, each pulling the pram back a little to slow its progress.

"You know you can have the keys to the Monmouth house if you want – I could go over with you in the morning and tidy up a bit," Laura was saying.

"No, really, I don't think it will be worth it for such a short time, but it's sweet of you to think of it. Besides, there'll be too much to do in the morning, and then I'll look after Selina for you in the afternoon while you're at the Red Cross, if you'll help Father in the evening for me." Jennie smiled at her sister. "I can hardly believe I'm going to see him after all these months – it feels rather unreal – Charles coming home on leave, as my husband! I saw him so often before we were married, but now we've been apart for so long that, well – I don't know whether I'm excited or scared!"

"Excited," Laura stated emphatically, knowing only how she would feel if it were Cyril coming home.

Jennie turned to her with quick sympathy. "I'm sorry it's not Cyril home on leave this time."

Laura shrugged. "It will be his turn next. At least he's up in Blackpool, away from what's been going on lately. Poor Charles has been in the thick of it." She grinned at her sister, transforming her rather matronly appearance. "If he's injured his hands you'll have to take *extra special* care of him!"

"He said it wasn't too bad when he 'phoned, mainly superficial cuts from glass, so I –" Jennie began seriously, before catching the wicked gleam in her sister's eye. The meaning of her words suddenly dawned on her. She gave Laura a playful push. "Ooh, *you!* I'll feel embarrassed all the time he's here, now!"

Both girls were laughing as they turned the corner at the bottom of the hill and headed for home through Nantyderry. They walked up past the station, which had become immensely busy since the outbreak of war, due mainly to the Army transit camp at Llanover, and past the Railway Refreshment Room, where often in the evenings soldiers would gather – but that too was quiet at this hour. The only people around were two soldiers deep in conversation with the stationmaster, but who still found time to smile appreciatively at the two young women; one so buxom that her floral print dress strained across her bosom, the other as thin as a lath.

When they reached the farm Laura went to gather in the line-full of nappies, which had become board-dry in the sun, while Jennie pushed the pram onto the front lawn. She looked around her with her usual feeling of pleasure at the farm basking in the afternoon. It felt like an island of tranquillity, surrounded on all sides by the evidence of war and yet strangely unaffected by it. Trains full of troops, lorries full of TNT, swept past and around it; evacuees filled many of the nearby homes where women were struggling without their menfolk; but on the farm life went on almost as normal, so that at times it was impossible to believe the war truly existed. Mother might moan, but so far they had had few shortages and Father's judicious bartering of the eggs and vegetables he took with him on the milk round ensured that they had most of what they needed.

She was loath to admit it, but if anything the war was providing her with opportunities to broaden her horizons that she'd never had before. She'd volunteered to help with the pathetic bands of evacuees which had arrived from many of the towns on the south coast of England, and a strange friendship had arisen between her and the officious Hetty Lloyd.

"How can you stand her?" Laura had asked early on, when Hetty arrived at the farm to take up Jennie's tentative offer of help.

But Jennie, at first, had felt sorry for the woman, and then grew to appreciate her considerable energy. She watched her with the children and realised that her gruff exterior masked a soul which deeply regretted being denied a family of her own. Her down-to-earth approach was often appreciated by the children, too – especially the older boys, who didn't always want the sympathy and protective-ness of well-meaning surrogate mothers heaped upon them.

"Come on!" Hetty would exclaim on fine summer holiday days. "Let's get some fresh air into these young lungs!" And, with Jennie as her willing assistant, she would proceed to round up the stouter-hearted of the children, march them up a mountainside, and intro-duce them to the thrills of slinging rope over high rocks and climbing up it. Or they'd go fishing in the river and become absorbed in select-ing worms and maggots, not caring a hoot when clothes became muddied or torn.

She also introduced Jennie to the body of women who ran the WVS in Abergavenny. "You can spare an afternoon to help out here, can't you?" she demanded in her robust fashion, and simply said, "Nonsense! She won't mind!" when Jennie intimated that her mother might object to even more time spent away from the chores around the farm. And Mother, aware that she'd only just won the battle over not taking evacuees and that Hetty's power and influ-ence were increasing as the war progressed, said little, although she remained tight-lipped and disapproving whenever Hetty appeared at the farm.

Jennie enjoyed the camaraderie, previously unknown to her, of the motley crew of women at the WVS and didn't mind the tedious-ness of sorting through piles of donated clothes at the Abergavenny clothing depot, or learning how to make camouflage netting. Stand-ing at a table covered with large squares of brown paper, which would each be made up into parcels containing efficiently listed assortments of garments, she listened to the talk which invariably centred on husbands, families, and coping with shortages. Some-times the discussions became more personal, especially among the younger women who were missing their husbands in more ways than just as someone who could bring in the coal, and then Jennie learned more about what married relationships should include than any amount of books could have told her.

"There'll be fleas in some of those clothes, I don't doubt," Mother sniffed when she first learned of what Jennie was doing, after Hetty had departed in the battered little Austin she'd acquired and which she drove in an alarmingly erratic style through the country lanes. "You don't know what sort of houses they've come from."

"Well, it's a pity you don't sort through some of *your* wardrobe, instead of criticising," Jennie retorted, as surprised as Mother at her own newly-found temerity, and walking out of the room before

Mother could recover and deliver a stinging reply.

The tension at home hadn't eased over the months since Jennie's marriage, although it had changed slightly in that Mother was able to fall out with Laura occasionally, which relieved the burden on Jennie and Father. Afternoons spent at Abergavenny were a welcome relief, and also taught Jennie something else: that she had a talent for clear-thinking organisation and with her gentle but firm manner could take the lead without upsetting the other women.

"Wasted on a farm," was Hetty's opinion. "The women's forces would snap you up, if you weren't married."

But Jennie only laughed. "Seeing as I've never left South Wales, they'd soon find out what a complete duffer I am."

Nevertheless, organising bands of women to issue drinks and cigarettes on Abergavenny station to troops returning from Dunkirk *en route* to requisitioned holiday camps in North Wales gave her a huge sense of satisfaction, as did her dealings with evacuees.

"I'm so much more sure of what I want," she confided to Laura. "I know Charles is keen to stay on here after the war and help run the farm, and that's fine, but somehow we'll have to have a home of our own. When I hear the other women talk about their homes – and when I used to stay with you at Monmouth – I realise that although I'm married, I've not experienced any of the day-to-day responsi-bilities which other married women have. And I never shall while we live with Mother and Father. We'll have to come to some sort of arrangement."

Laura was relieved to hear it. She'd had stern warnings from Cyril that should Charles become entrenched in running the farm, hers, Tom's and Emily's inheritances should be safeguarded.

Don't get me wrong, he'd written. *He's a super chap, good friend and all that, but everyone should be consulted if there's any sharing out to be done.*

"And children," Jennie had continued. "I definitely want chil-dren – lots of them, as soon as possible!" Little Selina had blossomed into a beautiful baby, sunnily disposed to all the attention that was heaped upon her, and in sharing her care with Laura as well as helping with all the small children who now filled the village, Jennie had become increasingly maternal.

The begetting of the 'lots of children' was the one thing that still bothered her. She'd longed to confide in the women at the WVS, who assumed that, as a married woman, she was as knowledgeable as they. But she couldn't bring herself to start a conversation along the lines of: "I may be married but I've only had sex once, and that felt like assault and battery, and will it always feel that bad?"

She couldn't speak to Hetty, either, no matter how friendly they'd become, because, after all, Hetty had never been married and so would know nothing of such matters.

She should have been able to talk to Laura, but something else held her back. Laura received many more letters from Cyril than Jennie did from Charles, which when they did arrive were exceedingly matter-of-fact. He'd been sent from Yorkshire to RAF Manston in Kent, and she consoled herself with the thought that, being right in the thick of the conflict, he was probably pushed for time and didn't want to alarm her by saying too much. Or perhaps he felt inhibited by the censor. But Cyril's letters appeared to be unashamedly romantic. Each one was received with a flutter of delight and snippets were gushingly read out at intervals throughout the day to a mystified Selina in her high-chair, with Cyril always referred to as 'Daddy'.

"Daddy says he can't wait to see his two best girls again, and when he does he's going to give us both great big kisses!" or "Daddy's being ever so brave and doing his very best to help win the war so that he can come back to us! Haven't you got a wonderful Daddy?"

"Absolute tosh!" Tom declared, on one of his infrequent visits to the farm, and followed this up with tart comments about 'Daddy' winning the war from his safe office desk, issuing RAF pay sheets.

These were also the days when Mother would become exasperated with Laura, who in her highly charged emotional state would spill Selina's breakfast milk over the spotless range, or be too slow helping with the chickens. The day would invariably end with Laura in tears, claiming that no-one understood the strain she was under and at this rate she'd have to go and live in married quarters with Selina, where they would undoubtedly be bombed out, and then wouldn't everyone be sorry!

"Too many women in the house, that's the trouble," Father would mutter, and take himself off to boil up the potatoes that weren't good enough to pass on to the War-Ag, turning them into pig-swill instead.

As she strolled towards the house now, Jennie went over in her mind last night's 'phone call from Charles. "Sorry I haven't written for a while. There's been a bit of an incident here at the airfield which made rather a lot of glass fly around. Some of it decided to embed itself in my hands – nothing very bad," he assured her, hearing her sharp intake of breath down the line, "but I've been laid up for a while and obviously couldn't write."

Everything these days, from minor spats to total devastation, was reported as an 'incident', so there was no way of telling how serious this one had been. "How are you now?" she asked, reluctant to be anything more than matter-of-fact herself when the operator at Pontypool exchange was probably listening in.

"Almost healed – that's why I'm calling. I've been given a bit of leave before I go back on duty – only thirty-six hours I'm afraid, but I should be with you the day after tomorrow."

"That's wonderful! Can I meet you at Newport?"

"No – no. I don't know yet what my travelling arrangements will be. I'll just have to turn up when I can."

She wished he'd call her 'darling', if only for the ears of the operator, but he rang off then, saying that someone else needed the telephone. But it was enough to lift her spirits to know that he was arriving home – and as each hour passed she was filled with a mixture of excitement and just a little bit of dread, which made her stomach turn over uncomfortably.

Laura was in the kitchen when she went in, looking solemn and listening to Gwyneth. "Don't know how she did it, indeed to goodness I don't. One minute she was down here, the next she was banging on the floor and calling for me. Gave me such a turn when I found her on the landing, it did. Could hardly move, she couldn't. Had an awful job helping her into the bedroom."

Laura turned to Jennie. "Mother's hurt her back. She's in bed. Gwyneth wants to call the doctor but says that Mother doesn't want her to."

"She says it's nothing a day or two in bed won't heal," said Gwyneth. "Perhaps you two ought to go and have a word with her. Listen to you, she would."

Jennie's heart sank. Mother in bed for a day or two would mean no end of traipsing up and down fetching and carrying for her, not to mention extra work around the house. Her prospect of a brief idyll with Charles began to diminish.

Laura was already heading for the stairs, and by the time Jennie reached Mother's bedroom she was half-way through her tale. "I think it's a touch of lumbago," Mother was saying. "I used to get it when you were all small. Rest in bed is the only thing for it, I know from experience."

Jennie couldn't ever remember her mother in bed with a bad back, but perhaps it had been before she was born. After a few words of commiseration she went down to collect Selina, who could be heard yelling in her pram, while Laura remained to take instructions from Mother for the rest of the day.

"I'm going to give her a hot drink and a couple of aspirin," Laura said as she bustled back into the kitchen. "Then we'll see what else has to be done this afternoon." She stopped at the sight of Jennie's closed face. "What's the matter?"

Hating herself for her lack of charity, Jennie shrugged. "It just seems ironic – when I was going to have a holiday with Emily, Father broke his leg, and now I've got the chance of just one day with Charles, Mother's laid up in bed."

Laura clapped her hand over her mouth. "*Charles!* Gosh, I'd forgotten all about him coming! Now don't you worry, you can still have some time together, even if it means taking Selina with you – I'll see to everything here. I can give the Red Cross a miss tomorrow, and if necessary I'll ask Nancy to come over – she's got plenty of time on her hands."

Nancy was a bone of contention that both Mother and Laura liked to chew on whenever they could. Childless, and in their eyes self-absorbed, she'd persuaded Tom to give up the smallholding – as Mother had always said she would – and encouraged him to work for the War-Ag instead, to avoid call-up. In the evenings he did his stint with the Home Guard, and there were rumours that on these nights Nancy went out dancing alone.

But Jennie ignored the dig at Nancy now, smiling gratefully at her sister instead, and pushing away the treacherous thought that, for whatever reason, Mother was doing this deliberately.

L aura was true to her word, and even Nancy was willing to help, cycling over the next morning and laughingly asking whether she could be given some task which wouldn't damage her nail polish. "It's my last bottle," she said, "and goodness knows when I'll get another."

"I suppose, as we know more of what's to be done around the place, you could see to Mother," Laura said doubtfully, knowing that Mother wouldn't be too pleased to be 'seen to' by her flighty daughter-in-law. But Nancy accepted the task with alacrity, revelling in the look on the face of the woman she privately dubbed 'that hard-faced bitch' when she appeared in her bedroom.

So it was that when Charles finally arrived in the middle of the afternoon he found three young women gathered in the kitchen.

"Well! I didn't expect such an excellent welcoming committee!"

Jennie jumped up from the table to greet him, overwhelmed at the impact of his maleness and his classic good looks which suited his uniform so well. "But how have you arrived now? There isn't a train due for another half-hour!"

"And she should know," laughed Nancy. "She's been checking the arrival of each one since early this morning!"

Charles laughed too, then hugged Jennie and kissed her resoundingly on the cheek. "I met a chap I knew and got a lift up from Newport. He dropped me at the top of the drive." He turned to the other two, his arm still encircling Jennie. "How are you both?"

"We're fine," said Laura, moving to the sink to re-fill the kettle. "But poor Mother's laid up in bed with a bad back, I'm afraid."

Across the room Nancy grinned and raised her eyes to heaven, and was surprised to see a response in Charles's eyes, which looked distinctly like relief. Strange, when she thought that he and Mother had always hit it off so well. Perhaps she'd been wrong; it was only a fleeting impression. Nevertheless, always intrigued by family conflicts, provided she could remain detached from them herself, she stored it for future reference.

"That's why I'm here," she said lightly. "So you two love-birds can have some time together!"

Jennie felt her face reddening. "We thought perhaps – your hands – you might need looking after yourself." She didn't dare look at Laura. "How are they anyway?" she gabbled on. "Are you in much pain…?"

He held out both hands. "Left one perfectly fine now – just a couple of scars for me to show off, and the right one – as you can see, still bandaged, but that's mainly for show – should be right as rain by next week."

Laura had set a tea-tray. "Why don't the two of you take this into the parlour, and we'll find Father and let him know you're here. No point going up to Mother at the moment – I left her sleeping not ten minutes ago."

She ushered the two of them out of the room, so that within minutes of his arrival Jennie found herself alone with Charles. She stood across the room from him. "You must be tired after the journey. Did it take you long?" He didn't look tired. He looked relaxed and – dared she hope it? – happy to be here, while she sounded like a polite hostess.

He smiled gently at her. "No it didn't take too long. Now stop looking like a frightened rabbit and come here and let me kiss you properly."

He held out his arms, and with a little cry she hurried towards him. His kiss was long and hard, his hands roving expertly over her body, filling her with the simplest of desires.

"I wasn't sure – what it would be like," she said at last, nestling her head against his shoulder. "After all these months apart, and with so little time after the wedding – I thought perhaps… well, that you might have changed your mind!" She didn't mention the curtness or infrequency of his letters. Some men just weren't natural letter-writers – she'd learned that much from the WVS women.

"Of course I haven't changed my mind." He began to kiss her neck, so that it tickled deliciously. "I can show you just how happy I am to be home later on. But for now, woman," he smacked her playfully on the bottom, "be a good wife and get your poor husband that cup of tea!"

She moved happily to do as he asked. It was going to be alright! All the doubts that had assailed her in the small hours of the night when, alone in the big double bed, she found it harder and harder to believe that Charles was truly her husband and truly loved her, were banished from her mind. She was suddenly filled with a glow of happiness. His leave might be short, but she was going to enjoy it, and show him that she was moving away from the young girl who knew nothing. For the first time she began to look forward to their night together.

They sat side by side on the sofa, catching up with each other's news, and she was aware of Charles's eyes approvingly on her as she told him about Hetty, and the evacuees, and the WVS. But as they talked and listened in turn, Charles fought down his surprise at her earlier words. She couldn't know how near the mark she'd been; or else she was more perspicacious than he'd realised. Whatever, he wasn't going to act a part this time.

It hadn't been as easy as he'd thought to push away the anxieties about the mess he'd got himself into over his marriage. The hours when Jerry was coming over and they were rushing about to get our own boys up in the air, or rushing to shelter from the bombs and incendiaries that were raining down on them, were distracting enough to banish all thoughts but those of sheer survival. But in between were the episodes of calm, when everyone was confined to base, and then there was plenty of time to think.

The admiring comments of his fellows when he had shown them the tiny snapshot he had of his new bride didn't help, either. How, he asked himself, could he possibly prefer *her mother?* As the months passed he began to convince himself that he'd been too hasty in mentally writing off his marriage, and the memories of his attraction to Katharine began to fade. He should do the honourable thing, he told himself, and stay true to his marriage. And with little opportunity to distract himself elsewhere, and so many young men doing the 'honourable thing' and flying to their deaths, his own honour, for the first time in his life, became important to him.

It still wasn't easy to quell all the doubts, however. He could have come home days ago, when his injuries first began to heal, but he'd put it off, not really wanting to put his new integrity to the test – until probing from the MO, who'd always fancied himself as a bit of a psychoanalyst, forced Charles to agree to spend the last couple of days of his sick leave at home.

He'd felt the gods were on his side when Laura said that Katharine was confined to bed. Without her obvious presence he could concentrate completely on his young bride and already a lightness of heart had enabled him to show the affection for Jennie which he knew she craved – and, he had to admit, he'd found himself enjoying her response far more than he'd anticipated.

"So what really happened to your hands?" she was asking him now.

"A complete shambles, I'm afraid. There was a big attack on the airfield and everything went: the buildings, the telephone lines … the runway ended up littered with unexploded bombs. And I just happened to get in the way of a lot of broken glass – or rather, fell into it. Put my hands out to save myself, so of course they got damaged. Luckily most of our planes were up at this point, and those of us on the ground were evacuated to different places. I don't think they're going to use that airfield any more, except for emergencies. And the poor devils in the planes were diverted to Essex, and then had to go up again later in the day when Jerry flew north of the Thames."

Jennie sat silently for a few moments. "So that's what they mean by an 'incident', on the wireless. It sounds quite innocuous, until you hear from someone who's been on the receiving end of one."

"I probably shouldn't have told you as much as I have," said Charles, "and I'm certainly not going to tell you any more, except that when I go back I'm being sent to Duxford to work on something new, which means that when I'm on duty I shall be underground."

Jennie wasn't too sure where Duxford was, but was thankful that he would be safe. She watched him drink his tea and found herself wishing he would kiss her again.

Edward came in then, saw the bandage on Charles's right hand, and made do with clapping him on the shoulder. "Good to see you again – this girl here's been worried about you!"

"Oh, I always turn up like a bad penny," he replied, turning a devastating smile on Jennie, so that she didn't mind any longer how spartan his letters were.

"I'm sorry Katie isn't down here to welcome you," Edward went on. "I expect you've heard she's laid up?"

"Yes… yes. I'm sorry she's not well, but they say rest in bed's the best thing for a bad back, don't they?"

A slightly awkward silence developed between the three of

them, as if, Jennie thought, simply the mention of Mother could put a dampener on proceedings. "Have you anything to unpack?" she asked Charles finally.

"Just a few things. I'll take them up now."

"And I'd better look in on Katie while I'm here," said Edward. "I expect she'll have heard my voice."

Jennie followed the two men up the stairs. Mother could be glimpsed lying tidily in the high bed as Father went through the door, although her face was turned away from them.

She saw that Charles was looking towards the room. "Should we go and say hello?" she asked, as the door closed on Father.

Charles swung round quickly at the top of the stairs and caught her arm with his good hand. "No! Later, perhaps." His voice was deep and conspiratorial as he moved swiftly with her towards their own bedroom. "We've got much better things to do!"

He closed the bedroom door behind them with his foot, put down his bag, and swung Jennie round into his arms in one practised movement. He began to kiss her as he had before, pressing her body close to his own so that she could be in no doubt of his need of her. His hand inched up under her skirt, easily freeing her stockings from their suspenders and caressing the soft skin on the inside of her thigh. She wondered if she was expected to undo his buttons in return, thought of Laura, and began to giggle softly.

"Do you think we should? *Now?* What if someone comes looking for us?"

"Too bad! I've spent many months waiting for this!"

His hands continued their exploration, until she felt herself relax and begin to respond.

"What about Mother?" she hissed, albeit half-heartedly, as he moved them both towards the bed. "She's only next door. She might hear us."

But this seemed simply to add to his sense of urgency. With clothing only half-removed he was on top of her, eliciting responses that she'd never felt before. She became aware that she was moaning softly as, with eyes closed, wave after wave of sensation engulfed her until she thought she would no longer be able to bear it. As she cried out she felt Charles's body shudder and then relax onto hers. She could feel his heart matching the rapid beat of her own, and held him close, loving him, a small, all-knowing, satisfied smile playing on her lips.

Now she knew. The talk amongst the other women, which had hinted at pleasures which had so far remained a mystery to her, now made sense.

Charles murmured in her ear: "Sorry that was so quick – tonight we can take our time."

She held him even more tightly. "It was wonderful," she breathed.

He lifted his head and grinned at her. "I thought from the noise you were making that you must be enjoying it!"

Her eyes widened in mock horror. "Do you think Mother heard?"

He grinned again. "What if she did? We *are* married, after all. It is allowed."

Jennie began to chuckle. "Yes, *but in the afternoon!* She would be so shocked!"

"Then let's go and see her and find out!"

But when they tapped on her door a little while later there was no answer, rather to Jennie's relief, as she was sure she would start to giggle again like a naughty schoolgirl if Mother had turned her disapproving eyes upon her.

Only Gwyneth was in the kitchen when they went downstairs, and she made no comment as to where they'd been – as, Jennie was sure, both Laura and Nancy would have done, to tease her. Charles went off for a stroll around the farm while Jennie began to help Gwyneth prepare the evening meal, already anticipating with a new eagerness the night ahead.

This is a bit different from the last leave-taking," Charles commented as they stood in the front doorway the next day, surveying the cloudless blue sky and the faint heat-shimmer already visible in the distance, although it was barely mid-day.

In more ways than one, Jennie thought, cocooned in the after-glow of being loved. For the first time in years she felt truly wanted, creating a well of happiness which was helping to ease the pain of saying goodbye this time. She felt nothing like the anxious, insecure girl who'd said farewell to a new husband all those months ago.

They'd seen Mother together earlier in the morning, the pain from her back apparently making her reluctant to talk for long, and after a few polite comments they'd been dismissed. The other members of the household had already said goodbye and scuttled off to carry out their chores, Laura beset by extra responsibilities as Nancy hadn't come over this morning, so she had to bite her tongue not to urge Jennie to hurry up.

Arm-in-arm, Jennie and Charles set off past the avenue of roses which continued to flank the front path and were now being gorged on by drowsy bees. Today they would walk through the ten-acre field to the station, as Jennie had done so many times in her life. As he helped Jennie over the stile Charles looked back at the house, admiring its solidity in a proprietorial way. Glancing up, he saw a face at the front bay window, and knew straight away that it wasn't Laura or Gwyneth. So much for a bad back.

It was too far away to see Katharine's face clearly, but nevertheless he felt her eyes boring into his. He slowly and pointedly gave a mock salute before turning his attention back to his wife, and didn't look again to see if Katharine was still there.

We had such a surprise a few days after you left. Without any warning Cyril turned up, having cadged a few days' leave. Of course Laura was over the moon and I don't think she stopped talking for the first hour he was here! (And since he's gone back she's hardly stopped crying! I'm sure she never used to be so emotional.)

Jennie paused and chewed the end of the pen, as she used to do when a schoolgirl. Did that sound as if she herself never shed a tear for Charles?

She was seated at her favourite place in front of her bedroom window, from where she could see the mountains beginning to take on their autumn hues. She'd had to wait until Charles had written to her before she knew where to send her letters, so it was already some weeks since his visit, but there seemed little of interest to write. She wanted to pour out the love she felt for him and the happiness which these days seemed to bubble inside her, despite the dreariness and uncertainties of war, but she found it difficult to be coherent on paper. How could she explain the warmth and security she felt after the way he'd loved her during their brief weekend together? She knew now that she had unlimited love to give in return, and at last she had an outlet for all that had been stifled and denied during her upbringing. But it was impossible to put that into a letter which might be read by goodness knows who. Perhaps better to stick to Cyril's visit.

Luckily Mother was up and about again by then, so Laura didn't have quite so much to do. Cyril didn't seem to have had it as rough as you so far – he had lots of funny tales to tell us of his time in Blackpool. That may all change now, though, because his Squadron was being moved – perhaps you might bump into him.

She wondered whether to say that Cyril was going to be in East Anglia, but wasn't sure about the Censor. Was family mail subject to random scrutiny, as well as that of the servicemen themselves? She wouldn't be surprised; the government seemed quite paranoid about keeping everything as secret as possible these days, if the posters one saw on every available hoarding were anything to go by. Perhaps, after exhorting Joe Public to switch him off, government ministers spent too much time themselves listening to Lord Haw-Haw.

Anyway, he was delighted to be able to see Selina and seemed terribly proud of her.

Should she say that she was hoping she would soon be able to make Charles as proud? No, better wait a few more weeks. It was still very early to tell, and she'd never been awfully good about keeping dates.

So after the excitement of a visit from each of you, life here now seems very mundane. Father is thinking of applying for someone from the Land Army to help on the farm, but is still battling it out with Mother as to whether that person should live in or out. Mother is convinced we'll end up with a brainless young girl with no morals who just wants to avoid working in a factory – but she wouldn't exactly have much chance to flaunt her lack of morals around here, would she? And perhaps you have to be brainless to prefer days of working in wet fields to the warmth of a factory!

She chewed her pen again and stared at the mountains until she began to feel her eyelids grow heavy. Over the past week or so she'd begun to feel unaccountably tired. She knew she should hurry and finish her letter before tea, but she was filled with a longing to curl up on her bed and sleep. Perhaps she should cut down on some of her activities with Hetty until the decision about extra help had been made.

18

K eating, ah! Come in! At ease!" Wing Commander Shaw returned Charles's salute perfunctorily and stretched his lips into a sort of smile as his WAAF assistant, who'd dragged Charles away from his meal in the mess, closed the door on them.

"Bit of bad news I'm afraid, Keating. Don't see any point in dressing these things up, as you know. Apparently Guildford took a bit of a hammering last night, and it seems your old home took a blast. Your mother still lives there, I believe?"

"That's right, sir. 49 Milsom Street. But she has a shelter in the garden. She should have been safe." His voice was flat, emotionless. He'd long ago schooled himself to keep his emotions regarding his mother well in check, and in recent years she'd been an embarrassment kept well hidden from the rest of his life. Only the RAF Admin knew of her existence.

His superior motioned him to a chair. "I'm rather afraid that this time she didn't reach the shelter. Seems the body of an elderly lady was found in the house, but as there's not much left of the rest of the street, no-one has yet identified her. Did anyone else live with your mother?"

"No, sir. She's been on her own since my grandmother died."

"Well it rather looks as if you're going to have to get down there and make some sort of identification – sort affairs out and so on. No-one else in the family?"

"No, sir. I'm the only one."

"'Hmm." Shaw leaned back in his chair, relieved that Keating wasn't the sort of chap to get all emotional about this sort of thing. "And your wife is down in Wales – I don't suppose she could...?"

"They've never met, sir." He went on hastily as the Commander's eyebrows shot up: "We only married last January and my mother was too frail to travel down for the wedding. I only had a weekend pass, so there was no time to travel up to her together afterwards."

"I see." Shaw hadn't realised that Keating's marriage had been so recent. He was of an age to have been married for quite some time.

Perhaps this was second time around. Whatever, he wasn't going to probe any further. Too much delving into his men's personal lives did nothing to help the job in hand.

He frowned thoughtfully for a moment. "We're still awfully pushed here, of course, but it looks as if you'll have to take some compassionate and get down there yourself. I can let you have five days, but no longer, I'm afraid."

Charles stood up. "Thank you, sir. That should be sufficient to make any arrangements."

They saluted and he was dismissed. He walked slowly back to his quarters, feeling unexpectedly numb. The burden that he'd reluctantly attended to from time to time had now, apparently, been lifted from him, but the relief he should have felt was strangely absent.

He kept seeing his mother as a younger woman, sitting by the fireside endlessly knitting pullovers for him, dressed in the black she'd worn since the news had come that his father had fallen in one of the first battles of the Great War. After that she seemed to become a frailer figure, overshadowed by the more forceful personality of his grandmother, who had moved in with them almost immediately. It all seemed so long ago, and quite divorced from the gummy, faintly musty-smelling old woman who'd clung to him during his rare visits in recent years whilst assuring him that she could manage as long as he was happy and successful.

Her face, when he found her among the corpses laid out in the nearby school, didn't seem so wrinkled in death. A fine layer of dust, like grey talcum powder, covered her, but there seemed to be no sign of injury.

"I found her myself," said a short, friendly ARP warden who'd just come on duty again in the late afternoon gloom. "Not crushed or anything, just lying by the back door. Perhaps her heart gave out as she was making for the shelter."

Charles nodded, not wanting to dwell on the picture of a lonely old lady moving stumblingly towards a solitary night in an Anderson shelter. "What do I have to do now?" he asked, as the warden gently pulled the blanket back over his mother's face.

"Come with me and we'll sort out all the form-filling, and then she can be moved to the mortuary. Then you need to see an undertaker and he'll make the arrangements from there."

The little man sucked in his lower lip before he went on: "Terrible few hours we had last night – nearly all your street gone. We pulled out a family of six from next door – all dead. I expect you'll know them?"

Charles, who'd had nothing to do with any of the neighbours for years, shook his head. "I think they were quite new here."

The necessary business completed, Charles went on his way. The warden watched him go, his own eyes red-rimmed with fatigue. Funny kind of chap, he decided. Didn't seem too upset at losing his mother, but then it takes people in all sorts of ways. Strange that he didn't know anything about the neighbours, though – the warden knew for a fact that they'd lived in that house for at least a decade. He shook his head at the vagaries of human behaviour, which surprised him daily, and went back to his work.

It was the next afternoon before Charles was able to visit Milsom Street and see the damage which had been done. He'd managed to get a room at the Station Hotel, but spent much of the night sleepless and uncomfortable in the hotel shelter. But at least there'd been hot water next morning, and a breakfast of sorts, before he made his way to the undertaker's. One end of the street had disappeared under a mound of debris, the houses on each side slipping into it in an almost symmetrical 'V', and on top of the mound a flag to show that the area had been searched. The house next to Number 49 had been wrenched away from it, to crumble on its side, so that the house where he'd grown up had its insides exposed indecently to the world.

The front door was still in place, though, and the front sitting room almost intact, if in complete disarray. Charles moved about the crowded little room, wrinkling his nose at the acrid smell of burning mingled with a faint whiff of gas, which permeated from outside. On the floor he found the photograph of his father, the glass broken and the photo itself slipping sideways out of the frame. He set it back on the mantelpiece and moved to the cupboard in the corner. It was here, he knew, that his mother kept all the important papers, and where he would find the insurance policy which would cover her funeral expenses. He lifted out the box – smothered, like everything else, in a thick layer of dust – and began to sort through its contents.

It was about half-way down that he found the letter, folded neatly in a sealed envelope marked simply: 'Charles'. The message, in his mother's large scrawling hand, was written in thick black ink, with many crossings-outs, and he had to read it twice before the full impact of the words hit him.

Dear Charles,

I have watched so proudly as you have reached adulthood and become a successful, handsome man who any woman would be pleased to call her son, and I thought it was time you knew that you are the living image of the man who was truly your father. Now that he is no longer alive, I feel it is finally right to tell you, and when you read this I will have passed on too, taking my shame with me.

You see, your real father was a well-to-do man, a solicitor who was some years older than me. I fell deeply in love with him, but he was already engaged to marry someone else. When I discovered that you were on the way I married Charles Keating, the man whose namesake you became, who had courted me for some time, and had no idea of my secret affair.

I never told Charles that you were not his son, and although he may have suspected when you arrived so early, he said nothing, and treated you as his own. For that I was always grateful, and I came to – (here a word had been crossed out) – care about him very much. When he was taken from us so tragically, I wanted you always to think of him as the man who was a good father to you and loved you deeply.

But I also, over the years, have felt more and more that you should know of your true origins. Your real father married the girl to whom he was engaged, but they had no children. I followed his successful career and want you to know that you are like him in so many ways. He, too, was debonair and a man-of-the-world, and I'm sure he would have been very proud to have you for a son.

I hope you will not think too badly of me. There was no other way at the time. Your true father was in a different class from me. We could never have wed, and in the few years that we were together Charles Keating was the best of fathers to you.

Your loving Mother

Charles sat on a battered chair, the letter on the table at his side. He gazed at it in blank stupefaction as children, clambering about the shattered street looking for shrapnel, broke the eerie silence. He rummaged in his pockets for cigarettes and matches, hands shaking slightly, eyes still on the heavy black writing which merged and danced on the page before him. As the import of the words penetrated his mind, he became filled with a burning anger which rose in his throat as if it to choke him.

Why had his real father never realised the result of his affair? Had he simply seduced her, used her, in the way that Charles had himself used so many women, and not given a jot about her afterwards? It was obvious from the letter that he'd never been told that a baby was on the way, so what reason had been given for the affair ending so abruptly?

As these questions flew around his brain he realised that now, with all the people involved in his childhood dead, he would never know the answers, and his anger became even greater – this time towards his mother.

Why, if she was ultimately going to tell him so little, did she bother to tell him anything at all? And why, after the death of her husband, did she not seek out the real father of her child and tell him that he had a son? He thought of all the years of grinding, back-breaking poverty, of his mother and grandmother making sure he was aware of every sacrifice they made on his behalf, but even those sacrifices amounting to very little in the way of comfort. How differ-ent everything could have been if his 'well-to-do' father had been exhorted to give them a helping hand!

He ground out his cigarette on the floor. All he knew now was what he was not. He was not the son of Charles Keating. He was not the person he should have been by rights, with comparative wealth and distinction behind him. He was not a man who could ever claim his true heritage.

Extracting the insurance policy, he thrust the box and the remain-der of its contents, including the letter, into the hearth.

All these years spent pursuing the life of a gentleman, perfecting the manners and accent which would carry him into the world of his betters, when all the time he should have been there with them, one of them by right.

Bitterly, he threw a lighted match onto the papers and stood holding the mantelpiece, his head bowed on his arm, watching the flames take hold, until it was all reduced to ashes. Straightening up, his glance fell on the photograph of Charles Keating, and he caught hold of it to consign it to the same fate. He remembered the years of honouring that picture, the poppies that would surround it every Armistice, and the entreaties to be proud of the man who'd laid down his life for his country issuing from the mouths of his mother and grandmother.

She'd probably been in on it as well, he decided; his grandmother. Part of the conspiracy to ensure that he would never know his real father.

He wrenched the photo from its frame and was about to tear it in two, when something made him pause. A recollection of skipping along a pavement, his hand held securely by the tall man at his side, who was taking him to some sort of treat – a carnival, a fairground? He couldn't remember exactly, but he could recall the good feeling inside. And he remembered long, capable hands showing him how to clean his boots, outside on the back doorstep, ready for school next day. "Fit for a soldier," the voice belonging to the hands had declared when Charles had finished.

He looked again at the photograph. "Poor devil. You were duped too, weren't you?" he said aloud. He tucked the photograph inside his jacket, picked up his hat and looked around him with distaste.

He was glad that he'd been able to arrange his mother's burial for the next day. He wanted to get away from here as quickly as possible, from every association with this squalid street and its surroundings. He knew he would never return.

He walked briskly back to the Station Hotel, ignoring the devastation of the streets he strode through, his mind still seething with anger and questions that would never be answered. There would still be two days' leave remaining after the burial. Suddenly, he wanted to go back to South Wales. Jennie, he realised, was all he had now, all he could be certain of.

He quelled the voice in his head which reminded him that even she had been gained under false pretences, and dwelt instead on the fact that she was the only true, untainted thing in his life. That she loved him he was in no doubt and now he wanted to return to that love, to be soothed by it and made to feel he was somebody – not an accident who knew nothing of the man who sired him, and little of the man who gave him a name.

If he was lucky with transport he could be down in Monmouthshire and back to Duxford in time. Down there, he knew, he could put all of this sorry mess out of his life and certainly, with determination, out of his mind – for good.

Frost crunched underfoot as Charles made his way through the little wicket gate along from Nantyderry station and into the lane leading to the farm. The journey had been hellish: he'd got as far as Reading, but the terrible bombing around Bath had meant a detour to Oxford, where he'd spent the night in a cold, cheerless waiting room before catching an equally cold, cheerless branch train down through Gloucester to Abergavenny.

Despite the early hour he spotted a red-haired girl he didn't recognise, wearing distinctive Land Army uniform, working at the far end of the ten-acre field – which brought a grim smile to his lips. So Edward had got his way, for once. Katharine must be losing her grip. She would doubtless be giving the girl a dreadfully hard time, and he spared a moment's pity for the youngster.

The rest of his pity he reserved for himself.

Committing his mother's body to the ground had been a hurried affair, conducted by a vicar completely unknown to the Keating family. Throughout the brief service, with only himself and the grave-digger in attendance, Charles had dwelt on the information his mother was taking with her which he'd now never be able to retrieve. The sense of injustice and betrayal by all those who had featured in his early life had continued to fester throughout his journey home, so that now, despite being tired and hungry, he wanted to shout out his anger to the whole world.

Of course, he'd remembered during the long hours at Oxford that Jennie and her family believed him to be already without either parent, so the true reason for his sudden appearance and state of distress would have to be explained in other ways. He would gloss over it, he decided, and possibly produce an illness if he needed to elicit more of the sympathy he now craved from Jennie.

He could hear raised voices as he approached the back of the house – singing and laughter, unusual so early in the morning. Walking in through the washhouse, he opened the door into the kitchen, at first unnoticed by those within.

Sat on a chair, with Selina on her knee, was Jennie, and beside her, his fair head close to her dark one, was Cyril.

With Cyril's arm around her shoulder, Jennie was bouncing Selina up and down as she sang: *Clap hands, clap hands, now Daddy's come home!* – to which the baby made a clumsy attempt to clap her chubby hands together, gurgling with delight as the two adults laughed. The picture they presented was cosy and intimate. "Wonderful!" Cyril was saying. "You're so good with her. Get her to do it again!"

Charles moved in the doorway, causing Jennie to look up, and, with a cry of delight, she thrust Selina into Cyril's arms, and flew to his side.

"Charles! Oh, how wonderful! What are you doing here?" Without waiting for a reply, she flung her arms around him and kissed his face. "But you're cold! Come in by the fire and get warm!"

She dragged him further into the room with a concern which should have been balm to his hurt. But all his tortured mind could think of was, *Jennie and Cyril… Cyril and Jennie…*

"Hello, old chap! What a wonderful coincidence! Only arrived myself yesterday. Missed you by a day or two the last time I was here!" Cyril was talking now, pumping Charles's hand up and down in greeting, as he held his daughter in his free arm.

"Cyril's being sent abroad, so he's got some leave," said Jennie, her eyes roaming over Charles's face, suddenly anxious. "Is that why you're here?"

"No." He turned to her now, seeing the healthy glow in her cheeks and the shapeliness of her body in the breeches and pullover she always wore around the farm. So much more attractive, he realised, than the matronly Laura, who had retained the plumpness brought about by Selina's arrival.

He reached his arm around her neck and pulled her close. "I had two spare days and wanted to see my wife!" He bent down and pressed his lips to hers, kissing her long and hard before releasing her again.

As he straightened up, his eyes bore into Cyril's. He had a sudden desire to punch his fatuous face. *She's my wife,* he wanted to cry. *My wife! The only thing I've got left!*

The sudden tension in the room was almost tangible. Jennie, flushed scarlet, stood floundering, while Cyril dragged his eyes away from Charles's gimlet stare and plopped Selina down to crawl on the floor.

"Quite right!" he cried. "My feelings exactly! Couldn't wait to get down here and see my two best girls! Laura's had to go into town, though. Quite a noise in the Red Cross now, and couldn't get out of it. So Jennie's been showing me Selina's latest tricks…"

Bluster, of course. Trying hard to cover up because I've caught the two of them together!

Cyril's voice trailed off as Charles continued to stare. "It was awful, darling," he told Laura afterwards. "He just appeared in the doorway, looking dreadful. Could hardly get a word out of him – I think he's been having a bad time in Duxford. *Some*thing's happened to the man, that's for sure."

At that moment Katharine appeared in the kitchen doorway. Immediately she seemed to size up the situation and moved forward with an alacrity she hadn't shown in Charles's presence for some time. "Well, what a surprise! Both my sons-in-law at home together! Jennie! What about getting this husband of yours some breakfast? He looks starving!"

Her eyes held Charles's as she spoke and, for him, there was no mistaking the triumphant message they held.

Didn't I tell you so?

Jennie hurried through her evening chores, eager to get back to Charles. It was only five o'clock, but already it was dark and very cold. The chickens needed no persuading to stay in the warm hen-house: they'd remained inside for most of the day. The cows and pigs were already seen to, and she'd been able to push away the tiredness that now tended to assail her most days.

She made her way back through the orchard and met Father coming out of the stable, his torch angled towards the ground because the zealous Warden on Star Hill would already be checking the black-out. She heard the smile in his voice. "Finished in record time! I wish Charles was here every day!"

"So do I!" she answered fervently. "For his own sake as well as mine. I don't think he's very well – he says he's had a touch of bronchitis and he certainly doesn't seem himself. If he was here for longer I could spend some time building him up."

Father's smile widened at the motherly concern in her voice. "Perhaps when you tell him your good news he'll feel a lot better," he murmured as they reached the house.

She spun round towards him in surprise. "How did you know? I haven't told anyone yet!"

He chuckled. "This might sound very ungallant, but I haven't dealt with cows and horses all these years not to be able to recognise very early when a calf or foal is on the way."

She laughed. "You're right, that doesn't sound at all gallant, but I'm pleased you know." She squeezed his hand as they went through the back door. "You won't say anything yet, though, will you? I want to tell Charles first, when we're alone."

That was less easy than it sounded, with the house so full of people. She was pleased to see Charles relax, though, as the day progressed. He'd looked so gaunt and grey, and behaved so oddly when he first arrived. But during the evening the small glow of love that had stayed with her since his earlier leave was fanned into a full flame as he showed a flattering need of her, holding her close to him as they all sat in the parlour after supper, regardless of Mother's disapproving stare. He didn't seem inclined to join in with Cyril's eagerness to recount escapades, however, which bore out Laura's whispered comment to Jennie earlier: "Cyril thinks he's been having a rough time," and explained his disinclination to make small talk.

Charles lay in the dark, staring up at the ceiling, Jennie's words echoing in his head but seeming to make no sense. Just as nothing during the day had made any real sense.

He'd watched himself going through the motions as best he could, as if he were someone else, talking to everyone and explaining his sudden appearance, but his mind had been in turmoil. He kept going over all the occasions he'd seen Jennie and Cyril together. The time he'd seen them kiss outside the house in Monmouth kept re-playing, like a cinema reel, the kiss becoming more prolonged and significant each time, with the voice-over of Katharine's words on his wedding night: *You're not the first, you know!*

Cheated again. Lied to by the people who were supposed to care about him. Duped whenever he tried to do the honourable thing. He forgot the number of times he'd duped other people, the lies and omissions about his own life which had gone into producing the picture of a gentleman by which he chose to live.

He'd tried not to let Katharine see that he'd read her telling look that morning correctly, of course. Whenever he found her watching him during the day, a Mona Lisa smile playing on her lips, he'd been openly affectionate and possessive towards Jennie, but the memory of the morning's little idyll that he'd witnessed refused to go away.

And now here was Jennie telling him that she was pregnant! And expecting him to believe it was his, when he knew from her letter that Cyril's leave had immediately followed his own. How much time had they spent together then, doubtless with Katharine's warped blessing, while Laura had been playing Florence Nightingale? The letter had gushed about how much 'fun' Cyril had been – this was obviously the outcome!

"I thought you'd be pleased?" Jennie's voice came to him, wavering, uncertain. "I'm sure I'm expecting a boy – I thought you'd like to have a son... especially when there's no-one else to carry on the Keating line."

The Keating line! If only she knew what a joke that was! His own birth had been one of complete deception, and now the next child to bear the Keating name would also be someone else's bastard.

"It's a bit of a shock," he managed to say at last. "I'll need time to think about it. I'm tired now – I need to sleep."

He forced himself to turn away from her, when in reality he had an overwhelming urge to put his hands around that slender little neck and squeeze it with all his might.

Jennie slipped out of bed and scurried to the bathroom just in time as a wave of nausea swept over her. When the retching finally ceased, she stood, exhausted and heedless of the chill of the room, and wondered what she should do next. Father had assured her that she wasn't needed for the early morning milking – he and Wendy, the Land Army girl, would see to it – so she could go back to bed. Yesterday she'd been looking forward to that prospect, but today she wasn't so sure.

Throughout the evening she'd hugged to herself the news she was going to impart to Charles, with a delicious feeling of anticipation of the night to come. But once they were in bed Charles had made love to her silently, hurriedly, with none of the affection and consideration that had brought her to such heights of passion during his previous leave.

As he rolled away from her, she recalled the wisecracks made by the younger women at the WVS about the urgency of a man's needs when he hadn't had a woman for a long time, and felt consoled. Snuggling up to him, and stroking the fine hair on his chest, she told him that he was to become a father the following spring.

His immediate reaction was simply a stiffening of his body, which made her put her hand back down to her side, and the ensuing silence was so long that she began to think he hadn't heard her.

After he'd turned away from her, muttering that he needed to sleep, she lay for a long time thinking about the reaction she'd expected from him every time she'd played this scene in her imagination. She'd seen Charles turning to her with incredulous joy, wrapping her in a cocoon of tender concern, and she sharing with him all the strange things that pregnancy was already doing to her body. It was to have been a time of laughter and togetherness, made all the more poignant by further separation, during which time he would pen loving notes admonishing her to take care of herself and the son she was convinced she was carrying.

She thought of this again as she leaned against the bathroom washbasin. *Too many expectations!* she told herself fiercely, to stop the tears that were hovering behind her eyelids. *You didn't even know whether he wanted children – the poor man has every right to be taken aback, especially when he was so washed out!*

She splashed her face with cold water and brushed her teeth to get rid of the acrid taste in her mouth. She would creep back to bed and doubtless discover that when he woke, Charles would be just as excited about everything as she herself felt.

Brimming over with the same sort of excuses with which she'd exculpated Mother's behaviour over the years, she tiptoed back into the bedroom.

But Charles was already rising, sitting on the side of the bed, his face devoid of expression.

"Oh!" she smiled at him winningly to show that she harboured no ill-feelings about his lack of sensitivity. "It's very early – I had to use the bathroom, but neither of us need get up just yet."

"I must," he said shortly. "I need to make my way back to Duxford today."

"But... but I thought you were going to stay until tomorrow!"

"I'm not due back officially until tomorrow afternoon, but it took me much longer to get down here than I thought, so I think it will be best to make tracks this morning." He avoided her eyes and reached for his dressing gown.

"I don't have to work today, with Wendy here – can I come to Newport with you?"

He turned ice-blue eyes upon her. "Just as you like." And then he left the room.

Jennie stood by the window as he pulled the door closed behind him in what seemed to be an emphatic gesture. She was reminded of the end of *Gone with the Wind* and Rhett Butler's: "Frankly, my dear, I don't give a damn!"

She and Laura had queued at the Pavilion in Abergavenny to see the film, and she remembered how she'd compared Charles to Rhett when she first knew him. Now the similarity was there again, his voice every bit as cold and clipped as Clark Gable's. But she was no Scarlett O'Hara! What had she done to produce such animosity? Surely he couldn't have failed to realise that a baby was the likely outcome of their uninhibited coupling of a few months ago?

They stood silently side by side on the noisy, teeming platform as the London train pulled in. The short journey from Nantyderry had been a difficult one. Jennie had tried to introduce all sorts of light conversation, but had received such off-hand monosyllabic replies that she began to wonder what the other people in the compartment would be thinking, and lapsed into an embarrassed silence.

As the London train drew to a halt soldiers and other Forces personnel stepped forward to open the doors, many of them lingering, one hand on the door, with a wife or sweetheart standing very close, heads bent in murmured farewells.

Jennie made one last attempt to reach Charles. "Before you go – we must talk! *Please!* The baby – if you stay in England, will you be able to get leave when it's born? I don't know when I'll see you – I don't know what to do! There are things I'll need to get, arrangements to be made – I don't know what you want! Names…"

He turned to her suddenly, eyes glittering dangerously, and grabbed her arm with such force that she cried out. "I don't care what you do, but if you have this baby, then the next time I see you, I'll *kill* both of you!"

He released her arm as suddenly as he'd held it, and without another word strode swiftly towards the train and boarded it. In the flurry of people she didn't see which compartment he went to, or whether he looked through the window towards her. The whistle blew, followed by a mighty slamming of doors, and the train began to chug gently away from the platform.

Jennie stood where he had left her, head held high. Numb with disbelief as all her dreams and her few small hours of happiness crumbled away, she did nothing to check the tears which streamed down her face, and was still standing there long after the train had disappeared round the bend in the line.

19

Harry

"Mam! Mam!" Harry called her name as soon as he pushed open the front door, but the house was suspiciously quiet. If she'd been there she would've come running at the first sound of his voice. He looked round the little front room. The black vases with their pink roses stood reassuringly on the mantelpiece, flanking the only clock in the house, its metallic ticking loud now in the silence.

Putting his kit-bag down, he glanced at the table and saw three neat piles of coins, each with a torn piece of paper underneath, labelled in Mam's spidery uncertain hand: *Rent. Insurance. Club.* He smiled to himself as he went through to the living room to put the kettle on. Of course – it was Friday! Mam would be out shopping, and the various money collectors would be expected to let themselves into the house and pick up the dues owing to them.

He swung the kettle over the fire and stood gazing out of the window, glad of the dingy sameness of the back yard. He made himself some tea and settled into his father's chair, the cushions permanently indented to fit his body.

This leave wouldn't be like the last. Then, he had returned from Dunkirk weary and thinner, with all sorts of horrors playing repeatedly in the cine-camera of his mind, but everyone had wanted to treat him like a hero, merely for surviving. In the pubs there'd been no shortage of people ready to buy him a drink with cries of, "You made it then, did you, Harry man? What you having?" – and he wanted to tell them that there'd been nothing heroic about crawling up and down a beach, hoping against hope that you would be in the next batch to be put on a boat. But if he'd begun he would have been like Coleridge's Mariner, and not have been able to stop until the whole tale had been told.

And now the heroics of Dunkirk had been superseded by the Battle of Britain, and almost everyone had a tale to tell about the war, even in a place like Blaenavon which was so far removed from much of it.

It hadn't been so bad when they'd first landed in France. His section was billeted in a little town called Ecachon and had quickly set about laying cables while the Phony War had played itself out. Mile after mile of cable spewed out of the lorries, while two men walked behind to lay them – with such efficiency that he heard later that 26,000 miles had been laid, and not one bit of it used. Then Hitler, having secured Denmark and Norway, turned his attention west and by the middle of May his mechanised armour was rolling through the French countryside. Harry's section had pulled back to Armentiers, and if he closed his eyes he could still see the chaos: the French, if they were able, scattering like ants, having first (for reasons known only to themselves) released all the lunatics from the local asylum; and those poor devils wandering the streets while bombs began to rain down on the civilians who had nowhere else to go.

His first sight of violent death, close-hand, had been while they were laying cable to blow up a bridge to slow the German advance. A queue of women and children outside a boulangerie opposite the bridge; there one minute, and then no more – just scattered bodies amongst the debris in the strange silence that followed an attack.

He was shocked by the suddenness of it; of life extinguished in a moment, without warning, with no chance to prepare, or say goodbye. Megan's lingering death, and even that of Nan, had at least allowed time for adjustment, and his grief had blotted out the sight of Ivor's battered body so that it had seemed he'd simply gone away. But here was immediate evidence of the frailty of human existence.

He went with the others and picked up the featherlight bodies of small children, their future gone in one swift blow, and as he lifted them all he could hear in his mind was Mam's voice when she was distressed: *Oh, dear, dear! Oh, dear, dear!*

The bodies of the adults were so damaged that all they could do was collect the pieces and, when there seemed to be sufficient, label them as one body. A body. Not a person any longer.

He didn't tell his family any of this. Sat at Lizzie's table for Sunday tea (amid what seemed to be a surfeit of women, with so many of the men having gone away), a child perched on each knee, there came the inevitable question: "What was it like?"

He told them of the lighter moments instead – the ones he hoped he would remember when this was all finally at an end. His unit going into a bombed jeweller's shop, and Jack Patterson helping himself to watches, so that for ages afterwards his mates would ask him: "What time is it, Jack?" and he would roll up his sleeve to display an assortment of silver and gold, and with a grin on his grimy face would answer, "What time do you want?" Or Ginger MacDonell prowling round the same shop muttering to himself, ignoring the silver and gold on display, and searching instead for razor blades, while the sound of bombs came ever nearer.

He told them about the large house they'd stayed in when they'd first reached Belgium, the doctor owner hurrying away as they arrived, with cries of, "It's all yours, boys!" in excellent English. For the first time in weeks there were beds and sofas to sleep on, if you were lucky enough to bag them first. Harry had spied an enormous child's cot, much larger than English ones. "I'll take this!" he said. "I can sleep with my feet through the bars." And so he had, a deep sleep from which he was eventually roused when those around him began to flee the building as bombs began to land with an ear-splitting noise. "Wait for me!" Harry had shouted as, in his panic, his legs would not free themselves from between the bars.

The family laughed at his explanation of how he had eventually toppled out of the cot, so he hadn't needed to tell them about the carnage at Dunkirk. He kept to himself the memories of men in the water desperately clamouring to get onto the packed boats, while those already on board knocked their hands away for fear they would all capsize, and of the Navy arriving and taking charge of the chaos, making the men line up properly, and shooting at those who didn't.

Instead, he spoke of the heroism of the everyday sailors manning their little boats, and of how good the buckets of tea tasted, and the bread and cheese that were brought round when he was finally put onto a naval ship at the end of the pier after five hungry days on the beach. And of falling asleep, and waking again in sight of Dover.

"We've got 'vacuees from Dover in our class at school!" piped up Lizzie's eldest, Bethan. "Mam gave them some of our clothes 'cos they didn't bring much with them."

He told them about befriending a young lad from Ebbw Vale, Taffy Briggs, but he didn't tell them about taking a blood-spattered tin hat from a dead officer and cleaning it out with sand before insisting that the hatless Taffy wear it. Nor did he tell them about him and Taffy taking a sick soldier to the Major-in-Charge so that he could be put on a Red Cross ship, only for the Red Cross ship to receive a direct hit as they were struggling back up the beach. And he didn't tell them about the bad dreams, with their recurrent element of looking up from the beach at the destruction of the town and seeing a dead horse, blown sky-high and swinging from an iron sign jutting out over a ruined hotel.

Bridget, who'd moved in with Lizzie since Archie had been called up, had seen the strain in his eyes and his determination to keep things light. She indicated the pair on her knee. "Sit next to these two, Harry," she said, in a voice that was now developing a curious Welsh inflection at odds with her London vowels, "and keep kissing them. They've just had mumps, and with a bit of luck you might catch it! That would keep you at home for a while longer!"

He'd just stubbed out his cigarette when he heard the front door open. He peered round the living room door first, in case it was one of the tally men, but it was Mam, shopping bags in hand and looking smaller than he remembered. He opened the door wider, so that she saw him as she kicked the front door closed behind her. Then the shopping bags were forgotten as she rushed towards him with a little cry of delight.

After she'd kissed him and held him for a second, she stood back and looked him over critically. "'Mmm. Not so bad as last time. They must be taking a bit better care of you. I suppose it's been a bit easier for you while you've been in England?"

Pictures of Sheffield engulfed in flames rushed through his mind, but he pushed them away. "Yes, while we were outside Doncaster. Goldthorpe Park – you remember I wrote to you from there? Beautiful place it is. Kept us there for weeks, they did, while they sorted us all out.

"How's everyone?" he went on, so that he could avoid telling her for the moment that this was embarkation leave.

"Not so bad. Lizzie's a bit worried because she hasn't heard from Archie for a while, but your Dad's happy 'cos he's been put on full time at the steel works." She glanced down at the meagre food packages in her hands. "And I'm wishing you were back in the Cworp, now that there's all this rationing! Mind you, it's teaching Bridget a thing or two – never known that girl cook a decent meal before the War, but she turns out all sorts of things these days."

Later, she pulled out an envelope from the sideboard drawer. "I thought you should have this, now, before all the others realise you're here and the house gets full of people."

"What is it?"

"It's what I got for selling the furniture – like you asked me to – after Megan died."

"Oh." He glanced at the fat wad of notes inside the envelope – along with a collection of photographs, all that was left of his time with Megan. Now that the whole world was being turned upside down, it already felt like a lifetime since she had died. But for an instant he saw her laughing face again, and the pain he'd thought he had under control now washed over him anew, in all its fullness.

He handed the envelope back to his mother. "Why don't you keep it for me? Not much use for a load of money at the moment. And if you need a few bob for something – well it's there for you. We can sort it out when I'm home for good."

She looked hesitantly at him. "I have wondered – since all this began – that perhaps you wouldn't make too much effort to come back again…"

He smiled wryly. "Don't worry. I'm too much of a coward for that. Scared stiff most of the time, when everything's going on."

She'd been right, though, as she usually was where one of her own was concerned. Army life had suited him well when he'd first joined up. Surrounded only by other men, he could put his emotions on hold and shut away the memories of loving and losing. Wearing uniform, responding to routine and following orders meant that he didn't have to think about how to organise his life, and concentrating on the minutiae of whether a belt buckle shone sufficiently brightly became more important than the question of what was he going to do with the rest of his life – or even whether he wanted it. And so he'd gone abroad viewing quite fatalistically the probability that he may not return.

But imperceptibly Dunkirk and the last couple of months had changed that; watching the maimed and injured clinging on desperately to life, often against impossible odds, had made him reassess his own condition.

Once regrouped and re-equipped, his section had been sent to Sheffield to re-establish communication lines after a series of devastating raids. Even the most hardened were unprepared for what met them. A pall of black soot hung over the city following the incineration of much of the centre, and people who survived were unrecognisable, with faces blacker than any miner working at the coal face. Those in charge had been convinced that, as Sheffield was in a dip and therefore protected from the sky by an almost ever-present mist, then the trams for which it was famous were safe to use and could continue to run. But two moonlit nights in November had proved this theory wrong, and in one lightning strike the main street had been hit with ruthless precision, and almost every tram, and those travelling on them, wiped out.

And in the midst of chaos and confusion Harry realised that his will to live was as strong as in those who were dragged out of collapsed buildings; that the inherent determination to survive had only been numbed, not obliterated, by Megan's death. As he watched bewildered children given shelter and witnessed the pathetic bodies of those for whom shelter was too late, he knew that he had no right to feign indifference to life and, with a certain amount of shame, that he was silently giving thanks that it was not he, or anyone close to him, who had forfeited theirs.

Mam took the envelope back and returned it to the sideboard. "I'll keep it safe here, then, until you're back... I expect it will be a while, won't it?"

He nodded. "I think it will. Going abroad again this week – I don't know where."

The predictable family get-together was no less boisterous for being dominated by talk of the War. It was interrupted in the evening by an air raid warning blasting out from the fire station. The family headed for the cellar in a leisurely way that made Harry hugely agitated. Mam decided to make a pot of tea to take down with them, while his father searched for the spare paraffin for the little heater they kept there. Harry discovered that he was far more bothered by the thought of Jerry coming over when it was his family involved than he had been at any time during the preceding months.

"Never for us, it isn't," his father said as they settled down by candlelight. "Worst part is knowing that some poor blighters in Coventry or Birmingham are for it, when you hear them all coming over."

"There was one German plane spotted during the day," Lizzie told him. "Looking for the Munitions Works at Glascoed, we think. Trouble was, lots of people thought it was one of ours, and all the kids at Forge Side School ran out into the playground to wave at it!"

Despite the heater, it was cold in the cellar. "It'll be even colder for Mrs. Isaacs in her special shelter!" said Dad, as the women tucked blankets round the children. He turned to Harry with a chuckle. "Runs to the lav at the bottom of the garden, she does, soon as the siren goes, and won't come out for hours. Doesn't matter who needs to use it – and they share with next door!"

"They ought to get her a proper Anderson shelter like the Williamses have got, over Capel Newydd," said Bridget, passing Harry a mug of tea. "He goes down there like a shot, the minute the warning goes, but she dithers about and gets him all agitated." She grinned, her teeth flashing white in the dim light. "Apparently he'd almost got her in there a few nights ago when we had a big one – and then she ran off back towards the house. 'Where you going?' he shouted after her. 'To get my teeth!' she said. 'You don't need your teeth,' he shouted back, 'it's bombs they're dropping, not bloody sandwiches!'"

Harry joined in the general laughter, as much at Bridget's excellent mimicry of a strong Welsh accent as at the story itself, and he was taken back to how she'd make Megan laugh, even when she had been so ill. He wondered how he'd have coped, leaving Megan to go to war, worrying about her while he was away. Perhaps it was better that she'd left him.

He had a few moments alone with Bridget when the 'all-clear' had sounded. "What news of Dai?"

Bridget put down her tea towel and fished in her apron pocket for a small paper sweet packet which held five Woodbines. Giving one to Harry and leaning forward to light her own, she said: "Africa still. I thought they might bring his Squadron nearer home during the Battle of Britain, but he's still out there, enjoying the life of Riley if his letters are anything to go by. He'd still like to be up there flying, he says, but I reckon he'd soon change his mind if he saw what was going on over here."

Dai hadn't made it as a pilot, so had settled for the blacksmith's shop instead. Harry made no mention to Bridget of the rumblings that were already going on in North Africa since Italy had joined the fray. Africa was a huge continent; there would be time enough for her to worry once she knew if Dai had been moved north.

He caught the train to Newport on a raw, late November morning. "At least if we're going abroad we might have it bit warmer than this," he said as Mam waited for his kiss on her cheek. He'd been up early to say goodbye to his Dad before he left for the morning shift at the steel works.

He looked up and down the length of Morgan Street, breathing deeply, as if by inhaling he could take a piece of it with him. Mam tapped him on the arm and thrust a package at him, wrapped in Saturday's bread wrapper. "Sandwiches for the journey. Ham, they are. Good job your Dad've kept a few of his pigs still." Her voice sounded as harsh as the wind whipping along the pavement, as she fought to master her emotions. He'd come back twice since the war started: did that mean that he had two chances less of coming back again?

"Take care then, Mam." The cloth of his Army issue felt rough against her cheek as he took her in his arms. "I'll write when I can – tell you about my suntan!"

She kissed him back, then pushed him gently away from her. "Go on! I've got all the washing to see to, can't stop here on the step with you all day." But she stayed at the front door, watching him to the end of the street. He turned then and waved, and noticed how grey her hair was in the wintry sun filtering through the clouds.

He thought he might meet up with someone he knew at Newport, but despite the throng of people he remained alone. There were all sorts of servicemen on the platform, as well as women, looking trim and efficient in uniform, but none that he knew. He managed to grab a window seat and lit a cigarette.

Somehow, he missed Megan more when it was time to leave Wales again than he did while he was there. Or perhaps it was the fond farewells that could be witnessed the length and breadth of the platform which made him long once more to hold her in his arms? He hadn't had anything to do with women since he'd joined up, although there'd been plenty of opportunity. Many of his mates had got to know the French Mam'selles during the Phony War, but somehow the smell of garlic and the thought of hairy armpits had been enough to put him off. Or perhaps these things were just a convenient excuse not to test his still far-from-settled emotions.

As the train pulled away many of the young women seeing off their loved ones ran alongside, waving. His eye was caught by one who didn't.

She stood very still a little distance from the platform edge, her face pale against dark brown hair, not unlike Megan's. But her eyes weren't Megan's. They were large and grey and held unutterable anguish as tears poured unchecked down her cheeks. She held her head high, despite the tears, as if oblivious to or uncaring of her distress being seen by those who jostled past her, but she didn't seem to be searching for a face at the windows that were rattling by her.

Her distress moved Harry in a way he'd rarely been moved by a woman since Megan's death. Lucky, lucky man, he thought, of the unknown recipient of all that emotion.

The train gathered speed until the station was left far behind, but the imprint of her face seemed to stay on the window glass, so that Harry remained staring thoughtfully at it until the train reached Bristol and he relinquished his seat to a pert little Wren.

Charles wandered down Regent Street towards Piccadilly Circus, where Eros was protected by a strange, pyramid-shaped shelter decorated with war slogans. He'd come in to the West End instead of going straight to a connecting train at King's Cross, feeling the need to be part of the anonymous bustle of the capital. There was a surreal atmosphere here which suited his detached mood. Oxford Street appeared to be in ruins, with all the major stores having been hit – John Lewis, D H Evans, Bourne and Hollingsworth, had all received direct hits but were still open for business, sometimes windowless: gaunt, sightless giants in the midday sunshine. Outside one of them was a heap of bare window dummies, at first sight a grotesque pile of bodies. Yet more people than ever were going about their business, apparently heedless of the devastation around them.

Charles turned into Leicester Square, where a building was still smouldering from an incendiary the night before, yet on the opposite corner stood a long queue of people waiting to see *The Wizard of Oz*.

As Charles stood surveying the scene and wondering whether he too should seek oblivion in escapist drama, the menacing whoop of an air-raid siren began to rise into the air and, like many others, he turned towards the Underground entrance.

As he reached the top of the steps, he stood aside courteously for an elderly woman to go before him, and in so doing stepped back onto a dainty foot in a very high-heeled shoe, causing a squeal of pain to be emitted by its owner.

"Oh, I'm so sorry!" Charles apologised as he swivelled round, to be confronted by an even louder squeal that made heads turn.

"Charles! *Darling!* It's you! I don't believe it!" Squashed toes forgotten, Sylvia flung herself into his arms – to the annoyance of the people behind her, who made a detour around the swirling fur coat she was wearing.

"How marvellous to see you!" Charles exclaimed, as he disentangled himself from her embrace and automatically took her elbow to steer her down the steps. As he looked at her animated face that seemed younger than when he'd last seen her, he realised that he meant it.

They found a corner of the crowded platform and began to exchange news. "You look wonderful," Charles told her. "Married life must be suiting you."

She gave a rueful laugh. "You mean *widowhood* is suiting me. Poor old Graham died in May. He was awfully keen to do his bit, so he joined the Home Guard, and then, poor dear, had a heart attack the very first time he had to 'stand to'. He was desperately worried about an invasion, and I think that's what did it."

She leaned towards him conspiratorially and he caught a whiff of her familiar perfume. "But I have to tell you, darling, that he left me a *very* wealthy woman!"

She sat back triumphantly, as if her inadvertent acquisition of a large sum of money was a considerable achievement.

"And what about you?" She smiled at him with a hint of coyness. "Have you missed me?"

"Of course!" But he couldn't bring himself to tell her that he was now married too. "I've moved around quite a bit, from one base to another – been bombed out of a couple – all some distance from

London, of course, and now I'm on a bit of leave. I had some family business to attend to." He had woven so many intricate stories to Sylvia over the years that it was difficult to recall them exactly, so now it was better to be as economical as possible with facts.

He scrutinised her afresh, taking in the carefully applied make-up, her expensive clothes with a hat whose brim tilted slightly over one eye so that part of her face was in shadow, and wondered – as he had so many times before – why he ever strayed from her side, and why, in the last couple of years, a country bumpkin family had held so much attraction for him.

"As a matter of fact," he went on, "I don't have to be back on duty until tomorrow afternoon, and I've been wondering what to do with myself until then."

"Well, I've got the perfect solution!" she exclaimed. "If the all-clear goes in time, you can come with me to the National – no pictures there, of course, and the roof's in a bit of a mess, but they're giving these *marvellous* lunchtime concerts with Myra Hess. She's all the rage, even if her name is a bit unfortunate!"

"Is that what brings you up to Town – to go to a concert in the middle of the day? Surely Headley-on-the-Hill is safer?"

"So it is, darling. And when all this first started I was very grateful that it is – but you know, it's so *dull!* Coming up to Town and feeling part of what's going on is much more *fun*, in a strange sort of way."

For the first time in days, Charles threw his head back and laughed aloud. Only someone as absurd as Sylvia could describe dodging bombs in a war-ravaged city in chilly November as 'fun'.

"And maybe afterwards we could go on to the Dorchester or somewhere – my treat, of course, when you've got to go back to a ghastly RAF base tomorrow – it's where everyone who's anyone goes at the moment. Or perhaps the Savoy – they've got a miniature hospital down in the basement, you know."

She'd simply assumed that he would spend the rest of the day in her company, and when the 'all-clear' sounded a little while later, he was happy to go along with that assumption.

The concert was excellent, the surroundings only adding a poignancy to the music, and later, dancing at the Dorchester, he wondered again at his brief episode of madness in thinking that the role of a minor country squire was ever one he could have shouldered.

Having thus dismissed the last eighteen months as a mental aberration, Charles was able, in the frothy company of Sylvia, to give himself over to forgetting the miseries of the recent past, and it seemed only natural that in these troubled times he should escort her all the way back to Headley-on-the-Hill.

20

Tom watched as his wife lifted a shapely bare leg to sit astride her bicycle, and smiled at the carefully pencilled-in seam and the sturdy shoes that still somehow managed to look elegant. He lifted his glance to take in the rest of her smart attire – from the neatly-belted dress which accentuated her narrow waist and the boxy jacket over it, to the carefully rolled hair which she was sure made her look like Dorothy Lamour. The smart clothes would be exchanged for a boiler suit and the hair bundled into a scarf the minute she reached the munitions factory, but Nancy didn't care. There was the evening cycle ride to Glascoed first, and the road from Llanover was so busy now with Army traffic and people going to and from shift work that it was important for her to look her best. And she would look just as band-box smart tomorrow morning on the return journey, her lipstick freshly applied, no matter how bleary-eyed she felt after a twelve-hour shift.

He smiled at her as their eyes met. "Same time tomorrow night?" he said.

She grinned back at him. "And the same place, if you like!"

She leaned forward to kiss him, leaving a bright red mark on his cheek, before pushing off along the narrow lane that would take her down towards Nantyderry.

Tom watched her go, reflecting, not for the first time, that they weren't doing too badly together through this war. He thoroughly enjoyed his job at the War-Ag, overseeing the distribution of supplies, which often necessitated his travelling around the immediate countryside to visit farms and meant that no two days were the same – and Nancy, with the challenge of doing her bit at the factory as well as running the home, was positively blooming.

He knew that some people liked to comment about her flightiness and her readiness to go dancing with whoever invited her, but they didn't know her like he did. When they worked opposite shifts, as they were doing at the moment, she would just be waking when he returned from work, and her arms would reach out, as they had this evening, and pull him into the bed, where her body was warm and inviting. And when she was on days and he'd been out all night 'doing his bit', she always welcomed him home with far more than a cup of tea. What more could a man want?

He nodded to himself as he sauntered down the garden, deciding to spend the mild spring evening in the greenhouse. Dazzled by the exciting lives of the film stars she read about so avidly might make her enjoy the attention of other men alright, but deep down he knew she was strictly a one-man girl.

Much the same thoughts were passing through Nancy's mind as she turned off the main road to take the short route through Nanty-derry. There might well be an evening convoy of trucks making its way ponderously along Rumble Street towards Glascoed, and, as she manoeuvred carefully to overtake it by cycling along the grass verge, one or two of the men might well call out, "Want a lift, love?" or, "Plenty of room in the back!" in strange English accents, and there might even be one or two wolf whistles, if there were not too many commanding officers about. And to all of them Nancy would smile, enjoying the stir she caused and tossing her head so they could admire her glossy hair and fine-boned profile – but who would actually need any of them, when you had a man as ardent and virile as Tom at home?

She passed the entrance to the farm, but even though she was in good time she had no intention of calling in there and getting the big freeze from Her Ladyship. Now *there* was a woman who could do with a bit more slap and tickle, Nancy decided, as she waved to the guard at Nantyderry Halt and then freewheeled carelessly down Star Pitch. She could tell from the way her parents-in-law behaved towards each other, never touching or engaging in light-hearted banter, that the old dragon wasn't getting it from her husband – and how could she, when they had separate bedrooms at opposite ends of the house?

That her mother-in-law was in need of something physical Nancy, endowed with much more than her share of natural feminine intuition, was in no doubt. There'd been something funny going on between her and Charles at one time, Nancy was sure of it, although she hadn't been able quite to work out what it was. Perhaps Katharine had made a pass at him and he'd turned her away – understandably, when she was so much older.

And then there was Tom's father, working away all day on the farm but with little to cheer him in the house.

"Such a pity for him," she'd once remarked to Tom, after subject-ing him to a long, tangled account of what she thought was wrong with his family, which left him none the wiser.

Tom had just laughed. "At their age they're both probably past it anyway! You're just being fanciful."

But Nancy had seen a tortured look in Edward's eye that she recognised – and he was such a nice man. He deserved to find some kind woman who would give him the comfort Nancy was sure he needed.

Rumble Street was quiet after all this evening, and she continued to chew over the situation at the farm. Things had gone from bad to worse through the winter, what with Jennie being pregnant but never able to get hold of Charles, so that everyone was wondering whether he'd left her – but no-one liked to say so. Of course, there were dozens of women having babies without their menfolk around, but mostly because they were serving abroad, not settled in this country and seemingly unable to put pen to paper or get to a telephone.

"It's all going to end in tears," she'd warned Tom after their last Sunday tea-time visit, when Laura had stupidly gone on about how frequently she heard from Cyril even though he was now risking life and limb while sorting out the whole of the RAF's presence in India or some such place. The rest of the table had become ominously quiet, until Jennie had said, "I think I've had enough to eat. I feel a bit tired – if you'll all excuse me, I'm going to lie down."

Even Katharine had said nothing as Jennie walked from the room, carrying her pregnancy awkwardly, as if the enormous bulge of her stomach was a separate entity from her, while her own body was becoming thinner than ever.

"And they needn't think they can call on me to help pick up the pieces," Nancy had continued, after Tom had agreed she was probably right. "Not after the last time I went over there to help, and all I got were ungrateful comments over my ability to clean a kitchen floor."

Nancy turned into the factory entrance, to be hailed by the other girls who were arriving for the night shift. She put thoughts of her in-laws away. Thank goodness Tom had turned out normally: tall, good-looking and – she smiled to herself as she put the chain on her bike and remembered his energy of a couple of hours ago – very hot-blooded.

Nancy had just missed seeing Jennie when she'd cycled past the farm. Had she been five minutes earlier, she would have spotted her sister-in-law walking disconsolately back to the farm, her pregnancy looking far too big a burden for her to carry.

Jennie had said nothing when she'd returned from the fateful trip to see Charles off at Newport, and at first the family thought her swollen eyes and quiet demeanour were a natural response to saying goodbye. But as the days went on and Jennie became more and more listless, made no mention of Charles at all, and took little notice of Mother urging her to hurry up all the time, meaningful looks were exchanged behind her back.

Finally, when Laura received a loving epistle one breakfast time from Cyril and began to read extracts of it to Selina, Jennie abruptly stopped buttering her toast and walked out heedlessly into the rain-spattered yard and across to the cow-shed. It was Edward who rose and followed her.

"Do you want to talk about it?" he asked gently, when he found her sitting on a milking stool in the far corner of the shed.

"There isn't much to say," she shrugged dully. "I told Charles that I'm pregnant and he doesn't want to know a thing about it." She turned to her father with such pained eyes that he flinched. "He said he would kill me if I didn't get rid of it. He hates me Dad, just because I'm pregnant, and I haven't a clue what to do about it."

Father pulled up another stool, to give himself time to think. Then he took hold of Jennie's hand. "Perhaps it was just a bit of a shock. Some men find it a bit scary, knowing there's a baby on the way – you know, extra responsibility, and so on. I remember when Mother... well, anyway, perhaps with the war and everything, and him being away so much, he was worried that it was too much for you both to cope with."

He put his arm around her and pulled her tense, rigid body to him. "He's probably feeling completely different now he's had time to think about it – and is too ashamed of himself to know what to write to you!"

The rest of the family said more or less the same thing after Father, to spare Jennie, told them what had happened.

"Of course he'll want the baby by now!" Laura cried. "I remember Cyril reacting just the same way when I told him about Selina!"

Which Jennie knew was a lie, because Cyril had been as proud as punch from the first, but it was a well-intentioned lie, and Jennie smiled at Laura gratefully. "You must keep writing to him," Laura went on, "and tell him all about the pregnancy – get him involved, so that he can write back and make plans for the future – he'll soon come round, you'll see."

All the things Jennie had been saying to herself, and now the comforting words from her family filled her with fresh hope. They were right! She had rather sprung it on him, after all, and he'd had a gruelling few months with all the heavy bombing that had gone on.

Who knew what that did to a person?

Mother's reaction was predictably more caustic. "Of course she should write to him! Make him see how ridiculous he's being! It's Jennie who's going to have to give birth and spend the next few years with a child tied to her, while he, like every man, can come and go as he pleases!"

Gwyneth and Wendy offered no advice, not being real members of the family, but made a point of being especially nice to Jennie and protecting her from Mother's increasing irritability as she took out her feelings about Charles on the rest of them.

Gwyneth had plenty to say to her own family, though, when she went home on her next day off. "Happy as pigs in muck, they were, when he was home that first time, which must have been when she fell. A different story it was, though, when he came home in November. I said that at the time, didn't I Mam? Wouldn't surprise me if he's taken up with some flighty piece in uniform. They say that's the only reason some of these girls have joined up –" Gwyneth, who kept thinking of the opportunities she might have if she could pluck up enough courage to don a uniform herself, pursed her lips censoriously – "and after all, he's a very handsome man."

Jennie decided to take Laura's advice. After all, despite at times sounding quite ridiculous Laura had managed to keep Cyril deeply in love with her, so she must know what she was talking about.

During the next few months of her pregnancy, she kept convincing herself that Charles would come round, as all fathers did, and tried in her letters to share the growing sense of wonder at this new life forming inside her. But as Christmas came and went with no word, and the weeks continued to pass, she gave up and kept her feelings to herself.

Mother urged her to contact Charles's commanding officer and get him to have a word with her husband, but Jennie resisted. What could any commanding officer do? Order Charles to pull himself together and start loving his wife and unborn child again?

At one point Jennie convinced herself that Charles might be ill – he hadn't seemed himself at all on that last visit, after all. So she sent a letter marked 'Confidential' to the Medical Officer at Duxford, and received a kindly reply saying that as far as he was aware Charles was in excellent health, and if there was anything further he could do to help she was to let him know. But she didn't write again.

For the first few weeks the whole family strained for the sound of post dropping through the letter box. "There!" Katharine would cry, having spent some time the previous night exhorting the Almighty to stop punishing her for her misdemeanours by treating her daughter so cruelly. "That will be for you, I expect, Jennie!" Then, when it wasn't, Mother became personally affronted that her entreaties had been ignored and took it out on whatever chore, or person, was to hand.

Jennie became confused by her mother's ambivalence. At times she could be almost kind, encouraging her to sort out Selina's old baby clothes in readiness, and making sure that Jennie had as many nourishing titbits as rationing allowed. But at others she would pronounce at length over what sort of man Charles was, that of course the marriage had been all wrong from the start, and that she'd known it would all go wrong – while somehow, to Jennie's tortured mind, managing to imply that considerable blame could be attached to Jennie's general ineptitude.

Aware of the increasingly anxious eyes and ears of the rest of the family, Jennie had taken to walking down to the telephone box next to the station whenever she steeled herself to renew her attempts to contact Charles. And this evening she would've been glad of the down-to-earth support of Nancy, whom she'd always liked, because for the first time in months she'd actually managed to talk to her husband.

Not that it had been much of a conversation. She'd hung on for ages, hoping that her money wouldn't run out while someone went to find him. Then, when she heard his voice saying a curt, "Hello?" her courage had almost failed her.

"It's me, Jennie," she said at last.

"I know who it is. What do you want?"

His voice was the same as it had been on the station the last time she'd seen him. Not a vestige of kindness, or even friendliness, in it.

"The baby is due in a few weeks' time. I've been trying to get in touch with you for ages, but you haven't answered any of my letters." She tried to keep her tone even and unemotional.

"I told you before: I don't want you to have this baby. I meant what I said when I told you to get rid of it."

"But he's going to be born soon! He'll be *your* son! You can't just deny his existence and walk away from that fact! We're married! Married couples have babies! What am I supposed to do on my own?… Why are you doing this to me?"

There was such a long silence at the other end of the phone that she thought they must have been cut off, but finally he spoke again.

"I have to go now. I'm afraid it's all been a terrible mistake."

This time the line did go dead. She stood in the telephone box for some minutes, staring at the instrument as if it might suddenly come to life again, but eventually there was nothing for it but to return to the farm.

A mistake. A terrible mistake.

The words were there again, haunting her. She trudged down the drive towards the house, the words echoing through her head, signifying, as far as she could see, her whole life so far.

She hadn't cried since the day Charles had left her on Newport Station, and unlike when she was a child and Mother had hissed with such venom that she'd been 'a mistake', she had no desire to cry now.

She felt numb and cold, despite the mild evening. She'd dreamed desperate dreams during the past few months, of everything being alright if only she could get to talk to Charles, but now they were as naught – had melted to nothing as soon as she heard his voice on the line. She'd contemplated getting on a train and travelling to Duxford – had even looked up where it was and planned the journey, but so many things confined her; the travel restrictions of the war, her lack of funds, the pregnancy, and most of all the deep, barely acknowledged anxiety over what she would do if he rejected her.

Well, now he had rejected her. She was no worse off than she'd been an hour ago, except that now she knew for certain what she was *not* going to be. She was never going to be a happily-married young mother.

The baby kicked inside her, as if to remind her of his presence, and she folded her arms protectively across her stomach as she walked. When she couldn't sleep at night she would stroke her stomach and tell the little being inside that everything was going to be all right. And as the time went on and wonder grew into an intense love, she became even more determined that her son – as she was sure the baby would be – should never feel that he, too, had been 'a mistake'.

The numbness continued to cocoon her from all thoughts of what she should do next. She went straight to the parlour. There was a play due on the wireless that she wanted listen to, and if she concentrated on that she might stay in this blissful state. She settled herself in an armchair with a cushion in her back – which always seemed to ache by this time in the evening – and tried to absorb herself in the story.

It was a good play, about life in the deep south of America, which made her think of *Gone With The Wind*, but she forced herself not to dwell on the memory of how she had at one time compared Charles to Rhett Butler. Besides, she knew that Rhett Butler would never have deserted a pregnant wife. The future loomed ahead frighteningly, and the past seemed only to hold disturbing memories, so she forced herself again to listen to the voices on the wireless.

She had almost succeeded when Mother came in. Hearing the deep drawl of a black slave, she crossed the room with a disapproving 'Tut!' Americans, especially poor ones, were high on her list of dislikes.

"Please don't turn it off," said Jennie, brittle. "I'm listening to it."

"This nonsense?" Mother's hand reached out towards the set. "I want to hear the news on the Home Service."

"You know that won't be on until nine o'clock, when this play will have finished. It's very interesting and I'd like to listen to it!" From within her cocoon Jennie heard her voice rise so that she was now talking quite loudly.

Mother looked at her in surprised indignation, but Jennie didn't give her time to speak. Her voice continued to grow as she went on: "It's difficult for you, I know, accepting that other people want to do something that you don't like, but that's a pity. I came in here purposely to listen to this play, I've been looking forward to it all day, and I don't see why I shouldn't do so just because you have walked into the room!"

It was suddenly desperately important that for once Mother should accept what she, Jennie, had to say.

As usual Mother responded sharply. "Don't you talk to me in that tone! This is only some old rubbish, you know it is! And I always listen to the nine o'clock news."

Jennie pulled herself to her feet. "Well, it will make a change for you *not* to have your own way for once, won't it? In case you weren't aware of it, I live in this house too, and have done for twenty years! But there has yet to come a day when something *I've* wanted has been given priority!"

The play was forgotten. The voices rose and fell from the wireless, but by now neither woman was paying any attention. Mother moved to the fireplace and lifted up the poker, then turned to answer Jennie, but as she opened her mouth to speak Jennie gave her no chance.

"What are you going to do with that? Hit me with it, because I've spoken back to you?" Jennie moved a step nearer. "Well, go on then! It's what you've wanted to do for years, isn't it?"

"Don't be so ridiculous!" Mother hastily replaced the poker in the grate, but Jennie wasn't listening.

"Oh, I was wrong! There *was* one thing I wanted that I was allowed to have," she cried: "Charles! I wanted to be married to him and live happily ever after more than anything else in the world. Well, I've got some news for you, better than anything on the wireless! I've finally spoken to Charles tonight, and he's told me categorically that he doesn't want me or the baby! That it was all some sort of *mistake!* But that shouldn't be any surprise to you, should it! I've been a *mistake* all my life!"

Hearing Jennie shouting, Father and Laura had both hurried to the parlour from different parts of the house and were just in time to hear Jennie's last words. Without looking at them, she stumbled from the room and headed for her bedroom.

For a long time she lay on the bed, staring at the ceiling, dry-eyed and thinking of nothing in particular. Some time later the bedroom door opened and Mother stood beside the bed.

"I didn't ever want this to happen to you," she said stiffly. "And I want you to know that after you've had the baby – if things stay the same – we will always keep a home for you here."

It was the nearest Jennie was ever going to get to an apology, she knew. It occurred to her that, once again, Mother had managed to get her own way – for years she had commented on how the young-est daughter should stay at home, and had held up royal examples as precedents. It would seem, after all, that this was what Jennie's future was to be.

"Thank you," she said, without turning her head towards Mother, and after a few moments Mother left the room.

Katharine made her way downstairs, bitterness welling up inside her. After all her efforts to resist temptation with Charles, to maintain her own reputation and that of her family, it seemed that they were to face the ignominy of a deserted daughter instead.

She was just as capable as he of ignoring the fact that her own jealousy and desires had played any part in the whole sorry story.

Push, Mrs. Keating... *push!*" The midwife's words seemed to be coming from a long way off. She needn't have bothered to urge so excitedly anyway; the whole of Jennie's body was contorting into an enormous contraction to expel the baby from her womb and she could no more have stopped it than fly. It demanded that she gave it all her attention, so that the midwife's ministrations counted for nothing. All that mattered was that she obey the dictates of her body.

She took in a great lungful of air, squeezed her eyes shut, pressed her lips together and responded to this overwhelming need to bear down. Just as she felt she must surely burst with the effort, or be split in two, she felt the baby's head emerge.

"That's it! Excellent! Rest now and breathe steadily for a moment. The head is here. Now, with the next contraction, just one more push and it will be all over!"

She opened her eyes, but had to close them again quickly as the next wave hit her. This time it was easier, though. As she pushed, the baby's body slid into the world, and she heard a lusty howl as her son raised his objections to the inconsiderate treatment he was receiving.

"It's a boy!" said the midwife, holding him aloft for Jennie to see.

"I know," she said, aware that her lips were tingling from the effort, while the rest of her body rejoiced at being relieved of its burden.

Later, when he was handed to her, wrapped so tightly in a flannelette sheet that it was no wonder his little face was like a boiled beetroot, she was pleased to see that he had her own dark hair.

"Eight pounds exactly!" declared the midwife as proudly as if this had been her personal feat. "And you were wonderful, my dear." She patted Jennie's arm. "One of the finest first deliveries I've attended, and a very bonny baby to boot."

Jennie glowed as she looked adoringly at the baby. For once she'd done something well. Despite all the tribulations of the past nine months, she'd carried this little chap inside her, nurtured and nourished him so that he was big and strong, and then delivered him with the minimum of pain and fuss.

He stirred in her arms and his face disintegrated as he began to wail. She looked quickly at the midwife for guidance. "Do what comes naturally and you won't go far wrong," she was told, as competent hands undid her nightie and guided the baby's face towards her nipple. Immediately he turned his head, latched on and began to suck.

"There now!" the midwife beamed. "You're definitely a natural! Hubby away, is he?" she went on sympathetically, to which Jennie just nodded while staring at the baby in fascination. "Well you make sure you tell him to get home safely so he can see what a fine boy he's got!"

When Jennie didn't answer, she patted her arm again. "Yes, well, you just carry on there for a while and I'll go and get you a nice cup of tea."

Both Mother and Father came at visiting time, when she was back in the main ward with all the other mothers.

"We've seen him in the nursery, through the window," Father told her. "Have you seen the size of his hands? Definitely cut out to be a farmer!"

"Did you have a dreadful time?" Mother asked hopefully in hushed tones, looking distinctly sorry when Jennie, still euphoric and exhilarated, shook her head and said, "Not a bit! It was the most exciting thing I've ever done in my life!"

Nothing was said of Charles until Mother and Father were back outside the Nursing Home, in the milk van, because there was no petrol for the car.

"I think we'd better call at the Post Office and send a telegram," Mother said, to which Father simply nodded. Once inside the building she wasn't sure what to put, but in the end decided on:

SON BORN THIS AM STOP ABERGAVENNY NURSING HOME STOP EIGHT LBS STOP BOTH WELL STOP

The views of the midwife who delivered the baby obviously weren't shared by the nursing home in general, which dictated that mothers could only do what came naturally provided it occurred on a four-hourly basis. The ward sister, a tall, mannish woman with very large feet in her regulation black laced shoes, would enter the ward at the appointed times with a baby under each arm, delivering them to the mothers as if they were the morning post. The baby belonging to the girl in the bed next to Jennie's had invariably reached the hiccuping stage of crying by this time, its natural inclinations to be fed unfortunately not corresponding to Greenwich Mean Time.

"Feed her up this time, Mrs. Owens," Sister would instruct the anxious mother, who had lain tensely listening to her baby's cries emanating from the nursery for the past hour or more and was now sufficiently distraught to be incapable of producing any milk: "or we'll have to put her on a bottle".

Jennie's baby, though, was declared a 'good little soul', sleeping from one feed to the next, producing a dirty nappy just when it was expected of him, and keen to suckle as soon as he was placed in his mother's arms.

"Just as well you've got used to this martinet," Jennie whispered to him as she stroked the soft hair at the side of his head, "because there's an even worse one at home – and she's not too keen on little boys, so you'll have to do your very best to charm her."

By the fourth day Jennie was producing milk in such copious amounts that she had to have a towel stuffed inside her nightie as feeding time approached. She liked being in the nursing home, with nothing expected of her other than to rest and tend her baby. The outside world receded, the only real one was here, in this room with five other young women – all of whom had husbands away, so that her solitary status was able to go unnoticed. She and the baby were safe in this tight little world, and the more she fell in love with her child, the less Charles or anybody else mattered.

And it was an enormous relief to be away from the farm, and the exhausting debates and discussions which had gone on after her outburst at Mother last month ...

The following day, after breakfast, when Wendy had gone outside to hose the yard down and Gwyneth was starting on the bedrooms, Mother had demanded: "I think you ought to tell us exactly what Charles said during your telephone call."

"Just what I told you last night," Jennie answered dully. "We didn't exactly have a riveting conversation. I asked him what he wanted to do about the baby and me, and he said that it had all been a terrible mistake."

Mother coloured at this. "So what happens now?" she asked quickly. "You've got his paybook at the moment, but what about when the war ends – what will he do about you then? You'll still be his responsibility."

"How should I know?" Jennie's softening towards her Mother ceased abruptly as she realised that the fact that he'd broken her heart was of less moment than the practicalities of financial support – and the fact that he no longer loved her seemed of no surprise to Katharine at all.

"Oh, I'm sure once the war is over and everything becomes back to normal he'll –" Laura began to say, but Father broke in.

"Jennie's home will be here, as it's always been, just as we agreed last night," he said with definition. "She's helped me run this farm as well as any man – better than her own brother, in fact – and if she comes back to it after she's recovered from having the baby, it will be time to start paying her a man's wage."

Jennie shot him a grateful look.

Katharine opened her mouth to say more, but then thought better of it. Perhaps now was not right, with Jennie looking as if her time could well come early, and plenty of other things to think about. Of course Jennie's place would still be at home, but for Katharine's benefit, not the farm's.

She would make sure, she decided as she rose to indicate that the discussion for the moment was at an end, that Edward would be fully aware of the extra burden all this would place on her. She hadn't wanted another child when Jennie was born, and she certainly didn't want one now! Nobody seemed to have thought that if Jennie was outside helping on the farm then she, Katharine, would inevitably be drawn into caring for the child. And Charles's child, at that! What if it looked like him, with the same piercing blue eyes, forever reminding her of her folly?

Nobody mentioned the fact that with the war so uncertain it seemed there would never be an end to it, plenty could happen which would ensure that none of them ever saw Charles again.

Over the next couple of weeks, although the dreaded word

'divorce' was never uttered, Mother, in between haranguing everyone – even her beloved chickens – about what she thought of men
who turned their backs on their families, began to drop heavy hints
about the necessity of seeing a solicitor in order to 'get your full due
if things get worse.' Jennie couldn't imagine how things could possibly get any worse, but refused to be drawn.

Another day, Mother said abruptly: "Would you like to have
a private room in the nursing home? It might be better to be in a
room by yourself when the other mothers are... well, some of their
husbands might get compassionate leave ... you know, if they are
serving in this country..."

"No, thank you!" Jennie had declared at once, before realising that
here was another of Mother's rare attempts at kindness." I appreciate
your thoughtfulness, but I don't want to have too much time on my
own – you know, in case I get to brooding. I think I'll be better with
company."

It was one aspect of her fortnight's confinement which Jennie
wasn't looking forward to. Despite all that was going wrong, the
thought of the birth didn't worry her at all – it merely filled her with
a strange excitement; but the prospect of staying in bed for the better
part of two weeks was far more daunting, as it gave so much time
for reflection.

She needn't have worried about that, though, in a ward of six
women. Caught up in the afterglow of the birth, she listened,
trance-like, to the chatter of the other mothers, ate everything that
was put in front of her – which was surprisingly good, considering the rationing – and dwelt on nothing more exacting than which
names to give the baby, or completing yet another matinée jacket. At
night they could hear bombers going over, heading for the Midlands,
but that too seemed to bear no relevance. If her mind turned to
Charles, it was only to wonder whether, if she could arrange for him
to see the baby – who was the most adorable in the whole hospital –
he might even yet change his mind.

This rosy glow was shattered just before lunchtime on the fourth
day, when a junior nurse came into the ward. "Post!" she announced
to the room in general, and began to distribute letters. Jennie's heart
missed a beat when she was handed one postmarked 'Cambridgesh-
ire.'

She opened it carefully and pulled out a single sheet of paper. It
took her no time at all to read the four words:

I have no son.

Automatically she placed the sheet back in the envelope, and then, in the quiet of the room, with the spring sunshine streaming in through a window at the far end, the tears which had been dammed up for the last six months began to fall. The terse communication had broken through her hormone-induced euphoria and brought reality crashing home to her. The tears became a torrent, pouring down her cheeks as her shoulders heaved, her breasts pumping out milk in sympathy.

The little nurse fled into Sister's office and asked her to come quickly, Mrs. Keating had just had some very bad news by the look of her and was getting hysterical.

Having been informed by Mother of the true state of affairs, Sister strode into the ward and, seemingly in one movement, whisked the curtains round the bed, fished an enormous white handkerchief from under her apron, and thrust it at Jennie before taking her into her arms, saying, "There, there, my girl. You let it all out. About time you did. Get it out of your system, you'll feel all the better for it."

She stayed, half-sitting on the bed, heedless of her cap being slightly askew and of the numbness creeping up one leg, murmuring nonsensical words of comfort (occasionally interspersed with a directive issued in a louder voice to any nurse she heard passing the curtains), until Jennie's sobs eventually died away.

"There now," she said finally, when the last tear was wiped away. "Let's get you sorted out, shall we? I'm going to fetch a bowl of water so we can sponge your face, then we'll change your nightie – what some mothers wouldn't give to have all that milk! – and then a nice cup of tea. Yes?"

Jennie nodded miserably. Satisfied, Sister went out through the curtain in search of hot water, fixing any enquiring look from the other patients with such a steely glare that they quickly turned away and pretended that they'd heard nothing.

"Now then," she said when Jennie had been washed and changed and her hair brushed soothingly. "We've a side room empty at the moment, which I think we should move you into. And then you might like to have that beautiful baby of yours with you for a while, and if you want, I'll stay and you can tell me all about it."

She smiled such a compassionate smile that her angular face was lit up. "Everything that goes in here," she pointed to her ears, "goes no further, and after thirty years in this job, you can be sure that there'll be nothing I haven't heard before."

She was surprisingly easy to talk to, making very little comment other than an occasional, "what happened then?" or, "and after that?" whenever Jennie came to a halt and the tears threatened again.

"So you see," Jennie finished, as the rattle of the lunch trolley could be heard in the corridor, "I'm completely baffled by the whole thing. I've wondered if it's simply that he's found someone else, but then, if that was the case, wouldn't it be easier, and kinder, just to say so?"

The baby, who'd been sleeping peacefully in her arms, stirred now and, sensing where he was, turned his head and began to search with his mouth. Despite herself, Jennie gave a little chuckle.

Sister looked at her fob watch. "I think, just for now, we'll forget what time it is, shall we? It will do both of you good." She watched silently as Jennie offered the baby her blue-veined breast, which his lips immediately seized as he made contented mewing sounds, almost like a new-born kitten.

When they were both comfortable, Sister said: "Whatever the reason for what has happened, you won't get over this until you accept that it's well and truly finished – you know that, don't you?"

Jennie concentrated on watching the baby for a few moments before raising her eyes to this calm, comforting woman. "I think I probably have accepted it, deep down. I think I knew that day on Newport Station that it was never going to work. I wanted to put off facing it, though – as if not only Charles but I, too, had failed the marriage if I didn't keep trying. It just became something else that I wasn't any good at... I don't think I've been very good at anything in my life so far, you see."

Sister nodded. "I'm quite sure marriage is something that you can't be good at on your own – and your husband is probably the type of man who should just never have married. Perhaps in a funny sort of way you should pat yourself on the back for being sufficiently attractive to make him even try it!"

Jennie leaned the baby forward to wind him. "He looks completely drunk," she said, as his head lolled forward and a trickle of milk escaped from the corner of his mouth."

Sister smiled. "I think one thing you *are* going to be very good at is motherhood, and I don't say that about many mothers who pass through here. I'm not pretending that the future is going to be easy for you, but there'll be many a girl bringing up a child on her own after this is all over. The time goes so quickly when they're small – try not to let it be spoilt by dwelling on what might have been, or you may find that it will become your greatest regret of all."

She stood up and became her brisk self again. "Shall I take him back to the nursery now, so that you can have your lunch? And when Staff Nurse brings him in for his two o'clock, we won't say anything!"

Jennie kissed the top of the baby's head and handed him over.

"Thank you, Sister – for listening and ... everything. I really shouldn't have taken up so much of your time."

"Nonsense! Now, after lunch, you make sure you have a rest, and then concentrate on what you're going to name this little chap. It's one thing us nurses calling him 'Baby Keating', but you really need to be calling him something else!" She turned in the doorway. "I'm going to ask Night Sister to give you something to make you sleep tonight. It's the best healer, you know, of mind and body."

"Thank you. And Sister... when my family come to visit, could you tell them... why I'm in here? So that we don't have to discuss it just yet?"

Sister nodded. "Of course."

The farm looked different, Jennie thought as the car pulled up in front of the house, and then she realised that her two weeks in hospital had been the longest she'd ever been away.

Father had driven home sedately because Jennie was in the back, nursing the baby – who was now named David, much to Mother's disgust because she was sure he would end up being called 'Dai', and that would be so common! (She had had to admit, though, that despite being a boy, he was a beautiful baby.)

Both Mother and Laura were on the front steps to greet them, and Gwyneth came rushing through from the kitchen as soon as they were inside, to exclaim over the baby, while little Selina tottered behind, her arms raised toward Jennie, to be picked up.

"She seems so big after dealing with this chap!" Jennie exclaimed, handing David over to Laura so that she could say hello to her niece.

"And he seems so tiny!" Laura laughed.

Jennie smiled proudly. "He's already regained his birth-weight *and* put on another six ounces!"

Father smiled. "Must be producing pure Jersey milk, like my best cows!" – which made Mother glare at him for being so vulgar; so he went off to put the car in the garage.

"You'd better put him on three-hourly feeds now that you're up and about," Mother declared, in the firm tones she'd used with Laura after Selina was born. "You won't be able to make as much milk as when you were lying-in."

"Oh, I think I'll wait and see what sort of pattern he falls into first," Jennie replied.

Laura saw Mother about to begin insisting so she butted in: "We've put the pram down here, so that you won't have to go upstairs every time you need to put him down for a sleep, and the little cradle I used for Selina is in your room. By the time he's too big for that, Selina will be able to move out of the cot and into a bed."

"Thank you – thank you all." Tears, which seemed to come unbidden to her eyes so readily since the day they'd started to flow in the hospital, welled up as Jennie realised the effort they were all making – even Mother – to make her feel that everything was normal.

Gwyneth stepped in. "I don't know why you're all still out here in the hall, indeed I don't! There's cups of tea going cold in the kitchen, and while you're all drinking them, it's my turn to have a look at this little fellow."

She held out her arms towards Laura and, taking the baby, exclaimed: "Why, look at this, Selina! He might have dark hair, but I can see he's the image of his –" she stopped and coloured slightly – "mother! Come on all of you – that tea's waiting, and I'm not making another pot!"

It was apparent as the days went on that there'd been an agreement in the household that Charles should never be mentioned. Mother no longer harangued about his relinquishing of his responsibilities, and Laura made no further reference to the fact that she and Jennie both had men 'in the War'.

Ironically it was now, in her heightened emotional state, that Jennie felt more in need of a chance to talk about how she felt than she had during her pregnancy, when all hope of a reconciliation had not yet been extinguished. To her great surprise, she found that the best person to talk to was Hetty.

When Hetty had called in to see her, Jennie had taken her into the parlour, away from Mother's continuing hostility. Hetty had eyed her critically. "I popped over to see how you were, and whether there was any chance of you coming back to the WVS in the near future? The girls are all asking after you – but you still look a bit peaky to me, so I think we'll leave it for a few weeks yet. How are things?"

"Fine, as far as the baby and I are concerned." Jennie stared down into her lap, then after a few moments lifted her eyes to Hetty. "I expect you know that it's a different matter as far as everything else goes?"

Hetty merely raised an enquiring eyebrow, but looked so genuinely interested that Jennie found herself telling her far more than she'd intended.

When she finished, Hetty sat with her hands planted firmly on her widespread knees. "Terrible business," she said, shaking her head. "I never knew your husband properly, so I can't comment there, but one thing I will say – at least you've got a baby out of it all, to give some meaning to your life. I would have given anything to have had a child when I lost my chap."

She grinned at the surprise on Jennie's face. "Oh, I know people think of me as a tough old spinster, but I've had my day! Only trouble was, it ended all too soon. He was terrified to go back to the front, you see, so I was happy to give him whatever comfort I could – and I know for a fact there were many girls who thought like me, only you never spoke about it – and he was dead before he'd been back there a week. I wouldn't have cared a hoot about the scandal if only he'd left me with a child to bring up, but sadly it wasn't to be."

She patted Jennie clumsily on the shoulder when she rose to leave. "Anytime, my dear, when you need a shoulder to cry on, I can be there. But don't give up – that baby's worth an awful lot."

It was perhaps similar sentiment to that which Laura would have expressed in an effort to get her to look on the bright side, if the whole subject hadn't become taboo, but somehow coming from Hetty it didn't sound so mawkish or false.

She tried to hang on to Hetty's words as she adjusted to a motherhood which both Mother and Laura seemed determined to share. Increasingly aware that David was now all she had, she wanted – and felt instinctively confident – to care for him herself, without the well-intentioned interference of either woman.

As in every other sphere of life, Mother had a litany of dictums regarding child-rearing that combined fact with fallacy, so that she was proved right as often as she was wrong, which made contradicting her so difficult. Jennie had taken little notice of her directives when they'd been aimed at Laura and Selina, but now she was feeling the full force of them.

– "You shouldn't talk to him so much, you'll tax his brain."

– "Don't stand behind him, he'll go cross-eyed looking up at you."

– "If you put a potty under him at every feed, he'll soon learn how to use it."

Jennie found herself resenting the simplest of Mother's actions. If Katharine felt the nappies which were drying on the overhead clothes airer in the kitchen, and declared them not yet ready, Jennie made a point of using them next. When Mother stated that all babies should be bathed after their morning feed, Jennie took to bathing him at night. When she said that Jennie should try him on a spoonful of groats when he was eight weeks, Jennie replied that she would wait until he seemed to need it. And so it went on.

Laura began to wear her down in a different way, praising the fact that David was so settled. "Of course, Selina was so difficult in those early months, what with colic and being awake through the night – I didn't have it half as easy! I was so tired most of the time!"

Which somehow seemed to imply that having a distressed baby to cope with made her a better mother.

Jennie took to spending as much time as she dared in her room with the baby, or else taking David for long solitary walks in the early summer sunshine, when she would occasionally allow herself to indulge in dreams of how things might have been, and she could then at least shed a tear in private. She even took him out when it was raining, regardless of Mother's warnings: "You'll catch a chill, and then you won't be able to feed him at all, never mind every time he whimpers!"

This last was a reference to a continuing bone of contention, because Jennie refused to leave him to cry if he stirred before it was officially time for a feed. It seemed preposterous to Jennie that when her body responded so immediately to his cries that the front of her blouse would quickly have two wet patches on it, she should make him wait.

"You'll form a rod for your own back," Mother warned. "You wouldn't be able to give in to him if you were on your own, with a house to run!"

Stung, because increasingly Jennie was wishing for nothing more than a place to herself, she retorted, "It's not a battle between me and the baby that one of us has to win! Besides, he doesn't know what time it is – he just knows he's hungry!"

Her thoughts were mutinous as she walked the dripping lanes on this particular morning, irritation with Mother making her step faster than was necessary. After every run-in they had, she was subtly made aware of how fortunate she was that under the present circumstances she was still provided with a home by her parents. That Laura was also enjoying her parents' bounty was disregarded because, after all, she had a home in Monmouth to go to should she choose, so that her presence was considered simply an extended stay – and anyway, there were far fewer areas of friction between Laura and Mother these days.

Jennie had tried to ease the burden of her and David's presence this morning by helping with the ironing. Mother had been in a particularly bad mood because this was the third day of rain, so the washing and everything else had fallen behind. But then David had started to cry, and she'd gone to pick him up, and the bickering had begun.

Nowadays Jennie found herself beginning to mutter under her breath when Mother started, or Laura twittered about Cyril and Selina. Nasty, unpleasant mutterings that contained many a word she would never dare utter aloud. Sometimes the mutterings developed into an urge to wreak some sort of havoc on her surroundings –

throw something against a wall, or sweep Mother's precious Willow Pattern off the dresser. She would clench her hands very tightly when these feelings came over her, lest they might begin to carry out such actions of their own accord, until her nails bit deeply into her palms. Another reason for escaping from the house whenever she could.

This morning the walk did little to lift her spirits, as it did on sunnier days. The views of her beloved mountains were obscured by low cloud, and the dripping hedges and trees made the landscape look as miserable as she felt. She toyed with the idea of talking to Father on her return, about resuming some of her duties around the farm. It would help to make her feel she was paying her way, but then it produced another problem: she would have to ask Mother to mind David while she was outside, and then Mother would delight in dealing with him in her own way, and Jennie couldn't bear the thought of that.

"I'd rather leave you with Gwyneth," she said aloud to the sleeping baby. "She'd sing you all those little Welsh songs she knows, and spoil you rotten, but you'd get far more love."

An all too familiar feeling of hopelessness enveloped her. Unable to stop herself, she re-trod the same ground in her mind as she'd done during every early morning when the dawn chorus, as she fed the baby, filled her with a poignant longing to be able to start again with the same joyousness as the birds greeted the new day – and this time not make such a mess of everything.

They were the same thoughts, with the same answers, but it was as if she had to torture herself with them almost daily, dragging all the hurt to the surface, examining it and suffering waves of mortification before she could put it away again and get on with the rest of the day.

Some of her thoughts had no answers, of course. Charles's determination to spurn David mystified her completely. Did his terse note, '*I have no son*,' mean simply that he refused to acknowledge him, or that he believed Jennie had been unfaithful? There would be no way of ever finding out, she knew, because his refusal to communicate during her pregnancy hadn't changed.

The natural progression of her thoughts was to the other mothers who had produced babies at the same time. They were imbued, in her mind, with perfect marriages – even if their husbands were far away – and were eventually going to lead enchanted family lives of the sort that would always elude her.

And finally, of course, her thoughts returned to the fact that no-one, throughout the two decades of her life so far, had ever truly wanted her.

Giving up on the wet weather, she plodded home, leaving the sleeping baby in the pram in the wash house. In the kitchen Selina was sitting on her potty, which she was encouraged to do for inordinate lengths of time in order to be 'trained', while Laura read to her all about Daddy's latest exploits from a letter which had obviously arrived with the second post.

"And Daddy says that when he comes home we're all going to live together in Monmouth, in our own little house, and we'll paint a bedroom just for you and…"

She looked up as she realised that Jennie had come in. "Oh! I didn't know you were back! I'll finish this another time. Come on, darling, have you done anything yet? Let's have a look." She thrust the letter into her apron pocket and lifted Selina off her potty.

"You don't have to stop," Jennie said, aware of a curious tightening in her chest which the picture Laura was painting for Selina seemed to have triggered. Another enchanted family when the war was over. "I don't need cosseting, you know, and I'm really pleased that you and Cyril are so happy and that he keeps in touch with you so regularly…"

Her voice began to wobble dangerously and the feeling in her chest wouldn't go away. She sat down abruptly at the table. "I'm sorry," she said to Laura. "I'm just feeling a bit down today."

"Of course you are," Laura said, leaving Selina and moving across to her. "Let me make you a cup of tea, while it's quiet." She gave Jennie a hug and crossed the kitchen to the range, and at the same time Mother came in from the hall.

Taking one look at Jennie's white face, she said, "I told you not to go out in that rain. Done you no good at all, obviously. You'll be down with something next and we'll all have to run round you! I hope you've not left the baby outside, it's pouring d –"

"Oh for goodness' sake, Mother, be quiet!" Jennie cried. "I'm sick of you going on and on all the time!"

Before Mother could reply, Laura moved to Jennie's side again. "She's a bit upset today," she said placatingly to Mother, before turning to her sister. "Try to cheer up, love. After all, it's a lot worse for some women you know, whose husbands have been killed in the war. At least Charles is still alive, and where there's life –"

Jennie jumped to her feet, sending the chair toppling over with such a thud that Selina began to cry. She heard a voice, much too strident to be her own, shouting at a bewildered Laura: "Shall I tell you something? I wish with all my heart that Charles *had* been killed! Killed before I told him I was pregnant. Then we could have all talked about how much he would have loved his son! Then at least I would have had a widow's pension to rely on, and a bit of self-respect! And I could have carried on fooling myself that he loved me! But as it is I've got nothing – no home of my own, not a stick of furniture to my name, no husband to speak of, alive or dead! Just a beautiful baby who's going to grow up with no stories of what a hero his father was, because his father won't even acknowledge that he exists!"

The voice was growing louder and louder, but Jennie couldn't stop it, and then it began to scream, and a blackness moved in from the corners of her vision, blotting out Laura's horrified face. It rushed towards her, and just as she realised that the screaming was coming from inside her own head, it enveloped her completely.

21

It was Emily who came to her rescue in the end. Told over the telephone by Laura that her youngest sister was having some sort of nervous breakdown, she arrived two days later, having travelled on two buses and three trains to reach Nantyderry.

"You're to come back with me and stay as long as you like," she told a listless Jennie, sweeping into her bedroom with the same sort of briskness as the Sister at the nursing home. "Ernest insists, and so do I. The sea air will do you a power of good – and you never did have that holiday with us. It would've been better if you had – then you mightn't have got caught up with that rat in the first place!"

"But what about –?"

"Mother? I've told her already why I've come. The dreadful Dr. Moxom agreed with me, so she was defeated on all sides, for once." She grinned. "And I think privately she's worried that next time you might go mad with the bread knife, or something! Of course, you and I both know that you're not in the least mad – well no madder than living with Mother all these years would make anyone – but it won't hurt to let her go on thinking that you might be! Much more likely to be able to do what we want then!"

Her no-nonsense style and matter-of-fact way of talking were more soothing than all the creeping around that had gone on for the past couple of days. When Jennie had sunk to the floor in a dead faint, Mother had immediately called Dr. Moxom, and Jennie had passively submitted to his oily hands examining her, but he'd only hummed and hawed and declared that she was probably a bit run down, so he would prescribe a tonic for her.

Father had come to see her when she was tucked up in bed and asked tentatively if she was all right, and had sat and held her hand when tears prevented her from speaking.

But here was Emily, acting for all the world as if it was perfectly fine to have hysterics one minute, tears the next, and long silences after that – all the while also assuming that Jennie would be quite fit enough to travel back to Devon with her the next day. The family had been bombed out of their home in Plymouth before Christmas, and had moved to Bideford, where Ernest's technical knowledge in the boat-building world was earning him considerable respect.

"We're renting this enormous flat on the ground floor of an old house," Emily told Jennie. "It's much too big for the four of us, so we won't even know you and the baby are there. And my two boys aren't going to mind another baby in the house – although the people upstairs might not be as keen," she added with a wink.

With what seemed the minimum of effort, Emily packed up Jennie's and the baby's things into two large suitcases, and before she knew it Jennie was saying goodbye to the family.

Throughout the farewells and the long muddled journey to North Devon, Jennie felt nothing more than a sense of unreality. But when they finally reached the house – even larger and more imposing, in a slightly decrepit way, than Emily had described – and Ernest had welcomed her affectionately and taken the baby from her in an experienced manner, she felt her shoulders ease and began to relax.

"I'm really grateful to you for this," she told him.

"Nonsense! We're delighted to have you! This war is keeping us all apart too much, and it will do Emily good to have some company, rattling around in this old place."

She noticed that his Welsh accent had begun to give way to a soft Devon burr, which suited his mild, unruffled manner. "Now then, Philip, quieten down," he said, largely ineffectually, to the little boy who was jumping up and down beside him.

Emily's younger son had just had his first birthday, but seemed nothing like his lively elder brother. He beamed at Jennie from where he was sitting on the floor, and then crawled off happily to examine something he had spied on the other side of the room.

"Michael's too lazy to get up and walk," Emily said, "And I'm not hurrying him – he'll only be forever falling over then; he's got that clumsy way about him."

The food was admired by Ernest in a way that brought home to Jennie just how fortunate they were on the farm, and when she asked whether leaving their home in Plymouth had been difficult, Ernest had just smiled. "We're still together, aren't we? That's the main thing – and it's much quieter here, safer for us all."

There was a comfortable air about the two of them, a deep companionship that transmitted itself in unspoken ways – a look here, an automatic deference to the other there, with neither one seeming to have ascendancy over the other. They'd both changed physically since Jennie had last seen them, too: Ernest had become a bit stouter, with his hair beginning to thin a little on top, whilst Emily was nothing like the up-to-the-minute young lady who'd caused such a stir when she'd had her hair shingled.

It was long again now, tawny, and tending to curl. Usually it started the day piled on top of her head with clips and combs, but as the day progressed these would slip, allowing soft tendrils to escape around her face. Sometimes when she was talking she would absentmindedly remove one of the combs, and then replace it haphazardly without recourse to a mirror, so it never looked quite as tidy again. When she went out she merely stuffed her hair inside a wide-brimmed hat that managed to convey a bohemian look which was distinctly attractive. She had maintained her athletically trim figure and managed to wear an assortment of clothes, flung on with complete disinterest, with the sort of dash that would be the envy of many a fashion-plate.

Jennie's room was tall and sunny, with French windows which overlooked a large walled garden. Each corner of the room was crammed full of bookcases, tables holding a weird assortment of household items, some boxes of clothing, pictures, tennis racquets and an old phonograph.

"I think it was probably the morning room when the house was first built," said Emily, "but it wouldn't have held half this amount of junk then! I'm afraid we've just used it as a storeroom for a lot of our things. We did make some attempt to tidy it up for you, and the wardrobe and dressing table are empty, but if you want to move anything or change it, just give Ernest a shout and he'll come and do it for you."

"No, it's lovely, honestly," said Jennie, wondering how Emily had possibly managed to acquire so many things. But in front of the French windows a space had been cleared for two armchairs and a small coffee table, which along with the sunshine streaming in gave the room a welcoming air, and nearby was a large old black pram. Emily pulled it forward. "This was the best we could do for the baby, but we can try to get a cot for you later on – Michael's still using ours, of course."

Jennie laid the sleeping baby in the pram. "I don't think there'll be any need, there's plenty of room for him in this." She gazed out into the tangled garden and wondered if she would eventually have the strength and energy to offer to clear it for Emily.

She turned back to her sister, easy tears threatening again, but she blinked them back determinedly and forced a bright smile. "I don't know what I'd have done if you hadn't turned up to rescue me."

"You would have survived, I'm sure of that – if only for the sake of that little one there – so we'll have no more of the grateful talk. Let's go see if Ernest's got the kettle on!"

Over the next few days it dawned on Jennie that for the first time in her life she had the freedom to do exactly what she wanted, with no responsibilities or obligations to anyone except herself and baby David. Such sudden freedom was awesome; she had no idea what to do, and even the simplest of decisions, such as whether to wash her hair, took on gigantic implications.

But with a wisdom that was more inherent than learned, Emily gave her space and time, offering her opinion in a down-to-earth way when it was sought but taking little notice otherwise of the perpetual dither Jennie felt herself to be in. Nobody in the household expected anything of her other than that she care for her baby, and there was no pressure on her to fit into any household routine.

Indeed, it appeared that there *was* very little household routine, other than Ernest setting off for work at a given time and returning many hours later, looking exhausted, but never anything other than pleasant to his family and quietly solicitous of Jennie.

Emily cheerfully carried out what household tasks she deemed essential, in a haphazard fashion that belied all the years of training by Mother – never mind the further years spent in nursing. Perhaps it was because of Mother's rigorous insistence on a place for everything and everything in its place, rather than in spite of it, Jennie decided as she watched Emily, cigarette dangling from the corner of her mouth, rinsing nappies at the large stone sink – at a time in the morning when Mother would have expected at least three loads of washing to be out on the line and almost dry.

"It's no trouble," Emily said, her eyes screwed up from the smoke, when Jennie protested that she should be helping. "It's just as easy to do two nappy buckets as one. You can sit there and sort my mending basket out, though, if you like. I hate darning and leave it forever, until Ernest hasn't got two matching socks without a hole in them!"

Sometimes she would stop in the middle of a chore to sit on the floor and play with the boys, and at others she would suddenly remember that she should be joining the queues at the shops to eke out their food rations, and she would stop what she was doing and fling her coat on, leaving the children to play with their aunt.

In the afternoons they took the children out – either up and down the steep, narrow little streets that led down to the harbour formed by the estuary of the river Torridge, or along the quayside, for Philip to admire the boats. There was even less evidence of a country at war here than there'd been in Nantyderry, which with the army camps nearby and the Munitions Works at Glascoed had seen a certain amount of activity. People still had the rationing and restrictions to contend with, of course, and there were plenty of things going on towards the 'war effort', but it was possible to feel that it was all happening much, much further away.

On hot days they went by bus to Westward Ho! where Philip and Michael could play on the sand and have a picnic of gritty sandwiches filled with plum jam. At first on such expeditions Jennie would be looking anxiously at her watch as the afternoon wore on, aware that no preparations for an evening meal had been made, and that Ernest would be home from work by the time they returned. But neither Emily or Ernest were bothered by such practicalities, and a meal of sorts would eventually be produced, tasting to Jennie, after lungfuls of sea air, like the best food in the world – even if it consisted predominantly of potato and beetroot.

One afternoon on the beach, as the baby kicked on a rug and Emily and the children built sandcastles with enormous energy, and if you ignored the dug-outs dotted around, it was possible to forget about the war, Jennie began to chuckle. "I remember Mother complaining years ago that you were going to turn out like Aunt Eunice," she explained to an enquiring eye from Emily, "and for once I have to say that I think she was right. You *are* just how Aunt Eunice would have been if she'd had children."

"And I said I would be lucky if I found someone like Uncle Frank – I remember! I think I have, too – we'll never have as much money, but that doesn't matter. Ernest's a good man."

Jennie nodded in agreement and then sat, her arms hugging her knees, staring out to sea. "It's a pity he has no brothers," she said at last.

Emily left Philip to flatten the castle turrets with the back of his spade while Michael squeezed handfuls of sand between his pudgy fingers, and joined Jennie on the rug. "I didn't really love him, you know, at first. I only married him because he'd been hanging around asking me for so long, it seemed only right to put him out of his misery."

"And now?"

"And now I love him more and more as each month passes. He understands me, he makes me laugh, and he lets me be myself." Emily looked down at baby David for a few moments, giving him her finger to grip hold of and pull inexpertly towards his mouth. "And he knows that he wasn't the first – that I'd made an absolute fool of myself when I was nursing, with a doctor who was married and had no intention of ever being otherwise – and still Ernest wanted me and waited for me. You wouldn't think such an unassuming man would be so determined, would you?"

Jennie was astounded. "I didn't know – I didn't think…"

"What? That anyone else could get it wrong except you?" Emily leaned across and gave her sister a hug. "I think we could do with a little bit of each other, you know. If I hadn't been so headstrong, and you'd had a bit more of my devil-may-care when it came to doing what you wanted, perhaps we wouldn't both have had to learn the hard way."

She lit a cigarette and took a long draw on it. "I haven't told anyone else in the family about what happened in Ross-on-Wye. I think Laura would have been much too shocked and would have agonised over whether she should ever invite me to her Conservative Club Coffee Mornings again, and of course one never tells Mother anything and wouldn't want Father to think badly, so we all end up bottling up all the things that really bother us. Silly, isn't it?"

Jennie nodded, reflecting that throughout her life it had only ever been Emily or Laura who'd put their arms around her. She couldn't remember Mother doing so, not even when she was a small child, and Father had always been kindness itself, but somehow not inclined to spontaneous shows of affection. On occasion, Charles had made her feel sufficiently confident to fling her arms round him in the sort of way she could never have done with her parents, and he himself had been highly affectionate towards her at times … and then, at others, so remote and cold.

"I feel so confused about myself," she told Emily now. "All my life I've never really understood what I've done to provoke Mother's rages, and now I don't know what I've done to make Charles stop loving me – if he ever did in the first place, of course, which has to be in grave doubt. I would have done anything, gone anywhere to make him happy, so it's not as if we disagreed about something. So I must have just not been the sort of person he really wanted, after all."

"Why does it have to be you?" Emily asked. She'd summed up Charles when first she saw him at Laura's wedding as the type who, twenty years earlier, would have been known as a cad. "Perhaps, like me, you simply made the wrong choice. Charles is probably the type who has always treated women badly, and always will, and as for Mother – well, she's always been odd. Look at her attitude about Hitler when this all started!"

She stood up and smoothed sand from her dress. "You have to just be yourself, you know. You're pretty, you're kind, and you're still very young. When you've got over all of this, and Charles is just a nasty memory, and this wretched war is over, there'll be plenty of men falling over you – you mark my words."

Jennie was quiet on the way home, and Emily wondered if she'd said too much too soon, but felt helpless to know what else to do. It was still such early days, she decided, assessing Jennie's progress as she would have done a patient who was being slow to recover. Lots of self-esteem building was needed for now, and if that took some time, well, it was no problem if Jennie continued to stay with them. She gave thanks again for Ernest's placid nature, and quickly squashed the memory of another man's hands running over her body.

In her room, Jennie examined herself critically in the dressing table mirror. She had almost regained her slim figure, except for a fullness in the bust which hadn't been there before, and for which she was quite grateful. Her face looked less pinched and was beginning to acquire a healthy summer outdoor look. She knew, then, that there was nothing wrong with her looks. *Be yourself,* Emily had said. But what if being yourself was the problem – that, despite physical appearances, you were just the type that other people found difficult to love?

David lay gurgling on her bed. She knelt on the floor and leaned over him, and immediately his eyes lit up and a broad dribbly smile spread across his face. She smiled back, in spite of herself. Here was pure, unquestioning love. "You don't care what I'm like, do you?" she said, and laughed aloud as his arms and legs moved in an unco-ordinated frenzy of excitement at the sound of her voice.

This was all she would need from now on, she decided. Forget what everyone else, including sane and sensible Emily, was desperate to tell her: that 'one day' she would get over this and meet someone else. Who needed another man who could just as easily tire of her as quickly as Charles had? No need to take that risk again. The love she'd felt for Charles was beginning to be replaced by seeds of hatred – for him, and for all charming, good-looking men.

From now on, it would just be her and David, together.

Edward decided not to tell Katharine where he was going until late the night before. He waited until Laura had gone up to bed, yawning and wishing that the bright summer light wouldn't wake Selina so early. He and Katharine sat in the parlour on opposite sides of the hearth, on which stood a large copper bowl filled with roses. He had a sudden memory of Jennie as a little girl, arriving home with armfuls of bluebells for her mother and then seeing disappointment shadow her face as they soon drooped and withered. He felt a pang at the loss of his youngest daughter – he hadn't realised how much he would miss her.

"I'm going up to Duxford tomorrow," he said into the gathering gloom.

Katharine's head shot up from the embroidery she had been absorbed in. "Whatever for?"

"To persuade that man to let Jennie divorce him quietly with as little fuss as possible."

Katharine's heart began to pound. The last thing in the world she wanted was for Edward to have discussions with Charles. The fine material slid unheeded from her lap. "Why ever do you need to do that? Jennie's not in any rush to do anything about the situation, and – well, you don't know... things may change..."

Edward waved his hand impatiently. "Nothing's going to change as far as Charles is concerned. She's heard nothing since that note after the baby was born, and that was months ago. Do you seriously mean to tell me that you would want her to go back to him if he suddenly announced that he'd changed his mind and wanted to play happy families after all?"

"No, of course not! I don't want *anyone* in this family having anything more to do with him," she said with feeling. "It just seems unnecessary to do anything at all at the moment. He might have been sent abroad, or anywhere, and your journey will be wasted. And we're told not to travel unless it's essential – why not write to him, or get a solicitor to contact him?"

Edward's lips set in a determined line. "If she divorces him for desertion she'll have to wait years, and in the meantime he could come back again and wreak more havoc. I want to see him in order to make a bargain with him – pay him if necessary, to provide her with evidence to divorce him for adultery. There's not much else I can do for her, but at least I can get all this sorted out while she's away – then perhaps she won't have to face so much gossip when she comes back."

He cast a sideways glance at his wife. "It'll be better for you as well. I'm sure you don't want the family dragged through the divorce courts, and at least while everyone is worrying about the war they'll maybe take less notice."

There was so much truth in what he was saying, and he was obviously so determined on his course of action, that Katharine admitted defeat – though what Charles, when cornered, might say about her, goodness only knew. She could only pray that Edward's opinion of the man was so low that he wouldn't believe anything he said.

Never one to flinch from the inevitable, she looked her husband squarely in the face. "What time are you leaving?"

Edward's leg, which had never set properly, ached if he sat or stood in one place for too long. He had caught the early morning milk train, which hadn't been too busy, but by the time he arrived in Paddington the pain was spreading up to his back, so that he walked along the platform with a pronounced limp, drawing sympathetic glances from one or two people who assumed that it was a war injury. They would have been forgiven, too, for thinking so, because his face had the drawn look that could be seen on many a serviceman's face. In fact, apart from the pain in his leg, Edward was trying to come to terms with the devastation he was seeing all around him. None of the reports on the wireless, or from people whom he met who travelled round the country more, had prepared him for what had happened in the capital.

He took a taxi rather than the tube to King's Cross for his connection, in the hope that what he'd seen as the train had drawn into Paddington had been a fluke. But he quickly learned that it wasn't.

"'Course, these parts aren't as bad as the East End," the taxi driver told him. "Whole streets gone over there – I've got a cousin whose house went while she was in the shelter, and when she went back, there was such a bleedin' big hole in the ground it took her hours to recognise where her house had been – and she'd lived there all her life!"

By the time he was sitting at a table in a cheerless little room with metal windows, where he had had to wait for an hour before he could see Charles, he was feeling thoroughly miserable and wishing he was back at home.

Finally Charles stood with his back to Edward, looking out through the window, although there was nothing to see apart from a strip of dusty grass and the window of the building opposite. "I don't know why you've bothered to come," he said. "You must know by now that it's all over."

"You've got a beautiful baby son. Things needs to be done to secure his future."

Charles turned from the window with something resembling a sneer on his face. "And how do you know he's mine?" he asked softly.

"Don't be so preposterous, man! Of course he's yours! Jennie hasn't looked at another man, before or since you came on the scene! You know that as well as I do!"

"Really? That's not what her mother seems to think! Why don't you ask Katharine what she told me on our wedding night? Or is *she* the one behind you visiting me here? Always did like to have everyone dancing to her tune, didn't she? Perhaps she's the one who wants me to come back!"

Edward's face suffused with anger. He stood up and leaned across the table. "It may surprise you to know, in your insufferable arrogance, that I haven't come here to ask you to return! I wouldn't want you to set one foot on my land ever again! I've come here to offer you five hundred pounds to provide Jennie with evidence to divorce you for adultery!"

Charles turned back to the window, momentarily lost for words. He needed to think rapidly. Sylvia still had no idea that he was married, and if he were to agree to this, it could all be done while he still saw her only intermittently. By the time this war was over he could be a free man again, and she would be none the wiser. And five hundred pounds would not go amiss, that was for certain. A nice little nest egg, should Sylvia's attractions start to wane again in years to come.

Edward spoke to his back. "If you are prepared to accept my offer, I want it done as soon as possible. There would be no further demands on you from your wife – and you would have no claims on the child. I don't want you coming back in the future and bothering any of my family again. I want you out of all our lives for good. Give Jennie a chance of a proper life."

Charles was quiet for a few minutes before he faced Edward again, hands in trouser pockets. "It has its attractions, I'll give you that. Except, of course, that as I'm convinced the child isn't mine, I could divorce Jennie. Which would be a shame, as both your wife and your other daughters would have to become involved in very messy proceedings. I don't think you realise how much damage could be done to your entire family."

With difficulty, Edward kept his hands at his side and his eyes fixed on Charles's face. "There is very little that has gone on in my household in the past few years that I have been unaware of, contrary to what you might think. So I know that any 'evidence' you might produce would have to be very shaky or downright untrue, which means you would be very foolish to proceed down that road. It could cost you rather a lot, whereas I'm offering you an escape from a marriage you obviously don't want, and a financial deal into the bargain."

Charles appeared to consider this for a moment. "Whichever way you like to put it, you're still buying me off. And you're good for more than five hundred pounds."

"Yes – but *you're* not!"

There was such contempt in Edward's voice that Charles flinched. Then he shrugged. Edward had obviously only come to issue ultimatums, not negotiate, but it had been worth a try.

"Very well. I'll make arrangements on my next leave. I'll go off to East Anglia, fix up a photographer, that sort of thing – I take it that's what you require?"

Edward nodded.

"And the money? When do I get that?"

"When you have sent me the photographs, and I've checked with my solicitor that they are suitable evidence, I will send you half the amount. You'll get the rest when the divorce has gone through its first stages uncontested."

There was little else to discuss. Edward picked up his hat and turned to leave, but Charles made no move to accompany him from the room. He lit a cigarette, then spoke just as Edward opened the door.

"Give my love to Katharine."

The words were said softly, with studied insolence, but Edward closed the door behind him as if he hadn't heard.

He took little notice of the city's carnage on his return journey. His mind was seething with anger at the insinuations behind Charles's words. He wanted to go back and have the satisfaction of punching his arrogant face and watching it bleed. Why hadn't he seen this in the man when he was planning to marry Jennie? *Because he was a good actor, of course, and he let you see only what he wanted you to see,* came back the answer. But Edward knew that was only part of it. Despite what he had told Charles, the rest consisted of his own willingness to stay out of the household affairs and immerse himself in the farm. And that was chiefly because of the situation between himself and Katharine.

Katharine! What had been her part in all this? That there was some element of truth in Charles's words he had little doubt. He'd known how much store Katharine had put by Charles's visits to the farm in the early days, but also knowing her reactions to all things physical he'd been happy to think of Charles's flattery as being merely a sop to her vanity.

Had it been more than that? *Had* she spoilt things for Jennie with her unruly tongue?

The more he thought about it as the train rattled on its way, the more he came to see the situation for what it had really been. Odd words and verbal exchanges came back to him with fresh meaning. Katharine, it was obvious to him now, had been jealous of Charles's preference for her daughter – why hadn't he noticed it then?

By the time he reached the farm his tired anger had spilled over to include both his wife and himself. He was surprised to find that Katharine was waiting up for him, even though it was extremely late. Her face was pale and anxious as she opened the kitchen door for him.

"Well?" She barely allowed him time to remove his hat and jacket. "Did you speak to him?"

"Yes I did." But he said no more until she'd placed a cup of tea before him. "He agreed to provide evidence for a divorce and I agreed to pay him five hundred pounds when it goes through."

"Five hundred pounds! The man's not worth five hundred pennies! There must be some other way! I'll write to Jennie and…"

Edward's hand shot out and caught her by the wrist. He fixed his weary eyes on hers and said in a slow, deliberate voice: "I offered him that money. I want this finished. Besides, I think you've done enough already, don't you?"

Her eyes widened and for a moment he saw – guilt, fear? He didn't know. He kept very still as she dragged her eyes away from his and made dejectedly for the door. Her hair and clothes were as immaculate as ever, despite the late hour, but he saw in the droop of her shoulders a middle-aged woman whose dreams and aspirations had never quite materialised, despite her strivings.

His anger left him as he remembered the fresh young woman he had fallen in love with. "Oh, Katie, Katie! Come here!" Rising, he pulled her towards him. For the first time in years she melted into his arms and began to sob.

Letters had flowed throughout the summer between Jennie and Mother and Laura; Mother's full of the difficulties that Father faced with increased demands from the War-Ag, and snippets about people at church, and Laura's much more newsy about the day-to-day doings of the household, making it possible for Jennie to imagine herself still there with them.

Mother's taken to being very nice to Gwyneth lately, Laura wrote, *because she's terrified Gwyneth will go off to a factory and we won't get anyone else, so she now takes out her wrath on Wendy instead. She came into the kitchen the other day just as Mother, for some reason, was going on about Wendy not being a proper name because Barrie made it up when he wrote 'Peter Pan'. There was a terrible row, with Wendy saying there were better ways to be a Christian than just having a truly Christian name, and it was a pity Mother didn't know some of them, and she didn't have to stay here – although I rather think the poor girl has little choice. But you should have seen Mother's face! The rest of us kept out of her way for hours of course, and I didn't dare catch Gwyneth's eye!*

Jennie wrote equally different letters back to both of them, always addressing both her parents in reply to Mother's letters, but even so it was a surprise when Father's letter arrived in his beautiful copperplate writing.

It came just as she and Emily were sitting down to their eleven-ses of Camp coffee – which was made mainly with chicory essence so that it tasted nothing like real coffee, but they were getting used to it – and pieces of stodgy home-made bread which Emily had felt compelled to make because Ernest had got hold of some fresh yeast.

Jennie scanned the letter quickly and then uttered a startled 'Oh!' and swallowed her mouthful on a choke.

"Anything wrong?" Emily looked up swiftly from the morning paper. Surely Father would have had the sense to send any bad news to her, not Jennie?

"Father has been to see Charles. He's… he's agreed to a divorce."

"Thank the Lord for that! How soon can you be a free woman?"

Jennie smiled, in spite of herself. A free woman! It made her sound like a chained African slave. "I don't know. It will probably take ages. Father wants my permission to see solicitors and things – here, read it for yourself, it's not personal."

She poured herself another cup of coffee and realised that this news made her feel nothing for Charles but a continued fuelling of contempt and hatred. She was determined to hold on to it in order to go through what she knew had to be faced: divorce courts, the gossip of all those in Nantyderry and Abergavenny who knew her family and for whom divorce was almost unheard of, and making a life for herself and David.

"Well?" Emily asked as she put the letter down on the table and lit a cigarette. "What are you going to do?"

She looked squarely back at Emily. Chin up, face the world, get used to it. "I'm going to write back to Father and tell him to go ahead with it as fast as he can. Then I'm going to get on with the rest of my life!"

Emily grinned. "Good girl!"

It wasn't too difficult, in the safe cocoon of Emily's carefree home, to galvanise herself into action again. She began by helping Ernest to sort out the garden, which he felt driven to do by the increased shortages and need for fuel for the winter. They chopped down two withered apple trees and stored the logs to dry out, and collected bags of garden rubbish for kindling. Then they dug over a vegetable plot and planted sprouts and winter cabbage, while the baby slept contentedly in his pram, the younger of his two cousins beside him in a cumbersome push-chair while Philip ran around beside his father, making enough noise for all of them.

It was good to be active again, feeling muscles that had grown slack becoming firm once more, and enjoying the damp, earthy smell of approaching autumn.

Sorting through the accumulated junk in her room, Jennie came across an old sewing machine, and with the threat of clothes rationing looming she set to, making clothes for all three little boys, who insisted on growing at an alarming rate. She used old curtains from the house in Plymouth, old sheets for romper suits and little shirts, and even managed to make Emily a three-quarter length coat for the winter out of two old blankets.

She kept to her room as she sewed through the shortening autumn evenings, despite Emily and Ernest's protests that she should stay in the sitting room with them. "I know I can't stay here for ever," she told them, "so I want to get used to the feeling of being on my own, while I know I've still got both of you around if it all gets too much."

She found that keeping herself busy was the best way to blot out everything that had happened. Sometimes she would glance up from her machine, gaze into the gathering twilight through the French doors, and be filled with nostalgia for home and the past; and the thought of how things might have been gripped her like a physical pain. Then she'd jump up and draw the curtains, as though in shutting out the garden she could shut out her old dreams and force back the hot tears lurking just behind her eyelids.

In the quiet afternoons, when the weather was too blustery to take the boys out, she found she was more able to confide in Emily, so that her solitary self-torture was lessened. But it was harder to control her dreams, and often she still woke from turbulent episodes to find her cheeks wet and her heart thumping wildly.

As December approached she began to wonder if she should make preparations to return to Nantyderry, but Emily and Ernest continued to urge her to stay a little longer, and she was happy to be persuaded. So Mother's letters, asking whether she should include Jennie in the preparations for Christmas, were answered with vague allusions to the difficulties of travel and the cold that baby David was suffering from as he began to cut his teeth.

Father sent postal orders to Emily and Jennie, urging them to buy whatever was available for themselves and the children, and Jennie found a slightly battered baby doll at a WI jumble sale, which she dressed and sent for Selina. Then she threw herself into Christmas preparations with Emily which were like nothing she'd known before.

"I've found this box under our bed – I forgot it was there!" Emily came into the large room that doubled as kitchen and living room one morning when she was supposed to be giving the bedrooms a thorough going-over. She plonked a cardboard box on the table and began to pull out pieces of tinsel and strips of gummed coloured paper. Housework was forgotten as she sat on the floor with the boys making reams of paper chains, and lanterns out of newspaper which she painted with very powdery paints that came off on their hands.

"I've seen a sweet little evergreen tree in the garden that Ernest can dig up," she said, "and then we can hang the tinsel and lanterns on it."

She sang Christmas carols to the children, in an off-key voice and with so many lines sung to 'la-la-la' because she couldn't remember the words that Jennie, who'd taken over most of the cooking, laughed and joined in, her face becoming prettily flushed from the effort combined with dealing with an ancient and contrary cooking range. The baby, propped up in the big old pram, watched all the activity and crowed with pleasure, and Jennie suddenly realised that she felt happy.

Ernest made toys for the boys carved from pieces of wood, sitting for hours by the firelight patiently whittling each piece: an engine for Philip and sets of farm animals for Michael and David. Coal was now in such short supply that Jennie was forced to join Emily and Ernest in the evenings, when they would discuss the progress of the war and listen to the wireless.

They were together round the fire when the first reports came in of the Japanese sinking of American ships at Pearl Harbour. "That's it!" said Ernest, his normally quiet voice raised with excitement. "They'll be in now, you'll see. Germany won't know which way to turn if the Americans are helping us and the Russians are still holding fast."

"And the Yanks will be able to boast how they've come to our rescue again, like they did the last time," said Emily caustically. "Let's hope they make some difference to the rationing as well." She held up a booklet she had been reading. "Have you seen some of these suggestions of what to do with carrots?"

Jennie smiled. "At least we can all see better in the blackout! Perhaps I should have gone home for a weekend after all, and scrounged some more things from Mother. She's probably still got a hoard down in the cellar."

"And what if she found some way of keeping you there?" Emily asked in mock horror. "How would I know what to do with all these carrots?"

Jennie's face grew serious. "I know I've said to you before about not staying here for ever – and I meant it, you know. I've been doing a lot of thinking while I've been sewing in my room, and I've decided that I must stand on my own two feet. Otherwise I shall spend the whole of my life dependent on other people's charity."

"But what will you do? How will you manage for money? And what about the baby? You surely don't want to put him in a nursery while you go out to work?" Emily's brow beneath her mop of unruly hair creased in concern for her sister. "I could always have him here, of course, but then you'd have to find a job and a home quite close, and that won't be easy –"

"I've worked out a plan," Jennie interrupted. "Well, at least an idea of what I could do. With all the call-up of women going on now, I might eventually be forced to do something, and then have to leave David in a nursery all day – and you're right, I wouldn't want that. But with so many girls going into factories and so on, there's a short-age of people to work in houses. You know, cook-generals, that sort of thing. If I could find a job like that I could have David with me, and have a home of sorts. Oh, I realise that it wouldn't really be mine, but at least I'd be providing for the two of us."

Ernest knocked out his pipe on the corner of the fireplace and spent a few moments filling it again with shreds of tobacco. He'd only recently taken to a pipe, and Emily teased him that he spent more time trying to light it than actually smoking it. When he had it alight to his satisfaction and its aroma filled the air – so much more pleasant than Emily's cigarette smoke, Jennie always thought – he spoke in his careful, measured way.

"Emily will have already told you that your home can be here with us for as long as you want, and it's important that you know she speaks for the two of us. But I do understand your need to make a home of your own – as long as you know that there is no urgency on our part, and you can wait until the right opportunity presents itself."

The passive brown eyes which still lit up whenever Emily entered the room now contemplated Jennie with compassion. She leaned forward and squeezed his hand. "I do know – and I'll never ever forget your kindness. I'm not sure what I would have done without the two of you coming to my rescue."

He waved his pipe in a dismissive gesture, but his mouth was set in a determinedly grim line. "It was nothing. No man should put a girl through what you've been through."

Jennie had often wondered how this very gentle, mild man would have fared had he been forced to join up and found himself facing the enemy. Now, though, seeing the set of his face, she fancied that he would have been well able to fight after all.

The 'right opportunity' presented itself in the New Year. The determination to enjoy Christmas had given way to the bleakness of the winter months yet to be endured before any hope of spring sunshine lifting the spirits. The three children seemed to go from one cold to another, which Emily dismissed as the usual childhood ailments, but Jennie couldn't stop herself fretting about David, and would lie awake at night listening to his snuffly breathing and bouts of coughing. In the end she decided to take him to the doctor's surgery, despite Emily's reassurances.

She found herself sitting in a packed waiting room, thick with cigarette smoke, and so many people coughing and spluttering that she began to think that Emily was right and David was in danger of catching something far worse from the other patients than if she'd kept him in the house.

The wait was a long one, and the baby began to grow fretful. At home Jennie would have simply put him to the breast, but there was nothing she could do here. She jiggled him on her knee, while a plump woman on her right wearing a hat tied on with a woollen scarf, like a Russian peasant, looked on.

"Are they keeping a little chap waiting when he's tired and hungry, then?" she cooed at him, in the sort of high-pitched voice some women reserve just for babies. She reached out her hand to him, nodding and smiling inanely, displaying several rather protruding front teeth and none at the sides or back. Emily thought she looked grotesque, but David immediately stopped grizzling and responded with a similar gappy smile.

"Are you living in the town?" She shot the question at Jennie, while still distracting the baby with nods and grimaces.

"Yes, with my sister, at Marston Court in—"

The woman swivelled her considerable bulk around to the companion with whom she'd been chatting earlier. "She's living at Marston Court – you know, that big house up on the hill – we'd wondered who'd moved in there, hadn't we?"

She turned back to Jennie, eyeing her wedding ring. "Staying long? Husband away?"

Jennie became aware that several other people in the room were listening. "Yes – um… my husband's in the RAF – I'm staying for a while – he's away…"

"RAF," the woman said to the other in an impressed way. "Not from these parts, then?" she asked Jennie.

Jennie began to wish that David would start to howl. "No. Wales. I was ill – after the baby – so I came here for a rest…" Perhaps she should have told the woman that Charles was dead, to shut her up.

The woman looked her up and down with a keen appraising eye that would have done credit to any doctor. "'Hmm. Some women aren't made as well as others for birthing. I expect you've got small hips. You had terrible trouble with your Alfie, didn't you, Bet?" She spoke to the other woman again, but didn't give her time to do more than nod before she turned back to Jennie. "Your husband seen this little one, yet?"

It was almost more than Jennie could bear. She wanted to stand up and scream at this dreadful woman to mind her own business, but there were too many other people in the room, and she didn't want to do anything that would give herself or Emily a bad name.

"No," she gabbled. "He's abroad – won't be back until the war is over – so I'm staying here. In fact –" she had a sudden inspiration – "I'm looking for a job. A housekeeper or something, so I can look after the baby as well."

The woman nudged Bet sharply. "She'd do well to go and see that music woman, wouldn't she? The one who's moved into the end of Abbotsham Road? She's not far from you," she turned again to Jennie. "It's a white house on the corner – she's looking for someone to live in. Very smart woman, she is – buys all her clothes from London, I shouldn't wonder. You ought to go and see her."

The doctor's buzzer sounded. "Go on!" the woman said. "That's you! And don't forget – the corner of Abbotsham Road!"

Jennie got up thankfully and scuttled into the doctor's room, leaving the two women to some very satisfactory speculation on the likelihood of her husband surviving the war.

22

Jennie probably wouldn't have taken it any further if a letter from Mother hadn't arrived the next morning. She took great pains to point out that it was getting on for six months since Jennie had gone to stay with Emily and Ernest, and didn't she think it was now time to return to Nantyderry and leave them in peace? Slipped in later in the letter was the news that Gwyneth was probably going to leave to join the ATS, and this, of course, Jennie quickly realised, was Mother's main objective in writing.

She thought long and hard about Father and the farm, and how much she would like to be back working alongside him again, until her nostrils were filled with the remembered aroma of the hay in the big barn, mingled with the warm pungency of the cows. But lurking in the back of her mind, alongside the nostalgic warmth of the cow shed and the beauty of the mountains, was the cold, soul-destroying atmosphere within the house, and Mother's voice constantly corroding Jennie's self-confidence.

She knew that her current sense of peace and security had been hard-won and was fragile, built on sand. To preserve and strengthen it she needed to stay away still longer, and the best way to prevent further haranguing letters from Mother was to follow up the plan of finding a job.

The following afternoon found her pushing David's pram along Abbotsham Road, until she came to the white house on the corner. She'd refused Emily's offer to look after David until she returned because it was important to make this unknown musical lady aware from the start that they came as a pair.

The house itself was wide and imposing, its front level with the road, while its back dropped down to accommodate the steep hill. Jennie stood on the front doorstep, which she noticed was in need of a good scouring, and pressed the brass button beside the door. After a few moments the door was opened by a tall woman in her early forties, Jennie guessed, with rather improbable blonde hair and immaculate make-up. She was wearing a simple blouse over a full bosom that suggested she might be an opera singer, and a skirt which from its cut made Jennie understand the remark about London clothes.

"Yes?" her voice was polite but impersonal, her face giving no clue as to her character, which immediately made Jennie's heart sink.

"I understand that you are looking for a housekeeper?" Jennie kept her chin up and her voice clear. "I would like to apply for the position, if it hasn't already been filled."

"No, it hasn't. Perhaps you'd better come in … Oh!" A slight frown creased her brow as Jennie stood back to reveal the pram. "I hadn't considered having anyone with children."

"I wouldn't be expecting any extra room for him," Jennie said quickly, "and he really is very little trouble."

Right on cue the baby, who could now sit very upright in his pram, peered over the storm cover and bestowed a beatific smile on the lady standing uncertainly on the doorstep. She looked at him thoughtfully for a moment as if making up her mind.

"Well, come in anyway," she relented, "and we'll talk about it."

Jennie lifted David out of his pram and followed the woman into a drawing room on the left that ran the length of the house. At the far end, in front of a big picture window which looked out over the town, stood a grand piano, marooned in a sea of boxes and bags, each with music books and manuscripts spilling out and seeming to swell towards the end of the room where they were standing.

The woman indicated a large wing armchair, which Jennie perched on, David on her knee. She must have been looking very apprehensive because suddenly the woman smiled. "Don't look so worried – it makes you appear much too young to be looking for any sort of job, and certainly too young to have a baby in tow! I won't eat you, my dear, but I must ask you some questions."

Jennie relaxed at the woman's softened features, although her voice still sounded rather brisk. She settled back further into the chair.

"Now then, introductions first. I'm Joan Meikle – Miss. I'm a professional pianist and singer, and I've moved down here for a while because I'm fed up with worrying about my house, and especially my piano, in London! And you are…?"

"Jennie Keating. I'm staying with my sister in Bideford – my husband's away in the RAF. I came here from Wales after the baby was born. I was ill, you see, and my sister has been a nurse. I'm fine now, but I would like to stay here, so I'm looking for a job where I can keep the baby with me." Jennie could hear herself gabbling, and her voice tailed away when she became aware that the woman was concentrating more on David than on what she had to say for herself.

"Does he always stare at people so steadfastly?" she asked, in a tone of voice that made Jennie unsure as to whether she was expected to apologise for him. "He's hardly blinked in the last few minutes."

Jennie removed his hat in an effort to distract him, and brushed her hand over the dark curls that now clung to his head, but still he stared at the woman. He began to make noises at her, as if willing her to talk to him, and suddenly, to Jennie's relief, she laughed – a deep throaty chuckle, which made the baby gurgle too.

"What a beautiful child!" she said. "I've had very little to do with babies, but this fellow seems particularly bright. Can you cook? I mean *cook well?* I shall be doing a lot of entertaining – many of my friends intend coming down to see where I've buried myself."

The question shot out, with a shrewd appraising look every bit as disconcerting as the baby's solemn stare. Jennie remembered her new resolve, and took a deep breath.

"Yes, I can cook. Not any thing terribly fancy, but with things the way they are you don't want someone with a *cordon bleu* qualification who is used to having lots of different ingredients at their disposal. What you need is someone who can make the rations appetising and stretch them as far as possible, with a good local knowledge of where little extras might be found." She crossed her fingers underneath the folds of the baby's clothes. "I can do all of those, especially if you like fish – and I shan't be wanting lots of evenings off to go out, which is what you might find if you employ a single girl."

Joan Meikle nodded. "And previous experience?"

Jennie had prepared herself for this sort of question. "I worked on my parents' farm until I married, which is excellent training for a cook-general. I can pluck and dress a bird, tell you anything you want about preparing hams and bacon, make home-made jams and purées, and I'm used to hard work. And Welsh farmers' wives are a house-proud lot, so I'm an expert at keeping everything clean and tidy!"

Her face held a tell-tale flush after such an unaccustomed self-eulogy, but she received another nod, more encouraging.

"I've just taken on someone who's going to come in and do most of the cleaning, so I would really want you for the cooking and general household management." She stood up with a quick, grace-ful movement. "Why don't I show you round, and then we can both decide whether we're suited?"

The house was quite luxurious, large and airy, with wall-to-wall carpet everywhere – most of it in a dull shade of pink. A formal dining room with a long mahogany table holding slightly tarnished candelabra was on the other side of the hall, and upstairs there were four bedrooms and a bathroom. The main bedroom, very feminine with windows heavily draped in a soft apricot, held more boxes and cases, which all looked as if their contents had been rifled through rather than systematically unpacked.

"Most of the furniture and fittings come with the house," Miss Meikle explained. "I've only brought my piano and personal belongings – I've left the rest in the basement of my London house. It's quieter in London now, of course, than it was last year, but I was away up north when the bombing was at its worst. Then when I returned I couldn't seem to settle any more."

A staircase led down from the hall to the basement kitchen, from where a door opened out onto a long, steeply terraced garden. The kitchen was square and well-lit, with a large scrubbed table in the middle, but like the bedroom it was littered with partly-opened packing cases.

"I'm afraid I'm not terribly good at all this." Miss Meikle waved a hand around dismissively. "Which is why I've always employed someone to do it all for me." She moved to the far corner of the room and flung open a door. "And this is what I thought would be the housekeeper's room. A sort of bedroom and sitting room combined – and of course the kitchen would be all yours too." She grimaced, then smiled. "I'd have very little inclination to venture down here, providing everything was running smoothly."

Jennie moved past her into the room. It looked out over the garden, and she noticed that the bed was covered in the same sort of chintz as the curtains, so that in the day it could double as a sofa. There was a Turkey carpet covering most of the floor, which reminded Jennie of the farmhouse, and the furniture was old but in good condition, and adequate for her needs. "It's very cosy," she said.

"Yes," agreed Miss Meikle, "but what about this chap? I hadn't allowed for him." She indicated baby David, sitting on the floor where Jennie had put him.

"There's room in here for his cot," said Jennie, "and he won't need anything else."

"'Hmm. I'll have to take your word for that. I know even less about babies than I do about housework. Not much of a home for you both, though, is it?"

Jennie took a deep breath. "Miss Meikle, I didn't get married until after the war began, and then my husband had to go away immediately, and I remained with my parents." She could hear the faint wobble in her own voice that still appeared whenever she made even slight mention of her marriage. "We – the baby and I – have never had any more than this."

Miss Meikle remained looking thoughtfully at the floor. *She's going to let me down gently by saying that she has other people to see,* Jennie decided, and braced herself.

But when Miss Meikle looked up she was smiling again. "Why don't we give each other a month's trial, starting next Monday? If we find we're not suited to one another, then I take it your sister will have you back until you find somewhere else?"

"Yes, she would." Jennie looked around her with pleasure. The thought that for the first time in her life she would have somewhere which was completely hers almost overwhelmed her. Alright, it might still be in someone else's house, but it would be her domain – hers and David's, and she had acquired it by her own effort. The house felt right, too. It was the appropriate sort of setting for this woman standing beside her, and there would be great satisfaction in seeing that it was properly maintained.

She nodded her agreement. "That sounds an excellent idea."

"Good. Now, if I can find some cups amongst all this mess, perhaps we can have a cup of tea and discuss your wages. Thank goodness the cleaning lady is starting tomorrow!"

Jennie looked around at the disarray and her fingers itched to start establishing order. "Would you like me to come along tomorrow as well, just for the day? I could leave David with my sister and give your new lady a hand."

"You wouldn't mind?"

Jennie found the kettle and moved purposefully towards the sink. "If this kitchen is to be my province I would prefer it to be organised in my way."

Miss Meikle bent down and scooped David into her arms, holding him awkwardly. "I think your Mummy and I are going to get on fine. And who knows, I might even learn a thing or two about little people like you!"

T he first thing Jennie saw as she approached the house early next morning was the very broad posterior of the new cleaning lady, who was on her knees scrubbing the front step. *A woman after my own heart,* Jennie decided with satisfaction, and then groaned inwardly as the woman heaved her bulk upright and turned to face her.

"I was hoping as it was you who'd got the job when she told me it was someone with a baby!" The peasant's headgear had been replaced by a tightly bound scarf done up in a turban, so that only a small quiff of greying hair poked out at the front, but there was no mistaking the toothless grin of the woman from the doctor's surgery. "Knew as soon as you said you was looking for a job that you'd be right for this place, and as *Madam*" – said with emphasis but no deference, Jennie noted – "had already told me I would be under the housekeeper, I thought it would be best if I had a bit of a hand in the choosing!"

Her voice rang with appreciation of her own cleverness as she gathered up her bucket and scrubbing brush. "Did she show you the back way in? It's round here."

Without giving Jennie the chance to say a word she was off, with surprising speed for one so fat, around the side of the house and through a tall black gate. "It goes down in steps," she said, holding the gate for Jennie, "but they're nice and wide, so you should be able to get the pram up and down them alright. She won't be wanting it in the front hall, will she?"

She bustled ahead of Jennie into the kitchen. "What about we start with a cuppa and get to know each other better? Madam's gone out into the town – to get some food in, she said, but I think she'll be in for a bit of a surprise. Don't seem to me as if she's done much of that sort of thing before."

She lifted the already-boiling kettle off a cream-coloured Rayburn which stood squarely in the middle of one wall, while Jennie removed her hat and coat and wondered whether she would be moving in next Monday after all. "Seen one of these before, have you?" the woman asked, pointing to the Rayburn.

"Yes – no – not until I was here yesterday," Jennie answered, still a bit dazed by the woman's presence. "It doesn't seem too different from a range, except the fire's inside."

"Nice lot of hotplates, too," the woman said, lifting up their lids admiringly. "I think the secret is never to let it go out – but it should burn anything, which is a blessing at the moment …

"There we are!" She put a cup of tea down on the table in front of Jennie and then stood the other side. Her breasts were sufficiently pendulous to sit comfortably on the bulk of her stomach, so that she could fold her arms over the top of them. "Dora Miles," she stated and jerked her head enquiringly towards Jennie.

"Jennie. Jennie Keating," she replied.

"Good. Now we know each other." Dora pulled out a chair. "Like I said, I'm s'posed to take my orders from you, which I'm quite happy to do, even if you are young enough to be my daughter, 'cos all I like to do is get my job done and then get away home. Haven't the sort of nerves to stand any more responsibility than that. Too sensitive by half, my Jack says." And she took a restorative slurp of her tea.

Jennie adapted her face suitably. "I'm sure we'll get along very well," she said in a voice that was a little too high pitched and, to her own ears at least, less than convincing.

"So'm I," said Dora. She leaned confidentially across the table. "Between you and me, I think we've got ourselves a tidy little number here. If we keep everything tip-top, Madam there's going to leave us alone. There's not many houses you can say that about, believe you me – and I've worked in quite a few. The stories I could tell!" She drained her tea-cup and then stared at the bottom of it for a moment, as if checking there were no dregs left. Then, with an energetic bounce that set the tea cups rattling, she stood up. "Now, you tell me what you want doing right off and we can have a good set-to. Then," she added ominously, "we can stop for elevenses and you can tell me all about yourself."

She's amazing!" Jennie told Emily when she returned home late that afternoon. "She's almost as wide as that doorway, but she goes through the work like a dose of salts! And defers to me about everything – imagine, me in charge of someone else, when half the time I don't feel capable of being in charge of myself!"

"But you think you can work with her?"

"Yes, I think so. She's only there in the mornings, and I've told her that I'll see to the cleaning of the kitchen and my room, so I'll only see her when we stop for a break. She's ever so nosey, of course, so I'm going to be very careful from the start what I say to her, but I think she's got a good heart."

"We'd better start getting everything packed up for you, then," said Emily. She looked at Jennie with the affectionate gaze that went right back to the days when Jennie was a little girl, running round the farm trying desperately to keep up with her two big sisters. "I'm going to miss you, you know. So will the boys."

Jennie laughed to cover up the sudden fear that she wasn't going to be able to manage on her own. "I'm not going into a convent! I should get most afternoons off, so I'll be round here like a shot, just you wait and see."

It was decided to move Jennie's belongings into the house after supper on Sunday evening, when Ernest was able to borrow a large handcart from a friend. Michael's old cot, which David now slept in, was dismantled onto it, along with a box of toys which Emily's pair had outgrown, and the old sewing machine. "It's no use to me," said Emily, "and if you've got it, I can carry on asking you to make things for me."

They entered the house the back way, Emily impressed with what she saw and extracting a promise from Jennie to show her round the rest of it when Miss Meikle wasn't there. When they'd gone, and she'd been upstairs to let her new employer know that she and David were now installed, Jennie sat beside her sleeping baby and looked critically around the room.

It needed more personal belongings, she decided, few of which she had in Devon. She would write home with a list of things for Father to send down to her: some of her books and photos, perhaps, and a few trinkets from her dressing table – and her old school Bible, which would please Mother. It dawned on her that she was already thinking in terms of being here for some time.

Dora arrived chirpily next morning, with her husband Jack and a large piece of wood, just as Jennie came downstairs from taking Miss Meikle her morning tea. Jack, it transpired, was a fisherman, with the same permanently tanned weather-beaten face as the men Jennie had seen down on the quayside. He was a man of few words, which wasn't surprising as Dora had more than enough for the two of them.

"I had a chat with Madam on Friday," Dora said, after a brief introduction. "It came to me that them stairs will be nothing but a trial once the baby starts getting about, so she says that it's alright for Jack to fix this bit of board across the bottom."

"That's a wonderful idea, thank you," said Jennie, smiling encouragingly at Jack, who merely nodded and moved towards the stairs. "But won't we break our necks stepping over it?"

"He's thought of that!" said Dora with a note of pride. "Hinges on one side and a hook the other, and we can come in and out no trouble."

She plopped a worn leather shopping bag down on the table and lifted out a large parcel wrapped in newspaper. "Fish straight off the boat." She winked broadly. "Ask no questions – brought in from Appledore this morning. Can probably get you a few other things as time goes on. They've been smuggling for centuries there, so getting round a bit of rationing is child's play!"

She turned to her husband, inoffensively getting on with the job in hand. "I'm starting on the spare bedrooms this morning, but Mrs. Keating here will give you a cup of tea when you've finished. Mind and don't get in her way, though; she's got that baby to see to as well as this place to run."

Many years later Jennie was able to look back on those war years, and the unlikely relationship that grew up between her and Dora from that first morning, as a time of contentment, even if a sentiment as strong as happiness was going a bit too far. They made an unlikely duo: Jennie with her native reticence from the years of Mother's insistence on ladylike virtues, and Dora with her ability to proclaim long and loud on everything and to winkle out of people pieces of information they didn't even know they knew. Yet within this strange symbiosis there sprang up a deep unspoken affection.

They worked as a team from the first, and Jennie's and David's lives quickly fell into a routine. During the morning, when Jennie was busy with chores in the kitchen, preparing lunch and planning what she could scrape together for an evening meal, she would take the base out of the cot and up-end it so that it became a playpen for David. There he would sit, happily banging wooden spoons on empty dried milk tins and gradually learning to pull himself up on the wooden bars.

In the afternoons Jennie would invariably call on Emily as she'd promised, often taking her a dish of something left over from the night before for the boys' tea, or some cakes from a batch she'd made once she had mastered the use of dried eggs. In return she came away with surplus vegetables from the plot which Ernest now tended with enthusiasm. By the following summer, though, she had her own supplies. The south-facing garden was a wonderful spot for ripening tomatoes, which she grew against the wall of the lean-to where David's pram was housed, and the bright red flowers of runner beans could be seen from the kitchen window climbing a makeshift trellis made from old fishing nets attached to the garden wall.

By this time David was beginning to toddle, and Jack's carpentry skills were needed again to confine him to the flat yard area immediately outside the kitchen, away from the steep steps leading down into the terraced areas, so he could stagger in and out on chubby legs while his mother worked.

Miss Meikle, as she'd predicted, kept very much to her own parts of the house, proving to be a fair, if rather distant, employer. She practised her singing and playing for several hours each day, which Jennie enjoyed but which brought a pained expression to Dora's face if the vocal exercises in her rich contralto went on a bit too long: "I'd rather something by the Andrews sisters, myself!"

Their employer soon made her mark on the town, however, and was in regular demand for charity concerts. This meant that people were constantly calling at the house, when pots of tea and coffee would be requested. As she'd also told Jennie, visitors from London were a frequent occurrence, and at such times Jennie needed all her ingenuity to produce satisfactory meals. Luckily, as her confidence grew, she began to enjoy the challenge of producing food from limited resources, and the continued supply of fresh fish from Appledore helped.

On warm summer afternoons Miss Meikle would often come down into the garden and sit on the lawn in a deckchair, content to observe the harbour below, or lift her face to the sun. Sometimes David would stand on his side of the barrier and watch her until she became aware of his gaze. Then he would solemnly hand her his toys one by one, which she just as solemnly handed back, until Jennie saw them and came running out to apologise for David being a nuisance and whisk him away.

But Miss Meikle always said she didn't mind David's presence. Indeed, apart from her passionate interest in music, there was little she did seem to mind about, as long as her household ran smoothly and her needs were catered for as unobtrusively as possible. She was always polite in her dealings with Jennie and Dora, and punctiliously thanked Jennie when a special meal for friends had been prepared, but she had no further interest in either of their affairs.

"Strange she hasn't got any men friends," mused Dora over their mid-morning break. "She's not a bad looker, after all, for her age, and that hair's natural. I haven't found any peroxide anywhere in the house. And she goes out enough, doesn't she, and meets plenty of people." She looked keenly at Jennie. "Which is more than can be said for you!"

Jennie was used to heavy barbs about her own life by this time, and was adept at ignoring them. "I think she just can't be bothered to get into any complicated relationship with a man – it would spoil the rhythm of her life, wouldn't it? And she'd have to think about someone else's likes and dislikes, and let's face it, for all she's not a bad employer, she doesn't go out of her way to do things for others, does she?"

Dora thoughtfully sucked a bit of lip into a gap between two teeth. "No, I suppose you're right. Still, I'd be tempted if I was her – some of those men she's had to dinner have been a bit of alright, haven't they? Especially done up in dinner suits!"

On evenings when Miss Meikle was having a dinner party, or had several guests down from London, Dora would come in and help Jennie in the kitchen, whilst managing to find a lot of time to stand at the bottom of the stairs and listen to what was going on above. Jennie couldn't believe that anyone could have such acute hearing as Dora, who seemed able to relate whole conversations from indistinct murmurings, so Jennie was never sure how much of it she made up. For her own part, the London visitors were more interesting for the things they brought with them. It seemed that if you moved in the right circles and had sufficient money, there was very little in the way of food and luxury items that you couldn't get hold of.

Much of the goings-on in Miss Meikle's life Dora was also able to glean from the letters which arrived, timing her cleaning of the front step as always to coincide with the arrival of the postman – and she wasn't above asking forthright questions of her employer when she asked Dora to slip some letters into the box on her way home at midday.

"Gets two letters regular as clockwork in those special Army envelopes, one from Italy and one from Canada. Her face perks up no end when she sees them, too, especially the Canada one." She took her empty tea cup to the sink and rinsed it out. "Don't see you getting none of those letters from the RAF, though. Not much of a writer, is he, your hubby?"

Jennie had had little sleep the night before, because David was cutting his back teeth and had been so fractious that she'd taken him into her bed, and then been unable to sleep herself. She felt too weary to fend off Dora's heavy hints any more, and besides, she was beginning to feel that Dora was owed an explanation – if only as a reward for her good-natured perseverance, no matter how curt Jennie's rebuffs had been.

"He doesn't write because we're not together any more. It hasn't worked out. We're getting a divorce." It was the first time she'd said those words out loud to anyone other than Emily and Ernest.

The suddenness of the flat statements had the startling effect of rendering Dora momentarily speechless, and she came back to the table and sank into a chair. It was no more than she had suspected – either that or, as she had told her Jack on several occasions, there had never been a Mr. Keating in the first place.

"So what was it, another woman?" she asked, in hushed tones.

"No, I – I don't think so." It was a question Jennie had pondered endlessly in the long reaches of the night, wishing in a way that it was, so that at least Charles's behaviour would be a bit more explicable. And she would rather have been deserted for the superior attractions of another woman, than know that being with no-one at all was preferable to being with her.

She took a deep breath. Dora was waiting, pop-eyed, to soak up all the details. "He was – is – a lot older than me, and – well, I suppose we had what you might call a 'whirlwind romance'. He urged me to marry him when things were hotting up after the Phony War, and I was swept off my feet. And then – then he just seemed to change his mind, especially when he knew David was on the way. I hadn't thought about whether he would want children – they just seem to be a natural progression after marriage, don't they?"

Dora, rapt, was alternately shaking and nodding her head at appropriate moments as the story unfolded.

"But from the moment I told him I was pregnant, he wanted nothing more to do with me – or with David – and I haven't seen him since." It didn't sound too bad, Jennie thought, if you missed out the bits about Mother, and about Charles threatening to kill her if she had the baby, and about his note after David was born.

Dora looked down at David, playing unconcernedly on the floor. "Poor little dab! Never to know his father! Mind, there'll be plenty of little 'uns growing up the same when this lot's all over, but you'd think he'd want to see him, wouldn't you? If he'd been killed, well, that would be different, but not to want your own flesh and blood, it's…"

Jennie knew from experience that Dora could continue in this vein indefinitely once she got going, which was the last thing she wanted this morning.

"Yes, well, nothing we say now is going to make any difference. It's finished, as I said, but I thought I should tell you, seeing as we've got to know each other so well."

Dora nodded, but Jennie could tell that she was still mulling it all over.

"Will you have to go to court?"

"I don't think so – I hope not. My father's sorting most of it out for me, and the Personnel Officer in the RAF is doing the rest. I think there'll just be some papers to sign – I'll probably have to go home for the weekend for that."

"Well, it's a rum do, and no mistake, and not for me to comment," said Dora, reluctantly taking Jennie's lead and rising from the table. "But I've said it before and I'll say it again – you want to get out and about a bit more. You're still a young woman and shouldn't be sitting in night after night on your own. I'll always come and sit with the little 'un, you know that, and my Maureen goes to the dances down at the Liberal Club every week – she'd happily take you with her."

"Such a pity" she told Jack that evening. "You should've seen her face when she was telling me – felt heart sorry for her, I did. There's more to it than she's letting on, I'll be bound." She pursed her lips in satisfaction at the challenge of finding out more of the details. "I wonder if he knocked her about? Anyway, I've told her she ought to forget about him and go out with our Maureen and maybe find someone else – she'd be quite a looker if she bothered to do herself up a bit. And she could do worse than find herself a man hereabouts with a nice little fishing business …" She glanced across at her husband, sitting puffing at his pipe and giving no indication that he'd listened to a word she said, and wondered if the advice she'd given Jennie was sound after all.

To keep Dora quiet, Jennie went to the cinema from time to time with Emily, where she found herself immune to the romance of *Casablanca* but unable to remain dry-eyed when they went to see *Bambi*. For the rest, though, she strenuously resisted Dora's persistent blandishments to pal up with Maureen, feeling only a sense of horror at the thought of going out purposely to find another man.

Distress at what she saw as her own failures was gradually being replaced by a slow-burning hatred deep in her heart for Charles, added to an increasing conviction that she never wanted to be in a situation of being beholden to a man again. The all-female world which she inhabited made her feel secure, and all the love she might have expended on a husband she was able to give to her small son.

She knew that not all men were cast in the same mould as Charles – you only had to look at Ernest and Cyril to realise that – but she convinced herself that having fallen for his type once, she could unwittingly do so again. Besides, she had no wish to re-kindle the see-saw of emotions that loving any man seemed to produce. If that meant living in a sort of emotional half-world, which Emily had suggested during an afternoon when they had foolishly strayed into discussing Jennie's long-term future, then so be it.

Emily had become quite cross at her imperturbability. "Make sure it's not just your version of sackcloth and ashes!" she warned, when Jennie announced her intention of finding a similar job after the war if Miss Meikle no longer had need of her, or possibly some sort of job in a boarding school. But Jennie refused to be drawn.

The running of the house and the raising of her child had become all-important by now. The visitors Miss Meikle entertained were almost all known to her, and she revelled in seeing to their needs and accepting their thanks before they left, when they would usually pop down the stairs and peer into the kitchen with a "Thanks for everything, Mrs. Keating," and a few kind words directed at David. It was easy to respond to them when she had a clearly-defined role to play: Mrs. Keating, the indispensable housekeeper, rather than Jennie, the vulnerable girl.

One evening one of the guests came down to the kitchen when she was still clearing up. It was a warm summer's night, and they'd all had drinks out in the garden before trooping back in through the kitchen and up into the dining room, smiling sympathetically at Jennie's hot face as she bent over the Rayburn. There were only three guests, so Jennie had managed on her own this evening. So she was surprised to hear a voice from the stairway say, "You look a bit cooler now."

She turned abruptly from the sink to see Gerald Kennedy leaning against the wall, watching her. A dark-haired man in his mid-forties, given to portliness, he was a regular guest along with his statuesque wife, who towered some inches above him. He'd always been most courteous to Jennie, and she returned his smile now.

"Yes. This kitchen gets all the evening sun, so it does get a bit warm at times. Can I get you anything?"

He shook his head. "No, thank you. I've come down here to escape for a while, to tell you the truth. There's some excellent brandy circulating upstairs, but it's a bit too much for me after the wine we've had, and the dining room's pretty stuffy." He moved towards the garden door, which was still open. "Thought I'd seek a bit of fresh air – I hope you don't mind?"

"Of course not. I was just going to clear the glasses away from the garden. It's still quite warm out there, if you want to sit for a while."

"That sounds like a good idea. But please – don't let me detain you!"

He stood aside with a small smile for Jennie to pass through the door before him, tray in hand. He followed her out, and stood between the garden table and seat, but made no move to sit down, and she was aware that he was watching her as she placed the tray on the table and collected empty glasses, cigarette packets and ash-trays.

"It must be a very lonely life here, just you and your little boy," he said at last.

"Not really," she answered without looking up. "My sister lives in Bideford, so I see her a lot. Besides, there are hundreds of women like me whose husbands are away."

She knew, without turning to see, that he was standing behind her now. "But a pretty young woman like you shouldn't be cooped up with a child all the time. You should be out enjoying yourself."

If she'd been in the safe familiarity of the kitchen she might have turned to him with a laugh and asked if Dora had been having a word with him, but out here in the encroaching darkness there was a feeling of menace about him that made her not want to joke at all.

As she went to place the last glass on the tray, he reached out and caught her hand, forcing her to turn towards him.

"We could enjoy ourselves together – now – here in the garden."

His eyes were glittering in the dusk. He seemed nothing like the safe, kind Mr. Kennedy who always complimented her on the food she'd prepared. Jennie began to pull away from him, unable to drag her gaze away from his, like a mesmerised rabbit – until she was leaning against a gnarled tree trunk, the knotty wood digging into her back.

"Please let go, you're hurting me – and I need to go back inside the house. This is silly –" She gasped as he moved closer to her, pressing his body against hers.

"Well over a year you've been alone, Joan says. A long time for a married woman to be without a man." His breath was coming in short pants as he forced his thigh in between her legs and clamped his hand on her breast, squeezing it hard, so she could feel the heat of his palm through the thin material of her blouse.

"Please, stop it!" she cried. "Leave me alone!"

"Now, now!" he said." I've watched you whenever I've come down into the kitchen, looking at people with those big soulful eyes! Asking for it! You know you want it as much as I do!"

He clamped his mouth down on hers. He tasted of wine and cigarettes. His hand moved from her breast and travelled down over her writhing body, before sliding her skirt up her thigh. As she twisted this way and that his other hand relaxed its grip on her as, unable to contain himself, he began to grapple with his own clothing.

Just as she felt as if she were drowning under the forcefulness of his intentions and was helpless to save herself, she thought she heard David calling out for her, and she became filled with a sudden, overwhelming fury. How dare this man – any man – treat her in this way!

Hatred mingled with her fury, hatred for Gerald Kennedy, for Charles Keating, for the arrogance of every man who thought that a woman could be there for the taking whenever it suited. Jerking her mouth away from his, she managed to take advantage of his fumbling and, summoning all her strength, pushed him hard. "Get away from me, you great oaf!"

Surprised at her strength, he staggered back from her, stumbled against a chair, and fell heavily against the table, hitting his head on a corner with a loud crack and knocking the tray so that the glasses crashed to the ground.

Not caring if he was alright, Jennie fled back into the house, through the kitchen and into her room. David hadn't stirred after all. He was sleeping peacefully. Anxious that Gerald might follow her in here, she returned to the kitchen, splashed her face with cold water, and tried to control her rapid breathing.

As she dried her face he staggered in through the back door, his hand to the back of his head. "My head!" he gasped. "I think it's bleeding!"

She picked up a heavy saucepan from the wooden draining board. "Then you'd better get up to the bathroom and sort yourself out." She held the pan threatening in front of her. "And if you ever come near me again, I'll make sure it's a knife I have in my hand!"

He glared at her for a moment, a look compounded of disbelief and loathing, before attempting to climb the stairs to the ground floor with exaggerated dignity.

She realised she'd been holding her breath while he was in the room, and now she let it out slowly, rocking backwards and forwards slightly as she wondered what he would tell the others if his head really was bleeding.

What should she do now? Should she tell her boss that her guest had tried to seduce her? She wasn't sure just how compassionate Miss Meikle would be, and he could always say that Jennie had led him on. *After all,* she told herself bitterly, *you did invite him out into the garden!* Anger rose in her again at the perfidy of men whom you couldn't even be pleasant to without them assuming they could take whatever liberties they wished.

She could still feel his hands on her body, the imprint of his mouth on hers, and she wished that she could soak in a hot bath, wash away every trace of what had happened. But that would mean going up to the top of the house, and she had no intention of doing so until the guests had departed.

After a few more minutes, when there was no sound except laughter from the dining room above her head, she poured water from the ever-ready kettle into the sink, grabbed a cloth and scrubbed and scrubbed at her face and arms, until the skin tingled.

Afterwards she sat for some time in the darkened bedroom, waiting for sounds of the guests departing. Her anger began to deflate and other emotions, masked by the vehemence of her fury, began to surface. *What if ...?* she kept asking herself. *What if I hadn't been able to get away? What if he had raped me, and left me pregnant? What if I tell Miss Meikle and she doesn't believe me?* "Asking for it," he'd said. What had he meant by that? She'd never been anything more than courteous to all the visitors. Did being friendly and helpful towards men mean that they thought you were 'easy'?

She wished she had someone to turn to, now, right at this moment, but she could tell no-one, go nowhere until tomorrow. And then she wouldn't tell Emily. Her sister's reaction would probably be to accost Gerald Kennedy, Miss Meikle and anyone else who was in the house on that night, which would mean the end of Jennie's job – and another job like this one would be hard to find, as Dora was often telling her.

Dora! She would tell Dora tomorrow – could she get by until tomorrow? – and ask her advice. Until then she would force herself not to think about it. She rose, re-entered the kitchen and automatically began to clear away, her thoughts veering between shock at what had happened and surprise at her own strength of reaction. There was something reassuring about carrying out the regular chores that soothed her, although she would only collect the broken glasses in the morning, and tell Miss Meikle that she'd dropped them when washing up.

The only person to come downstairs after the front door had banged closed was Miss Meikle, to tell her that her that the guests had gone and she herself was retiring.

"Right. I'll just clear away the dining room," Jennie said, to which her employer nodded and turned towards the stairs. Then she suddenly turned back again. "Are you alright? You look a bit peaky."

"Yes. I'm fine. Thank you. It's just been a bit of a warm evening."

"Then why don't you leave everything else until the morning, when Dora's here?"

"No. Honestly. I'd rather finish up for the night." *And not go to bed too soon because I know I won't sleep for hours.*

She willed Miss Meikle to go away, before she blurted out that one of her favourite friends from Barnstaple was a drunken swine who tried to seduce defenceless women. But perhaps Miss Meikle already knew that – perhaps he'd tried to seduce her, or even succeeded, and that was why they were so friendly. After this evening Jennie felt that anything was possible, although there was something about Miss Meikle that would prohibit such advances before they began.

Which begged the question that perhaps there was something about Jennie which encouraged a man like Gerald Kennedy.

Miss Meikle yawned. "Well, I'll turn in. Thank you for this evening." She scrutinised Jennie's face, and said, with unusual concern: "Perhaps you need a break. You must say if I'm working you too hard. Any time…" Her voice faded away as she climbed the stairs.

It was the sleepless night Jennie had known it would be. By the early hours she'd decided three things: that she would tell Dora about the incident because it would be unbearable not to tell anyone; that she would ask Dora to come in to help whenever the Kennedys were invited to dinner; and that last night's episode confirmed the fact that nearly all men were swine who could not be trusted, and she was better off without one.

As it turned out there was no chance to tell Dora anything next day, as she didn't appear for work. Jennie took on the extra cleaning chores in the afternoon when David was having his nap, glad of the opportunity to keep busy, stopping only when Emily arrived to wonder why Jennie hadn't gone round as planned. Emily waited as Jennie finished sweeping the already spotless path outside the back door with swift, impatient movements, one of Dora's voluminous aprons tied round her middle. "You look just like Mother!" she said, and then wished she hadn't when Jennie suddenly flung the broom down and scowled at her, looking, if only she knew it, even more like her parent.

"Dora's not been in today," she said shortly, "and I wanted to keep on top of things in case she's not in tomorrow either." She just stopped herself from saying that Emily could probably do with a bit more of Mother in her. She forced herself to smile instead. "Don't mind me! I get a bit crabby when I'm here on my own. Shall we take the boys for a walk?"

Dora only appeared the following morning, just when Jennie had decided that she wasn't going to arrive at all – looking so dreadful that all thoughts of telling Dora her woes left Jennie immediately.

"Dora! What on earth's the matter? You look terrible!" Jennie cried when Dora appeared in the kitchen doorway and heaved her body onto a chair beside the table.

"It's our Joss! His ship went down – I don't know when, but they told us two nights ago. We got a telegram. They were all lost! My boy, lost at sea!" Tears trickled in rivulets down the deep gorges that had suddenly appeared in the face that had been as round and smooth as a full moon.

"Oh Dora, no!" Jennie hugged the bulky body as Dora's shoulders heaved convulsively. "Why on earth did you come in today? You should be at home with Jack!"

"He's gone out. Down to the bay to be with his mates. They'll all understand, see – there's many of them's lost someone in the water at sometime. He's no good round women crying. He's sat himself at the window ever since the telegram came, not saying a word. So I'm glad he's gone, but I couldn't stand being in the house on my own."

"What about Maureen?"

Dora blew her nose loudly on a spotless white handkerchief and tossed her head in a disparaging way. "Wailed like a banshee for hours, enough for all of us, until the doctor had to come and give her something to knock her out. Slept the clock round and then I packed her off to work this morning. Couldn't stand it if she started all that up again, so I thought she'd be better with the other girls."

"And did the doctor give you something as well – to help a little bit?"

Her face now devoid of tears, Dora drew herself up in the chair. "It wouldn't make any difference, would it? He'd still be gone when

I woke up, like he'll still be gone every day for the rest of my life. I'll have my bit of a cry when I need to, and keep hoping that they might find his body so's we can say a proper goodbye, but there's no sense running away from it, is there?"

She spoke with a quiet dignity at odds with her tortured face. Jennie moved away to make a pot of tea, while David ran in and out of the kitchen on his sturdy little legs, and she only just managed to resist the urge to take hold of him and hug him to her very tightly indeed.

There were dark days and better days for Dora after that. Joss had been in the Merchant Navy, while her other son Hugh had joined the Royals, and the good days occurred when she heard that he was still safe and well. Miss Meikle had been sympathetic to her loss, telling Dora to have as much time off as she needed, but backing away from any signs of emotional distress. Very gradually Dora became more her old self again, but Jennie noticed a dullness in her eyes that hadn't been there before. She was only too happy to come in during the evenings to give Jennie a hand with visitors, saying that it was preferable to being at home with an increasingly morose Jack and worrying what Maureen was up to, since she'd taken to going over to the army camp near Barnstaple.

Jennie never did tell Dora what had happened with Gerald Kennedy, even when the man had the cheek to poke his head round the corner of the stairs and say, "Thank you, Mrs. Keating, for a delicious meal," as if nothing had ever happened. Inwardly she fumed and strengthened her resolve never to have anything to do with a man again, and sometimes she even managed to laugh at herself because the opportunity to meet another man had little chance of occurring, but she never mentioned anything of this to Dora. Compared with losing a son, being the object of a drunken man's lust was small beer, and Dora had somehow lost her appetite for chewing over salacious gossip.

Occasionally Jennie made the journey home to Nantyderry, when guilt over not seeing her family and the desire to be back on the farm among the mountains overwhelmed her, but the visits were not a success. Mother insisted on referring to David as 'the boy', which always set them off on the wrong foot, and Jennie was never sure whether she was meant to behave like a guest, or pitch in and become one of the family again. She would sit at the tea-table and make polite conversation about Emily and Ernest, while suffering agonies lest David should spill something or behave less than perfectly under his grandmother's critical eye.

At first, anxious that there'd be talk, she was reluctant to venture out into Nantyderry, but in the end the divorce had been very low-key, and she realised that there were few, if any, acquaintances who knew about it. No mention was ever made of Charles, but she felt he was there, unspoken but still between them, every time Mother wondered aloud: what was Jennie going to do with herself and 'the boy' after the war was over?

It was evident by this time that the war *would* soon be over. Jennie had listened with bated breath to the news of the D-Day landings, and shed a little tear when Glen Miller's death was announced, remembering the times she'd listened to him on the wireless at home in spite of Mother's rantings about the terrible *American* noise his band made. She hugged Dora when the blackouts were finally done away with and some of the clothing restrictions lifted, and she breathed a guilty sigh of relief when the doodlebugs falling on London halted Miss Meikle's plans to return to the capital.

But the day came, as she'd known it would, early in 1945, when Miss Meikle announced that she would be going back to her house in London within the month and, regrettably, it was not a suitable house for a live-in housekeeper who had a lively little boy in tow.

Part Three

1946 ~

23

For Harry, coming home had been much harder than he'd anticipated. His unit had been one of the last to return to Britain, so it was well into 1946 before he was re-united with his family. Mam had cried and laughed at the same time as she hugged the son she hadn't seen for over five years, and then pushed him away from her to get a better look, while his Dad had pumped his hand up and down with a rare smile on his face, as if he'd come up on the pools.

There was so much to catch up on that they veered from all talking at once, so that no-one was listening to anyone else, to awkward little silences when there seemed so much to say that no-one quite knew where to start.

For Harry it all felt slightly unreal – as unreal as he felt in his de-mob suit, the jacket of which was wide enough in the chest but inches too long in the length, so he found himself walking with his shoulders lifted somewhat to make up for it. He'd dreamed of this homecoming, of course, throughout the whole of Africa, the heat and the deserts, and throughout the beauty marred by terrible destruction in much of Italy. He'd taken part in the merciless bombardment of Montecassino, seen Italian peasants, their livelihood shattered, desperately trying to sell cigarettes to the British soldiers, and then, months later, stood in awe amidst the splendour of the Vatican. None of it made sense, so best always to keep home in one's mind's eye, until it became the embodiment of all the things that could be relied upon to remain constant and unchanging in this shifting world.

But, of course, so many things had changed. He came back to an England of austerity and utility, with grey-faced people in the devastated cities who, after the euphoria of VE Day and VJ Day, had had to come to terms with the fact that hard work, shortages, and 'make-do-and-mend' were to continue to be their war legacy for the foreseeable future. Even when the little branch train drew up alongside the platform at Blaenavon, it didn't feel quite how he had imagined it.

He was pleased to be home, there was no doubt about that, but there were all the small differences – a shop that had changed hands here, a pub that had closed down there, council houses going up where he and Megan had strolled through Coed Woods, and prefabs in Church Road; differences which had come gradually to the town and been assimilated by its inhabitants, but left Harry feeling uneasily a bit of a visitor when he longed to be a part of the place again. And Mam and Dad were older, greyer, and smaller.

Both Archie and Dai had come home almost a year before him. Archie, thin and wiry beside the plump Lizzie whose shape hadn't seemed to have been affected by rationing, had resumed his place in the family with such gusto that by the time Harry arrived home Lizzie had presented him with twins, a boy and a girl. Archie walked around the house with a baby in each arm, pleased as punch with his achievement and as oblivious as his wife to the problems of two extra mouths to feed and two extra bodies to fit into their tiny house.

Dai had declared his intention of staying in the RAF and wanted his family to move away with him, but Bridget put her foot down and said that for now they would move into one of the prefabs which she had already secured for them. And that the farthest she was prepared to go was to Cwmbran, where plans were afoot for a whole new town, and then he could look for work in Newport. The rest of the family had held their collective breath while row after row erupted between the couple, but Dai had suddenly capitulated. He curbed his wanderlust, went to work in the blacksmith's shop at the Foundry, and settled down in the little two bedroomed bungalow that actually gave them more space than they'd had in the whole of their married life.

As he made himself comfortable in the tiny back bedroom in Morgan Street, Harry envied his brother and sister their family life, no matter how turbulent it might be at times. He felt that he'd come full circle, back to the same position he'd been in when he was sixteen – except there was an older face now staring back at him in the shaving mirror, more experienced but not necessarily any wiser, with a harder look in the bright blue eyes which continually questioned what he was going to do with the rest of his life.

He knew that he was ready to find a companion again. He wanted the satisfaction of his own home and children, with someone to share it and give his life some purpose. Whether he could ever love anyone again the way he'd loved Megan he wasn't sure, but he was now prepared to try at least. The war had separated Megan and all that had gone before, so that while he could still mourn her and miss the life they'd shared, it had been another life in a time long ago, with a Harry whose emotions and reactions had not been irrevocably altered by nearly seven years of war and army life.

Gradually he took up the reins of his social life again, playing cards at Uncle Fred's house, where Uncle Joe now lodged and was kept busy by Fred's wife Violet, who found him all sorts of jobs to do in and out of the house to keep him from being under her feet. He went to the Rolling Mill with his father, two men out together as equals now, to enjoy a pint and meet many of his old friends. He sought out Arthur, who'd been invalided out of the army when he lost a leg in France, and found him settled in Bryn Terrace with a tin leg, a pretty wife and child, and a job in Fowler's Men's Outfitting.

Arthur, the lad who had always outstripped the tongue-tied Harry when it came to chatting up the girls, was keen to see his old friend settled down again. "Fancy a shop job again, Harry? I think old Fowler will be looking to expand when clothes rationing finally ends – got his eye on Woodley's place the other side of Broad Street. I could put a word in for you as an assistant, if you want?"

Harry shrugged. "I don't know what I want, to tell you the truth, Arthur. Or at least, what I want and what's available don't seem to match up. I don't think I want to work in a place again where you've got to watch yourself all the time because the boss is around." He grinned. "I spent too much time on 'Jankers' for answering back, I think, to put myself in that position again!"

One weekend his friend Ronnie, who'd become his bosom pal in the army since Dunkirk, arrived out of the blue. Ronnie had gone back to Edgware, where he knew from the letters that had flowed throughout the war that his girl was still waiting for him. He arrived in Blaenavon in an open-topped car, with all the flamboyance that had attracted Harry to him in the first place, and an invitation to his wedding.

"So she really had waited for you, then?" Harry smiled, as Ronnie immediately set about charming Mam with a bunch of flowers and tales of what a good friend her son had been to him – which included exaggerated stories about bravery but nothing about the poker schools they'd set up between them, or the drunken nights spent in Italy and France.

"Yes, she waited – just like she promised!" He lowered his voice and dug his elbow into Harry's ribs as Mam bustled out into the scullery: "Trouble is, I couldn't wait, once I got home – knocked her up straight away! Not that it matters, we were getting married anyway – I just needed to convince her old man that I was back to stay."

Ronnie was already making headway with the big plans he'd begun to formulate when they were waiting for de-mob. "The housing market, that's the place to be, Harry, after the war! All those people who've been bombed out will be clamouring for somewhere to make a fresh start. There'll be new housing estates popping up everywhere."

He'd formed his own small company – knowing Ronnie's penchant for gambling, Harry didn't dare ask where he'd got the money, but Ronnie told him that his prospective father-in-law had been persuaded to make a large donation. "I'd like you to come in with me," he told Harry. "There's plenty of work to keep the two of us going, and you can't go wrong in London."

But Harry was adamant that he didn't want to go to London now that he was just settling in back home.

"But you can't sit here twiddling your thumbs forever!" Ronnie protested, his exuberance and bonhomie seeming too big to be contained in the little house.

"I've got plans, same as you!" Harry protested hotly, but found it difficult to explain to Ronnie that those plans were vague notions which included finding someone with whom to share his life and have a family.

He decided to take Ronnie out for a drink.

"Excellent idea!" said Ronnie. "You can take me to all those places you kept talking about!"

"Right!" Harry grinned. "Then we'll start at the top of the town and work our way down!"

It was Saturday night and the town was busy. As they walked the length of Broad Street their conversation was constantly interrupted by people calling a greeting to Harry.

"Blimey!" Ronnie exclaimed. "Do you really know all these people?"

"Of course." And as he'd done with Ivy – so many years ago, it seemed now – he began to reel off the names of those they met, and some of their family histories. "And that's why I want to stay here," he said as they entered the Vine Tree and ordered a couple of pints.

When another couple of weeks had gone by, though, and Harry still had found nothing that he wanted to do, he began to wonder whether he should have gone with Ronnie after all.

"The only way to prosper, Harry, is to work for yourself," Ronnie had told him. "Set yourself up in a little business now, like I'm doing, and you can't go wrong."

The more he thought about it, the more he realised Ronnie was right. Neither of them had responded very well to always being under orders in the Army – Harry had lost his corporal's stripe a couple of times for insubordination when the futility of some of the things they'd had to do when times were quiet had made him utter some angry retort.

Finally one evening, when even Mam had begun to get fed up with his aimless mooching about, and: "Too bloody choosy, that's the trouble. You wouldn't be so picky if you had a family to feed!" came from his father, which earned him a surreptitious kick under the table and a black look from Mam, Harry sat down with a pen and paper to work out what he wanted.

Blaenavon was beginning to enjoy a post-war prosperity, brought about in part by the bus-loads of workers now employed by British Nylon Spinners down in Pontypool, and the promise of open-cast mining which was just starting up on the Blorenge. Factory work didn't appeal to him at all, but he thought long and hard about what would be needed up on the mountainside. As an idea began to formulate in his head, he jotted down some figures and checked the balance in the Post Office savings book where Mam had assiduously kept his 'nest egg' throughout the years he'd been away, and which he'd now added to with money saved during his time away. Then he wrote everything out again, as neatly as he could, and carefully put the papers away.

Next morning he was up early, dressed in his suit, and out of the door with a wink and a "See you later!" to Mam. He came back that evening saying nothing about where he'd been, but with a pleased expression on his face.

The following day he was off early again, and Mam heard no more from him until four o'clock that afternoon, when she was brought to the front door by the persistent harping of a horn to see the narrow street almost blocked by a large, flat-bed lorry – and sitting at the wheel, a huge grin on his face, was Harry.

"What do you think?" he asked, but before she could answer he went on: "Put the kettle on while I get this thing parked somewhere, and I'll tell you all about it!"

During his procrastination two nights before, Harry had realised that one of the difficulties in open-cast mining was the wide terrain covered by the workforce. Lorries would be needed for everything – from transporting the soil being lifted by an enormous machine they'd had to be bring onto the mountain in pieces and then construct, to transporting food for the men who were working too far away from the canteen to come back for their midday break.

Harry had gone straight to the managers' offices that morning, discovered that the transport issues hadn't been fully worked out yet, and put his proposal to them. It helped that the senior manager he spoke to was also an ex-serviceman, keen to give his fellow soldiers a break whenever he could.

"I was dying to tell you last night, but they wanted to think about it and let me know today. I told them to give me an answer quickly, 'cos I had another company down Cardiff way interested in using my services. So, now you are looking at the new transport manager, who will not only be running all that side of things but will also be doing so with his own lorries – which, of course, I told him I already had at his disposal!" Harry told his surprised parents.

"But you didn't have any lorries then," his Mam said, pouring another cup of tea and trying hard to keep up with his excited account of events.

"No, of course I didn't. But I thought of how Ronnie would have gone about this, and it's all bluff, really, just like playing cards. And I knew Jones's garage had had a lorry out the back of their place for ages, so when the company said 'yes' today I went straight down there and picked it up from him, cheap. He's getting me three more by Monday. Not brand new of course, but they'll do fine for up the mountain. I expect I'll do some of the driving myself from time to time, so I won't be stuck inside all day."

His parents could only give a sigh of relief that at last their Harry had found something to do that might soak up the restlessness he'd shown since his return.

24

When Miss Meikle had said she was returning to London, Jennie had been determined to find another situation where she could continue to bring up David, but it had proved impossible within Bideford, and she'd been hesitant about starting again somewhere unknown. And then fate had intervened in the form of a letter from Mother, saying that she was laid up in bed with goodness-knew-what – the letter had been most unspecific in that way – with no-one to help. Laura had left for a joyous reunion with Cyril, who had returned bathed in glory, at least in Laura and Selina's eyes; Gwyneth wouldn't be returning because she'd made an indecently hasty marriage – Mother spent some time commenting caustically on the need for it; and although Father had a boy to help him on the farm there was no-one to help Mother. So didn't she, Jennie, think it only fair that she should return to the bosom of her family?

Fair or not, Jennie did feel compelled to return to Nantyderry, particularly as Mother's letter had included several paragraphs about how she and Father were not getting any younger and it seemed dreadful that there was now no-one on whom they could rely.

There were emotional farewells between herself and Dora, who cried almost as copiously as when her son had been killed. "Like a daughter, you've been to me," she said more than once. "I'm going to miss you, and your little 'un – and you'll miss your Auntie Dora, won't you, middear?"

"We'll both miss you," Jennie assured her, trying not to cry herself. "But think how busy you're going to be once Maureen's baby is born – you won't know yourself when you're pushing your grandchild around Bideford in his pram!"

"And if our Maureen stays as flighty, I expect I'll be doing plenty of that," Dora agreed as she wiped her eyes. She sighed. "I suppose it all works out for the best, doesn't it? I can't say I like that lad she's wed, but it could have been worse – she could have been one of those going off to America to marry, and then I'd never see her again."

"And once Hugh's home, there might be more wedding bells in the family."

Dora nodded and then they were both quiet for a few moments, each thinking about Joss, who would never come home.

Emily took a robust view of Jennie's departure. "Well, you certainly look a lot better than when you first came down here. It's time you moved on to something else, you know – stopped burying yourself away. So mind you don't do that when you get back home; get over to Laura's and join in with whatever those two get up to, and let Mother babysit for you... she'll get the work out of you in return, won't she? And remember, you're your own boss now, and you're going back to help *her* out – so make sure you stick up for yourself!"

There was a heavy, dragging feeling in the pit of Jennie's stomach all the way home, brought about by the dread that she was making a huge mistake in returning, but she overrode it with the concern that perhaps Mother was very seriously ill indeed, and if so it was time she really made her peace with her, and put aside all the memories of the hurts and insults inflicted since childhood.

She and David were welcomed back enthusiastically by Father, who came to meet them at the station and immediately endeared David to him by promising he could ride on the tractor when they got back to the farm.

"How's Mother?" Jennie asked anxiously as soon as all their belongings had been stowed in the van. "Has she had the doctor out?"

"Lord, no! It's only her old lumbago playing her up again! A few days off her feet and she'll be right as rain, I expect."

"So... she's not seriously ill? But her letter said – at least it implied – that this was something else, that she was really poorly, and wouldn't be able to manage on her own in the house any more!"

Father chuckled. "Well, you know your Mother. Laid up for a while and she thinks it's the end of the world! She's had Laura back over here till yesterday, but she had to go back to Monmouth for some do that Cyril wanted to take her to, and..."

He stopped, and his face fell as he saw the expression on Jennie's. "So you didn't really want to come home, then? I didn't see the letter, but your Mother said you had to come back because you had nowhere else to go ... that we needed to take you in, in a manner of speaking, because your Miss Whatever-her-name-was you were working for was going back to London."

"No – I mean, yes! I mean... Oh!" Jennie hopped from one foot to the other like a small child needing the lavatory, furious with Mother, but not wishing to hurt her Father. "Let's get in the van and talk!"

She pulled David onto her knee on the passenger seat and waited for Father to get in beside her. "It's not that I didn't want to come back, exactly… or that I didn't need to. Mother was right about the job finishing, but then I understood from her letter that it was vital that I came back as soon as possible because she was so poorly, and there was no-one else to help. I just feel a bit… used, I suppose. I would have liked the decision to have been wholly mine."

"I see." Father turned the key in the ignition ponderously. *Katie, Katie,* he thought, *when are you going to learn that you can't force everyone to do exactly what you want?* "We've both missed you, you know, and missed seeing our little grandson grow up – especially with Emily's two being so far away as well. We're very pleased that you're back."

She patted his arm as he pulled out of the station. "I know, Dad – and I'm grateful for all that you did – with the divorce and all that. I just get worried that I'll always be shifting from pillar to post and never have anywhere to call my own."

"You might yet. You're only twenty-five now – once everything's back to normal you might find someone to settle down with, have a proper home of your own. And until then this will always be your home, you know that."

"Yes, I know that."

She smiled at her father, despite the sinking feeling in the pit of her stomach. He didn't really understand – neither of them did, she was sure of that. How could she explain to them that she didn't want another man? That marriage was not on her agenda at all… she just needed to be in charge of her own life?

"At least I'll be able to get David sorted out for school here," she said at last, in the silence that had fallen between them.

Her spirits began to revive at the familiar sights she'd always loved as they turned into the farm. David jumped out of the van, demanding his promised tractor ride, but first he had to have the grime of the journey wiped away at the kitchen sink and then go and see Granny in her bedroom. He kissed her obediently when his mother told him to, but he didn't get the same warm hug in response that he'd got from his grandfather.

Nothing had changed; Jennie had been foolish even to suppose that it would. A complete change of personality, as well as heart, would have been necessary on Mother's part for there to be any difference, and she wondered sometimes whether Mother even had a heart.

Oh, it *seemed* different for the first few weeks, when they were all getting used to one another again – smiling over David's excited discoveries on the farm, which had just been a backcloth on his previous best-behaviour, tightly-controlled visits – and while Jennie still felt like a visitor, and Mother still treated her like one. But this false situation had a short life. The humdrum of daily life throbbed on, and Jennie found herself slotting back into the routine – an apparently necessary part of which was still to meet Mother's exacting and often contrary standards.

But this was a different Jennie from the physically and mentally weak girl who'd fled the farm under the ignominy of a broken marriage. This was a Jennie who'd held down her own job, brought up her child satisfactorily, (even Mother had to grudgingly admit), and who had no intention of playing the victim to Mother's dictator any more.

It took Mother some time to realise this, of course. She'd assumed that Jennie would be so grateful to her parents for providing a roof over her head (as she frequently pointed out, disregarding, as she always did, her own manipulative actions), that she would willingly take up the role of daughter-at-home which Mother had designated for her long before Charles had played such havoc with all their lives. Jennie's stance on everything was over-ruled; from wanting to use the cooker – Mother's cooker! – to prepare meals, to objecting to David being swiped round the ankles with a wet floor cloth because he had inadvertently stepped on the still-wet kitchen floor which Mother had been down on her hands and knees cleaning.

And that was another thing. Mother had envisaged Jennie taking over the chores that Gwyneth had been called upon to carry out, and was not prepared for Jennie's more democratic view of sharing all the tasks, both dirty and pleasant, between them.

"How did you manage to stay there so long, on your own?" she asked Laura when she had escaped to Monmouth for the day. "Didn't she drive you daft as well?"

"Oh yes," Laura answered, "but Mother knew that if she pushed me too far I could always return here – and I threatened to on more than one occasion, I can tell you; I even packed to go to Lancashire once when Cyril was stationed up there... and it suited her to have me at home at the time, so she used to back off."

"And that's the difference, isn't it?" said Jennie. "She's got me over a barrel."

"Give it a bit more time," Laura advised. "It's difficult for both of you when you've been used to running a house yourself. Remember, when I first went to stay I was pregnant, and at that time I didn't give a hoot about helping out so she didn't feel invaded by my presence – and she does have her good points, you know."

Jennie didn't care to ask what those were, in case she found herself falling out with Laura as well. All she knew was the contradiction that was Mother hadn't changed.

There was no denying, though, how much this new way of life suited David, which encouraged Jennie to stick it out. It brought a lump to her throat to see Father fish out the old wheelbarrow from her own childhood and give it to David, so that he could solemnly follow his grandfather around the farm. There was equal joy on Father's face when he praised his new assistant. "He's a great boy," he told Jennie. "You've done a good job with him."

Jennie only wished that she could change places with the lad who helped outside, and work on the farm with Father too.

In September she took David along to the little school in Llanover, one of the few times she'd ventured into the local community since her return. She still had it in her mind that people would point her out as the woman who was now a divorcée on account of her husband leaving her, but luckily most of the other mothers were too taken up with settling their own children into school to do more than smile welcomingly. Thankfully David, who had been missing some of the rough-and-tumble he'd enjoyed with Emily's boys, took to school immediately, leaving Jennie with a manly smile in the mornings and regaling her with all sorts of often incomprehensible tales, holding echoes of her own time there, as they walked home together in the afternoons.

Father insisted that Jennie be paid an allowance, which Mother agreed to providing the word 'wages' wasn't used, as Jennie had requested.

"It's just that if I feel I am earning a wage for the work that I do, I can also feel justified in taking proper time off to do whatever I want," she'd tried to explain as reasonably as possible.

"But it makes you sound like some sort of servant," Mother said, her face indicating just what she thought of that demeaning role.

"And an allowance makes me feel that I'm a charity case, dependent on every bit of bounty that falls from you and Father in order to survive," Jennie argued.

Mother simply raised one eyebrow, sufficient expression to demonstrate that her parents' charity was really all that Jennie could expect.

Father spoke up. "Whatever you call it, Jennie deserves reasonable pay for what she does. Gwyneth was paid, after all, and so –" he continued quickly before Mother could point out that Laura hadn't needed to be paid when she was under their roof – "I shall reimburse Jennie from out of the farm accounts, so you need have nothing to do with it."

He fixed his wife with a sterner look than Jennie had seen him use for a long time, and to her surprise, Mother piped down. Jennie realised in a flash of discernment that this was what Mother had wanted all the time – a man who would overrule her, dominate her from time to time... and probably, she realised with even greater insight, that domination should extend to the bedroom as well. She felt herself grow hot as she pictured Father manfully sweeping up a protesting Katharine and striding up the stairs to the bedroom before... but nevertheless, she wished she was able to share her thoughts somehow with Father.

"Well, I still think it's a ridiculous idea," Mother grumbled as she backed down, "but if you two want to do it, then get on with it. I shall say no more."

She said plenty, of course, in a roundabout way. Comments were made about how hard Father continued to work, when he ought to be thinking about slowing down, just so that he could continue to keep a roof over all their heads. And when Jennie wanted to go to Abergavenny to spend some of her 'allowance' on new shoes for David, Mother saw fit to fetch the Zebo, tie an old apron round her waist, and set to black-leading the range in order to make Jennie feel guilty about sloping off when there was so much work to be done.

The worst winter of the century came almost as a godsend, because irritations were forgotten as they all cleaved together to keep the farm going. Jennie spent more time outside helping Father to feed the animals and keep the drive clear for the milk lorries, while Mother fretted about her hens, and the snow that found its way through the rafters of the dairy and then dripped down on her clean surfaces.

But when the thaw finally set in, in the spring of 1947, Jennie knew that she had to find work away from the farm, or her nerves would be in the same state they had been six years previously. Sometimes, when she sat in her old bedroom, it was as if those six years hadn't existed – except for the small, intense, dark-haired child sleeping peacefully along the landing in the little bedroom that used to be Gwyneth's.

In the way that these things often do, her chance came when she met up again with Hetty Lloyd. The war years had changed Hetty considerably; she was bluffer, coarser – in body and in voice – since Jennie had last seen her. Disgusted at being considered too old when women were first conscripted, she had persevered and eventually ended up training as a mechanic, sorting out Army lorry engines with a deftness that brought whistles of admiration – the only admiring whistles she was likely to get, she knew! – from the men around her.

She bowled down the drive one morning in the same old battered car that Jennie remembered, its sweetly-purring engine giving testimony to Hetty's skill, and thumped on the front door with such gusto that Mother was sure it must be a delivery boy – and hurried to answer it so that she could tell him in no uncertain terms to go round the back.

"'Morning!" The two women eyed each other with well-remembered antipathy, increased on Mother's part by her distaste for Hetty's bulky body being attired in trousers, an old army jersey, and heavy men's brogues. "Heard that Jennie was back in these parts, so thought I'd come to see how she's getting on … Ah! There you are!" She pushed past Mother as Jennie, hearing Hetty's loud voice, emerged from the kitchen. "How are you, m'dear? Looking very well, I must say! How's that baby of yours? Not such a baby by now, of course!"

Jennie ushered Hetty into the parlour, delighted to see her old friend, and they quickly fell to catching up on each other's news. Any hopes she had of Mother bringing them tea came to nought, but Hetty didn't seem to notice, and as she had just lit a Woodbine on which she was inhaling deeply, it was probably just as well.

"I'm living in Pontypool now," she told Jennie. "Got a bit restless when the war ended – thought there'd be nothing for me to do, y'know, but I've landed a nice little job, working for a firm which supplies canteen staff for various companies. Just finished a big contract with British Nylon Spinners - set up a large canteen there. Could have done with a few more workers like you, I can tell you!"

"I don't suppose you have any more in the pipeline?" Jennie asked hopefully.

"Why?" Hetty tossed her head towards the door, in the general direction of the kitchen. "That old bird giving you gyp, is she?"

Jennie spurted with laughter at Hetty's succinct but not too subtle grasp of the situation. "You could say that! I suppose I'm a bit like you, though… I miss doing a proper job, like I had in Devon."

"Well, I might have just the thing, as it happens. Open-cast mining outfit on top of the Blorenge needs a new canteen supervisor – or would that be too far for you to travel? You'd be able to pick up the Works Bus at Abergavenny."

"That should be alright, if I can get back here at a reasonable time to see to David."

"Early start and early finish, all these jobs – you'd be finished after the dinner-time rush."

"That sounds ideal – if you think I could do it! How big is the canteen?"

"Oh, it caters for about three hundred, if I remember rightly," Hetty said breezily. "But you can manage that alright – there's a team of girls working under you, so you won't be short-staffed. It's just that they haven't been too happy with the manageress so far. Bit too slapdash, and that soon transmits to the rest of the team.

"Tell you what," she went on, before Jennie could point out that her previous experience was limited to providing meals for one most days, and rarely more than six when she was busy, "come and see me on Saturday – I'm due a visit from the Personnel Manager then, and we can talk about it more." She fished in a capacious handbag that was almost a hold-all until she found a slip of paper and a stubby pencil. "That's my address, over Belli's cafe in the main street – door at the side, you can't miss it. Come over about ten."

Father took her to Pontypool, without telling Mother why, and sat in Belli's cafe with David while Jennie climbed the stairs to Hetty's flat. She knocked twice before she heard Hetty's voice: "Come on in, the door's on the latch!"

There was no sign of Hetty in the big square room that Jennie entered. "I'm through here," she called. "In the bedroom – didn't realise that was the time, I'm afraid. Come through!"

Hetty was struggling to get out of a large unkempt bed, her hair sticking on end, wearing a voluminous winceyette nightgown. She began to cough as she sat on the edge of the bed and reached for her Woodbines.

"Had a bit of a late night, to tell you the truth," she smiled ruefully at Jennie. "Some of the lads from the Transport Depot turned up and we all went for a drink – well, quite a few drinks, actually."

Her feet were searching for her slippers under the bed when there was another knock at the front door. "Come in, Jeff!" Hetty shouted. "We're through here!" And to Jennie's acute embarrassment she appeared completely unconcerned that she was about to entertain a man in her bedroom while in a questionable state of dress.

Hetty read her mind and grinned. "It's alright m'dear – he's seen me plenty of times before like this!" Which only increased Jennie discomfiture as Jeff, the Personnel Manager appeared in the doorway.

"This is the gel I was telling you about," Hetty said without preamble. "Jennie Keating. Hard worker, excellent organiser – soon sort out that lot over there, I can promise you."

Jeff shook Jennie's hand as he looked her up and down. She

had scraped her hair up into a bun under her hat to make herself look older – and had been mortified at the amount of grey hair thus exposed, but at least it gave her an increased air of maturity. She wore a plain grey skirt just touching her knee, and a white blouse with a Peter Pan collar over a peachy short cardigan which fitted into her trim waist, under a three-quarter length swing coat. It was all several years old, but the effect was clean and neat.

Jeff seemed to approve. "Hetty tells me you worked together early in the war?"

"And she's done all sorts of things since then," Hetty said before Jennie could open her mouth. Hetty had retrieved her slippers by this time and pulled a hairy dressing gown off the bedpost. "Why don't you two sort out the details together while I make a cup of tea? I've got a mouth like sandpaper!"

Jennie's eyes danced as she told Father about her strange interview on the way home.

"The main thing is, I got the job," she said finally. "I can start a week on Monday, so all I have to do now is tell Mother about it." Father had known, of course, the reason for the trip to Pontypool and endorsed it fully. He'd seen the strained look begin to re-appear on his daughter's face and wanted it banished again as soon as possible.

"Oh, your Mother will rant and rave a bit, no doubt," he said, "but if she needs someone else to help her she should be able to get a woman in from the village for a couple of days a week. I can pop David along to school in the mornings, and you'll be back to fetch him in the afternoon, so I think we'll both just keep out of her way a bit until she's got used to the idea!"

25

The sheep, bony and angular with its newly-shorn coat, lifted its head disinterestedly at the sound of the lorry's horn, staring before reluctantly moving away with an almost fully-grown lamb bleating behind it, still with a thick coat and so looking much more appealing. Harry wondered, not for the first time, how any records were ever kept by the farmers whose sheep roamed the hillside as to how many their flock actually contained.

It was good to feel the early summer sun through the windscreen and appreciate the many shades of green in the fresh moorland grasses, after the months of snow that for weeks had all but cut Blaenavon off from the rest of the world. It had been piled up to the bedroom windows of the little house in Morgan Street, and even the trains had come to a complete halt.

He sniffed the air appreciatively through the lorry's open window. It was clean and tangy and filled him, for the first time in many months, with a feeling of optimism. It had been a good choice to set himself up here on the open-cast mining, where there weren't too many people looking over your shoulder to keep a check on what you were doing.

Sometimes, out on the rough tracks that now zigzagged across the mountain, Harry almost felt he was back in the army. There was the same atmosphere of camaraderie amongst the men working in this remote area, so that it became a self-contained community. Even the canteen at Pwlldu reminded him of the Naafi.

It all suited Harry very well. Not only did it give him the sort of freedom to plan his day that he'd always wanted, but it also gave him the use of a tiny office at the back of the canteen. It was the ideal place to run a horse-racing book, and, as men were in and out all day, the bosses could be none the wiser.

He'd been interested in horses since the days when he used to watch the pony races up at the new recreation ground, and during his early adolescent years, when his body was stubbornly refusing

331

to grow as quickly as those of his friends, he'd fancied himself as a jockey. But then he shot up a few inches almost overnight, and that dream was put away before it was even uttered.

But horse-racing and its accompanying gambling had continued to fascinate him, and he'd learned much about running a book and working out odds during the time before the war when he had moved rapidly from one job to another. Here, now, surrounded by like-thinking men but away from the restrictions of Forces life, was the perfect opportunity to earn a bit of money on the side and indulge his favourite pastime.

In a short time he'd organised a system of collecting bets from the men as he drove around in the mornings, returning to the office with them at dinner-time, and telephoning any bets too large for him to handle to a bookmaker in Brynmawr. Payouts would be made next day, after he'd listened to the results on the evening wireless. It was a system that worked, without interfering unduly with his job, and he enjoyed the fact that he was doing something for himself – which had made him realise how much he would like to be his own boss.

That what he was doing was illegal didn't worry him unduly. Even in the height of the Depression there had been gambling going on in the town – so much so that the Workmen's Institute had taken to removing the racing pages from the newspapers left for the general public in the reading room, to prevent the place being filled with bookie's runners. Those in authority usually turned a blind eye, providing there was never any trouble, and Harry saw to it that his venture was strictly controlled so that no man could call him a cheat and draw attention to the enterprise.

He pulled in behind the canteen as usual, jumped down from the cab, and strolled through the door directly into the office. There was just time to deposit the morning's money in the bottom drawer of the desk before going through to the kitchen to collect the dinners for the men.

To his surprise a young woman was standing behind the desk, opening the drawers with a slight frown between her eyes. She jumped slightly when the door banged behind Harry, but stayed where she was.

"Good morning," said Harry, politely but distantly. He didn't know the woman, and he certainly didn't want anyone rummaging through his desk. "Can I help you?"

"I don't know," she said coolly. "I'm Jennie Keating, the new canteen manageress. I was told that this was to be my office, but it looks as if someone else has been using it."

"So they have. Not someone – me. I was given this office last year." He took his cap off and extended his hand. "Harry Jenkins, I manage the drivers."

He watched her as she shook his hand for the briefest of moments and moved away to the other side of the desk. She was probably in her late twenties, with large grey eyes which seemed to dominate her finely featured face, a slender body swamped in the wrap-around pinafore that all the canteen women wore, and dark hair tugged sharply back into a bun beneath her white cap. He noticed traces of premature grey where the hair was pulled tightly behind her ears. There was something about her that seemed familiar, but, unusually for him, he couldn't place her.

"You don't have to glare at me," she said in icy tones. "After all, this is the office attached to the canteen. It would seem sensible, therefore, that I should use it."

He realised he'd been staring and pulled himself together. "I'm sorry – it's just that I'm sure I ought to know you, but you're not from Blaenavon, are you? I don't think there's anyone in the town I don't know."

"No, I'm not." She relented a little. "I'm from Goytre – Reg Stollard brought me up this morning in the Works Bus from Abergavenny. I've never been to Blaenavon."

"And I haven't been down to Goytre for years – I wonder where I've seen you, then…?"

It looked as if he was going to ponder the question for hours. Jennie squared her shoulders and said briskly, "I can't imagine. But back to this business of the office. I'm supposed to be sorting this canteen out – apparently it's been in a dreadful mess, and – oh, gosh!" She remembered what he had just said about knowing everyone, and suddenly looked slightly embarrassed, and much younger. "The last manageress wasn't a friend of yours, was she?"

He smiled at her awkwardness. "No, not particularly. And you're right, the place has been in a mess… it was about time she went. It's affected the food, too. Some days it's been very good and others it's been little more than bloo— than pigswill. It needs someone to sort it out. The girls are good, mind, they're just a bit young. Need someone ol— more experienced, to keep them up to the mark."

He couldn't believe how uncomfortable she made him feel, standing there surveying him with those grey eyes which were so difficult to read. He wouldn't have cared about the odd swear-word up here on the mountain – although he didn't swear in front of his family – and as well he'd nearly insulted her by saying she was older. A bit like a school marm she was; had the right sort of voice for one, too.

"So you agree I do need the office, then? There are bits of paper all over the kitchen, which makes it impossible to keep track of anything properly."

"Ah, now! I didn't say that exactly. I need somewhere for my bits of paper, too." He could feel the weight of all those folded bits of paper and coins in his pocket. He was sure she wouldn't approve if she knew what they were.

"But this is part of the canteen! Isn't there somewhere more appropriate that you could use?"

"I don't think so. Anyway, at the risk of sounding childish, I was using this office first, and nothing has been said to me about you needing it. No-one from the kitchen has ever wanted it before."

"Yes, well … as you've just agreed, no-one seems to have organised the kitchen properly before. I need somewhere to keep the order books and so on, and a kitchen window-sill is not the right place."

Her face had become tinged a healthy pink as they spoke, softening her rather haughty appearance. He decided to be kind on her first day.

"What about we share it, then? There's just about room for another desk, and as long as I've got a few drawers and a wall-space to pin up the rotas I can manage."

She bit the corner of her lip as she thought for a moment. He could tell from the expression on her face that she didn't relish the idea of sharing the space with him.

"Are you in and out of here a lot?"

"No, not really. Pop in first thing in the morning, then again at dinner time, like now, and then I spend a bit of time here late afternoon."

"I finish at half past two," she said consideringly. "So perhaps we wouldn't get in each other's way too much. We could give it a try, I suppose. It's just that when I'm working I don't like to be disturbed."

The school-marmish note was back in her voice, irritating him into replying more cuttingly than he had intended. "Don't worry, I can't think of any reason why I should need to bother you." He looked her up and down coolly. "And you certainly won't disturb me!"

The colour in her cheeks deepened, and she looked so uncertain for a moment that he regretted speaking so harshly. "I've come to collect the meals for the boys at the far end. Twenty-five I need – are they ready yet?"

"Of course," she said, no more coldly than he probably deserved, and led the way through to the kitchen, where six young women in their late teens and early twenties were clattering about amidst steaming pots and pans as they prepared for the first influx of workers.

"Has she given you lines or extra homework, yet?" Harry asked Val, the liveliest and the unproclaimed leader of the girls, as she helped him stack the canisters in the back of the lorry.

"Oh no, she's really nice," said Val. "Made sure we all had a proper break for our elevenses, and she doesn't mind rolling her sleeves up and mucking in. Why... don't you like her?"

Harry shrugged and pulled a bit of a face. "Don't know her properly, do I? She just seems a bit straight-laced, that's all."

"I think she's a little bit awkward with men," Val whispered as she left him, with all the worldly-wise experience of her twenty years.

Jennie's head was whirling as she sat in the ramshackle bus, trying not to look out of the window as it made its nail-biting descent down the twisting road, which had a perilous sheer drop on one side and seemed to necessitate a lot of heavy shifting of gears and sharp braking, even in this fine weather. Goodness knows what it would be like in the winter.

She leaned back against the seat, pleased to have it to herself. Already the air was blue with smoke and full of the sound of rapid chattering and laughing, but she didn't mind that she wasn't part of it – she needed this time to unwind and reflect on the day, and she doubted whether there'd be much opportunity for that once she got home.

As a first day it hadn't gone too badly, she supposed. The girls were friendly and willing to work hard, although some of the sloppy habits they'd developed would have given Mother a fit. But there was plenty of time to change all that – she had the sense to realise she had to make sure the girls were on her side first, before she cracked the whip too much.

The place itself was rougher, harsher than she'd expected, although she'd exclaimed with delight when they reached Pwlldu early this morning and she had turned to look at the view down the mountainside. The little hamlet, swelled now by the offices and buildings hastily erected by the mining company, was desperately poor – just two long rows of stone-built cottages from which far too many more children seemed to pour than you would think they could hold, with a little chapel, a schoolroom, a shop that had obviously been someone's front room, and a pub. But the valley it overlooked was breathtakingly beautiful, and directly opposite was an unbroken panorama of all the mountains of her childhood – the Sugar Loaf dominating them, with the Skirrid to one side, and all the others stretching out towards Brecon, as far as the eye could see. When that man – what was his name?... Harry Jenkins – had returned in the afternoon with a desk for her, she'd asked him to put it under the window, so that she could see the mountains whenever she looked up.

She closed her eyes. It already felt like the end of a very long day, although it was only mid-afternoon. She hoped she wasn't going to feel this tired every day, when there was David still to see to when she got home.

Behind her eyelids swirled a confusing kaleidoscope of people – so many had passed in and out of the canteen that she had little hope of remembering any of their names just yet. They all called to each other in loud voices, speaking rapidly in a more staccato Welsh accent than she was used to, even though it was only a few miles from Abergavenny. It was as if the Blorenge was the huge demarcation between accents, ways of life ... everything.

And so many of the men had strange nicknames – there was even one called 'Basket-bum', which none of the girls seemed to mind screeching out from the other end of the canteen. Her lips twitched involuntarily as she tried to imagine herself doing the same one day, or even referring to him at home!

Home. It was funny how she still called it that, and thought of it as that, even though it held very little comfort for her at present.

She was the only one left on the rickety bus by the time it swung into Abergavenny bus station. "Thank you very much," she said to Reg Stollard as she stepped down. "You could have left me at the War Memorial, you know, and I could have walked through the town."

"No trouble," said Reg, his narrow wizened face peering out from under a cap whose peak was so large that she wondered how he managed to see to drive the bus. "You'll be in good time to catch the Goytre connection now – got to fetch your little lad, did you say?"

"That's right, he's not long started school at Llanover." Disappointingly, she said no more except, "Thanks again. See you tomorrow."

"Tarrah love!"

Reg turned the old bus around to head back up to Blaenavon. He'd have to ask the girls in the canteen more about her tomorrow, so that he could satisfy his wife's desire to hear all the gossip about anyone working on the mountain, so that she could pass it on when she was shopping in the Cworp.

26

The tea's fresh, and I've just put your toast in!" Val spoke over her shoulder, bustling across the canteen kitchen as Jennie went to hang her hat and coat up in the little office.

"Thanks, Val, I'll be there now." There was no sign of Harry Jenkins, so she spent a few moments tidying her hair before donning the white cap which made her look so severe. Perhaps Val and the other girls were right; she should wear her hair loose, like they did, with the regulation cap perched so far back on their heads as to be almost useless as a hygiene precaution. She quickly applied a touch of lipstick – she hadn't done that, either, when she first came to work here – and made her way back into the kitchen.

Val was buttering two slices of toast. "There you are, get that down you – starved, you look. Lily's already started on the fish, so we're in good time this morning."

"Thanks, Val," Jennie said again before tucking in. There was something about this first cup of tea and toast which tasted better than anything else all day. Perhaps it was because she'd been up several hours before she could enjoy it, so she appreciated it even more.

She listened to the five girls clattering and chattering around her as they prepared for Friday: fish-and-chips day. Val had gone back to spreading margarine on an enormous pile of bread, which the men liked with their chips, as she told Lily all about the film she'd seen the night before.

"That Frank Sinatra was in it – lovely voice he's got, but he's not very big, you know. Not that he's little either – slightly built, I suppose you'd call him. Nice smile, though, sort of lop-sided."

"Who was the girl in it with him?" Lily, as fair as her name suggested, and only reaching up to Val's shoulder, slapped fillets of fish into dishes of beaten egg before coating them with breadcrumbs. These two were great partners, having worked in the Men's Department of Briggs's outfitters during the war, and now armed with many a joke about inside legs.

"I can't remember – one of those blonde American actresses. He kept lighting two cigarettes and handing one to her, which I thought was ever so romantic." She deftly split open each empty bread wrapper and used them to cover the plates of bread and marg. "How are those potatoes looking, Marina?"

Fifteen-year-old Marina was exotically named, as many of her age were, after the Duchess of Kent, but there the resemblance ended. Recently left school, she was small and insignificant apart from heavy eyebrows that looked as if they were doing their best to meet in the middle. This morning she was at the sink, peeling potatoes for all she was worth before putting them in the chipping machine, as she listened to Val and Lily, her mouth hanging slightly open.

"I'm getting through them – not too many eyes they haven't got." Her last words were muffled as she dived once more into the sack at her feet to extract another armful and thrust them down on the worktop along with a layer of dust and soil.

Across the other side of the room worked the other partnership: Branwyn mixing the sponge pudding, while Glenys reconstituted pints of dried milk ready for the custard. Friends since Hillside Junior School, they were not quite so loud as the other two, but just as intent on enjoying themselves after the restrictions of war-time.

They were a real team, Jennie noted – not for the first time – with some satisfaction. If it hadn't been for their friendliness she probably wouldn't have persevered through those first few months, when Mother had been so determined that she shouldn't succeed with this job, and the long days had made her so permanently tired. But she was used to it now. Mother she ignored as best she could, getting David ready for school before Mother was even up, so that he only had to have his breakfast before Father took him to school. Now that it was the long school holidays and he was 'under Mother's feet all day' – although in reality he was out on the farm pestering Father for most of it – Jennie would happily have given him breakfast as well, but Mother had taken it into her head that the range wasn't to be messed with before she got up. Which was why Jennie now enjoyed this tea and toast every morning.

"No breakfast, not even a cup of tea until we have our elevenses?" Val had shrieked in horror when Jennie had admitted to her one morning that she felt quite faint with hunger. "We'll soon see about that!" And from then on the kettle was always boiling and the toast ready when Jennie arrived each morning.

Gradually, through persistence and a deliberate policy of appearing thick-skinned, the girls had managed between them to wheedle out of Jennie most of the circumstances of her life, so that collectively they thought of Charles as a brute, Mother as slightly mad, and Jennie as someone who needed their protection and help. Their current campaign was to get her out and about a bit more, and – although they knew this would be an uphill struggle – interested in men again.

As soon as she'd gulped down the last of her tea, Jennie set to with the rest of them. She fetched a large bowl and handed it to Marina. "Why don't you fill this with potatoes from the sack – then you won't have to keep bending down so much, and the work-top will stay cleaner."

"Right – sorry – thanks, I will." As always, Marina looked almost ready to curtsey because Jennie had spoken to her.

She smiled at the girl in a vain attempt to make her relax. "We'll have these windows open, too or we'll be as fried as the fish this morning. I think we're in for a scorcher today."

She was right. By the time they all sat down for their midmorning break they were red-faced and their hair hung in limp strands on their shoulders.

"Doesn't matter. Washing mine before I go out tonight," Val said.

"Who with this time?" Marina asked. Val's varied love-life was a constant source of discussion amongst the girls, and her ability to attract the men so easily had quickly filled Marina with unstinting admiration.

"Ted Probert."

Lily's carefully plucked eyebrows disappeared under her fringe. "Again? Getting a bit serious between you two, isn't it? Three Fridays in a row that'll be! Asked you round for Sunday tea with his Mam yet? Big in Wesleyan Chapel, she is, lots of hymn-singing in the evening, mind!"

"I know her," Branwyn joined in the teasing. "Hefty woman she is, built like a prop-forward, and face like a torn dap, even on a good day!"

Val pulled a face at them good-naturedly. "Well, her son might just be worth it... but I haven't made my mind up yet. I'll let you all know!" She turned to Jennie. "You going anywhere nice this weekend?"

"I don't expect so," Jennie replied, as she always did. "David's been asked to a birthday party tomorrow, so I'll have to take him into Abergavenny, but that'll be about it."

"There's a dance on at the Mostyn Hall tomorrow night," Lily told her. "Most of us are going, why don't you come along too?"

Memories of dancing in Charles's arms on a Saturday night at

Little Mill came unbidden into Jennie's mind. She hadn't been to a dance since then, and she supposed she never would again. Those days were long gone.

"Oh, I couldn't!" she said quickly. "It's too difficult to get over to Blaenavon on a Saturday, and, besides, I haven't got anyone – you know, a boyfriend – to go with."

Glenys laughed, a horse-like sound that belied her fastidious appearance. "Neither have we! That's the whole point! We all go together and, well … see what happens."

"Yes but it's different for you… you're young, and…"

"Oh, listen to grandma! You're not that much older than us, you know! And if you came to Blaenavon, no-one would even think about…"

"What? That I was a gay divorcée, out looking for a good time, when I ought to be at home with my child?" Jennie's eyes hardened and her mouth was pulled into a thin line. "Well I can tell you now, that might not be what they would be thinking, but it's what *I* would be thinking, and what my mother would be saying!"

Flustered, Glenys stammered, "I didn't mean – I was only trying to…"

Jennie's face softened again. "Look, I know all of you are only trying to help, and can't bear the thought of me not being out till all hours enjoying myself, but I'm fine, honestly! And I really appreciate your concern – like I've said before, you're a great bunch of girls, and if I wasn't tied the way I am I'd be out there with the best of you."

She pictured herself at a dance, trying to cope with the attentions of a man, and the only image that presented itself was of Gerald Kennedy and his sweaty little hands. She hadn't told the girls about him – they would probably have laughed at how badly she'd handled the incident, which they would have fended off so adroitly in its early stages that they would never have ended up in the position that Jennie had.

She stood up, to signal that the break was over. "Now let's start frying that fish or it'll be dinner time before we know it."

There was no more time for chit-chat for the next couple of hours as they dished up endless plates of fish-and-chips and bowls of pudding, while Marina and Branwyn cleared the tables and struggled with a mountain of washing-up. The girls could fill the plates deftly while keeping an eye on who was coming next and maintaining a nice line in banter with the men as they queued, Val giving them a broad wink every time somebody said, "Got a bit of sauce, love?"

Harry Jenkins came in for his dinner, stopping to chat to lots of the men before making his way into the office to sort out all the bets.

Jennie had been told by the girls what he was up to, and couldn't decide whether or not she approved, but as she didn't need to have anything to do with it she simply decided to ignore it.

She tried her hardest to ignore him, too, along with the rest of the men. She would have loved to take part in the free-and-easy chat which seemed to trip so effortlessly off the girls' tongues, but as soon as the men began to appear she felt herself clam up, staying in the background as much as she could, her tongue sticking to the roof of her mouth if any of them directed some light-hearted comment towards her. They probably thought she was a miserable old bag to work for, and she knew that one or two of them considered her a mite hoity-toity, but there was nothing she could do about it.

Harry Jenkins carried on chatting to her when he came into the office, regardless of whether or not she responded, but then he chatted to everyone and was, she thought, just so full of himself that he probably didn't even notice her limited replies. Sometimes, though, he asked her about David – she guessed that Val would have filled him in with much of her background – and then he seemed genuinely interested, and she found herself talking quite freely about the little boy who was her pride and joy.

"I would have liked a son myself," he said one day, "but there you are, that's the way it goes. Spend a lot of time with my sister's brood instead, to remind myself what a handful they can be!"

"I'm sorry… about your wife." Val had, of course, told Jennie just as much about Harry.

He shrugged. "We were very happy, but what with the war and things, it seems a long time ago now. We wanted kids, though – but perhaps it was just as well we had none. Been spoilt by the women in my family all my life, I have – I'd have been hopeless looking after a little one on my own!"

He'd smiled at her then in a way that suddenly made him seem much more vulnerable. She'd never thought of a man as vulnerable before …

Her thoughts jolted back to the present as Val's voice intruded into her thoughts. "We need another tray of chips!"

"Oh, sorry – I was miles away." She slid a fresh tray of chips out of the large warming oven and brought it over to Val. "Sorry to keep you waiting," she said to the man standing in the queue.

"That's all right. Quite happy standing here listening to these lovely girls for a minute," the man said, a broad grin on his lined face. "Get up to things we'd never have got away with in our day, don't they, love?"

Jennie coloured as she realised that the man, easily in his mid-forties, was including her in his generation, but before she could reply Lily butted in. "Get away with you, Huw Mathias! 'Our day' indeed! Mrs. Keating here's only in her twenties – need your eyes testing, you do!"

"Oh – oh, I'm sorry…" Huw began to stammer, making matters worse by showing that his mistake was completely genuine. "Just with you being the boss and all – didn't think they'd give the job to such a young woman, like…" He grabbed two slices of bread and moved away quickly with his tray.

"We seem to be slackening off now," Jennie said, only her colour betraying that she minded. "I think I'll go and finish up in the office."

Val followed her through a few minutes later.

"You don't want to take any notice of Huw, you know," she said in her direct way. "Always was a bit stupid, especially where women are concerned."

Jennie gave up struggling with the requisition forms for goods that were still on ration, put her pen down and leaned back in her chair. "He's right, though. I feel about a hundred sometimes when I'm standing next to you lot, and I'm sure by the end of the week I must look it!"

"Don't be silly…" Val began to say, but was stopped by a direct stare from Jennie. "Well, to be honest, I think it's only your hair, you know – where it's showing grey when it's pulled back"

She drew up a chair next to the desk. "Why don't you and I have a day out together – in Newport, next Saturday? Your Mam and Dad could look after your little boy just for one day, couldn't they? We could go and get our hair done, look round the shops… a proper girls' day out. What do you say?"

She sounded so bright and eager that for once Jennie didn't have the heart to refuse. "I think that would be very nice – I'd really like to come. And David's going to my sister's in Monmouth for a week, so it would be a good time to go. Only don't tell the other girls, or they'll spend all next week suggesting different styles for me to try!"

Harry was whistling jauntily as he headed for the office. He was feeling relaxed after a pleasant weekend, and ready to face the week. Saturday had been a good day at Cheltenham races with Uncle Fred. He'd picked out several winners and won enough for a good meal on the way home, had been able to slip his Mam a bit extra, and still had a few pounds to spare in his pocket. Life was definitely looking up.

His hand was already on the door handle when, glancing through the window at the side of the door, he saw that Jennie Keating was already in there, standing in front of the mirror. At least, he supposed it was Jennie, although she hadn't the familiar tightly-drawn bun. This girlish figure, in a button-through dress hugging her body before flaring provocatively around her knees, was turning this way and that, surveying her hair, which fell in soft, very dark, velvety waves on to the white collar of her dress.

He peered more closely through the grimy window, convinced once again as he watched her that Jennie was familiar to him from some time back, but still he couldn't place her ...

What he did know was that she wouldn't like to think she had been spied upon, so he resumed his whistling and made a deal of noise opening the door. Even so, she'd been so absorbed that she turned a startled face towards him, both hands flying immediately to the new hairstyle.

"Oh, it's you! I was miles away!" Her cheeks were already tinged with the give-away pink which always made her look vulnerable and today made her seem very young, as she made a grab for the unbecoming wrap-around pinafore and hat.

"I wondered who was in here for a moment. You look different... your hair... it's very nice."

She looked up from tying the strings of her pinafore firmly round her waist, her grey eyes large and unsure, and he was suddenly dumbstruck as recognition swept over him.

At last he could place where he'd seen her before – it had been puzzling him for months! Now, with the new softer hairstyle framing her face, she was the girl on the station again, the one who had wept such desperate tears, and who had come to his mind unbidden at times during the discomfort and desperation of the next few years!

He opened his mouth to share the revelation with her, but then closed it again as he remembered what Val had told him about her husband. Perhaps he'd been wrong in his assumption as to why the tears were being shed, and she wouldn't want to be reminded of it.

She was uncomfortable with the intensity of his gaze upon her. "Val persuaded me. We went out together on Saturday. I'm still not used to it yet... and I don't know how I'm going to get this cap to stay on. I think I'll have to tie my hair back after all." She fidgeted with the cap and two large black hairpins.

"No! Don't do that!" He spoke so hurriedly and firmly that she was startled. "It makes you look a lot younger... not that you looked old before, of course... it's just more – well, up-to-date perhaps..."

She smiled at his discomfiture, which was almost matching her own. "What you mean is that the grey has gone – which was the object of the exercise of course. I still don't know what to do with this cap though."

"Well, I don't think you would be able to tie your hair back now. It would probably be too short to pin back easily anyway … it would just keep falling down and get on your nerves all day." He laughed as her eyebrows rose in surprise. "Listen to me! Sounds as if I know exactly what I'm talking about, doesn't it! Spent too long surrounded by women in the family, see – my sister, my sister-in-law, Mam, gran, cousin … so I've listened to an awful lot of hair talk!"

He wanted to keep that open look on her face, not the tight-lipped shut-away expression that was often there whenever he spoke to her. 'The Man-hater', some of the men called her, and one or two had made much lewder comments until Harry had told them in no uncertain terms not to be so filthy, which had surprised him as much as it had surprised them. Now he was pleased he'd defended her so strongly. If the other men had seen her breaking her heart on Newport station perhaps they too would have understood her behaviour a little more.

She plopped the cap back on her head. "Well, it will just have to do like that for today – I'm running late already."

She'd spent about ten minutes parading around the kitchen for the other girls while Val had told them about the day out they'd had and described the clothes for which Jennie had, in the end, used her precious clothing coupons – which she'd been intending to save, to buy new clothes for David after the summer.

"Turn round," Harry ordered now, "and give me those pins. I can see better than you trying to do it with your hands behind your head."

Holding her lightly by the shoulders and ignoring the way she seemed to flinch at his touch, he turned her to face the mirror again while he pushed the hairpins firmly into place, and fought the sudden urge to turn her back towards him and press his lips against hers.

At the same time Marina peered round the door from the kitchen to tell Jennie that her tea was getting cold, but catching sight of the two of them so close together she scuttled back instead to tell the others importantly that it looked as if the new hairstyle was working already.

Harry couldn't get Jennie out of his mind for the rest of the morning. The eyes that had watched him in the mirror had reminded him of an injured bird that struggles to escape whenever you try to help it, because it can't quite bring itself to trust you, even though it knows that your help is what it desperately needs.

He ended up giving himself a stern talking to. From what Val had told him, the husband had obviously been a complete bastard and left Jennie totally screwed up about men. Not to mention the problems she still had at home. Not the sort to get mixed up with at all. She'd thawed a bit towards him in recent weeks, especially when they'd talked about kids, but would probably scream blue murder if he made any sort of pass at her. And there was also the child to think about. There had got to be less complicated ways of finding someone to settle down with!

By lunchtime he'd convinced himself that he was simply being unnecessarily sentimental in his sudden upsurge of feeling for Jennie, born of the realisation that she was the girl on the station. Real life was never like the things you imagined or dreamed about, and that distraught face on the platform had become so idealised over the years that now he was imbuing Jennie with all sorts of qualities she probably didn't possess at all.

Nevertheless, to his chagrin, he was pleased when she followed him into the office – something she usually avoided as much as possible – so that he didn't at first register the embarrassment on her face. She thrust a small piece of paper and some coins towards him with schoolgirl awkwardness. "One of the men came in with a bet for you, so I wrote down what he told me – I don't know whether I should be getting involved in all this, you know, or even whether it should take place in this office. I am aware that it is illegal."

Her voice was as cold as on the day she had first arrived. He'd been right – any warmth she had appeared to display towards him recently was all in his imagination.

"I'll mention to all the men that they are not to use you to pass bets on to me," he said in a similar manner. "Then whatever *I do* at *my* desk needn't concern you."

She nodded and headed for the door as he unfolded the piece of paper. The hoot of laughter that he let out stopped her in her tracks. On the paper she'd written, in a neat careful hand: *3 o'clock, Doncaster. 2 shillings each way – Cat Shit.*

"I'm sorry, I'm not laughing at you," he said, between chuckles. "You weren't to know, but the horse's name is 'Catch It'!"

Her eyes widened, she struggled with herself for a moment, but then she too was laughing. "I thought it was funny when he said it, but he was adamant that it was right, even when I asked him to repeat it! It's been on my mind all morning!"

"It's the King's horse," he told her, "Can you imagine them walking round the paddock, and the wireless chap saying: 'And now we have the King's Cat Shit!'"

They both exploded again. The newly-waved hair bounced around her face as her whole body shook and her cheeks turned a healthy colour, from merriment for once, rather than embarrassment. She could be very pretty, he realised. Not with Megan's delicate, ethereal sort of looks, but with a wholesome, outdoor sort of prettiness that spoke of her country upbringing.

"I hope you've got a special occasion lined up this weekend to celebrate your new look," he said, when they'd finally stopped laughing.

"Not at all. As I told you, this was all Val's doing. Very persuasive, Val is, when she sets her mind to it." Val hadn't succeeded in fixing her up with a date to make a foursome with her and Ted Probert, though.

"I thought it might have been with someone particular in mind – new boyfriend, or something ..." He mentally cursed himself the moment the words were out as the expressive eyes clouded over and a faint frown appeared between her eyebrows.

"The only man in my life is David," she said, "and that's the way I like it. I can't understand why everyone in this place is so keen to organise my life for me."

He shrugged, and kept his voice deliberately light. "Valley people, see. Like to keep tabs on everyone and pair them off whenever they can – makes it all nice and tidy like, and gives the old women something to talk about when they're sweeping out their front pavements!"

She wished she hadn't been so sharp. For a moment she'd been worried that he was leading up to asking her out, but that obviously wasn't his intention. She really must try to stop being so suspicious of everyone, when they were just trying to be friendly.

She tried a smile. "I thought it was only country people who gossiped, because there isn't much else to do after a hard day's work."

"Don't you believe it! Favourite occupation for my mother and my aunties, it is – sitting on a Sunday evening and listing who's died recently. Then they go back over all the family – usually find out that we're related to them somewhere along the line, and all the skeletons are brought out of the cupboard. Keeps them happy for hours, it does!"

The awkwardness had passed. The openness was back on her face. "You don't have to tell the men not to bring their bets in here, you know – I'll just give them a pencil to write them down themselves in future!"

She was still smiling as she returned to the kitchen, just as Glenys was about to despatch Marina to listen at the door. She told the girls about the mix-up over the horse's name as they were tidying up the kitchen at the end of the day, and made them all laugh as she recounted the tale.

"Looks like Marina was right – she is getting on very well with Harry," Lily said to the others as they waited for the bus which would take them down into the town.

"Well, I wouldn't get too excited, girls," Val said as the bus pulled up. "They've both had a rough ride once already – you know what Jennie's like about men, and I can't see Harry finding it that easy to start going out with someone else after what he went through, even if it is a few years ago now. He hasn't exactly been a Romeo since he's been out of the army, has he? Not for lack of opportunity, either. Someone told me there's a girl over in the wages office makes eyes at him every time he's in there."

She boarded the bus behind the others, thankful that the only problem she had with Ted Probert was making sure she wore clothes that were difficult for his wandering hands to undo.

27

So what do you and young David do at the weekends?" Harry asked Jennie a few days later. The sunny weather had changed abruptly, so he'd come in to the office earlier than usual in the afternoon, to escape from the driving rain.

She put down her pencil, glad of the excuse to stop stretching her ingenuity to produce something different for next week's menus from the same tired ingredients. Rationing and shortages seemed to be more severe now than they had been during the war.

"Oh, this and that. I try to take him out from the farm if I can, on Saturday at least, so we can spend some time together on our own – I think more for my benefit than his, because he adores being with his grandfather. Sometimes we just walk down to Llanover if the weather's good, and have tea in the little tea room next to the Post Office. Or we might go to visit my sister in Monmouth – although he's just come back from there, and he finds his little cousin Selina a bit difficult at times – she's not as keen on getting filthy dirty as he is!"

She turned back to her work, so he made an attempt to do the same, although there wasn't much on his desk that needed his attention.

After a few minutes he said, "I sometimes walk down to Llanover on a sunny day."

"All the way from Blaenavon? It must be miles!" The menus were forgotten again.

"It is if you follow the road, because then you have to go all the way round Abergavenny – the same way the buses take you home. But there's a little track out over the mountain, Llanover Road, that takes you all the way there. Only a couple of miles that way, and a beautiful walk."

"Ah, I see." She scribbled a few more words on the pieces of paper in front of her and then glanced at her watch. "Time I was making a move, or Reg will be wondering where I've got to."

He watched as she donned a raincoat and sou'wester style hat. "Will you be walking that way this Saturday, if the weather clears?"

She turned to him speculatively for a moment.

"Possibly," she said, with just a slight twitch of her lips.

All the way home she wondered why she had said that. Did her 'possibly' constitute accepting some sort of date? Perhaps she should arrange to go to Laura's this weekend, and then she could mention that to him before Friday. Or, with a bit of luck, it might still be pouring with rain on Saturday.

Don't be so ridiculous! she told herself, in Mother's scolding tones. *You haven't made any definite arrangements to meet him, and besides, David will be with you – and after all, he's not exactly a threat is he?*

That was true, she decided. She had no difficulty now sharing an office with Harry. He wasn't the tall, handsome type like Charles had been, who made you to want to impress him terribly so that he'd turn his devastating smile upon you, and he didn't have the smarminess of Gerald Kennedy. He was just an ordinary sort of man – average height, dark hair, blue eyes – even they weren't like Charles's. They were a deeper, brighter blue, with lots of crinkles at the side where he smiled a lot …

He was probably just a bit lonely, and she could sympathise with that. "Beautiful girl, his wife was," Val had told her. "Looking back, she always had a touch of that consumptive appearance about her I suppose, but she was really classy-looking too. Took it awfully badly, he did, when she died. Nursed her himself, and then joined the army straight away – long before war was declared. I don't think he could bear to stay here, with all the memories."

Marina had sighed over the romance of it all, although she wouldn't have placed Harry Jenkins as a romantic lead… but it would make a lovely story with, say, Gregory Peck, who by rights of course would die after some amazing feat of bravery, with her photo clutched in his hand.

There was really nothing for her to worry about, Jennie decided finally when she recalled Val's words. She would certainly be no match for the beautiful, sweet-natured girl Val had described.

Nevertheless, she avoided him as much as she could over the next few days, in case he should want to make a more definite arrangement, and made sure she didn't see him before she went off to catch her bus on Friday afternoon – when, as predicted, the weather had already improved again.

She spent all of Saturday morning giving her and David's rooms a thorough cleaning and deciding that they'd stay at home this afternoon and play cricket. But at lunchtime he was just as adamant that he wanted to walk to the canal so that they could throw sticks off the little bridges that regularly punctuated it, carrying narrow tracks to the farms which flourished on the lush lower slopes of the Blorenge. David's insistence was building to a full temper-tantrum under Mother's anticipatory eye, so Jennie relented and agreed that they would go just as soon as he'd eaten every mouthful of the prunes which he didn't care for very much.

In the end they followed the canal all the way to Llanover, dawdling at every bridge to play 'Pooh Sticks' and watch the sun sending dappled rays to play on the water through the overhanging trees. Jennie was happy to linger much longer than usual, in the hope that if they arrived at the tea room – which was an inevitable climax of the afternoon and could not now be avoided – Harry would have been and gone.

But he was still there when they walked in, sitting at a window table smoking a cigarette, an empty pot of tea in front of him. David was in good form, bounding energetically into the cafe in his wellies and asking exuberantly if he could have sandwiches *and* one of those big buns because he was really hungry – so that he didn't notice at first his mother speaking to the dark-haired man already sitting at the window table.

"Come and say hello to Mr. Jenkins first, David, then you can decide what to have," Jennie told him.

David said hello politely, and then asked: "Did you know that this is our favourite table?"

"I thought it might be," Harry answered, "because it's mine too."

"There are lots of other tables we can sit at, David," Jennie said quickly, gazing around the almost empty room.

"I hope you won't," Harry moved his chair back so that David could sit nearest the window. "I would very much like this to be my treat – after all, I feel I owe you something for putting up with all my little transactions in the office."

"Oh, that's really not necessary," Jennie replied, but then he said: "I don't often get the chance to have a small child to spoil," conveniently forgetting the hours he spent as genial uncle to Lizzie's brood.

And then David was already wriggling across into the window seat, and the waitress had come over to take their order, so Jennie felt it would be churlish to make a fuss. She subsided into the chair opposite Harry whilst he and David embarked upon a deeply serious discussion over what they should order.

"Did you walk along the canal as well?" David asked, as soon as the waitress had been despatched.

"No, I walked here from over the other side of the mountain," Harry told him. "I work on top of the mountain with your Mam."

"But we don't usually see you here."

Harry chuckled. "That's because I usually have a drink and a sandwich at a place called the Goose and Cuckoo on the way here." His glance flickered towards Jennie. "But today I fancied a change …

Have you ever been to the Goose and Cuckoo?" he asked her.

"No, but I hear that it's very pleasant."

"It is – tucked away up a little country lane. It's got a garden outside, so children can play, which is useful." He turned to David. "And late in the evening badgers come out from their homes and play in the garden, too."

"Can we go there, Mum, can we?" David asked immediately.

"I expect so, one day," she answered.

"Perhaps we cou—" Harry began to say, then changed his mind. "I'm surprised there's not a pub in Llanover," he said instead.

"Old Lady Llanover is dead against strong drink, so she won't let a pub be built on any of Llanover estate land," Jennie told him. "You seem to be very interested in public houses?"

He grinned. "Not to drink in. I only like the occasional pint. But I am interested in having one of my own one of these days. I like being my own boss, you see – discovered I really didn't like taking orders from other people when I was in the army, and suffered for it once or twice, too! Running a little pub somewhere would suit me very well, I think."

His stronger Welsh accent seemed more pronounced in the genteel surroundings of the tea room, but he spoke well, Jennie thought, and his manners were excellent … and then she felt cross with herself for analysing him in the way Mother would.

The adults drank their tea but ate little, whilst David tucked in blissfully to the gargantuan feast which Harry had ordered.

"I didn't ask you afterwards," Jennie said eventually. "Did it win – the horse?"

"It did. Came in at ten to one, and I thought the joke over its name was such a good omen that I put five bob on it myself!"

Seeing the puzzled look on Jennie's face, he refilled her cup and began to explain the intricacies of the betting system. But when he came to Yankees and Trebles she smiled and shook her head. "You've lost me now. I think I would just be tempted to play safe anyway and stick to 'each ways'."

He regarded her speculatively for a moment. "I suspect you play safe in most things."

She returned his gaze steadily. "Yes, I probably do. You have to, you know, when you have a small child to consider."

"I see." He nodded, but he didn't look convinced, and somehow Jennie detected a hint of criticism.

Stung, she retorted: "People always say 'I see' when they don't see at all. When they have little understanding of the things which shape and influence a person's life." She turned to David and wiped some jam from the corner of his mouth.

Harry seemed unmoved by the sharpness of her tone and continued to sit back lazily in his chair, encouraging David to eat his fill.

"I'll tell you what I see," he said at last. "I see a pleasant young woman still beating herself up about events in her life which, being a betting man, I would lay a hundred-to-one weren't her fault, and thinking that from now on she has to take a back seat in life to make up for it. And she'll continue to do so for the next twenty years, until she eventually finds that life has passed her by completely and she has nothing to look forward to but a lonely middle age."

She was just about to respond sharply that she hadn't come here to be preached at, when he suddenly leaned forward and grinned disarmingly. "And do you know how I know that? Because I'm doing exactly the same. Hopeless pair aren't we?"

"But your wife died!" she cried. "You can't hold yourself responsible for that, surely?"

He made a little grimace. "I couldn't stop her getting TB, I suppose, no. But that doesn't stop me forever wondering if I should have got her to a specialist sooner, or whether I should have been more insistent that she went to a sanatorium, or whether even living with me instead of being cosseted by her family actually made her condition worse. That's just what I mean, see – I'll never know the answers to any of those questions, so I'm silly to go on pondering over them – but I still do. And I suspect you've had more than one sleepless night going over all the things that have happened to you over the past few years, and torturing yourself about them."

She thought of the endless nights when she first went to Devon, when David would wake for a feed and afterwards she would sit in the chair by the French windows, waiting for the dawn, when the demons would be banished by the rising sun.

She nodded at Harry. "I suppose the girls have given you all the details of my situation?"

"Only when I asked them. They're a good bunch – very little gossip goes beyond their own little group."

A silence fell, until David broke it by saying he had had enough to eat now, and could they please go back outside? Harry insisted on paying the bill, despite Jennie's protests, then joined them outside, blinking rapidly in the late afternoon sunshine, which hadn't penetrated the interior of the cafe.

"May I walk back with you, until I turn off?"

"Yes!" said David excitedly, before Jennie could reply. "And then I can show you the rope swing – Mummy won't let me go on it because she can't swim!" He'd already caught hold of Harry's hand and began to tug him along the tow-path.

"Alright! Alright!" Harry said with a laugh. "But your mother's right. You can't go on it if it isn't safe."

David scampered on ahead like a young puppy when he realised that Harry wasn't going to be hurried.

"It probably is quite safe," Jennie told him. "It's just that I'm extra cautious, I suppose. It's difficult to know where to draw the line between letting him be a proper boy and not being too over-protective."

Harry pulled out his cigarettes and watched David running along the path. "You seem to have got it right so far – he's a lovely little boy." He held out the packet to her, but she shook her head.

"Very wise, it's a terrible habit," he said solemnly, as he took out a cigarette for himself and lit it.

"I've sometimes been tempted, just to shock my mother," Jennie said, "but somehow I've never been able to get the hang of it."

"Bit of a terror, is she, your Mam?" Harry asked, having already heard a tale or two from Val.

Jennie's brow wrinkled as she sought to find words to describe Mother. "I've never really understood her," she confessed at last. "She's always had a lovely home, beautiful clothes, a good husband and family, and she's still a handsome woman, but... it's like she's never been really happy. There's a sort of restlessness inside her that comes out as discontent with just about everything around her."

She grinned, suddenly looking very girlish. "Her discontent even changes from day to day, which certainly keeps you on your toes! When I was in Devon she was really keen to have us both back here, but now that we are here, I just get the feeling that we're a burden to her that she would prefer to do without. And I think with me... being the youngest of the four children, and a long way after the others – well, I suppose I *was* an extra burden, when she thought she'd finished with all that. And then I haven't exactly turned out the way she would have wanted."

The words from her childhood came back to her, with a clarity that belied the years between: *Never wanted... a mistake!...* so that she shivered, despite the warmth of the sun.

Harry noticed, and assumed she was dwelling on her broken marriage. He stubbed his cigarette end out on the ground and sought to change the subject. "Did you like living in Devon?"

"Yes I did, on the whole. My sister and her family live down there and were very good to me, and I worked for a kind employer – and I made friends with the cleaning lady, Dora, who I suppose you would describe as 'salt of the earth' . She could talk the hind leg off a donkey – she'd beat Val and all the girls put together, but she was a wonderful friend!" Her face, which had lit up as she described her old ally, became serious. "It was the best thing to do – after my marriage... you know – it made me grow up and learn to stand on my own two feet, I think."

Harry nodded. "I know what you mean. That's why I joined the army – had to get away for a while and sort myself out. Mind you, I didn't expect to be away for the best part of six years!"

"And did you – sort yourself out?" She coloured slightly, in the rapid way he had noticed before. "I'm sorry – that's a very personal question."

"Not at all. Yes, I think I did. I saw so much – not just the horrors of war, but different places, the different ways people lived. I met so many of them who had lost everything, but they were dusting themselves down and quietly doing their best to get on with life again – and that certainly stops you feeling sorry for yourself! And, like you, I made friends with people – not just army mates, but ordinary men and women in the places we were stationed. It made all the difference to how well I survived the awful bits. I'd pushed people away at first, after my wife died – but that was no way to get over it. I realised that I couldn't do it by myself. I'll never underestimate the importance of friendship again."

He knew that he was beginning to sound too sombre, too. "Come on." He nearly grabbed her hand, but stopped himself. "Let's stop dawdling and catch David up – looks like he's reached the rope swing he was on about."

They approached the tree which hung out over the canal, a thick rope dangling tantalisingly from one of its high branches.

"Do you want me to help him?" Harry asked Jennie.

"If we're not keeping you," Jennie said, unable to resist David's mute appeal.

"Right, then." He pulled the rope back to the bank and tucked it under his arm as he lifted the small boy up. "You sit on this thick knot here, and hold on with both hands, very tightly, just here – that's it! Now I'll swing you very gently, but you mustn't let go until I catch you again, alright?"

David nodded. "Can you swim?" he asked, anxiety and excitement mixed in his voice.

"Like a fish," Harry lied solemnly, knowing that the water was only about three feet deep at this point.

He let go of the rope so that it swung slowly out over the water and back again. David squealed with delight. "Keep going! Keep going!"

Harry pushed him again, a little harder this time, and again and again while Jennie watched the dark, unruly curls of her son and the equally dark hair of the man bobbing back and forth, closer and farther and closer again. Some people on the little stone bridge up ahead stopped to watch them, and smiled at the small boy's pleasure. *They probably think we're a happy little family out for a stroll,* Jennie thought, and found herself wishing suddenly with all her heart that it was true – that they would be going back together to one of the stone cottages on the hillside surrounded by fields, where she would bathe David before Harry read him a bedtime story, and then she would cook supper for the two of them, and…

The people moved away, and she forced herself out of her reverie as she realised how ridiculously personal it was becoming.

She heard Harry say, "I think that's enough for today, or the rope will begin to hurt your hands." He caught hold of the swing for the final time, and lifted David back onto the ground. Retrieving his jacket from where he'd placed it on the grass, and brushing it down before slinging it casually over his shoulder, he nodded towards the bridge. "This is where I turn off."

"Can we go on the swing next time?" David asked eagerly.

"Hush, David," Jennie said quickly, catching hold of his hand to stop him jumping up and down.

"I expect we'll meet along here again at some point," Harry said, looking directly at Jennie.

But she said nothing more, just held out her hand towards him. "Thank you very much for the tea, and for giving David such a nice time."

Her voice suddenly sounded so formal that he only just managed to stop himself from laughing. Instead, he took her hand equally formally and said, "It was a pleasure." Then he turned to David and ruffled his hair. "Goodbye, David. Be good."

He climbed the steep side of the bank up to the bridge. His shirt sleeves were rolled up, and Jennie noticed that his arms were strong and muscular as he grasped tree roots to pull himself up. At the top he stood on the bridge and watched as they walked underneath it, then waved to them both when they emerged on the other side, beneath him, and David tugged at his mother's hand and made her turn to wave as well.

Jennie was quiet as they strolled back to the farm, David's energy flagging now so that he matched his pace to hers. She realised as she re-lived their conversation that she'd said far more to Harry in one brief afternoon than she probably had to any other man. She couldn't remember feeling so free to talk to Charles. You could hardly call Harry Jenkins sophisticated, or particularly good-looking, come to that, but he was certainly easy to talk to. Like a friend. Definitely like a friend. Perhaps all men were easy to get on with if you could be sure that friendship was the only thing they had on their minds.

"We met Mr. Jenkins, and he pushed me on the swing right out over the canal," David announced as soon as they entered the kitchen, "and there were sharks and crocodiles in the water, but they didn't get me!"

"That's good!" said Father immediately, "because I've been waiting for you to come home, to show you a new lot of kittens in the barn. Go and get changed, and we can go and see them."

"Mr. Jenkins?" Mother queried when they were alone together.

"Yes. Harry Jenkins. The man I told you about who has a desk in my office. He was in the tea-room at Llanover, and walked part of the way back with us. David persuaded him to push him on a rope swing."

She decided that she would keep David off the subject of the huge tea Harry had bought for the two of them when he came back in with Father. Somehow she didn't want Mother's raised eyebrows and cynical questions to spoil what had been a lovely afternoon.

"And what have you been doing this afternoon?" she asked Mother brightly instead. "Have you been out in the sunshine?"

"Good heavens, no! I've had far too much to do in the house for me to go outside!"

"Well, I'll go and change too, and then get supper ready, so you can have a break. Why don't you go and see to the chickens, and then you'll have some fresh air as well?"

She smiled at her mother, refusing for once to accept the guilt that the older woman was trying to pile on her because she'd had a pleasant afternoon out, and went upstairs.

Harry didn't meet a soul until he was on top of the mountain, where there were people picking late whimberries, and courting couples trying to look nonchalant as they sought secluded spots amongst the little tumps of heather and ferns. He'd been trying to imagine Mam being discontented if she lived in a beautiful house with a garden, and plenty of food on the table and good clothes to wear. It took all sorts, he supposed, and there'd been plenty of women with tales of woe when he worked in the Cworp, but, to be fair, most of them had had plenty to complain about.

He looked down over the town, basking in the sunshine that had even made the breeze warm today, and wondered anew at how it had taken a World War to make it prosperous again. More employment about now than there'd been for years, with plenty of new factories springing up down the valley. A few more private cars on the roads as well, and one or two families had even bought their houses from the coal board and were building on bathrooms at the back.

He smiled to himself as he strode down Llanover Road into the town. With his father still insistent that he wouldn't have electricity in the house, Mam would probably never know the luxury of an indoor bathroom, but now that Lizzie was living in one of the new houses at Capel Newydd she went down there once a week and had a bath. Afterwards she sat like a queen in Lizzie's front room, with a cup of tea and a biscuit while the children ran riot around her. "Lizzie!" she would cry each time. "Can't you get these children to hisht? I've come down here for a bit of peace and quiet!"

On the same afternoon, Charles Keating was also making his way home. The grandiose house at Headley-on-the-Hill was home now, to him and Sylvia. If it hadn't been ungentlemanly, he would have liked to whistle as he walked along. He'd had an easy war, Sylvia's arms had always been warm and welcoming to return to, and with the money he'd been given to turn his back on Jennie he'd been able to keep himself very comfortable during the stretches that he and Sylvia had been apart. And once the war was over Sylvia had produced that special pout of hers whenever, for form's sake, he had suggested that it was time he found some regular employment.

"Darling," she would say, "the last few years have been so awfully *dreary*! Let's just enjoy ourselves for a little while."

Sitting in his desk drawer was a Special Licence, which he'd procured earlier in the week, which meant that he could finally make an honest woman of Sylvia. Not that he had any real taste for marrying again, but Sylvia wasn't getting any younger, and at the moment everything was still in her name. He could picture the look on her face when he sprang the surprise on her, and she'd be too excited to look at all the documentation too closely and discover that he had been married once before…

He turned into the gate and studied the front of the house. He hadn't been that keen on the place when he used to visit Sylvia here, but somehow possession put a very different slant on things. He'd already suggested some improvements – or he might even be able to persuade her to sell up and move to somewhere they could choose together.

At least a new front door, definitely, he thought, as he pulled his key out of the lock with some difficulty. "Darling! I'm back!" It was a beautiful day; she was probably waiting for him in the conservatory.

She was. Lying on the rug, her body twisted into a strange shape and her mouth into a grotesque one. A side table and lamp, which she'd grabbed at as she went down, were lying smashed beside her, and there was a dark stain beneath her, spreading out over the rug.

"Oh my God! Whatever's happened to you?"

He knelt beside her, but all she could do was make a strange moaning noise from her skewed mouth while her eyes implored him to *do something!*

"I'll phone the doctor … an ambulance! I'll be right back!"

He hurried out into the hall, his fingers stumbling over the telephone dial. And as he waited for an answer, all he could think of was that fate had cheated him once more.

28

There was no-one in the office when Harry arrived at work the following Monday. He'd come in early on purpose, but she must have already been in and beaten him to it. He sat down at his desk, lit a cigarette, and picked up a pile of papers. He'd never particularly liked paperwork, much preferring to be out and about meeting people, and he noticed ruefully how evident this was by the state of his desk compared with Jennie's – which probably contained an equal amount of paper, but on hers it was neatly stacked into efficient piles, and there were slim, sharpened pencils laid out in a row at the side.

He decided to start the week by sorting it all out, telling himself firmly that it needed doing badly, and wasn't simply an excuse to linger, waiting for the door from the kitchen to open.

A stack of discarded paper was growing steadily on the floor beside him when the door suddenly flew open and Jennie bustled in.

"Oh, hello! I didn't think you'd still be here! Reg's bus broke down just as we turned off the Keeper's road, so we had to walk the rest of the way." She was taking off her hat and jacket as she spoke, revealing a dress underneath which seemed to skim the outline of her slender body, ending just on the knee – which did justice to her well-shaped legs, Harry thought. Perhaps the government ought to be congratulated for calling on women to wear shorter skirts in their continuing efforts to save cloth.

She was still talking as she bent over to take a clean overall from the basket she'd brought with her. "Ieuan Williams decided we could get here faster if we took a footpath around the Lamb and Flag, which I'm sure wasn't any quicker really, and all I seem to have done is tread in sheep's mess!"

Her cheeks glowed from her exertions, and her eyes glinted merrily, so that the grey in them deepened, turning them almost black as she began to laugh. "Marjorie Pollock, off the switchboard, started to complain because she was wearing high heels, so he threw her over his shoulder in a fireman's lift and carried her most of the way. It's lucky we're away up the mountain, because she was shrieking her head off!"

To his relief, the body which he had an overwhelming urge to fling his arms around and crush very tightly was now hidden beneath a swathe of overall. His mind went back years, before Megan even, to when Ivy used to tease and tantalise him with the promise of her body. Ivy had got her wish to become a barmaid, in the end, by marrying a publican, and was now stuck out on the lonely road to Garndiffaith, grown blowsy from a succession of children and, Harry suspected, a fondness for gin.

He dragged his mind back to the present, where Jennie was still talking to him. "David and I enjoyed our afternoon very much," she was saying. "It was good of you to give him so much attention."

He smiled. "He's a great little boy – a credit to you. You're obviously doing a marvellous job bringing him up alone."

She smiled back. "Thank you. But I do get a lot of help from my parents, of course – and Mother's a stickler for good manners! But it does him good to spend some time with a man – someone younger than his grandfather that is. Someone who can join in a bit of rough-and-tumble with him; more of a father-figure…"

"That's me! Everyone's favourite uncle, stand-in father – anything you like, really!" His voice was brittle, his smile less genuine.

Her hand suddenly flew to her mouth. "Oh dear! That sounded terrible – I wasn't hinting, you know – that he needs a father… you were right what you said – about friendship – that's all I meant. Gosh! Is that the time? I must go and give the girls a hand… and I'm interrupting your work…"

He said nothing, but he was no longer smiling. He stood up. "I'd better go and give Reg a hand with that bus."

She nodded. "The girls will be wondering where I've got to." But still she made no move to leave.

She watched him go out of the door, cursing herself for her stupidity. Just when she thought there'd been a bit of a chance of having a friendship with a man, she had to go and make that stupid remark, which meant he would now think she was after a man – any man – to be a father to her child.

Her jaunty mood left her as she made her way through to the kitchen, where she spent the morning haranguing the girls in a way that even Mother would have been hard pressed to live up to. Fortunately they knew nothing about her Saturday meeting with Harry, so no questions were asked. Instead, they pulled faces at each other when she wasn't looking.

"What's up with her?" Glenys muttered to Val after Jennie had declared that the counters were not fit to serve food from. "More trouble at home?"

"Dunno." Val shrugged. "She hasn't said, and from the look of her this morning, I'm not going to be the one to ask. Perhaps it's the curse."

"Yeah, and she'll have all of us cursing if she goes on like this," Glenys said grimly, heaving a bucket of hot water from the sink before going in search of a scrubbing brush.

Jennie would probably have overcome her embarrassment at such a minor gaffe if she hadn't had the dream on Monday night. In it, she and Harry were in the little stone cottage she had idly thought about during their walk, but David wasn't with them. They were alone, and Harry was doing things to her that she'd never have thought of in her waking hours – and what was worse, she was enjoying it.

Travelling on the bus, the dream was still with her, unsettling her and filling her with a dread of seeing Harry and betraying herself. And she was angry with herself for allowing it to play on her mind. She was done with men – that had been decided several years ago, and she was determined to school her body to accept the fact. She wasn't prepared to risk going through all that heartbreak again, and inexorably drag David through it as well.

A pleasant young woman… thinking that from now on she has to take a back seat in life… until she eventually finds that life has passed her by … Harry's words from Saturday came back to her. Dammit! She was thinking about him again!

She forced herself to pick at the old scab of injuries which Charles had inflicted upon her. That was what really happened when you got yourself tangled up with a man – at least, that's what would happen to her, she was sure of it. She'd suffered rejection from her mother and a husband she'd been prepared to adore – there was not going to be a third time.

Nevertheless, she could feel the blush beginning to rise when she stepped into the office and saw Harry sitting at his desk. She grabbed her overall and swept out again, muttering about having to catch a delivery van. Harry was wearing a new jacket, she just managed to note, but in her dream he hadn't been wearing anything at all – and neither had she.

This is ridiculous! she told herself, as she thanked Val absently for her tea and toast and wondered if Harry would come out of the office this way. She decided an inventory of the store cupboard was a must, in case he did, and refused to acknowledge her disappointment when he didn't.

By Wednesday she'd managed to avoid him almost completely, by spending any spare minutes re-organising the kitchen, and by taking her paperwork home with her.

By Thursday Harry had had enough. He came into the kitchen at lunchtime earlier than usual, before they had started to dish up, walked over to Jennie and announced: "I need to talk to you."

Branwyn nudged Lily. "He'll be lucky. Not exactly in a chatty mood this week, is she?" The clatter of dishes continued, but there was an air of expectancy as the girls all strained their ears to listen, while appearing to take no notice at all.

"It's rather inconvenient at the moment – the men will be in any minute now." Jennie had barely looked at him as she deftly cut large trays of corned beef and potato pie into squares.

"I'm sure the others can manage for a few minutes." His voice was firm, almost angry.

Jennie became aware of Marina hovering nearby, her mouth slightly opened, a ladle of beetroot salad suspended in mid-air. "If that beetroot goes down your apron, you'll never get the stain out," she said sharply to the girl as she followed Harry through to the office, not looking at any of them.

Immediately, as the door closed behind them, chatter replaced clatter.

"I said all along those two had fallen out. That's what's been wrong with her all week, I reckon." Lily folded her arms in satisfaction.

"But what is there to fall out with Harry about?" Glenys asked. "Not exactly the bad-tempered sort, is he?"

Marina held the ladle closer to her, placing her apron in even more danger. "Perhaps they've been having a clandestine romance which has ended in a lovers' tiff," she said dreamily. She'd recently discovered a publication by the name of *True Love Stories*, which held her entranced every Friday evening when she bought a copy out of her pay packet, and which then coloured her thoughts and her speech for the following week.

"She's had a go at him again about running a book from the office, more like," said Val. "She never has been too keen on him doing that." She glanced at the big clock on the wall. "Whatever it is, we won't find out standing here, and we'd better get a wiggle on, or there'll be a queue out to the door before we know it."

Inside the office, Harry sat Jennie down on a chair, pulled another opposite it for himself, and lit a cigarette. The dream had begun to fade by now, so Jennie had her emotions well under control. She would explain, as well as she could, that she wasn't cut out for friendships with the opposite sex.

"I don't understand it," he was saying. "We had a pleasant afternoon together, which you thanked me for very prettily on Monday, and since then all you've done is cold-shoulder me – just when I thought we were starting to get on well together. So come on – what's it all about? What have I done? I can't share an office with a sulker!"

"I don't sulk!" Jennie said at once. "And you haven't done anything." She paused. What to tell him? That she'd had an erotic dream about him that kept intruding into her working life, simply because he was the only man in over six years who had paid her the slightest bit of attention and by whom she didn't feel threatened in any way? How pathetic it made her sound!

Gathering her rapidly fragmenting resolution, she spoke in a rush. "I thought I'd spoilt things – Monday morning, when I said that David needed a father-figure. I thought that you'd think that I was trying to hook you... you know, just so that David could have a father – and I wasn't. Not that you wouldn't make a good father, I'm sure, but you'd said about friendship, and that's all I was wanting too, but it didn't sound like it – and you went out without saying anything, so I thought I had... you know... made you think I was after you... and I'm not, because I don't ever want to get mixed up again – in that way... but I didn't know how to tell you that – just like I'm not making a very good job of telling you now... and that's all... really..." Her voice tailed away, leaving her staring at her hands in her lap.

He reached out, and for a moment she thought he was going to pull her towards him. His nearness sent a thrill through her body which belied everything she'd just said and made her keen ever so slightly towards him. But his arm went past her, towards an ashtray on the desk behind.

"And that's really all this is about?" His voice was warm and friendly. She nodded.

"Silly girl, then, aren't you, to have worried like that? I hadn't read anything into your remarks at all. And if I didn't make that clear at the time... well... I was probably thinking about what I had to do next – Reg's lorry, or whatever." He wouldn't admit that her gratitude for the attention he'd paid to David *had* irked him, just a bit.

She raised the large grey eyes which had been haunting him all week, and which had driven him out of the office on Monday morning, and regarded him steadily.

He smiled at her. "So why don't we return to where we were on Monday – both having enjoyed our excursion on Saturday – and plan to do it again?"

She gulped, determined to hang on to her resolution. "That's very kind of you, but I don't think quite honestly that it's a really good idea... people would see us and talk... put the wrong meaning on things..."

He cut across her with an impatient wave of his hand. "Can I ask you a question – a rather personal one? Had you had many boyfriends before ... you know... your marriage?"

"Boyfriends?" she echoed, as if he'd said *'aliens'*. "Well ... none, really. There wasn't anyone – out in the countryside – and I was very young when I married... so ... no, none."

"That's a pity."

"It is? Why?" There was a warning note of frostiness in her voice.

"Because if you'd had a few boyfriends, you might have known that there are some men in this world who are capable of treating a woman well. And you wouldn't be so convinced that every man who tries to be friendly towards you is out to seduce you, and then cast you aside!"

He was so near the truth that she felt furious with him. She stood up quickly and moved round behind the desk. "That's not what I think!" she hissed vehemently.

"Isn't it?" He was standing too, leaning across the desk so that his eyes directly challenged hers. "Well, you've nothing to be afraid of then, have you, if two lonely people, albeit of opposite sexes, find that they can get on sufficiently well to spend a few pleasant hours together – and to hell with what anyone else thinks! – especially when they are carrying around as much past baggage as we two are?"

She remembered then about his wife, and Val's assertion of how much he'd loved her. Of course Harry, of all people, would not pose a threat to her! That dream had evidently had too much influence on her conscious mind. And she certainly didn't want him to think that she was arrogant enough to believe she could compare herself with his dead wife.

Her shoulders relaxed with a sigh, and she offered him a sheepish smile. "I seem to be very good at getting it all wrong, don't I?"

He stood up straight again as the tension in the room evaporated. "It's called 'inexperience', an increasingly rare commodity, I think, since the war. Anyway, what I've wanted to say to you since Monday is: how about a trip out with David this Saturday or Sunday? I thought I would borrow my uncle's car and we could ..."

"Oh, we can't!" Jennie said. "Or the weekend after, I'm afraid... not because I don't want to," she went on hastily, as his face darkened. "It's just that I'm away on holiday for the next two weeks. I'm taking David to Porthcawl with my sister and her little girl."

"But when you come back?"

"That would be lovely. I'm sure David would thoroughly enjoy it."

And by then, she vowed silently, *I shall have myself completely in check.*

Harry missed her more even more than he'd thought he would. He'd got used to her enquiring face at the end of the afternoon, looking up from her desk to ask him whether he'd had winners or losers that day, and he hadn't owned to himself completely just how much he looked forward to seeing her each morning. He found himself listening for her quick, light footstep in the corridor outside, and felt irrationally irritated with himself for the excited way he glanced up when he heard footsteps one morning – to be disappointed when it was only Val's face which popped round the door.

"Had a postcard from Jennie this morning, we have," she told him. "Lovely weather they're having, apparently."

"That's nice," he said equably, even more irrationally annoyed because he hadn't received one.

He thought perhaps he could do with a holiday himself. He had days due to him, but with no-one else to make plans with, it didn't seem worth it. Porthcawl suddenly seemed exceptionally attractive – but he couldn't just turn up there. He'd had difficulty enough already in persuading her as to the platonic nature of his intentions. To seek her out now where she was holidaying just because he was missing her would contradict everything he'd said.

No. Better to settle for a day at Chepstow races with Uncle Fred and Joe instead.

The sun shining on the righteous!" Jennie told everyone who commented on her healthy tan and how lucky she'd been to have two weeks of such glorious weather. She didn't tell them how she'd veered between irritability and boredom for a great deal of the time. It had been good of Laura, of course, to suggest the holiday, which Cyril had been unable to accompany them on because not only was he hectically busy climbing the insurance ladder once again, but he was also standing for the local council elections in September and was determined to ingratiate himself with as many people as possible. But her irritability stemmed from realising that she was tired of having to be always grateful to others for what they did for her and David.

Mother had taken to giving her a daily bulletin of everything that had been done for her child and herself while she was out at work, although Jennie had said repeatedly that she would happily take care of her own and David's needs after she returned each day.

"Don't be so ridiculous! I don't want everything about again at the end of the afternoon just when I'm getting straight. And how could you dry all the washing then?" And she would shake her head at the lack of common sense in this daughter who trooped off to some ridiculous job each day, while her parents slaved to keep a home for her and the child.

Jennie had remained firm at first, cleaning her and David's rooms and washing their clothes on Saturday mornings, but Mother had complained long and loud that this interfered with her weekend baking – even though she was in the kitchen and Jennie was in the wash room – and had ostentatiously gone over the kitchen floor with a cloth every time a drop of water was carried through, until she could legitimately complain of backache.

It was easier in the end for Jennie to acquiesce; to grit her teeth and be grateful, whilst reminding herself that this was all part of Mother's strategy to get her to give up work and become the dogs-body at home.

And now she was having to be grateful to Laura for organising this holiday, even though she'd tried to insist on paying her way. "Cyril won't hear of it," Laura had said. "He's only too glad to help when we're doing so well!" This declaration of the gulf between their situations only added more salt, but she'd agreed to go because David was so delighted at the idea; thrilled to be going to the seaside which he already knew so much about, which gave him automatic superiority over his older cousin.

The boredom arose from the sort of holiday it turned out to be. They stayed in a gloomy little boarding house which gave itself airs by being described as a private hotel, filled with such respectable middle-aged people that even Mother would have approved. Jennie and Laura shared a room at the back of the house, with an adjoining room for the children, both facing north, so that the sun never penetrated. To compensate, the floors were each covered with a square of alarmingly patterned carpet which shrieked against the fussy curtains, and cabbage rose wallpaper which had evidently been on the walls for some time, as David kept finding little corners of it peeling off which were simply irresistible to his small fingers.

All over the building were polite notices such as, in the porch: 'Patrons are requested not to wear sand shoes in the hotel'; and, in the bathroom: 'Please leave this room as you would wish to find it'. They were signed by 'The Management', which consisted of Mrs. Oates, who prepared the meals with a great clattering of pots and pans that could be heard through the swing door from the dining room, as if she were working under protest, and her husband, a despondent Neville Chamberlain look-alike who served the same dun-coloured soup of indeterminate flavour at dinner each evening, and manned the reception desk with a tight-lipped smile. (This was in an effort to retain his cream-coloured false teeth, which to the children's delight tended to drop when he spoke, with a clicking noise that punctuated his speech.)

The sea-front, the wide stretch of sandy beach and the rolling, surf-laden waves under a persistently blue sky, were all that David could have wished for. He and Selina were happy to gambol about on the beach all day, squealing as they jumped over the smaller waves which swept up the beach, and making intricate sand tunnels. Laura was also content, sitting in a low-slung calico chair, her skin glowing from an evil-smelling concoction to ward off sunburn, with the accoutrements necessary for a day at the beach packed around her so that she could dispense anything needed without raising herself from the chair. By the end of the first week her ample cleavage, squashed between the straps of a flowery, short-skirted garment that seemed too long to be a bathing costume and too short to be a sundress, had turned a deep brown, while the backs of her legs remained lily-white.

But Jennie was filled with a restlessness which refused to be quelled. She played with the children in the water and took them for long forays amongst the rock pools for interesting shells and tiny shrimps while Laura serenely kept camp, a wide straw hat shielding her eyes as she absorbed herself in an Agatha Christie. But the restlessness in Jennie remained, making it impossible to sit for long beside her sister and do nothing more than flick through the daily newspaper, which Laura insisted upon buying each morning during their laden journey to the beach.

"Do you ever think about the future – I mean the distant future?" she asked Laura one afternoon, as the children ran up and down the beach with buckets of water in a fruitless attempt to fill the deep trench they'd dug. "You know – what you'll be doing in ten or fifteen years' time?"

"Heavens, no! There's too much going on at the moment to think very much of the future." She considered for a moment. "I suppose we might move to a bigger house as Cyril gets on, that sort of thing."

"And what about more children?"

They both watched the dark, tousled head of David against the sleek, blonde one of Selina, each absorbed in their task.

"I don't think so," said Laura carefully. "Once Cyril's on the council he'll go far, I'm sure of it, and he'll need me beside him – I don't think I could give him as much if there were more children to distract me."

"When I dreamed my youthful dreams, I was going to have a

houseful of children," Jennie said. "One every couple of years, so there was always a little one at home with me as the others grew up. And the big ones would come home from school each day to this wonderful, smiling mother, and a plateful of freshly-baked scones!"

Laura turned to face her. "If that's still your dream, it's not impossible, is it? There's still plenty of time to find a decent husband – and you're good with children. Remember the hordes of evacuees you and Hetty used to gather about you? They all thought you were wonderful. You just need the right man to come along."

It was the song Laura had been singing since before Jennie went to Devon, and who could blame her? They'd been schooled by the nuns to find fulfilment in the sacrament of marriage to a good man.

Unbidden, Harry's face appeared in Jennie's mind's eye, and was resolutely pushed away. "The trouble is, though, that I wouldn't trust myself to know whether it *was* the right man – and once you're married and find out it isn't, it's too late. So it looks as if we're both going to have only children."

Laura opened her mouth to speak again, but Jennie stood up abruptly as Harry's image refused to go away, and called to the children: "I fancy a walk up on the cliff-top. Do you want to come?"

They both gave the briefest shake of their heads and went back to their game. "Do you mind if I go?" Jennie asked Laura. "I'll only keep interrupting you otherwise, and you look as if you've nearly found out whodunit."

Laura smiled affectionately, making Jennie remember that for all her staidness she still loved her sister. "Of course not. The children will be fine, and by the time you come back I'll know whether it was the Major or the American heiress!"

It was breezier on the headland. Jennie walked briskly into the wind, glad of the energy required to push against it, and wished she was back at work so that, amongst the noise and camaraderie, she wouldn't feel so heartachingly lonely.

Once or twice in the evenings they took the children for a stroll around the town, but it wasn't a great success. Tired from their day's exertions on the beach, they became whiny and fractious, ready to argue even though the day had been spent in complete harmony. So once the children were tucked up in bed, most evenings were spent in the stultifying atmosphere of the hotel lounge.

Among the guests was a party of elderly ladies from Bristol who played endless games of whist, and bickered gently amongst themselves as they confused one another by talking at cross purposes because each was only interested in her own thoughts and words. Snippets of their conversations would drift across to Jennie as she sat in the window watching the melancholic setting of the sun. Royalty and bodily functions featured heavily.

"I saw pictures of King Farouk at the Royal Wedding ..."

"I shouldn't have had that lettuce. It always gives me wind in the evenings ..."

"No dear, that was the Shah of Persia ..."

She saw herself forty years hence in the same situation, Harry's prophecies all having come true. It seemed as if, no matter how she tried, either the man himself or things that he'd said kept cropping up, so that it was impossible to forget about him.

They played a few desultory games of cards and dominoes in the evenings, but Jennie found her concentration flagging.

"It's all the sun and sea air," said Laura. "Cyril will be so sorry to have missed it. Do you mind if we put this away and I go and phone him? – just to see if he's eating properly on his own."

"Of course not," said Jennie with relief, as Laura padded out to the telephone in the corner of the entrance hall.

Jennie glanced out of the window again and wondered if the same pink sky was casting a glow on her mountains.

At the beginning of the second week a wiry little man with miner's lungs, and his even shorter wife, arrived from Blaenavon. Jennie was tempted to ask whether they knew Harry, but was suddenly worried that they might say 'yes', and then mention something unflattering about him. So she didn't mention that she worked at Pwlldu, or anything about the canteen girls. It was left to Laura to tell them about Goytre and Monmouth and the relationship between the two small children, whom they admired with lots of: "You'd never think they were cousins, would you, one so fair and the other so dark?" – followed by a silent, mouthed, "Poor little thing!" to one another, when they discovered that David had no father.

You look like a pair of gypsies!" was Mother's unflattering comment when a tanned Jennie and David arrived back at the farm, but then she softened it by telling 'the boy', surprisingly: "We missed you while you were away".

"What did you get up to, then?" Branwyn asked when Jennie returned to work with a feeling of relief, and the girls were gathered round her for the early-morning cup of tea.

"Nothing you would approve of!" Jennie chuckled, and watched their faces fall in disbelief as she recounted the tedium of the holiday. "It was really for the children, though," she said defensively. "And David had a wonderful time, so it was worth it."

She went into the office reluctantly, almost shy of seeing Harry again, but perversely wanting him to be there. He had his back to the door as she entered, and there was no mistaking the look of pleasure on his face when he turned round.

"Look like you've been to the French Riviera," he said admiringly.

"Well it's just as well I haven't, or I might not have been so pleased to be back," she laughed.

"Don't tell me you missed us!" he said in mocking tones.

"Shall we just say that my sweet but very respectable sister chose a hotel so equally respectable that it seemed to house everybody's maiden aunt!"

She told him about some of the other guests, exaggerating their idiosyncrasies so that he laughed.

"And there was I thinking you might get swept off your feet by some tall dark stranger. I had a few days off myself, and nearly came over to Porthcawl – but I thought you might not be too pleased to see someone who reminded you of work, when you were supposed to be relaxing." He picked up a clipboard from his desk, not looking at her as he spoke.

She took a deep breath. "I think I would have been very pleased to see you," she said, "and not just because everyone else there was so tedious!"

His head shot up, his eyebrows raised in surprise. "I think this holiday has done you good," he said after a moment.

"I made some new resolutions during my solitary walks – summer ones, instead of New Year's."

"And…?"

"And… I know that I can't keep pushing friends away, or I'm going to end up like those old biddies in Porthcawl. So – before I left, you suggested more excursions together at weekends. If that offer is still there, I'd like to make the most of it."

He nodded thoughtfully before he answered. "And what if … just supposing – I'm not saying it will, of course – our friendship deepened into something … well, a bit more than just friends, say? What would you do then?"

She took another deep breath. "I think I would try very hard to let things take their natural course – although I couldn't promise that I would always do it very well. *Inexperience,* you said, remember?"

He nodded again. They stood regarding one another seriously for a few moments before he spoke, softly, a small smile playing about his lips. "Well then. I've got some men off on holiday, so I'd better get cracking, and you'd better start thinking about where you would like to go this weekend."

J ennie clattered the last cup and saucer onto the shelf of the dresser. "Careful!" Mother cried. "You'll break them! What are you in such a hurry for, anyway? It's not David's bedtime yet."

"I want to go and listen to the wireless," Jennie said as she dried her hands on the kitchen towel.

Mother pursed her lips. "Racing results for that man, I suppose."

But Jennie left the room without answering, went into the parlour and switched on the wireless. A horse called 'David's Day' had been running at Kempton Park, and she'd asked Harry to put a shilling on it for her.

"Each way? Or are you going to be a daredevil and put it all on the nose?" he teased, her caution in such matters by now a source of much bantering between them.

"Each way," she confirmed, smilingly handing over a florin.

She smiled a lot these days, she reflected as she waited for the results, although mainly when she was at work, or alone with David.

Her growing friendship with Harry hadn't been well-received by Mother, who, as Jennie had anticipated, could see no further than the broad Welsh accent and down-to-earth manner.

The dark, dusty green leaves of summer were turning to burnished copper and flaming reds and yellows when he'd first bowled up the drive in Uncle Fred's car to take Jennie and David to Hereford for the day. He was earlier than expected, so Jennie was still upstairs making an impatient David keep still while she did her best to tame his unruly hair and create some sort of a parting in it. She heard Mother go to the front door and was suddenly as agitated as David, straining her ears to listen to the murmur of voices below.

"Go down and talk to Grandma and Harry, while I just powder my nose and find my shoes," she told a relieved David, relinquishing all efforts to make him look as tidy as she'd wanted. Knowing Mother, she would probably keep Harry waiting on the front doorstep and regard him with her lofty, superior face.

But Harry was more than a match for Mother's disdain, and coped by simply ignoring it.

"Good morning. I'm Harry Jenkins – I expect Jennie's told you all about me."

"Yes, she has," Mother replied, in tones which indicated that she hadn't been impressed with what she'd heard, while taking his outstretched hand for the merest moment. "I'm afraid she's not quite ready yet."

"That's alright. My fault – I'm earlier than I said I'd be. But don't worry, I can wait. There's nothing to be in a hurry about." As he spoke, Harry stepped nearer to Mother, so she had no option but to open the front door wider and allow him into the hall.

"I hope our jaunts at the weekends don't inconvenience you too much," he went on, with his most winning smile.

"Not at all. We're used to running the farm and house throughout the week when Jennie's at work; Saturdays and Sundays make little difference."

He nodded, ignoring the barb in her voice. "Like my Mam – always in the back kitchen, she is, busy with something. She always says she only goes to Chapel for a good sit-down! But Jennie's a great girl – she deserves the odd treat – and this young man's a great fella too," he continued as David came boisterously down the stairs.

"Yes," said Mother icily, as she watched David fling himself at this man dressed in a showy blue pin-striped suit which made him look like an American gangster. "His grandfather and I are very fond of him. I understand you are from Blaenavon?" she said, making it sound like some far-flung savage-ridden corner of the Empire.

"That's right. Good little town it is, too. Not as beautiful as all this countryside you've got around you, of course, but the people are all very good-hearted – but then, most of them are related to one another if you go far enough back!"

"Tidy place you've got here, mind – fair play!" he went on. "Don't know much about farming myself, although my Dad's always kept pigs on a sort of allotment he's got. I know plenty about horses, though – especially when they're running round a track! Not so keen on the dogs, though – the ones I put my money on always seem to run backwards!"

"Really?" Mother replied faintly.

"Ah! Here she is!" Harry exclaimed irrepressibly, before Mother could think of anything else to say.

"Sorry to keep you waiting," Jennie said as she descended the stairs, aiming a piercing look at Harry which he managed to ignore completely.

"That's okay," he said. "Your Mam here and me've been having a bit of a chat." He turned to David. "You ready then, butt? Say tarrah to your Nan." He placed his hat at a rakish angle on his head, before turning back to Mother with the faintest suggestion of a wink. "Nice to meet you, Mrs. D. I'll bring them both back safely."

Jennie's eyes were twinkling as she swept past Mother, but she managed to keep a straight face until the car had turned out of the drive.

"You did that deliberately!" she spluttered.

He took his eyes off the road for a moment to look at her with a wide-eyed innocence. "What, me?"

"Yes, you!" Jennie laughed. "I could hear you as I came downstairs, going on about dog-racing! And what was all that 'butt' and 'tarrah-to-Nan' business? I've never heard you sound so broadly Welsh!"

"We-e-ll, I couldn't help myself. She does have a bit of a look about her, like Queen Mary with piles, doesn't she?"

"Ssh!" Jennie said quickly, turning to see whether David was listening, but there was still a grin on her face. Fortunately David was too busy looking out of the window to listen to the boring conversation of adults.

"Anyway," Harry went on, obviously unconcerned about the impression he had or hadn't made on Mother, "one of us had to do the talking, and she wasn't saying much."

She'd had plenty to say when Jennie and David returned home, though. "A dreadful man!" she exclaimed with an exaggerated shudder. "And so common! I don't know how you can bear to be going about with him!"

"Oh, Mother!" Jennie replied. "Where's your sense of humour? He was putting it on a bit for your benefit, and it worked. You should have seen the look on your face!"

"Never mind the look on my face – I certainly saw the look on his when you were coming down the stairs! He'll have you in the family way before long, you mark my words! That'll be the next thing!"

"That's not true, either. I've told you that neither of us wants that sort of relationship. We're just friends, that's all."

Mother stared hard at her. "He's a man, isn't he?" she said darkly.

Mother would have been gratified to know that her observations were not so far off the mark. It was becoming harder and harder for Harry not to take Jennie's arm when they were out together, or put his arm around her when they were talking in the office, and the desire to simply grab her and kiss her fiercely was becoming ever stronger. What still held him back, apart from David always being with them if they met at weekends, was a slight stiffening of Jennie's body which he was aware of even if their bodies brushed accidentally, or he took her elbow to steer her across the road.

He pondered these things as he urged the little black car up the lane from Llanover, where the trees on the steep banks on either side, dressed in their autumnal glory, formed an arch overhead through which the low evening sun glinted gold on gold. Underneath, thick gnarled roots, exposed where endless winter rains had washed the soil away, intertwined relentlessly in a brown web, in dark contrast to the beauty overhead. As the car chugged protestingly to the top of the mountain the trees fell away, exposing views over three valleys, each basking under a blue sky – so that, cocooned inside the car away from the biting tanginess of the air, you could be forgiven for thinking that it was still summer.

Harry drank it all in, even while his mind was full of Jennie. Majestic in the distance sat the Sugar Loaf, its body now clothed in ambers and browns, with ribbons of green. Jennie's favourite mountain. She'd told him how much a part of her childhood it had been – the keeper of her secrets, she'd said. "Were there many?" he'd asked her lightly, and she'd studied him sombrely for a second or two before answering: "A few."

He wished more than anything that she was with him now, so he could share his feelings of melancholy which the scene evoked. There wouldn't be many more evenings like this. Very soon the mountains would be covered in swirling, raindrop-hung mists, or smitten with heavy storms which sent the wandering, bedraggled sheep in vain search of shelter under rocks. The carefree days of summer would be a faint memory as they struggled to and from work, gasping as the cold air hit them when they stepped out from the warm fugginess of the paraffin stoves that heated the Works buildings.

Jennie would understand if she were here with him now. The grey eyes would deepen thoughtfully as he explained the heavy sadness which the timeless beauty all around them seemed to invoke in him at this time of year, and she would nod and smile a small sympathetic smile, with a stillness about her that was comforting.

He thought of her now, probably putting a tired David to bed, enjoying the warmth of his trusting little body nestled up to hers, listening to his prayers. So much of his own life at present seemed to be spent in vicarious pleasures; observing the Spartan contentment of his parents' old age, playing surrogate parent from time to time to the growing broods of his brother and sister, becoming the dependable ear for many of his friends and relatives as they coped with the small crises which arose in their lives, of the type which rarely impinged upon his own.

He turned his back on the Sugar Loaf and pointed the car down the mountain in the direction of Blaenavon. Something would have to be done, he decided. He remembered Jennie's assertion, when she returned from her holiday, that if their friendship began to develop into something else she would try to let things take their course... but would she?

He pictured her again, in her real surroundings now, not in the ones which had previously been a figment of his mind's eye. That was another thing. If he was truly serious about her, what could he offer that bore any comparison to the sort of upbringing she'd had on the farm? It was certainly larger and more luxurious that he'd imagined – would she want to trade that for the sort of two-up, two-down terrace filled with utility furniture that was all he would be able to afford? There didn't seem to be an ounce of snobbishness in her, but surely all the years spent with that martinet of a mother would have rubbed off a little bit – and *there* was an out-and-out snob for you, if ever there was one.

He tried to see the narrow streets and higgledy-piggledy assortment of houses through her eyes, as he pulled the car into Market Street garage to fill up with petrol before he took it back. Not much to look at, really, he supposed, but it was difficult to be objective because of the love he bore the place.

He would have to bring her here, introduce her to the family, and then it would be up to her. If she began to make excuses to end their little outings together, he'd know.

He got out of the car quickly as the garage hand came towards him. The thought of Jennie turning him away suddenly filled him with a greater awfulness than he'd experienced on top of the mountain.

It's only for one night. We can look after the lad for one night, surely," Edward said, wishing that he'd stayed outside for his elevenses.

"Of course we can look after the boy," his wife snapped at him, clattering cups and saucers into the sink. "That's not the point, is it? The point is, where's it all going to lead? He's after her, there's no mistaking that, and she's silly enough to fall for it! She'll take the boy away from us, and end up living in that dreadful hole! Is that what you want for your precious daughter?"

Edward carried a plate to the sink. What *had* he wanted for this daughter who'd been his soulmate for so many years on the farm – the daughter he'd missed so dreadfully during the war? Someone who could have given her the sort of life she'd always enjoyed, he supposed – like Ced Griffiths's boys, who each had their own farms now, creating a sort of dynasty around Goytre. But she'd never shown the slightest interest in them, or they in her, except as a tennis partner to play at Penpergwm.

"I know what I don't want," he said now. "I don't want her to fall for another character like Charles Keating, and have her breaking her heart again over someone who doesn't give a damn about her! And you have to admit," he went on as he knelt by the door to lace up his boots, with a smile twitching on his lips which he knew would infuriate Katharine, "Harry Jenkins is nothing like Charles Keating, is he?"

"Out of the frying pan and into the fire, that's what it will be!" she exclaimed, resorting to clichés, as she tended to do when she wanted to press her point. "If she must think about marrying again, why couldn't she rely on Laura to find someone for her? There must be some decent man in Monmouth prepared to take on a woman and child!"

"Or, alternatively, we could take her to the cattle market on Tuesday, and see who would bid for her!"

But Katharine had moved away into the larder as he spoke, and missed the heavy irony. "It will all end in tears, you mark my words," she said as she came back into the room.

Edward was ready, and thankful, to return to the fields by now. "It certainly will if you keep on at her," he said. "She's only going to Blaenavon to meet his family – nothing's been said by anybody about marrying. Come to think of it, I don't think I've even seen them touch. You're the only one who's taking it seriously, and if you make too much of it you'll only push her further towards him."

"Oh! So then it will be my fault, will it?" Katharine's voice began to rise. "It's amazing how everything that happens to Jennie ends up as my fault!"

And then she stopped suddenly, as Edward went out through the door and she remembered that last time, it probably was.

Harry's nervousness had transmitted itself to his Mam. She'd spent ages debating with Lizzie as to whether she should prepare high tea, with sandwiches and cake, or an evening meal, which the men in her family preferred. If it was high tea, then she could use the cake-stand she'd inherited from Nan and which usually only came out at Christmas.

"But if we have a proper meal, our plates don't all match," she said, her brow furrowed with the perplexity of it all.

"I could lend you some of mine," Lizzie suggested, "if you really think it'll make a difference. And it's no good asking Harry, 'cos men never see the niceties of these things anyway."

"But then, she's a cook herself, isn't she?" said Mam. "She might not think our plain-and-simple is good enough."

Albert, having heard variations of this conversation for at least three days, grew exasperated then. "She's coming to meet *us*, not give you a cookery exam," he said. "And she won't have been giving them bloody caviar on top of the Keeper's, will she?"

Mam and Lizzie pulled faces at each other as Albert stomped off to the Rolling Mill for some sensible male company, renewed their debate, and in the end settled for high tea.

Lizzie was waiting with her parents to greet Jennie, having left her brood at home with Archie. She was reminded of the first time Dai had brought Bridget home, and taken her around the family like a prize exhibit.

She liked the look of Jennie, and felt envious of her slenderness, but found her shyness a bit daunting. The first cup of tea was drunk amidst efforts at polite conversation on either side, encompassing the weather and the increase of traffic since the war, with Harry trying too hard to gee things up – rather like the warm-up man for the main act.

Just as the conversation lulled again, there was a commotion in the back kitchen, followed by two little faces appearing round the door.

"I told you to stay with your Da!" Lizzie cried in exasperation, especially as both faces were none too clean.

"Oh, let them come in!" Jennie said. "They look adorable!"

Which immediately raised her several notches in Lizzie's estimation.

"Great!" said Bethan, Lizzie's eldest daughter. "I'll go get the others! Save us some of the sandwiches, Nan!"

The arrival of the children, shepherded by Archie, broke the ice completely, and by the time Dai and Bridget turned up and squeezed into the tiny living room there was already an animated conversation going on about the difficulties of keeping growing children clothed and fed, into which Bridget entered automatically.

Harry knew that Jennie was being accepted into the fold when Lizzie said, "You should bring your David over to play with our lot one Saturday."

"He'd like that," Jennie answered. "He misses the rough and tumble he used to have with his cousins in Devon."

I'm so glad you suggested the pictures tonight as well," Jennie told Harry later that night as they emerged from Top Hall. "It made the prospect of meeting all your family a lot less daunting. Not that they were at all daunting, really... it's just that there's so many of them."

He chuckled. "I know what you mean. It doesn't help when they all live so close, either, does it? Everyone gets to know what's going on, and they all want to join in. Extra curious, they all were tonight, as well – it's the first time I've taken a young lady home since... well, for donkeys' years. They wanted to pass on their sympathy to the poor victim!"

"Is that what they think I am – your 'young lady'?" she asked.

"Would you mind very much if they did?" he countered.

They walked on a few steps before she answered. "No, I don't think I would ... except that we don't really go out... in that way... do we?"

He took her hand firmly in his, pleased that she didn't immediately pull away. "That could soon be remedied."

She looked down at their entwined fingers and then back at him, and noticed the anxiety in his eyes. "I suppose it could," she agreed.

They both laughed and walked on companionably in the darkness.

"So, what did you think of them all?" Harry asked.

"Lovely people," she said at once. "And so... well, different, I suppose – but in a nice way. A *good* way." He didn't say anything immediately, so she went on: "You're all so free and easy with each other, and always joking and pulling each other's legs. Do you always get on so well, or was that for my benefit?"

"No, no... we're always the same on the whole. Can't say I've ever thought we were any different from anyone else, though. We have our little spats from time to time – my brother Dai and me don't always see eye to eye – and there's an aunt in Ebbw Vale that Mam hasn't spoken to in years, but that's families, isn't it?"

"Not mine, it isn't" she said emphatically. "My Aunt Eunice is good fun, but Mother's always called her a flibbertigibbet – and Emily, my sister in Devon, is full of life, but I don't see her very much now." She chuckled. "And all the nicknames! I thought it was bad enough at work, but once your family started talking about different people, nobody seemed to have a proper name at all! Where do the nicknames come from?"

He shrugged. "Dunno. But it's the same through all the valleys, isn't it? Perhaps you lose it a bit when you get to the more country areas. Some of them have meanings, though – like Cag Jones. He's left-handed, see. *Cag-handed,* they call it round here, so he became Cag Jones. And then my Mam was talking about Bonar Hewitt – he's been called Bonar as long as I can remember, because he talks so much – just like Bonar Law, the old MP."

"And what about *Gobby* someone-or-other they were mentioning? Does he talk a lot as well?'

He laughed. "Oh, as in having a big 'gob' you mean? I didn't think a refined young lady like you would use a word like that! But actually it's because he starts nearly everything he says with, 'I gobbee honest...' So he became Gobbee Matthews!" He pulled her nearer to him, their hands still entwined, so that their heads were nearly touching. "And up at the Works, 'Basket-bum' speaks for itself, doesn't it? – You *gobbee* honest!"

She gave a long gurgle of laughter, so that he wished there weren't so many other people about and he could take the plunge and kiss her. Instead he waited until they were in Uncle Fred's car, heading for home.

The initial plan had been for Jennie to stay the night at Uncle Fred's, but her mother had been so awkward about the whole thing that in the end Harry had said he'd run her home, in case the evening was called off completely. And it had gone well. Jennie had seemed a bit shy and awkward at first, and he was worried that Bridget or Lizzie would label her as 'posh', but she soon relaxed when the kids all piled in, and then his Dad started asking her about the farm. He could see from Mam's eyes that she approved of this genteel young woman. Over the next few days there'd doubtless be lots of comments about it being time he found a place of his own.

He didn't stop the car at the top of the mountain, but waited until they'd passed the Keeper's pond, which gave off a ghostly shimmer in the moonlight. On the other side of the mountain the nearly full moon shone down into the valley, casting a blue-grey sheen over the smaller slopes and roof-tops of Govilon, and throwing the hulk of the Sugar Loaf into sharp relief.

Harry pulled up in a little inlet at the side of the narrow twisting road. "Looks beautiful, even at night, doesn't it?" he said, before Jennie could ask why they'd stopped. "Do you fancy a little stroll – it's light enough?"

"Why not?" she replied. "I feel like a naughty schoolgirl who's absconded and doesn't want to go back yet to face the music!"

She turned to open the car door, but suddenly gave a strangled cry and grabbed Harry's arm. "There's somebody out there!" she said urgently. "I've just seen a face – perhaps it's a drunk, or something!"

"Well, he's a long way from the nearest pub! Hang on, there's a torch here somewhere." He leaned across to open the glove compartment, acutely aware of her body pressed to his. "Here we are!"

He shone the torch out through the passenger window. Jennie gave a little gasp of surprise, and then began to laugh in relief as it illuminated the large, bony head of an old ewe, staring into the car with a persistent but vacant expression.

Harry switched off the torch. "Probably interrupted her beauty sleep, poor old girl. You alright?" He slid his arm around her as he spoke.

"Fine," she nodded, and chuckled. "I just feel a bit silly."

He kept his arm where it was.

"You're not silly. You're beautiful."

And finally, after all the long months of careful restraint, he began to kiss her, savouring the gentle feel of her lips as slowly, hesitantly, she began to respond.

29

Jennie plumped up the pillows on her bed with far more vigour than was necessary, her mind racing ahead as to what she could do next. Mother's bedroom, perhaps – she could get it completely turned out before Mother came home, which might actually bring a smile of gratitude to Mother's lips, but even if it didn't, no matter. It would have kept Jennie occupied and away from the thoughts that constantly churned in her mind, and which only intense physical activity seemed capable of blotting out.

It was a strange way to spend Whitsun Monday, but Jennie didn't care about that, either. It was a relief to have the house to herself for once. Father had driven Mother in state to Monmouth first thing that morning, to spend the day with Laura, dropping David off on the way to play with a school friend at Raglan, and now, with Father busy as usual outside, Jennie was alone. She could have spent the day with Harry, but for once she'd declined, needing some time to think things through. But it was no good. Her mind just went round in unending circles, always with no solution – which was why she'd driven herself to spring clean where it wasn't even needed.

She and Harry were regarded as a steady couple now, by almost everyone – except Mother, of course, who continued implacably to refer to him as 'that man' and disliked him even coming to the house.

Harry remained completely undeterred, seeing her opposition as some sort of a challenge, but Jennie was unable to shrug off the hostility between them as easily as he could. It had resulted in them spending Christmas apart – Mother had decided on holding a big family Christmas at the farm, to which Harry, naturally, was not invited as he wasn't family, and Jennie, keen for David's childhood Christmases to be joyful ones, had desisted from arguing about it. Emily and Ernest had brought the children to stay, which had been wonderful, but she would've liked Emily to have met Harry.

"You'll have to bring him down to stay with us," Emily had said when Jennie had explained about Mother's hostility. "He's obviously doing you good – put a bloom in your cheeks."

Jennie had insisted on spending the New Year in Blaenavon, though, this time taking an excited David with her, who quickly fell to playing rowdy games with the other children that involved a lot of running in and out between the legs of all the grown-ups squashed into Lizzie and Archie's front room for their customary New Year's party.

Harry had carried an exhausted little boy back to Morgan Street, moved by the trusting way two little arms were wound round his neck and a small head nestled comfortably into his shoulder. "I'd hate to miss seeing this little chap grow up, you know," he told Jennie.

She watched as he tucked him tenderly into the big old iron bed in the back bedroom that he was to share with his mother while Harry took the sofa downstairs.

"The three of us boys used to sleep in that when we were little," he whispered to Jennie as they tip-toed downstairs to put the kettle on for when his Mam and Dad returned. "And Ivor used to snore something shocking!" His face grew sombre. "Never really liked New Year, I haven't," he said, pulling her close to him. "I always find myself thinking about times gone by, instead of the year about to begin. Not always a lot to celebrate about another year having passed, is there? You're older, not a lot wiser, and no further forward than you were this time last year."

"We weren't as close this time last year," she said. "Perhaps that's something to celebrate."

He smiled down at her. "I wasn't really including this year – been the best one for a long, long time." He began to kiss her, and once again she found herself unable to stop her lips responding to his, sinking deeper and deeper into his embrace, until his hands were roaming over her body and she could sense the urgency of his need of her.

And then, as always, she was pulling away from him, hot and afraid... of what?

She sat on Mother's bed now, her ambivalent reactions to Harry's lovemaking foremost in her mind, as it had been for the last few months. She loved him, she knew that, with a certainty which continued to grow as he poured his affection over her. And it wasn't the timid, hero-worshipping love which she'd felt for Charles, when she'd been grateful to receive whatever crumbs he'd thrown at her. This was deeper, stronger, more mature. She didn't need to wonder whether she was boring him, or try to decipher his mood or anticipate his reactions. He was constant in his love, relaxed in his relationship with her, and best of all they could laugh together.

Which was why she hated to see the hurt, quickly veiled, in his eyes when she reacted the way she did.

He'd told her repeatedly that he loved her, but she was much more guarded in giving expression to her feelings. It was as if, at the eleventh hour, she couldn't let go. All the careful restraining of her emotions which had been necessary over the years since her disastrous marriage – and even before that, with Mother, come to think of it – when she had determined to be in control of her life and not be swayed again by any man, came rushing to the fore again whenever she felt herself succumbing to Harry's passion.

She'd tried to explain, and he'd tried his best to understand. He filled her world with plans for the future – incorporating everything she'd ever wanted; a happy life together with David, whom he already loved as his own, a home of their own ... but it seemed to make little difference. While her head longed for everything he was offering, her body held back.

"Perhaps we should just go ahead and get married," he'd said. "Which isn't the most romantic proposal in the world, admittedly, but you know how much I love you. I'd get married tomorrow if it was up to me. And perhaps everything would be alright then."

"And what if it wasn't?" she'd whispered sadly. "Another marriage down the drain immediately."

And another failure, said Mother's voice inside her head.

Now, as she sat with the confused thoughts which she'd done her best to avoid all day pressing in on her, her eyes alighted on the old wooden sewing box which still stood in the corner of Mother's room.

Staring at it, she was transported back till she was a solemn little girl again, with two muddy brown plaits, and she could hear Mother's angry voice spitting words of rejection at her. She'd tried to look for the tin again a few times during her childhood and early teens, but something had always stopped her: either fear of being discovered, or fear of what she might discover – she wasn't altogether sure which.

But now she intended to find the secrets which the red tin held.

Suddenly she was kneeling in front of the sewing box, lifting its lid and the top tray inside, and there, sure enough, was the square box with its red and gold embossed lid. Just an ordinary box, really, nowhere near as fancy as her memory had insisted. Nevertheless, she was moved to open it and examine its contents.

She lifted out a batch of documents, the records of their family life. Baptismal certificates for each of the children, birth certificates, and, at the bottom, the marriage certificate of her parents. She unfolded it carefully and saw their names written there, and Father's signature in his firm, exquisite copperplate hand. How many times over the years had she watched him write out his bills and invoices in the same beautiful writing?

She studied the names of the witnesses, but didn't recognise any of them, and wondered idly who had given Mother away when her own father would have been already dead. Strange, too, how her parents never celebrated their wedding anniversaries. "A lot of nonsense, brought in by those Americans to make you spend more money!" she recalled Mother declaring once, and the subject had never been broached again.

She folded the marriage certificate carefully and returned it to the bottom of the box, and then looked at the birth certificates, but there was nothing of particular interest there except to note that they followed one another through the months, from Emily's birthday in August to her own in November. The fact of a birthday tea each month in the lead-up to Christmas had been well-marked throughout her childhood.

She was about to put the box away, as puzzled as she'd been in her childhood as to Mother's agitation regarding its contents, when a date which she'd barely registered suddenly sprang into her mind's eye. Quickly she tipped out the contents of the box again and spread the marriage certificate out on the floor.

It was dated 4th March, 1913.

But it couldn't be! She scrabbled about for Emily's birth certificate again, to check that she hadn't made a mistake. But no, there it was – Emily May Davies. Date of birth: 17th August, 1913.

Jennie leaned back against the side of the bed, dumbfounded. So that was it! Into her mind leapt all Mother's diatribes over the years about girls who led young men on, and the terrible consequences which were no worse than they deserved, leaving her daughters to vow that if ever such a fate befell them they would throw themselves in the river rather than come home and face Mother. Tales of how she'd turned back at a stile when she and Father were courting, so that he wouldn't have a glimpse of her ankle … and all the time she'd been four months pregnant when they'd married!

Still stunned at Mother's hypocrisy, she didn't hear the footsteps on the stairs, but when the bedroom door opened she turned with the same sense of alarm at discovery – heart thumping wildly in her chest, face reddening guiltily – as she'd done all those years ago.

But it was Father's smiling, gentle face she saw – Father, who had seduced her mother over three decades ago! Why, then, didn't she feel the same anger at him?

"Here you are!" he said, oblivious of her distress. "I thought I'd have a quick cup of tea before I go to fetch your mother and David."

"I was spring-cleaning," Jennie babbled, indicating the disarray on the floor. "I found these."

She held out the marriage and birth certificates.

"Oh," Father said, and sat down heavily on the side of the bed. "Well, you'd better not let your mother know that you've seen these. Her best-kept secret, this is. She'd be mortified if she thought anyone had discovered it."

The pounding in her chest continued. "I nearly did, once before – when I was a little girl. I'd been putting some threads away in the sewing box. Mother went mad when she saw me with that red tin – even though I wouldn't have understood anyway! She... she said some terrible things..." Even now, so much later, the memory of that morning was almost too painful to recount.

Father had been gathering the different papers together, but something in Jennie's voice made him stop and turn to her.

"She gets carried away when she's in a temper – and I can imagine what sort of temper she would have been in if she thought you'd seen these. But she doesn't mean it, you know – she's always let her tongue run away with her."

"Oh, she meant it that day," Jennie said with bitter emphasis. "I can't remember any other day of my childhood as clearly as that one. She told me in no uncertain terms that I hadn't been wanted... *a mistake,* she said. Eight years old, and to be told that I was someone's *mistake*... and now I find that underneath all that virtuous exterior, she was worse than any of us! How could she have spent all these years condemning everything and everybody who didn't come up to her expectations?"

Resentment was oozing from every pore, and she began to shake with the vehemence of her emotions.

Father put his arm around her and gave a long sigh. "She's difficult to understand, I know. It's taken me years to work out what goes on in that head of hers, but I've more or less got it sorted out now – I think. She's been punishing herself all these years, that's the long and short of it. No... I'm not just making excuses for her." He pulled Jennie back towards him as she tried to move away with an impatient gesture.

"You see," he went on, haltingly, "she never could accept that she liked it... wanted it... the physical side of things, I mean. It wasn't a one-sided affair – me taking advantage of an innocent young girl. We were desperately in love... but she seemed to think that it was wrong to enjoy it – that it wasn't ladylike, or maidenly. Not just over slipping up before we were married, but afterwards as well. She grew to resent the fact that her body wanted to do things her mind told her were... I don't know... common, or disgusting, or whatever. And three babies in as many years just made it worse."

He was becoming acutely uncomfortable as he spoke. "I shouldn't be saying these things to you."

But Jennie held on to his arm. "It's important – for me, it's important."

He was silent for a moment but then continued, looking into the distance, back over the years when everything which could have been so right had started to go wrong. His voice was bleak.

"She stopped everything then – all physical contact; insisted on separate bedrooms. She always wanted to *be* someone, you see. And you couldn't *be* someone if you had a child every year and stayed on an out-of-the-way farm that no-one of any importance ever came to. But we did stay – you have to be much more of a business-man than I ever was to become the sort of 'gentleman farmer' she would have preferred. So as time went on, she became as disappointed with me as she was with herself. And because she wouldn't allow herself to be driven by her physical needs, she became driven by all sorts of other things – like those missionary nuns or spinster headmistresses do, I suppose – and ended up blaming everything and everyone else for her discontent."

"And that's how I was 'a mistake'," Jennie said quietly.

He nodded. "We'd been out somewhere, to a bit of a do, and she'd had a good time – and just that once she let me back into her bed, and it was like we were newly-wed again. But then, of course, she found out you were on the way and she was horrified. She'd allowed herself to lose control again, you see, and by then being in control had come to mean so much to her."

He planted a kiss on his daughter's forehead. "But how could someone who has given her father so much joy ever have been a mistake?"

She managed a wan smile, while she tried to imagine her mother as a young woman overtaken by passion. It was impossible. All she could see was the discontented face, disappointment etched in deep lines weighing down her mouth.

"You still love her, though, don't you?"

He nodded again. "Never stopped. I've just always hoped that as both of us get too old to be passionate about very much at all, she'll perhaps settle down into some sort of acceptance, and even some happiness. That's all I've ever wanted – for her to be happy." He gave a thin smile then, as much at his own vain hopes as at his wife's.

"But the fires seem to be taking a long time to burn out!"

He made as if to stand up and end the conversation, but then seemed to think better of it. "She blames herself, you know, for things going wrong with your marriage. No need for me to say how, but as is her way, she hates having to admit to it – takes it out on everyone else instead! What I'm really trying to say is... don't let what she says influence you over Harry. If you think he's the right man for you, then take your chance. Don't let your head rule your heart, and then live to regret it. Don't make the same mistakes your mother has made."

"Do you think I might?" she asked.

His warm brown eyes looked levelly into her troubled grey. "These past few months, when it's obvious that Harry is head-over-heels in love with you, you've been ... distracted. And all this ..." his arm swept around to take in the room; "all this activity – as if you don't want to face up to things, or maybe let go – you know, *lose control*." He smiled sadly. "I've seen it all before."

When she didn't answer, he shrugged. "But then, maybe your old father has got it wrong, after all."

"No... no, you haven't." She was surprised at his perception. "I'm glad we've talked like this. It does help to explain Mother's behaviour ... well, a bit at any rate!"

They sat on for a while, each absorbed in their own thoughts. Then Father did stand up. "I'm going to make that cup of tea now. Shall I bring you a cup while you clear this lot away?"

Jennie nodded, and tried to gather her wits just as she gathered the scattered papers.

She was still upstairs, watching from the landing window, when Father carefully drew the old Ford up outside the front door and walked round to open the passenger door for Mother. Looking down on her, she seemed smaller, and Jennie could see how her always luxuriant dark hair was beginning to fade where it parted in the middle. To her amazement, she found herself starting to feel sorry for Katharine.

Sorry! For the woman who'd made so much of her life difficult, if not downright miserable, and continued to do so whenever she could!

But now it wasn't her mother she was seeing, but a woman who'd squandered all the happiness she could have had in her life. A good man had been prepared to give her everything he could and it had still not been enough.

And I've got a good man waiting for me, she told herself. *And I'm in just as much danger of losing everything with my stupid way of carrying on!*

She could see similar traits to her mother's in herself – heaven forbid! She'd been so determined to prove she could live her life without a man that now, when Harry was hers for the asking, she couldn't let go of that determination, and she was spoiling the best chance of happiness she'd ever had.

She watched Mother tip the front seat forward so that David could climb out of the car, and then, to Jennie's surprise, as Father went back round to the driver's side to put the car away, she saw Mother lean forward and plant a kiss on the top of David's head.

She really does love him! she thought incredulously. Mother, who'd pitied every woman who produced a son, and had spent the past few years referring to David as 'the boy'! Mother, whom she could never remember kissing any of them spontaneously!

Perhaps, after all, she was beginning to mellow, and Father wouldn't have to wait so long for the 'fires to burn out'.

She watched as grandmother and grandson walked towards the front door together, until her view of them became obscured by the arches of roses which lined the path, and the further revelation hit her that Mother was probably more reluctant to lose David than her daughter, and that could explain in great part why she was so opposed to Harry – only, being Mother, of course, she would never confess to such frail feelings.

She was about to turn and go down to meet them when another car suddenly roared into view, screeching to a halt far less sedately than Father's had. It was Uncle Fred's car, and within seconds an excited Harry had leapt out and was bounding up the path.

She hurried downstairs to open the door. She could hear Mother and David talking in the kitchen.

"I know that we weren't supposed to be seeing each other today," Harry said, after a perfunctory kiss on her cheek, "but there's something that I need to talk to you about. Do you think we could go out somewhere for a while?"

"Of course. But David's only just come home – I haven't seen him all day. I'd better sort him out first. Can it wait a while? – I take it it's good news?"

He grinned. "I think so. But yes, it can wait. I'll spread my charm over your Mother while you do whatever you want first!"

They went into the kitchen, to be greeted by an excited David, who wasn't the least surprised to see that Harry had arrived, but immediately included him in a garbled account of his day.

"I've got tea all ready. There's plenty for Harry to join us," Jennie told Mother, a new firmness in her voice. "Then Harry and I want to go out for a short while – I'll make sure David is settled in bed first."

Mother was quiet but not openly hostile during tea, and Jennie and Harry managed to keep up sufficient small talk with Father for the meal to pass quite equably. Fortunately, David was tired after his day out and quite happy for Jennie to take him off to bed as soon as they had finished.

"Take your time," Harry told her. "It's a beautiful evening. I'll stroll around the farm, perhaps, with your father."

When she descended the stairs again, having quickly changed into something more appropriate than the old skirt she'd been wearing, she found Mother alone, moving between the table and sink with intense concentration.

"David's almost asleep already," she said, "so we'll be off."

Her mother merely nodded, and then, as Jennie reached the door, said, "He's telling your father his intentions, you know – out there by the barn."

Jennie turned back. "Well, Father will be the first to know, then, because Harry hasn't told me yet."

"You'll have him, though, won't you, if he asks you?" Mother's voice was flat, almost defeated.

Jennie didn't answer directly. "It won't work for ever, will it, this arrangement?" she said instead. "Two grown women sharing a house isn't ideal, and I think –" a new revelation, this, and difficult to voice – "I think in some ways we're too much alike for it ever to work. Far better for me to have a place of my own."

Mother turned her back as she folded tea-towels with great deliberation. "Your father paid out *five hundred pounds* to get you out of the last mess," she said. "He'd pay twice that much to keep you out of this one."

Jennie had been prepared to be kind, understanding, even to stress how much Mother would still see David; but trust Mother not to allow her to do that. She always managed to have a little something up her sleeve, to ensure that one's pity, or any feeling akin to it, did not last long.

"That won't be necessary," Jennie said coolly, determined not to show how this latest revelation had thrown her. "I'm not a silly young girl any more, and Harry has no other motive than that he cares about me. *If* he wants to marry me –" *and, please God, let him still want that!* because suddenly she wanted it more than anything else in the world – "then I intend to say Yes, and I'll go to Blaenavon and live in a house you would consider not much more than a hovel, and be blissfully happy!"

Not quite as cool as she wanted to be any more, but voicing her decision made her want to be with Harry as quickly as possible. She headed for the door again.

Mother remained by the sink, staring out of the window.

Harry wouldn't tell her what was on his mind until they were in the garden of the Three Salmons in Usk. His air of suppressed excitement had been infectious, though, and the narrow leafy lanes, the sparkling water of the river as they drove over Chainbridge, and the splendour of the scenery as they bowled along the old Abergavenny road into the sleepy little market town, were all imbued with a feeling of optimism, of summer just around the corner, and – hopefully? – of a new life about to begin.

"Drink first, or stroll along the river bank?" Harry asked once they had parked the car.

"I don't care as long as you hurry up and tell me what this is all about!"

"Drink it is, then," he said, and settled her on a bench in the hotel garden while he went to find a waiter.

A shaft of late evening sunshine fell onto the seat between long shadows, where clumps of geraniums and columbines were clustered in dusky shades of blue and pink, in muted contrast to the splash of roses in their first flowering, splayed across a trellis separating the garden from the car park. Jennie pondered for a moment Mother's declaration about money paid to Charles, and then realised that she didn't care any more, except to feel even more gratitude to Father for extricating her from the situation with no hint of what it had cost him, either financially or emotionally.

She probed experimentally at all the old wounds which still troubled her from time to time, and discovered they truly hardly hurt at all. She felt lulled by the tranquil scene around her, and the warmth of the sun on her shoulders, and more relaxed than she had for months.

Harry appeared, followed by a waiter with a tray, but he didn't speak until the man left. Then he spoke without preamble.

"There's a pub come up in Blaenavon. At the bottom of the town – The Greyhound. Nice little place it is. Lots of living space upstairs, too. I've been given first refusal."

"But that's wonderful," she said cautiously, hoping there was more. "It's what you said you always wanted."

"And of course, the open-cast won't last much longer, you know. Another year or so and we'll all be out of a job..."

"... So it would be best to grab an opportunity like this while you can, wouldn't it?" she finished for him.

He nodded and took a long slurp of beer. "Almost be a fool not to."

A thought occurred to her. "What about applying for a licence – don't you have to prove that you are of good character? Always law-abiding, that sort of thing?"

He grinned. "I've already seen Sergeant Roberts. He said there'd be no problem as long as I gave up my 'other business interests'! Couldn't do it anyway, if I left the mountain – it'd be much too risky down in the town."

She sipped her drink. "It sounds as if you've already decided."

"Well, like you said, it's a good opportunity." He placed his empty glass very squarely on a beer mat.

"With plenty of living space you said... so presumably there would be room for a wife?"

His head shot up. "And for a seven-year-old boy with dark curly hair," he smiled.

For the first time ever, she took the initiative and leaned across the table and kissed him. "I love you, Harry Jenkins," she said.

More people came into the garden. "Come on," he said, grabbing her hand. "Time for that stroll along the riverbank."

It was much later when they began to head for home, when ambitious plans for renting out a large back room for meetings as well as catering for wedding parties had been laid, alongside the providing of a stream of brothers and sisters for David.

"Of course, Mother will have a fit about us living in a pub," Jennie said, when they were discussing how to tell everyone. "Especially taking David to live there. It was only today that I realised just how fond she's become of him, in her funny way. She'll never come to visit us."

"She probably wouldn't have visited us wherever we chose to live, if we stayed in the valleys," said Harry.

Which was true. Ever since Jennie had come to know Harry's family, she'd tried to imagine Mother sitting amongst them, still wearing her hat to show she was an official visitor, her eyes darting around in silent condemnation.

"Anyway," Harry went on, "We can make sure we visit Goytre every week so both your parents can still see David – we'll probably be glad of the break, once we get going."

They were nearly back at the car. Harry turned to her in the gathering dusk and took both her hands in his. "I wouldn't really have taken it without you, you know. You were always a much bigger part of the plan than anything else. But I want you to be completely sure – about everything, you know, not just about taking on the pub... but about us."

He waited a moment. *"Are* you sure?"

She could hardly see his face, but it didn't matter. She knew it would be full of the sort of love for her that she'd never expected to find. There would be no more rejection, no more mistakes. She could let go of the rigid self-control she'd imposed on herself for so long, and replace it with trust.

For the second time that evening, she kissed him. Long and lingering this time, telling him all he needed to know.

"Yes," she said.

THE END

The Author

Julie McGowan is an established short story and feature writer for national and international publications, and has won numerous writing competitions over the years. Her writing credits also include educational features, pantomimes, sketches and songs and newspaper columns. Well known in her home town of Usk for her work in the community, Julie runs a theatrical group which performs variety shows and her witty pantomimes to sell-out audiences every year. She also co-directs *Is It?*, a theatre company which runs young people's drama workshops and tours schools in Wales with productions covering health and social issues.

Born in Blaenavon, Julie left Wales for Kent at the age of 12. She trained as a nurse at Guy's Hospital, London, and then as a Health Visitor in Durham, living there for 4 years after her marriage to Peter. The couple now have four adult children and have lived in Surrey, Lincolnshire and Hertfordshire before returning to Wales in 1992. Julie has had a variety of jobs including teaching piano and a stint as Town Clerk in Usk.

Julie's next two books, *Don't Pass Me By* and *Just One More Summer*, are also available, both in print and digital versions.

Julie loves to be in contact with her readers. Please do visit her website at:

www.juliemcgowan.com

or email her at:

juliemcgowanusk@live.co.uk

ROSE & CROWN, BLUE JEANS, BOATHOOKS, SUNBERRY, CHRISTLIGHT, and EPTA Books

MORE BOOKS FROM the SUNPENNY GROUP
www.sunpenny.com

A Little Book of Pleasures, by William Wood
Blackbirds Baked in a Pie, by Eugene Barter
Breaking the Circle, by Althea Barr
Dance of Eagles, by JS Holloway
Don't Pass Me By, by Julie McGowan
Far Out, by Corinna Weyreter
Going Astray, by Christine Moore
If Horses Were Wishes, by Elizabeth Sellers
Just One More Summer, by Julie McGowan
Loyalty & Disloyalty, by Dag Heward-Mills
My Sea is Wide (Illustrated), by Rowland Evans
Sudoku for Christmas (full colour illustrated gift book)
The Mountains Between, by Julie McGowan
The Perfect Will of God, by Dag Heward-Mills
Those Who Accuse You, by Dag Heward-Mills
Trouble Rides a Fast Horse, by Elizabeth Sellers

COMING SOON:

A Whisper On The Mediterranean, by Tonia Parronchi
Fish Soup, by Michelle Heatley
Moving On, by Jenny Piper
Raglands, by JS Holloway
The Stangreen Experiment, by Christine Moore
Sudoku for Sailors (full colour illustrated gift book)
Sudoku for Bird Lovers (full colour illustrated gift book)
Sudoku for Horse Lovers (full colour illustrated gift book)

Rose&Crown
Inspirational Romance
www.roseandcrownbooks.com

BLUE JEANS BOOKS

(Romance imprints of the SUNPENNY PUBLISHING GROUP)

BOOKS FROM ROSE & CROWN, and BLUE JEANS BOOKS

Uncharted Waters, by Sara DuBose
Bridge to Nowhere, by Stephanie Parker McKean
Embracing Change, by Debbie Roome
Blue Freedom, by Sandra Peut
A Flight Delayed, by KC Lemmer

COMING SOON:

30 Days to Take-off, by KC Lemmer
A Devil's Ransom, by Adele Jones
Brandy Butter on Christmas Canal, by Shae O'Brien
Redemption on the Red River, by Cheryl R. Cain
Bridge Beyond Betrayal, by Stephanie Parker McKean
Heart of the Hobo, by Shae O'Brien

Lightning Source UK Ltd.
Milton Keynes UK
UKOW05f1107030114

223923UK00002B/22/P